"We—that is, the girls and I . . . we want to hire you to collect the murderer."

My stomach flipped.

Zylphia squeezed my fingers, then let me go. "We can offer coin, but not enough," she said hastily, as if by giving me time to think, I'd say no. "So we've gathered what we could together, and we can make up the difference with a ball of opium.

I wanted it. It was the only thought that filled my head as Zylphia's offer registered. "What size?" I asked.

She held up thumb and forefinger, creating a circle big enough that I'd be set for at least a season.

But even as my greedy body yearned for it, I knew it didn't matter. There was such hope in my friend's eyes. Such fear.

And I'd already decided, even before the offer of payment.

"You an[d]   [co]llector," I said,   [b]risk to my own e[   ]

This wou[   ]

By Karina Cooper

The St. Croix Chronicles
TARNISHED

Dark Mission Novels
ALL THINGS WICKED
LURE OF THE WICKED
BLOOD OF THE WICKED

Coming Soon
SACRIFICE THE WICKED

Dark Mission Novellas
NO REST FOR THE WITCHES
BEFORE THE WITCHES

KARINA COOPER

Tarnished

THE ST. CROIX CHRONICLES

AVON
An Imprint of HarperCollinsPublishers

AVON BOOKS
An Imprint of HarperCollins*Publishers*
10 East 53rd Street
New York, New York 10022-5299

Copyright © 2012 by Karina Cooper
ISBN 978-0-06-212764-8
www.avonbooks.com

First Avon Books mass market printing: July 2012

Avon Trademark Reg. U.S. Pat. Off. and in Other Countries, Marca Registrada, Hecho en U.S.A.
HarperCollins® is a registered trademark of HarperCollins Publishers.

Printed in the U.S.A.

10 9 8 7 6 5 4 3 2 1

Tarnished

Chapter One

I was nine years old when I picked my first pocket. A fog shrouds much of my childhood, but I do remember this: that cold spring night, I lifted threepence, a small pocket watch, one embroidered handkerchief, and the torn stub of the gentleman's circus ticket.

The watch was nothing more than engraved brass and tooled numbers, but I was allowed to keep it. A reminder, not just of what I could do but who I belonged to. Eleven years later, miles from Monsieur Marceaux's Traveling Curiosity Show, I still carry it with me.

Perhaps that says something about me.

My name is Cherry St. Croix. I am a collector, one of the many who are employed to acquire, kill or investigate for bounties. My rules are simple: I don't collect children, and I don't murder for coin. Truth be told, I've never killed for any reason.

In the fog-black streets below me, the cobblestones gleamed wetly, painted yellow by one lens of my goggles. The fog crept in silence, dark as pitch and thick as pudding through the damp alley, and it burned with every inhale. Living above the drift as I did, I never developed the tolerance—or, rather more specifically, the lung scarring—to breathe the coal-ridden air.

To combat the choking stench, I'd developed a set of protective goggles and a detachable respirator, which now covered much of my face. The yellow glass comprising one leather-wrapped lens cut a swath through the air clear as any light. Clearer, since on nights like these, the fog bent light like a blinding sheet. I enjoyed unfettered vision.

My quarry was not so lucky.

Allez, hop! I dropped like a stone from my uneasy perch above the narrow alleyway. With only the faintest clatter of broken grit, I landed behind Mr. Bartholomew Cummings, ready on the balls of my feet, knees bent, balanced with a gloved hand to the damp cobbles in case I needed to move quickly.

He wouldn't turn. I knew that my boots were soundless, but even had I misjudged the uneven street and stumbled, Cummings was far too deep in his cups to care. He was singing. Or he thought he was singing, but it sounded more like the eager shriek of an alley cat in heat to me. As his ribald shanty bounced from brick to brick around us, I rose to my full height—unimpressive even when at my most confident—and slipped into place behind him.

His wavering, unfortunate falsetto didn't so much as hitch. Through the yellow glass, I could see that he had no cloth over his mouth, nor any means by which to see in the blasted dark that was as much devil-fog as night. He was probably used to the air, as most of the lower London denizens eventually became. The old barber likely knew the feel of each cobble beneath his thin boots.

It was a shame he didn't know the feel of trouble the same way.

I'd never met Bartholomew Cummings, but I knew of him in passing. He was a barber, a bit of a peacock when it came right down to it, and a congenial drunk. But the man was also up to his carefully waxed mustache in debt.

The Midnight Menagerie did not forget them what owed money. Many of the bounties I pulled from the collector's wall came from the Menagerie. They paid well and often, unfortunately for Mr. Cummings.

I winced as his lofty praise of an unnamed foreign woman's bosom hit an ear-shattering note. Quickly, I withdrew a smooth, wrapped cudgel from my belt. It was the work of moments to wind up and let fly.

The wood connected with the back of my quarry's capped head. He dropped like a stone, foreign woman's bosom only half remembered. A thick, gummy silence slammed into place; a dramatic breath, a humming watchfulness.

It wouldn't last, I knew. More drunkards would stagger by, eager for a bed. Anybody's bed, for that matter, and the East End prostitutes knew it. Even as I knelt to check that my quarry still breathed, I could sense the eyes around us.

I sighed, shivering. The early autumnal chill leveled over London was only made worse by the damnable fog. Three parts smoke and one part bone-chilling damp from the rotting Thames, it had a way of sinking skeletal fingers into your skin and curling in. I longed for a fire and a hot cup of tea.

I would have settled for my warmest cloak, but I'd left it at home. Such finery wasn't for this world. Down below the drift, I wasn't Cherry St. Croix, daughter of a dead madman. I wasn't the ward of a wealthy guardian or even a well-heeled miss on walkabout.

I wasn't anyone. Just a collector. Most people didn't even have a name for me.

I knelt, shaking my head as I sifted through Cummings's pockets. I could have stolen his jacket. The old brown corduroy was patched through, but the fabric looked sturdy. It was certain to be much warmer than the woolen shirt and high-necked corset I wore now.

Tempted as I was, the contents of his pockets revealed little more than the dog-ended stub of an old cheroot and a half-empty box of matches; not even a shilling to his name. That he'd likely gambled it on a poor hand of cards was only a secondary thought. I should have accosted him coming instead of going.

"Aren't you fortunate?" I muttered, the respirator muddling my voice to something unrecognizable. Winding my usual braided cord around his wrists, I tied it tightly with complex knots guaranteed to vex even the most patient of souls.

Cummings snored through his gaping mouth. Loudly. Poor bugger.

No matter how cold I was, I had no intention of stealing clothing from a man the Menagerie had claimed. He'd be lucky to escape in the morning with his skin intact, much less the genteel remains of a fraying coat.

My sympathy fled as I thrust my shoulder under his dead weight. A handful of coarse words sprang to my lips.

He was too skinny by half, but a head and then some

taller than me. My shoulder strained under his bony weight, feet skittering in the wet road as I struggled to drape him at an angle that wouldn't send me flying into the gutters.

I liked to think I was stronger than most women my size, but I wasn't made for heavy lifting.

Still, I'd managed worse, and we weren't the only pair of "drunks" to be staggering home by light of the flickering gas lamps. My clothing was deliberately designed to let me pass as a man if one wasn't looking too closely, and most of the inhabitants of Blackwall would think twice before attempting to take on two "men" without greater numbers at hand.

Fair was not a word used lightly below the drift, if used at all.

Few observers would even consider that I was a woman, and I used this knowledge gleefully. A woman in trousers? Absurd. By the time they saw my specially armored corset wasn't a waistcoat of any design, it'd be too late.

Although awkward to maneuver my unfortunate friend, we weren't far from the district where the Menagerie set up shop. Limehouse, so named because of the local lime kilns located by the river, is a very strange kettle of rather interesting fish. The district is known for its rampant immigrant population, practically run from top to bottom by the Chinese who'd taken it over as their own. The Menagerie borders the southern edge of the district, arrayed along the river but miraculously free of the fog that plagued the city.

I'd never understood how. Once, I'd looked for air-moving wheels or devices and found none, and the ringmaster only laughed when I asked.

The rest of London below wasn't so lucky. Or so clean. The journey from Blackwall and across the Isle of Dogs reeked of rotting fish and musty coal smoke. Cummings was entirely unhelpful, and more than once, I had to pause for breath. Although I sensed more than a trace of interest from the yawning shadows surrounding us on our half-hour journey, no one had tried to halt our meandering procession.

Which was lucky. I didn't have the energy for a brawl, and lacked entirely the desire to leave my quarry behind. I needed him.

Or rather, I needed his bounty.

One of the unfortunate circumstances of my existence is that although I am considered a wealthy heiress, I am wholly dependent upon a stipend allotted by my guardian every month. Unfortunately, I am a creature of expensive habits and necessity. The tools of science are not cheap. My stipend was nearly gone and I'd another fortnight left before I would be allowed more.

Among other reasons, I collect to supplement a miserly income.

Mr. Cummings would provide enough of a bounty to afford me relative peace for the next fourteen days.

Eventually—finally—we arrived at the tarnished gate that marked my destination. Beyond the fence, the Midnight Menagerie waited.

Years ago, after Vauxhall had lost favor and become instead the preferential haunt of footpads and ruffians, rumors of a new pleasure garden began to circulate. It wasn't long before the Midnight Menagerie became *de rigueur* for all comers with coin to spend and pleasures to acquire, above or below the drift.

Although the ringmaster of the Menagerie was as

English as I, the truth of it was much more complex. The Menagerie was actually run by a mysterious organization known as the Karakash Veil—an enigmatic name for what I was sure amounted simply to a criminal association of Chinese origin.

I wasn't positive. I'd never met anyone who claimed to be part of the Veil, and rumor suggested no one else ever had, either. No one, perhaps, but Micajah Hawke, the Menagerie's dark and imposing ringmaster. Him, I'd dealt with. Unfortunately.

The man was a brute, for all his raw polish. And too bloody pleased with himself by half.

I sometimes entertained the thought that he, in fact, was the leader of the Karakash Veil, only masquerading as a servant. But the very name itself, Karakash, had its roots deep in China. It was the name of a river filled from bank to bank with rolling, polished boulders of jade.

Hawke, for all his savvy, didn't strike me as a man to hide behind a mask. Or a veil.

Arms braced over my shoulder like some awkward dancer, Cummings stirred, moaning something that I'm sure would have been better received by a woman not me. My ears burned, but I set my jaw.

His was not the first advance I'd received in these dark streets, sober or otherwise. Although I'd never taken up with any who'd offered, I doubted it'd be the last time a man tried. In his defense, I assured myself, he was quite gone on—my nose wrinkled as his sour breath wafted through my respirator—gin and the wrapped edge of my cosh. And he had no other recourse but to half lean against my body, which although corseted tightly in place, could not be mistaken for a man's at such close quarters.

I stiffened as one heavy hand came down on my backside. "I think not," I gritted through my clenched teeth, shaking strands of black hair away from my face. "Get your hand off—"

The rebuke sizzling on the edge of my tongue died as chimes rippled out through the fog. The jaunty tune seemed almost laughably out of place, and my head snapped up.

It seemed to me as if London—all of London, from the Underground rails to the canals above the drift— lived and breathed by the ruddy Westminster clock. Although the clock face was entirely obscured, towering high over the bank of fog thick as pea soup, the sound reached even the Menagerie.

Was it finally four?

The largest bell, affectionately termed Big Ben by just about all in London anywhere, bonged four slow, baritone notes, and I held my breath.

It hissed out on the fifth bell. "Bloody hell," I swore. I'd missed the four-o'clock warning. I was late! And given the distance I'd need to cover in a very short amount of time, I'd be later still by the time I made it home.

"Your pardon," I told the lolling Mr. Cummings, who did not care. I shrugged him off with little grace, and grabbed his lapels to steady him against the gate. Ensuring that his bonds remained in place, I coiled a second length of rope around his waist and through the rusted bars behind him. "I'd walk you farther in," I told his chapped red cheeks and fluttering parchment eyelids, "but I simply can't. Be a good sport and remain here."

He didn't care what I said. I doubted even that he'd

waken completely before the Menagerie groundskeepers found him, but my need to get home on time superseded even my need to get paid.

I had no choice. I'd have to return as soon as I could to collect my bounty. Quickly, I slid a swatch of black cotton from my right boot. It wasn't nearly as nice as the calling card my chaperone preferred I used above the drift, but it would have to do.

I couldn't leave Cherry St. Croix's calling card down here, after all. People would talk.

I grinned as I tucked it into the unconscious man's front coat pocket, half out to ensure that the ringmaster's sharp eyes wouldn't miss it. Micajah Hawke was many things—enigmatic, keen of mind and of razored wit; most decidedly a bastard of the highest order—but he wouldn't cheat me.

At least, he never had before. That I knew of, anyway. I felt it only prudent to leave a wide margin of error.

As the last echoes of Big Ben's predawn chastisement rolled away, I sprinted into the fog. Cummings's snores dogged my steps.

I knew the London streets like I knew my own home, and I deviated from the main thoroughfare as quickly as I dared. I ran through the rat's maze of alleys and dirty, muck-filled lanes, scolding myself soundly. How could I possibly miss the four-o'clock bell? I *had* to be home before the servants woke for the day.

As I reached the West India docks, I paused in the shadow of the alley. My hair, usually tightly pinned, released tendrils to stick to my forehead and cheeks around the goggles. Given the dampness lingering in tonight's gritty miasma, I likely had soot and probably worse smudged across my face.

No ferryman in his right mind would give the likes of me a lift above the drift. No ferryman, that is, but the caustic captain of the *Scarlet Philosopher*.

A rather pretentious name for a rotting canoe.

Captain Abercott was a man who had never set foot in Her Majesty's Royal Navy, despite his claimed designation. Nor would he, I imagined, unless it were for a gallows in his honor. But he was also a greedy man with a working sky ferry, so he suited my purposes nicely.

I stripped off the protective goggles and attached respirator, blinking furiously as the stench stung my eyes, and jammed them into the tooled leather pouch hanging from my hip. I had brought no change of clothes, intending to return home much earlier than five of the clock.

If I were careful, and as long as I kept to the quiet paths, I might get mistaken for a manservant in the dark.

Around me, I could all but feel London coming to life. The shop owners would soon be setting out stalls and goods, and the workers would be trudging to the factories. I needed to hurry, and as I stepped out of the shadows and strode for the *Scarlet Philosopher*, I hoped that God was feeling kind this morning.

Once upon a time, the West India docks had been the stopping point for ships sailing the Thames. Mostly merchant vessels, slave vessels and the occasional secretive pleasure barge, each owing a tithe or employed by the East India Trading Company.

I had never seen the docks as they were then. I only knew them as they were now: mostly empty at this time of morning, the water lapping thick and befouled against the wooden supports. Slowly, the dockworkers would begin to gather; the poor and destitute eager for the threepence earned for an hour's worth of work.

A docker could garner sixpence for an hour above the drift, plus extra if they worked fast, but the unfortunate men below couldn't find a way up as long as they remained poor. The divide was horridly real, and fodder for rumors of strike.

A tragic conundrum all the way around, but not, at the moment, my concern.

On higher ground, well out of the reach of the black tides, the ferries rested on iron frames, flat bottoms nestled securely in place. Lines held them as they would any other boat, but they were more for show and I suspect a bit of nautical pride than real necessity. Even the sails and rigging flown proudly from a few of the more ostentatious boats were superfluous.

The boats were entirely mechanical in nature, designed to rise as coal burned in the furnace to produce steam. Enough steam would have to build up to power the mechanism that made the ship's innards churn. They would sink again as the steam was released; a less complex and yet more unstable version of the aether engines that powered the ships in Her Majesty's Royal Navy.

They were air vessels, albeit ponderous things that traveled no faster than the speed of a horse and carriage on promenade. And only up or down. But they were one of only two methods to travel between London above the drift and the miserable London below.

The other involved attempting to scale the enormous mechanical stilts that lifted London proper above the fog banks, and this often ended in little more than a long scream and red mess. I'd only ever met one man who'd *almost* done it. His amputated legs told a fable more grisly than any penny dreadful.

Lucky for me, that meant a greedy bloke like Captain Abercott would man a barely sky-worthy boat and accept whatever extra coin at whatever cost. He'd expected an early morning, and his stack was one of three already blowing a wisp of white steam into the cool air.

No sign of him, however. I frowned.

"Hello?" I called. My raspy voice flitted through the heavy fog, wrapped in cobwebs and swallowed. "Are you there, Captain?"

"'Oo be you?" I heard, barely a guttural growl from somewhere beyond the railing.

"Your usual fare." I had to swallow hard, clearing my throat as it prickled uncomfortably. Damn this fog. One could always tell an upsider from the constant throat-clearing.

"We ain't ready t'leave," returned the disembodied voice, sour and dismissive.

I shook my head. I wouldn't play this game; not tonight. Today, rather. Blast it.

"I've coin for you," I said, my customary greeting as I traversed the narrow gangplank without permission. Wasn't it bad luck to step on board a ship without it? Maybe, but I didn't care. "And more," I added meaningfully, "if you keep quiet and move quicker than this."

Although I wasn't sure he could. I stopped at the top of the plank, gloved hands braced on the railing, and stared at the mess in front of me. Rope lay in chaotic coils across the small deck; sails had been left slung haphazardly across timbers I wasn't sure weren't needed for some function of the ferry.

A clatter to my left drew my eyes, and I narrowed an accusing gaze at the tattered man oozing out of the narrow door that led to belowdecks.

Captain Abercott was not a thin man, given more to portly indulgences. Nevertheless, the man was unusually spry. He lacked any hair at the top of his head, but made up its loss by a fine tuft of dingy white fringe that stuck out like a drooping wreath from beneath a jaunty sailor's cap. His winter overcoat was patched, his fustian breeches tucked into boots more suited to the life of a pirate than a ferryman. And the flask in his hand winked as he raised it in my direction. His version of recognition.

"You are drunk," I observed. Wryly, too. It wasn't the first time, but I always hoped it'd be the last. Drink kept his memory fuzzy, but it did nothing for the steadiness of his boat. Or my innards.

Red-rimmed eyes glanced up to the sky, though not a trace of it could be seen through the fog, and he smiled. He had, much to my dismay, four teeth missing. Just two nights ago, it had only been three. "An' painless, thank y'fer askin'," he slurred.

I stepped onto the deck, well away from chapped, grasping hands. My un-bustled backside had been fondled one too many times already, thank you, and the good captain had made a lasting impression once. "So I see. Can you fly?"

"Sure as a chicken," he assured me, puffing his barrel chest out. Though I noted that he had to seize the door frame to do so.

I cleared my throat. "Chickens most assuredly can *not* fly."

"Ah," he said, staggering across the deck. "Ah. But 'as anyone tol' em that?"

"Dear God in heaven."

My options were few. As Abercott made his stumbling away across the deck of the small boat, I thought it over. Try another ferryman, one possibly less soused? But also more likely to flap his gums at any passenger with a bit of gossip to tell.

Or?

I tucked my fingers into the front of my special-made corset. Fabricated of waxed canvas, it was slatted with the thinnest metal I could possibly find and of the same color as my plain woolen shirt. A long, thin blade could be inset into the plating at the front and the back. My modest design had protected me from some of the unfortunate injuries I could have received while pursuing meaner quarry, and caught more than one particularly vile ruffian off guard.

And it was a gem for hidden pockets. The smallest of them just by my hip gave way, releasing my small brass pocket watch. The engraving had long since worn away, but the gears inside ticked faithfully as I opened the facing.

Twenty minutes after Big Ben's last bell. I would barely make it home as it was.

I seized my courage in both hands and prayed to all the gods of modern science that the ferry, uncomplicated even by my standards, would fly itself. "Then please," I said as I sidled to one of a half dozen seats nestled along the rail. "Take us up, Mr. Ab—"

He turned on me so suddenly, black-grimed shovel held in one filthy hand and reddened eyes wild, that I startled, tripped over the trailing edge of a loose rope, and sprawled across the thinly padded bench.

I may have delivered Cummings with my hide intact,

but my dignity would take a beating now. Laughter bubbled to my lips, and I sucked in a burning breath, felt my ribs tighten beneath the corset stays. Now was not the time to show my amusement at the bloated sot threatening me.

I could send him headfirst over his own bloody railing, but I wouldn't. Because he was, despite appearances, kinder than I had any right to expect, and it was *his* ferry, after all.

"Captain," I corrected myself. "Of course I meant Captain. Your pardon, sir."

"Hmph." Abercott turned again to his shoveling, and the flames leapt in wild orange and searing blue. The trickle of steam from the stack slowly became a banner, and the old man spryly ambled over the deck debris to throw off the unnecessary lines.

I held my breath when I could, turning my face to the heat given off from the furnace, and muffled my coughing against my gloved hands when I thought Abercott wasn't paying attention. I could have easily just put on my respirator, but such things invited attention. Speculation.

In the five years I'd played the role of collector, I'd learned a most interesting fact. To wit, those average folk who lived below the drift treated collectors as just another facet of an already dangerous life.

Above the drift, collectors were something else entirely. Generally speaking, those gentlemen who claimed a collector's occupation—I thought of them as Society collectors, gents who dabbled for the fun of it—were considered only *fashionably* dangerous. Popular, and certainly exciting. Invited to all the soirees for that certain element of mystery.

Nobody wanted a collector on business in their home, so the Society collectors rarely seemed to work. Merchants, traders and the occasional respectable ferry captain were their targets; folk not powerful enough to threaten a well-to-do lifestyle. There were, as far as I was aware, no *real* collectors among them. Except for myself, of course, and certainly no one knew that.

The ferry shuddered, and I gripped the edge of the seat as it lurched like a drunken cat. Whether it was the reliability of a well-oiled ship or whatever angels I had entertained, the ride up was as uninteresting as I could have hoped. The ferry rose slowly, steam hissing in caustic chorus from an array of tarnished copper tubes as Captain Abercott worked the multitude of brass and copper levers at the wheel.

As the ferry broke through the fog drift, I groaned. The typically cloudy sky had lightened, streaked with pink and wicked purple as the sun rose above the horizon. Blinking hard against the sudden surge of light, almost painful after the noxious shadows below, I inhaled the clearer air gratefully while the sotted captain navigated his floating brick into place at the upper docks.

I could not exit the ship fast enough.

Several shillings lighter, to say nothing of the indent I'm sure my white-knuckled grip left on the rail, I hurried away from the curious eyes of the dockworkers already well into their labor. Several sky ships had come in while I'd been below.

Nothing I could pry into now.

I stopped on the edge of the wharf district and surveyed the road ahead of me. London above the drift was vastly different from London below. Picturesque, even, with its staggered silhouette framed in the dawn's rosy hue.

Decades ago, the Queen's Parliament had gathered to address ongoing complaints from the peerage forced to endure the black smoke pouring from the factory districts. It was the very beginning of Her Majesty's reign, and the Queen had definite *ideas*. At the end of the debate, Parliament chose not to move London or force the factories to relocate. Instead, the municipal decision to raise London above the fog brought the finest minds from all across the world to bid on the project.

It was a minor German baron and his son who'd won the right. Almost four years after the bidding ended, the plans were completed and construction finally began. London was set on its collective ear as whole districts were cleared for construction. Refugees flocked to the river banks.

Baron Irwin Von Ronne went mad before the first stilts were finished, but his brilliant son took over the project and completed it rather more quickly than anyone had expected. The end result was the cleaving of London's well-to-do from its poor, its immigrants and those who couldn't maintain appearances. Historical buildings and those belonging to the peerage were raised by mighty steel stilts, cranked high by accordion girders and leaving channels between districts spanned by attractive walking bridges.

It was as if select bits of London now hovered like mountain peaks amidst a sea of fog. I could run, keeping to the bridges. It would garner suspicion, of course. No one would recognize the raven-haired servant dashing madly across the cobbles, but they *would* talk if that servant slipped into the home of the mad doctor's unmarried daughter.

Alternately, I could flag down a gondolier; those men

who guided the smaller sky boats along the fog canals. This would involve speaking with another thinking person, and no matter how respectable the gondolier, I knew for a fact that many of them gathered for drinks and worse. I didn't need the gossip from that angle, either.

Bloody bells and damn. Tripped up in my own propriety.

I'd have to walk, and quickly. I kept to the shadows as much as I could, my head down as if I were in a hurry. It took far too long, with far too many of the working classes passed along the way, but eventually the cobbles paving the pedestrian crossings changed abruptly underfoot. They curved in shape, familiar as I traversed the boundary into London's West End.

I lived in Chelsea, a neighborhood known for its wilder ways and all-too-Bohemian residents. The district catered to the artists, the wastrels, those of lighter thought and consequence. I'm told that when my mother chose the house, it had been a neighborhood more suited to scholars and thinkers, but such things change.

The pink sky tinted the pale path in shades of mauve and shadowed purple, and I followed it at a brisk clip. The Cheyne Walk residence that served as my home was not mine. Not yet. In the strictest of terms, it was one of three that belonged to my father—by all accounts, a doctor touched by more than a hint of genius. Or madness, to hear the talk. This townhome was one property, the second was an isolated estate in the countryside. They say my father refused to step foot in it after his own father's death.

Common drivel claimed it haunted.

The third, a marvelous castle in isolated Scotland, had been engulfed in a terrible fire. This was the inferno that took my father's life. My mother, Josephine, had the unfortunate luck of perishing beside him. I don't remember her at all, though gossip suggests I look like her. I have her infuriating shade of deep, ruby-tinted auburn hair, they say—one of my many disadvantages, they typically add in the same breath—and my features are similarly highbrow. Though I lack her height and stature. And, of course, her grace, wit, charm, and talent on the pianoforte.

With both my mother and father burned to death, I was left in the arms of a Glasgow orphanage already too full to worry about the origins of a mildly singed child. I only vaguely recall my time there, and this in snatches of memory and impressions. Generally, I get the feeling that it was overwhelmingly depressing. This may in part be due to the cordial given all the children to keep us sedated and out of trouble.

My whereabouts were unknown for years, and the whole of Mad St. Croix's estate was left to his executor, and my current guardian. I only have the vaguest impressions of Mr. Oliver Ashmore, but I can assure you with the utmost of earnestness that I don't like him. Not only is he never about—a circumstance I view as a favor—but he terrifies me.

I'd only ever met him once in all my seven years under his tenure, and I've never gotten over it. However, I've been told that he scoured heaven and earth to find me, and I think that he might have succeeded sooner were it not for Monsieur Marceaux's talent scouts.

This is not a point in Mr. Ashmore's favor. While I don't remember the orphanage very clearly, I do remember what life was like in Marceaux's traveling circus rings.

Frightening. Difficult.

And, if one played one's game very well, a child could live as free as a Gypsy in those colorful tents. But it required time, effort and clever instinct. Although the details of my childhood are terribly unclear, I know that I served as acrobat at times. A pickpocket among the crowds at others. I could climb just about anything, had never learned to be afraid of heights, and with patience, I was taught how to contort my way through nearly anything.

In short, Monsieur Marceaux turned me into the perfect thief. And as long as I continued to bring in goods and crowds, I was worth more as a performer than I was as another girl in the auction rings.

I was thirteen and a cunning little criminal when Mr. Ashmore's barristers finally located me. God only knew how. The damage had long since been done. I was a thief and a pickpocket, and already dependent on opium to keep nightmares at bay.

I understand it took some effort to wean me from the noxious concoction foisted upon me, both by the orphanage and the circus. Godfrey's cordial, it's called—an old trick of opium and treacle often utilized by orphanages, nurses and impatient governesses. To compound matters, Marceaux, no gentleman by any stretch of the word, liked to keep his children supplied with raw opium.

As a tool for good behavior, there's little better. Because of this, my first months in London were terrible. Fraught with nightmares and with illness.

Yet, in London I remained.

I slipped through the decorative grate separating the property from that of Lord William Pennington beside it. The man didn't live there—what upstanding gentleman in his right mind would choose to reside in a neighborhood teeming with Bohemian wastrels and dreamers?—but his lady wife's mother had no such complaints. She enjoyed the privacy of thick, towering shrubs, which worked especially in my favor. How many times had I come through the property? Dozens. Hundreds.

I made it six steps into the side yard when a familiar whistle caught my attention. I looked up.

Betsy braced her hands on the windowsill two stories above, her round face set in disapproving lines. "There you are," she hissed. She'd been watching for me, then, and that meant I was dangerously late.

Elizabeth Phillips had been my maid from the moment I was too old for a nanny and too much a handful for one governess. As mischievous as I was, Betsy was often complicit with my many schemes; perhaps not the sort of helpmeet a concerned lord and master should have chosen for his young charge.

Betsy threw a twisted rope ladder out of the second-story window, and I caught it easily in both hands. I had smuggled the ladder into my room ages ago, and had used it more times than I could count as I flitted between lives.

"Quickly," Betsy urged, and withdrew back into the room. Concealed by Lord Pennington's looming shrubbery, I seized the twisted rope. Scaling it was the work of moments, and Betsy caught my hand as I eased over the sill.

"*Allez, hop,*" I said cheerfully as I leapt lightly down. "Am I terribly late?"

"You're cutting it dangerously close," Betsy said, rebuke clear on her apple-cheeked features. "Let's get you clean a'fore you stain the pillows."

"Just the hair," I began, and froze as I caught a glimpse at myself in the mirror. "Bloody bells!"

Betsy gasped. But unlike her, who glared reproachfully at my adaption of the lower class's uncivil crudeness, I was more appalled by the state of my appearance.

As I feared, the lampblack I coated through my hair had smudged over my forehead and cheeks, leaving sooty fingerprints across my dirty face. Only the circular seal of my fog-prevention goggles had kept the pale skin around my eyes clean, giving me a wide-eyed, startled effect. Even my mouth, unfortunately full by nature, bore a black smudge across the lower edge, which gave every impression of losing a fight with a brick wall.

"I have to find a way to change my hair," I said fervently. "It smears like ink at the first sign of damp."

"It's *always* damp. And you need a bath, first," she corrected sternly, and plucked the rope from my hands. "Quickly."

"A bath, then," I agreed. I shed my belt, draping the pouch across an elegant rose-patterned chair, and carefully assured it wouldn't slide to the floor. I didn't have the components to fix either my goggles or my respirator should they break.

Betsy spun me around. "Did you get your man, miss?" Her quick fingers loosened my stays, and I took a deep breath as the constricting panels fell away. Idly curving one hand around my aching breast, I rubbed at the pained curve as she helped me out of my collecting uniform. Buckled corset and accompanying knives, same color shirt, the camisole I wore beneath. Trousers, worn leather boots and underthings were all separated into two piles. One for her to wash and mend at her own home, and one for the less suspicious items to be washed with the rest of my things.

I grimaced. "More or less," I said, but kept my tone to a hush. Through the soles of my now bare feet, I could feel the fine tremors as the household staff prepared for the day.

I'd sleep through most of it, and as Betsy helped me into the now lukewarm bath, I sighed with pleasure. My eyes eased closed. "Lovely."

"So you were paid, then?"

This made my eyes snap open, and I frowned. "Not yet. I had to leave him by the gate," I admitted. "The time—Oof!"

Betsy's fingers pushed on my head. I submerged beneath the surface, squeezing my eyes shut again as a sooty cloud floated into the scented water. Heedless of my stinging scalp, she pulled and scrubbed and wrung until the bathwater turned nearly black.

She was talking as I surfaced, sputtering. "How on earth will you gain your fee?" she asked baldly, her mitigated Bow Bell accent sharp and flat and entirely informal.

That was my fault. Betsy was my friend, and I'd always encouraged her independence in my rooms. But I glowered at her as she helped me from the tub. "I'll go back tonight and collect it."

"That's so soon!" Her eyes were dark and wide, like a sweet calf's eyes, but they frowned at me now in consternation as she took a towel to my freshly clean skin. She was so serious beneath the fringe of rumpled brown curls over her forehead that I grinned, tucking my wet hair over my shoulders.

"You worry too much," I told her. "It's a lark, that's all."

"It's dangerous, is what it is."

"That, too." Of course it was. On many, many counts. "But I want my bounty. The Menagerie has it."

Even mentioning the decadent pleasure garden was enough to make my friend shiver and fall silent. I sat on the vanity stool, tucking my soft robe around me, and waited patiently as she dried my hair between two towels.

I was filled with energy. With the knowledge that not only had I successfully completed another bounty, but that I'd been unhappily forced to leave him on the Menagerie's front stoop.

As if I were afraid to face the garden's dark host.

Gooseflesh crawled over my spine, and I shook my head hard. I wasn't afraid of Micajah Hawke. He annoyed me, like a gadfly.

A particularly handsome gadfly, but a stinging insect nonetheless. He'd give me my due. He had no reason not to: after all, I'd delivered Mr. Cummings as the bounty note requested. Maybe not personally, but there'd been nothing about personal attendance in the request.

My eyes focused on my reflection, now all but glowing with cleanliness and good health. My cheeks were pink, and my green eyes shone vividly now that my hair was once more back to its natural color.

As Betsy worked my auburn hair through her hands, the daylight creeping through my window picked out gleaming strands of jewel red and uncanny hints of near violet. A fashionable fringe draped across my forehead, but the rest fell nearly to my waist in unruly curls.

I hated it, my hair. Not only was it a terribly unfashionable color in the social mores of London above, but it was entirely too memorable anywhere else. I had my mother's hair, for better or for worse, and it was for this reason I ran lampblack through it when I escaped below. Dark hair was so much less noticeable. If I could, I would have cut it as short as a boy's for easier tending, but I didn't dare.

Betsy met my eyes in the silvered glass and tugged on a loose curl. "Stop that."

"What, exactly?"

"You're scowling, miss. Something fierce."

I stuck out my tongue. Betsy sighed in deep-seated resignation, but I chuckled as I rose from the vanity seat. "You sound like Fanny."

"She's got a point, she does," my maid warned. "You'll look like that weathered old bat in Lord Pennington's loft."

"Would that I had but half her talent." I giggled. The bedclothes were already turned down. I slid beneath them, and Betsy tucked the bedding around me, dark eyes glinting merrily.

"Would that you had half the view," she said, tongue-in-cheek.

Lord Pennington's mother-in-law was of great amusement to us both; a wily woman who had taken to painting the most extraordinary nudes from the not-impenetrable privacy of her veranda.

"Hush." I laughed. "You're a wicked girl, Betsy Phillips, and I'll be the first to tell your husband."

"If he doesn't know by now—"

I covered my mouth. "Stop, stop," I pleaded, laughter muffled. "Before Fanny comes barging in demanding to drag me to her early markets."

"That one's sound asleep this morning," Betsy assured me. Her smile faded as she tucked the blankets up around my shoulders. "Will you sleep all right?"

My eyes flicked to the crystal decanter on my nightstand. Ruby liquid glinted in the lamplight, as brilliant as the jeweled glints in my hair, and my pulse skittered.

Laudanum. I didn't sleep well as a rule. Fanny thought it had to do with the boundless energy that had demonized this house from the moment I first set foot in it. She was only half correct. The nightmares I suffered when I attempted sleep without opium had kept the household up for months before the physicians had prescribed laudanum to help. They assured Fanny I'd grow out of it.

The nightmares had lessened, it's true, but the laudanum had not.

But Betsy didn't like the idea, and my chaperone kept a close watch on my use. I'd had to hide my opium grains from Betsy before, and I'd learned to measure out my requests for only the most difficult nights. I shook my head, settling back against my pillows. "No laudanum tonight, I think." I smothered a false yawn, and Betsy smoothed the blankets.

"Dream sweet," she said. "Perhaps of broad shoulders in naked marble?"

I smothered a snort. "Wicked girl," I repeated.

"And well you love me."

"Mm." I turned, wrapping my arms around the lacy edge of my pillow, and closed my eyes. "Good night, Betsy."

"Good night, miss," she said, and I heard her footsteps ease toward the door. "I'll be in again, come after noon."

Plenty of time for rest, I thought, and sighed into my soft pillow. I waited for a good long time, measuring the pulse of my house as the staff set to work. When I was sure that Betsy wouldn't be returning, I sat up.

The crystal decanter waited, its garish color winking innocently. I picked it up, its faceted edges unyielding in my hands, and pulled the stopper free. The fragrance curled through my lightening bedroom in wisps of spicy cinnamon.

I tipped a portion of the contents into my mouth, barely aware of the still-bitter taste of the draught as it slid through my throat, into my chest. My stomach. It pooled there like a warm balm, and I sighed as I settled back into my bed. I relished the feel of the liquid sleep as it curled through my insides.

I would run out of the laudanum soon. My store of opium grains was gone, used already, though I don't recall using it all.

If I didn't collect my bounty later tonight, I'd have to face my night terrors alone.

But that was something for later concern.

It wasn't long before the laudanum took effect. The sounds of my staff downstairs blurred into a gentle ocean of calm routine. I slept. And as I soared on the heavenly wings of God's own heralds, I dreamed.

But I never remembered what I dreamed. At least, not when laudanum cushioned my head.

Chapter Two

I don't wake happily. The promise of pain shooting through my forehead came to fruition as I cracked open eyes gummed with the detritus of hard sleep.

I squinted in the dim light. Bless her, Betsy had drawn the heavy drapes before she'd left, leaving my bedroom swathed in murky shadow. Dusky rose and lavender faded to shaded brown and gray; much less offensive to my waking sensibilities.

I rolled over, drawing the bedclothes around my shoulders, and groped at the night table without fully opening my eyes.

Glass rattled. Cold edges slid over my fingertips, and blearily, I found the chain I'd been looking for. Grumbling wordlessly, I drew the watch as close to my face as I could and opened the case.

Only minutes before noon.

What was I doing? My mind beckoned as if through tangled webs of woven fog. I'd had plans. Or was it that I deliberately had made no plans?

Was it so very important for me to get out of my warm bed now? I didn't think so. With a sigh, I closed my eyes firmly and damned the day to fend for itself.

A precise rap shattered my ruminations. The door opened, utterly without sound thanks to the lamp oil I frequently applied to the wide hinges. "Good morning, miss!"

I groaned and threw the covers over my head. All the better to drown out Betsy's gratingly Cockney cheer.

"Oh, no, you don't." She seized the edge of the blankets in both hands. Cold air speared through my thin cotton nightgown, and I swore before the rest of my mind could properly take form.

Betsy's appalled expression only partially salved my pique. "It's deucedly cold," I pointed out.

"Ladies don't say 'deucedly,'" she shot back, and flung the bedclothes into a corner. "You are going to be late for breakfast, miss, if we don't hurry you in."

She made an excellent point. Frances Fortescue was a woman of impeccable propriety.

Or at least, I thought uncharitably as I stood and allowed Betsy to take charge of me, Fanny was an old widow whose propriety extended only as far as the employ of a madman's daughter could. My governess since I was thirteen, and a widow for as long as I'd known her, she now served as my chaperone in polite society.

An unmarried girl without a mother could not be choosy.

Betsy whipped my nightgown off and quickly helped me dress. For all my waking unkindness, I loved Betsy and Fanny dearly. It only tweaked my conscience a smidge to think such unkind thoughts while Betsy prepared me to face the light of day.

I sat in front of the vanity and studied my reflection as Betsy arranged my hair into a collection of upswept curls and high knots. She used more pins than I suspected necessary, but we'd learned long ago how unmanageable my thick hair could be.

"What is for breakfast?" I asked, pausing midway to yawn behind splayed fingers. "Tell me there's strawberry jam?"

"You'll have to ask Mr. Booth." She smacked my offending hand. "Don't start yawning now, you're just out of bed. Didn't you sleep?"

"Not enough." My God, it was as if my thoughts were hiding from me deliberately. I shook my head hard, wincing. Waking hadn't always been this difficult. It seemed as if the older I got, the harder I found it to wake up. I wondered if I'd ever be allowed to sleep through the day entirely.

As if Society didn't think me odd enough already.

Betsy worked quickly, and within moments, I found myself corseted, bustled, and wearing a pale blue day dress trimmed in peacock green. My shoes were much more delicate than the kid boots I wore below the drift, but my toes complained immediately at the pinch.

Such was the life I led.

Betsy stepped back, beaming. "You look lovely."

"Who's to notice?" I muttered, and swept my skirts out of the way as I made my way into the hall. She snorted behind me, but said nothing.

My home has no name, though I'd always envied the lovely titles the peerage gave their estates. Unfortunately, most of the names I imagined as a child included the words "mad" or "deathly" or "tombs." Terribly morbid.

So nameless it is, but it is no less elegant for it. I stepped into a hall laid with rugs carried from the farthest Orient, furnished with items carted from the heart of Egypt and icy reaches of Viking lands.

My father had enjoyed dark woods and foreign taste, and every room mirrored this leaning. Mr. Ashmore had changed little; in fact, he only added to the mystifying collection each time he visited. The staircase boasted newels carved into life-size lions, mouths agape and hungry eyes glaring. My skirts rustled across the hardwood floors, and I made a face at the brilliantly polished mirror at the other end of the hall.

Rumor suggested it had been a gift from a Russian czar. I silently called bollocks on the idea.

A czar from the steppes would be far more likely to give horses, wouldn't he?

Through the elegantly papered walls, I could hear the whisper of movement. China delicately clinked as I stepped inside the dining room.

The table was large enough to seat twelve comfortably; however, I rarely bothered with such events. Fanny was seated already, her thin figure wrapped in a demure navy blue day gown. Her gray hair was swept up into an elegant chignon, not a hair out of place.

"There you are. Come sit, my dear, and eat." Fanny set her tea down beside her plate. Her mouth smiled, papery skin wrinkling, but her pale blue eyes raked over me from top of my pinned hair to the tips of my shoes.

I resisted the urge to curtsy. She'd only explain, unperturbed as ever, that curtsying was reserved for more elegant times or some such social rubbish. I didn't care to sit through another lecture, so I swept into a seat with as much restraint as I could muster.

Paper crinkled under my elbow.

Bless the butler who had managed this household for as long as I'd lived in it. Washington Barrett Booth and his wife, Esther, had always been here. They hadn't raised me in the same way as the hired nannies, but I loved them both as if they had.

And Booth never failed to supply me with the morning paper.

Fanny thought it the dominion of gentlemen to be bothered with the news. I thought *that* archaic and useless. Still, I gave her the courtesy of a smile as I replied, "Good morning, Fanny. Did you sleep well?"

"Quite, thank you. And yourself, my dear?"

Terribly. "Just fine, thank you," I lied. Bold, black print caught my eye. My fingers itched to open the paper, but the uneven *step-thunk*, *step-thunk* of Booth's familiar approach halted me. "Good morning, Booth," I chirped.

The butler was at least sixty years old, if he was a day. Unlike many men of an age, he had a full head of thick, white leonine hair, and the most impressive sideburns I'd ever seen. His clothing was never anything but distinguished and neat, his hands gloved, and his manner impeccable.

Only the ornate brass crutch affixed to the carefully hidden stump of his right knee marred the effect. He'd lost his leg at war. I felt it gave him the appearance of savage nobility, like a gentleman pirate, and told Booth so when I first met him.

He hadn't laughed. Very gravely, he bowed and thanked me graciously for my assessment, thereby winning my thirteen-year-old heart forever.

Now, his gray eyes twinkled quietly as he set a silver

tray at my elbow. "Good morning, miss," he replied. "Madam."

Fanny sipped at her tea, inclining her head, but I gave the man my brightest smile. Meal laid out, he turned and once more faded out of sight. *Step-thunk, step-thunk.*

"You aren't going to read that swill while you eat, are you?"

I looked up from the paper I had unfolded across my lap, blinking as innocuously as I knew how. "It's not swill, Fanny. How else is a girl to understand what's happening in the world around her?"

She grimaced, lips pinching together the way she did when she swallowed an argument, and waved a weathered hand at me. "If you must. At least eat. It will be a long time until dinner."

"I'll be sure to take tea on time," I said, but my eyes were skimming the print across the newspaper. The *London Times* spared no ink for the broadsheet. "'Ghastly Murder in the East End,'" I read aloud. "Dreadful mutilation of a woman."

Her teacup clattered loudly. "Cherry, really." The reproach in Fanny's voice was enough. I shrugged, reaching around the paper to collect a wedge of toast, smeared liberally with jam. Strawberries, I noted with pleasure. My favorite.

"Sorry," I said.

"Shall we focus on today's schedule?"

I knew better than to speak with my mouth full, so I said nothing, knowing the woman could carry a conversation all by herself with ease.

The paper called the murderer "Leather Apron." Hardly helpful. That could be any one of a number of working-class men below the drift. Betsy's own husband was a journeyman blacksmith, and I was sure he owned at least one apron made of leather to keep the sparks at bay.

"Now, we have an appointment with Madame Toulouse this week," Fanny continued briskly. "Be sure to consider carefully your wardrobe. We'll want at least three new dinner gowns and as many day dresses as pique our interest." She paused to sip at her tea. "The *Ladies' Monthly Review* has featured a new gown from Paris. The Directoire fashion is returning."

"I want tea gowns," I mumbled around the sweetened toast.

"Not with your mouth full." I winced behind the paper and swallowed hastily, but she was already adding, "Absolutely not. Tea gowns are nothing more than indecency cloaked as fashion. They are not appropriate for an unmarried lady, and we've better things to purchase for you than gowns that will never see the light of day." Without missing even a breath, she added, "And speaking of going out, the Honorable Theodore Helmsley has sent an invite to a formal."

I rolled my eyes from behind the safety of the paper. "He's just Teddy."

"He is a viscount's son, albeit the youngest of three and unlikely to inherit anything." Fanny's china clinked, this one a firm sound that suggested she was once more following her own path of conversation.

My chaperone's every gesture was a dialect in and of itself.

"Which baffles the mind," she continued. "Your relationship with him defies explanation. Why on earth are you wasting your time on a man who stands to inherit nothing?"

"I don't intend to marry him, Fanny," I said, but only absently exasperated. My attention focused on the article. A woman, one of many prostitutes in the East End, had been found with her throat brutally slashed. Gruesome.

"Well, if he hasn't asked for your hand by this time," Fanny said briskly, "it's unlikely that he'd be so inclined to offer anytime soon. You're twenty years old, my dear, and take it from me—"

The prostitute's entrails had been wound around her neck? I grimaced, the toast suddenly ash in my mouth. I swallowed it down with effort, but the details in the print were too horrible to put down. Organs shredded like so much raw meat. Vast quantities of blood, as if murdered in a rage.

"—Are you at all listening to me?"

"Yes, of course, Fanny," I murmured.

I knew a great many of the streetwalkers of the East End. Not all, of course; there were far too many women selling themselves for me to know more than a passing face or recognize a distinct call in the night. Women driven below by the higher wages earned turning tricks for coin, or exiled from a society unable to forgive the transgressions of independent thought.

I couldn't turn my back on them.

Especially since I knew I was only an outed secret away from the same fate.

"Cherry."

I scanned the broadsheet again. It didn't give me a name. Who was killed? The odds were low that I knew her, but then again, such a brutal murder had to have clues. Perhaps I could investigate.

"Cherry?"

And who was Leather Apron? Was it in any relation to the terrible murder of the August before? The broadsheet seemed to suggest that the two were related, and certainly the details were equally as gruesome—

"Cherry St. Croix!"

I jerked the paper down, crumpled it in my lap and sat straighter in my chair. "Yes, madam," I said smartly.

Fanny's eyes glittered in dangerous warning. Her rigid posture never bent so much as a millimeter, but I could sense her genteel bristle even from across the long table. "You haven't," she said with the icy control I'd learned to recognize at a young age, "heard a single word I've said, have you?"

I wracked my memory. Cinnamon-peppered clouds of laudanum and the newsprint words were all I found. "No, madam," I replied. Very quietly, I pushed the newspaper off my lap and reached for my tea.

Fanny's eyes slitted. "Earl Cornelius Kerrigan Compton is returned from his station with Her Majesty's Royal Navy. He is, as you might have known if you paid any such attention to the news that matters, the eldest son of the Marchioness Northampton."

It took every iota of control I had not to cringe.

"She is, much to London's delight, throwing a ball in honor of her son's successful return," Fanny continued. "The Honorable Helmsley has requested your company." Every word dropped between us like the most delicate of hammers; finely made and damnably hard.

I set my jaw. "I don't want to."

"We are going," Fanny pronounced firmly, with the finality of a sealed bargain.

"When is this ball?" I demanded.

"Tonight."

My stomach twisted. "Fanny, I don't—"

"We are going," she repeated, no louder but much slower, "tonight."

I would have slumped, but my corset refused the allowance. As the toast I'd managed to eat surged back into my throat, I swallowed hard and managed, "As you wish."

Fanny waited until I'd picked up my tea, unaware that I was trying to drown the knot of hysteria gathering in my chest, before returning her own attention to her meal. "Now," she continued lightly, "we must think carefully on your gown. It will take all day to prepare."

I wanted to groan. Instead, shifting in my seat, I glared at my food and attacked it with as much restrained savagery as I could get away with. I had to find a way to sneak away from this rotted ball. I had no interest in this pompous Earl Compton, and even *less* interest in his mother, who had decided early in my social appearances that I was something to be pitied, watched like a squirming bug, and as she put it, *kept from my own ambition.*

The Marchioness's little salon was known in Society columns as the Ladies of Admirable Mores and Behavior. The gossips referred to their vicious circle as L.A.M.B.

I entertained fantasies of taking the slaughter knife to the whole lot of them.

No matter how well-intentioned Teddy's request, I knew no such invite could have gone through without the Marchioness's approval. The very lateness of its arrival suggested her hand in it. For some unknown reason, she wanted Mad St. Croix's daughter at her ball.

And Fanny, bless her ambitious heart, was going to serve me on a silver platter.

As the woman droned on about colors, fabrics and style, my fingers tightened on the delicate handle of my teacup. I wanted to be anywhere but that ballroom.

Specifically, I wanted to be below the drift and collecting my bounty, talking to the street doves—bloody bells, I would have settled for Micajah Hawke's smug scrutiny.

"And, Cherry."

I blinked, mouth smiling automatically. "Yes, Fanny?"

Her blue eyes met mine, as direct as an admiral at his own helm. "If you make one misstep, I'll see that your books are locked away for a fortnight."

My throat ached from holding back my temper. It lanced into a sharp pain behind my right eye, and my free hand fisted into my skirt. "Yes, of course," I murmured.

It wasn't her fault. I'd always been a difficult child.

But for this brief moment in time, I seriously considered setting fire to her skirts.

With no more warning than Fanny's imperious directive, I found myself upstairs after breakfast, stripped down, scrubbed from head to toe and draped in a robe as Betsy and Mrs. Booth collaborated on the design of my hair.

Esther Booth was the reason the house didn't fall to disrepair. She ran it with an iron disposition disrupted only by the subtle indulgences of her husband, and although they were lacking in children, she'd done all right by me.

Even if I was forced to sit still for hours as Betsy and Mrs. Booth argued, debated, experimented and improvised on my waist-length tresses.

"You could cut it all off," I offered, angelic innocence.

My housekeeper gasped. "Saints preserve us," she muttered under her breath, even as Betsy shot me a quelling frown.

I shrugged.

Finally, my hair was pinned and fresh flowers acquired for the crowning touch. I hate, hate, *hate* flowers in my hair. They invariably fall off at the most awkward of moments. Like into my soup bowl at a social parlor or crushed to a perfumed death on the ballroom floor.

And the fragrance of lilies makes me sneeze.

Nevertheless, as the sky darkened and afternoon tea came and went with nothing but a few delicate cakes to sate my growing hunger, I watched as if from a distance as my maid and housekeeper dressed me like a paper doll.

I enjoyed listening to them chatter, but I was nervous. Worse, I was annoyed that I'd be trapped in a stifling ballroom, enduring gossip and speculation and study like some kind of caged animal, while my bounty remained below. Unclaimed. Unspent.

"And we are done!" announced Mrs. Booth, but I wasn't given much time to inspect my appearance before I was hurried from the room, all but stuffed into my cloak and elbow-length gloves, and guided out into the night.

London gleamed prettily in the dark. Lights shone from the Chelsea square, especially with the gas lamps flickering merrily. The city above the drift glimmered and danced; a glittering dowager festooned with diamonds.

Below, she was pocked and diseased, her skirts hanging torn and stained around her roughened knees, but only the faintest roil of fog wafted over the edges of the elegantly decorated canals to remind the peerage of the impure dregs beneath them.

The time of the horse and carriage as emblems of status was long gone, passed now to rustic country estates or idle pleasures at Hyde Park. Our carriages were gondolas, as they have in Venice, and our footmen gondoliers. Slimmer than the ferries that only moved up and down, these vessels could float like a ship on air.

The night was filled with the soft hum of the aether engines installed at the bottom of each. They sucked in air and steam, filtered it through a process developed by the late Dr. Angelicus Finch, and extracted—so the science periodicals explained—the aether found in the very atmosphere.

Because of this, the discharge expelled through the array of finlike pipes inset into the tail was colored blue, and you could mark the business of an evening's road by the flares and shades of azure lighting the night. Chelsea was often lit by a subdued blue glow.

The St. Croix carriage was not one of the more spectacular, lacking in gilt and trim and boasting only one pan-flute array of pipes at the tail, but it offered a private box with curtains. More important, it was also outfitted with a clean-air machine. Useful for those occasional days when the fog shifted up.

As I gathered my skirts around me and took Booth's steadying hand, the houseboy at the front of the gondola caught my eye. He grinned a gap-toothed smile and winked.

"Face forward, Leviticus," Booth directed solemnly.

I couldn't help my smile as I settled into the box. I knew little enough of the brat affectionately called Levi, but he'd earned an extra coin or two from me over the few months Booth had taken him under his tutelage. I asked him his age, once. He'd claimed sixteen.

I'd called him a bald-faced liar and sent him to the kitchen.

We have reached a sort of truce. I no longer force him to scrub the pots, and he refuses to go lower than twelve.

Booth handed Fanny into the padded box seats beside me. The widow was lovely in a silk mauve gown and matching lined cloak. Her gray hair had been swept into a clean chignon, with only a few thick curls draped beside it. A spray of feathers bobbed delicately by her subtly powdered cheek.

I arranged the folds of my yellow skirts and tried not to think about what was coming as the gondola lurched into motion.

I knew I looked fetching enough. Betsy and Mrs. Booth had simply outdone themselves, choosing the vivid yellow gown to contrast with the fire buried in my hair. Ivory lace frothed from the gown like a spill of cream, drawing attention to its low waist, small bustle and length of the hem. I wore no rouge, even secretly as many women did, and the gown's color turned my eyes to a brilliant shade beneath the curls Betsy had created with hot tongs and paper.

Sunshine yellow was my favorite color.

My cloak was ivory, not white, my dancing slippers

bronze, and a single, wide yellow ribbon trailed from
my throat. My gloves were also ivory and elbow-length;
my fan was draped on a ribbon from my wrist, and the
yellow and white flowers in my curled and coiled hair
were pinned viciously in place.

I was as ready to meet the enemy on the field of battle
as any soldier facing unrelenting odds.

Fanny said nothing, perhaps unwilling to rock the
uneasy truce we'd settled upon, and it wasn't long
before the gentle sway of the gondola eased to a slow
halt. I knew without pulling back the window curtains
that we'd moved into the flow of traffic. There would be
many gondolas making for the Marquis Northampton's
fine London estate. The occasional patch of blue light
flared around the curtain rim, and a vague din of conversation trickled through the thick box walls.

My fingers clenched in my skirts.

When out and about in London proper, you could tell
a great deal about a family by their gondola. Whether
covered in gilt or carved in dark, rich mahogany; layered in trim and tassels or plain and unadorned, each
gondola was as unique as a flower.

There were craftsman who excelled at gondola
design, and whose trade many wealthy families desperately vied for.

But it was *how* a gondola traveled that claimed the
most significance. If she sat too low into the drift or
too high out of it, if your gondolier was too unskilled to
keep her steady on the fog as if it were real water, then
you bore the label of *faux* sophistication. New money,
no sensibility.

Anyone who was simply anyone hired a gondolier
who could keep his boat steady.

Fortunately for my already fragile reputation, Booth was an excellent gondolier.

"Cherry, you are frowning," Fanny said abruptly, and I realized that as I'd concentrated on the noises outside, my eyebrows had pulled together.

I deliberately relaxed my brow, but my fingers only tightened into my gown. "I still don't understand why we're here," I said sullenly.

"For the love of all that is holy," Fanny sighed, and I caught myself before I frowned again. Ladies of good breeding didn't frown. They didn't scowl, or pout, or twist mouths into anything more offensive than a quiet smile.

Ladies were to be silent and gracious and understanding.

Ladies certainly—I smothered a sudden giggle as it welled into my throat—never climbed walls with the intent to wriggle through tiny windows. They didn't steal from a gentleman's pockets, cosh ruffians over the head or deliver men for bounties paid.

They certainly didn't enjoy the fine flavors of Oriental opium.

I was no lady. But I didn't say this aloud. Instead, I held up a gloved hand and promised, "I shall behave, Fanny. I'm not so stubborn that I'd destroy my reputation because of one marchioness."

"*The* marchioness," Fanny corrected. I watched the artfully frayed feather dip and sway with every bob of her head. "The only marchioness who matters. If she turns on you, my dear—"

"I know." A cut from the Northamptons was as deadly to a reputation as arsenic to a drunkard. I had no choice but to be on my best behavior.

I could give two tosses what the vile woman had to say about me; I enjoyed my solitude. But anything that marked me would mark Fanny, Booth and the others. I wouldn't force them below the drift for anything in the world.

And it was that I had to repeat to myself with every passing minute.

The gondola eased once more to a stop and rocked gently. Within moments, the door to the box opened, and I accepted the white-gloved hand as it appeared in my vision.

"You look stunning," Fanny said reassuringly as I stepped into the twinkle of a thousand lanterns.

The Northampton home stood like a majestic queen at the far end of a drive lined with lamps. The cobbles were pristine, already filled with the slow plod of guests mingling, conversing and greeting one another along the way. The night sky seemed lit to gold, an aura of light and music and sound hovering just over the tremendously large manor.

Blinded, I barely noticed as the hand in mine tightened. Then a familiar laugh forced me to shake the stars from my eyes. All at once, I realized that Booth was helping my chaperone out of the gondola, and the hand in mine belonged to my dear friend instead.

"Ted—!" Fanny cleared her throat behind me, and my instinct to seize his hands in both of mine quickly transitioned to a small, graceful curtsy. "My Lord Helmsley," I demurred instead. Lace pooled around my feet, but I peeked up through my lashes to see Teddy bend slightly at the waist, head inclined, in form-perfect propriety.

Theodore Helmsley was not the most handsome of

London's bachelors, but I'd never held that against him. To be truthful, he was rather hawkish in appearance, with a blade-thin, hooked nose and a build far more suited to the life of a circus juggler than a viscount's son. Still, dressed to the nines for a ball, he cut a far more interesting figure than the fat old men and milquetoast dandies that often filled the floor. His black tailcoat was perfectly tailored, his waistcoat and trousers also black and just as fine. Like all of the gentlemen, his white shirt collar was winged and his bow tie white.

His dark brown hair retained a natural curl, cut long enough to leave a hint of it but short enough to salve fashion's demands, and his features were razor sharp and slightly off center. A keen intelligence hid behind the fashionably languid expression he often wore. He was nobody's fool, my friend, and we'd spent many a visit poring over the science periodicals together.

When we first met, he caught me attempting to create fire from two sticks, as the Indians in America were reputed to do. I'd been invited to a summer soiree at his mother's home, but wandered away when the adults failed to notice my utter boredom. That I am Mad St. Croix's daughter only cemented our friendship.

The mores of Society frowned on too close an association, but as the youngest son, Teddy had no illusions as to what his future held. He'd have to marry up, enlist as an officer in military service or go into a respectable trade if he expected to live well. As of yet, he'd met no girl he wanted to marry, and I was secretly grateful.

I knew any debutante he married would frown on me.

But for tonight, he was my escort, and I smiled up at him brightly. "Miss St. Croix." His greeting was subdued, but his hazel eyes snapped devilishly as they studied the hem of my gown. He guided me out of Fanny's path with his free hand, the other curved under his top hat. "May I say you look utterly charming?"

"You are most kind, sir."

"Mrs. Fortescue, you honor me with your presence," he continued, not breaking stride as he bowed shortly to a suddenly fluttering Fanny.

I didn't need to look to know that the eyes closest to us were taking in my every detail. I resisted the urge to look down at myself. The cut of my gown was fashionably low, but not as daring as other gowns I had seen. The extra flowers arrayed along the décolletage helped. My cloak was new and artfully draped. I was fine.

Nervous, but fine.

"Shall we proceed to the ball?" Teddy's voice in my ear jarred me from my musings, and I swept my skirt into one hand. "I'm glad you came," he added as he fell into step beside me.

"I wish I hadn't," I murmured to him.

His lips twitched. "I wasn't going to invite you, but father insisted."

Viscount Armistice Helmlsey III was one of the peerage's many indulgences. Besotted with the finer things in life, it was no small secret that he lived the life of a hedonist—and encouraged his sons to do the same.

In his mind, I was a fine match for his third son.

In mine, I'd rather drill holes through my fingernails than marry. In less than a year, I would inherit everything of my father's. If I married, common law dictated that everything that was mine would belong solely to my groom.

Bugger that for a lark.

I loved Teddy, but not in that way. And certainly not *that* much.

"I owe your lord father a debt," I replied sweetly, and Teddy raised a gloved hand to his mouth before the laugh escaped.

Fanny watched us carefully as we traveled the lengthy path. Once inside, I'd be sure Teddy kept her glass full. I wouldn't enjoy this night, but I silently vowed that my chaperone would.

As if reading my mind, Teddy's head dipped closer to mine. "I'll be sure she is escorted around while you dance."

"I have to dance?"

"Of course," he said, eyes twinkling. "You don't think the gentlemen would miss a chance to spin Mad St. Croix's daughter about the floor, do you?"

My back teeth ground. "I wish they would."

His laugh told me I'd find no help from him. He enjoyed watching the peerage deal with, as he put it, the blemish that was me in their midst. It wasn't hurtful. I *was* a blemish; a curious boil on the face of the upper class.

One part curiosity, one part irritation. Like a colicky thoroughbred.

From what little I'd been told, my mother had been the darling of the upper class. Rumor had it that the Queen had favored her for a time, although all invitations stopped when she accepted my father's proposal. My father's reputation for towering intellect and eccentricity was as well known as my mother's beauty. They'd been a strange match, I gather. A love match, even, which would explain why she married beneath her station.

My mother had been beautiful. I was only a pale imitation.

Soon enough, we stepped into the most lavish entry I had ever seen. I had no chance to admire the décor before Fanny spirited me into the ladies' cloakroom, where I was swiftly divested of my outerwear. Fanny gave hers to the waiting maid, fussed with the folds of my gown, and snapped up the trailing fan I left dangling from my wrist.

"Enjoy yourself, my dear," she ordered.

I would rather eat live bugs, but I firmly arranged my mouth into a demure smile and stepped into the ballroom at Fanny's side.

Right into my own personal level of hell.

Chapter Three

The heat swept over me like a tide. Conversation, the faintly irritating whine of the orchestra and the oppressive humidity of so many bodies crushed into one enormous room conspired to steal my breath, and I flinched.

Fanny cupped a hand under my elbow. "There's Lord Helmsley," she said in my ear.

Grateful for the reprieve from having to decide what to do, I let her lead me across the room, pardoning ourselves as we sidled around knots of gaily dressed girls and festively gowned matrons. I kept one hand in my skirts, constantly worried that my lacy train would end up beneath the foot of one of the many powerful elite.

That was all I needed. To be accused of sending a duchess or some earl sprawling.

Teddy's smile was equally as pained as we met near the dance floor. Divested of his hat, stylish walking stick and overcoat, he looked both wealthy and elegant. And like he belonged in this mess. He bent his head so I could hear him over the music. "I understand the marchioness and her family are not here yet."

"What, to her own son's ball?"

He shrugged his thin shoulders. "Fashionably late, don't you know."

"Rude," I muttered.

Teddy fought back another one of those cheeky grins and cleared his throat, proffering an elegantly beribboned card. "Your dance card, Miss St. Croix."

"The devi—" I caught myself before Fanny could, although she was already distracted, searching the crowd for faces she recognized. I was not the only unmarried lady at the ball, and many of the married women and chaperones were acquaintances of hers.

Teddy dangled the card like a magician's watch, and I snatched it out of his hand. "Thank you, sir," I said through my teeth, but I channeled retribution into my eyes.

He was unapologetic. "I shall seat Mrs. Fortescue, and return to claim a dance. Save an entry for me, won't you?"

"Only if you're extremely fortunate," I told him, but without heat. I liked that he doted on Fanny at these events.

Still, I thought as I turned and studied the press of gentlemen and ladies, I turned out all right. My dress was much richer in color than strictly fashionable, but my coloring allowed me to skirt the boundaries of the preferred hues. My eye picked out gowns of azure blue and stunning green, each on the most lovely brunettes, though the dominant color by far was white and cream. Blondes were the absolute height of fashion, with my own fiery coloring primarily cultivated by actresses and ladies of the opera.

Not exactly a mark in my favor.

The heat battered at me from every direction, and I very much wanted a drink of something cool. That I was wilting so soon didn't bode well for my flowers, and judging by the overly sweet fragrance filling my nose, mine weren't the only bouquets at risk.

I barely kept from grimacing as I fought back a sneeze. I wouldn't stand out in the middle of a crowd waiting like some doe-eyed girl for a dance. I intended to a find a wall and stay there, come hell or damnation. I'd dodged the master of the house before, avoiding the meddlesome principle that forced the appointed man to ensure all ladies danced. It wouldn't be difficult to lose whomever it was tonight.

It was already a crush, and so early, too.

I gathered my skirts in hand and took a step, only to jerk to a stop as my gown tightened around my hips. I staggered, flailed as my slippers skidded on the slick floor, and found my arm firmly held in large gloved hands. The room rocked, my hip drove into something solid and warm, and I gasped.

"Oh, dear. Forgive me."

The voice in my ear was rich and polished; as fine as red wine and laced with the civil notes of an excellent education. Eton, I thought vaguely. Certainly rounded by some time spent abroad.

My gaze traveled from the elegant hand at my elbow to the sleeve of a tailored black tailcoat, up the fine seams of a wide shoulder that needed no padding, to the starched wings of a crisp white shirt and white tie.

He was lovely. And wholly unfamiliar. His sandy blond hair was brushed off his forehead, and a small, groomed mustache decorated lips set into a concerned line. His chin was strong but not bullish, his nose noble, and his eyes put me in mind of the jade statues Mr. Ashmore had once brought from China.

They narrowed now, troubled. "Are you unwell?" he asked, and the fingers tightened at my elbow as if I would wilt to the floor should he let me go. "I'm terribly sorry, I had no intention of stepping on your gown. I feel quite clumsy."

I found my voice at the same time as I remembered how to direct my limbs to move. I extricated myself with no trouble, sinking into a small, graceful curtsy. "Your pardon," I said, somehow remembering my social graces. Fanny would have been so proud. "I seem to be in your way."

He bowed in kind, the formal gesture sharp and extremely precise. "Then fortune looks favorably upon me tonight," he replied. "Might I ask the pleasure of dancing with you in apology?" His eyes met mine without reserve or curiosity. "It's a poor trade, I admit, but perhaps I may yet climb at least a whit in your esteem by the end."

Dance? I didn't want to dance. I didn't want to step onto the floor where so many eyes would watch my every step, but my would-be assailant didn't appear to be in the habit of waiting for a rebuff. He took my hand, and before my mind could catch up with my body, we were among the dancers.

The heat seemed less intense on the ballroom floor, perhaps due to the movement. Gloved hand around mine, my partner lead with masterful grace, easing into the fluid steps with ease. My skirts swirled in a froth of lace and tulle, and the music surrounded us as cozily as the dancers around us.

His eyes remained with me, not roaming the crowd as so many gentlemen would when my lack of artful conversation bored them, and my cheeks burned. "Do you read the periodicals, sir?" I blurted, desperately grasping for something to converse about.

His smile was controlled, but kind. "Often. Do you mean to say you do?"

Oh, thank God. A commonality. "Every morning," I told him, watching as his eyebrow twitched. Just enough. "Does that surprise you, sir?"

He had the grace to think on it as he guided me into a docile turn. "It shouldn't," he finally allowed. "Tell me, what have you read of late?"

Somehow, I didn't imagine the murderous Leather Apron fit conversation, especially between strangers in a ballroom. I blindly cast for something, anything. And brightened. "Have you heard about Her Majesty's new flagship?"

The hand at my waist slid to the small of my back as he led me into a quick-paced promenade. I clasped hands with a gentlemen beside me, turned and circled again.

My unnamed partner caught my hand and guided me expertly back into the pace. "The *Ophelia*," he continued smoothly. "Yes, I've heard of her. A beauty of a sky ship."

"I hope to see her before she launches," I said, and his eyebrow shifted up. Quizzical? Disapproving? I didn't know. He said nothing, and as the silence stretched between us—as I stared into pale jade eyes and floundered for rational thought—I seized on a new topic. "You dance quite well, sir."

His eyes crinkled ever so slightly at the corners. "One of many such talents," he said without modesty.

But it charmed me, and I found myself curious to know more. "Many?"

"I shan't give away too many secrets," he replied, "lest you think me uninteresting and leave me behind."

I chuckled.

His gaze touched on my unpainted mouth, then flicked again to my eyes. "You dance elegantly," he added.

"One of few such talents," I replied, twisting his own words, and the corner of his mouth quirked. "I'd best inform you now," I continued lightly, "lest you think me actually interesting."

"Aren't you?" My foot glanced off his, a shade too quick for the step, and his eyes flicked down to my skirts. Then up, twinkling. "I find you decidedly interesting."

"Boldly spoken," I returned. "You don't know who I am."

"An oversight I intend to rectify, I assure you." A shiver ran up my spine at his serious words, and I took the time to study the crowd around the floor. Many were staring at us. Women's fans were up, and a good deal of their eyes were affixed with such interest, dismay or outright contempt that I stumbled.

My partner's hands tightened, turning me so gracefully that I doubted my own misstep, much less that anyone had seen it. His gaze flicked out over my head, then returned to me. That corner of his mouth quirked again. "The dance will end, and I'm afraid I shall have to prevail upon someone to facilitate an introduction. To whom shall I ask?"

I didn't want to tell him. Bad enough that two strangers were dancing without an introduction. As soon as this unknown gentleman learned he took a madman's daughter around the dance floor, he wouldn't look at me nearly so kindly.

And he was handsome. My heart fluttered as his feet moved beside mine, guiding me, spinning us both.

My silence only caused him to dip close to my ear to murmur, "I shall prevail upon the master of the house, then. We are acquainted, he and I."

I opened my mouth, but before anything could be said, the strains of music died away. The gentleman stepped back, bowed smartly, and took my hand to lead me to the base of the grand stairway at the far side of the room.

"There you are," Fanny called as I curtsied again.

"I return this young lady to your safe care," my strange partner said, and bowed.

I watched Fanny stop, stare and barely manage to curtsy before the man turned and strode through the crowd. Murmurs followed him, swirled around me, and I frowned at my chaperone.

"Why is everyone staring?" I whispered.

"Stop frowning," she whispered back, but her thin cheeks were pale. "Do you know who that was?"

"Certainly not the prince," I said crossly.

Fanny gave me a look designed to quell my temper as thoroughly as an ice bucket, and I resisted the urge to rub at my throat. I was hot, overcrowded, and I disliked not knowing what was happening.

Suddenly, an orchestral flourish wound its way through the ballroom, and I looked up. Fanny took my arm, tugging me aside.

Fashionably late to his own ball, His Lordship Benedict Kerrigan Compton, the Marquess of Northampton, stood at the top stair. He was splendid in his ballroom finery, but all eyes certainly were pinned on his lady wife in ice blue beside him.

The flutter in my chest plummeted to an arctic pit in the base of my stomach as I gazed upon Lady Almira Louise Compton. The Marchioness of Northampton. She had been, once upon a time, fair. Her hair still held the gentle shine of golden hues faded from age. Her features were still striking, even from a distance.

And, I noticed with a sudden wash of dread, her steely gaze was fixed on me.

Behind her, a handsome gentleman with sandy blond hair bent his head to listen to His Lordship's quiet words. What parts of my stomach hadn't given over to ice now formed into a solid knot of spikes.

I almost took a step back, but caught myself and raised my chin instead. A delighted murmur spread through the crowd at my back. As the marquis and marchioness stepped down the stairs, I watched my handsome stranger trail in their wake, studied the set of his fine shoulders, and recognized what I should have seen then.

I had danced with His Lordship Cornelius Kerrigan Compton. The marchioness's cherished son.

If looks could be daggers, I would have been skewered and bloody under Her Ladyship's scrutiny.

"My lord and lady," murmured others beside me in greeting. They were met with regal nods, smiles.

"Your lordship." Fanny eased into a curtsy beside me.

Her grip tightened on my arm, and as the noble family stopped in front of me, my knees gave way enough that I could mirror her greeting.

My eyes sank to the floor.

Gasps began to trickle through the crowd. Then a single sound, as if the entire ballroom had collectively inhaled and now waited to let it out.

I looked up, briefly wondering if I could be so lucky that one of the many glass chandeliers had dropped lamp oil on my hostess's head.

And met steely green eyes. He had his mother's eyes, I thought, but couldn't frame any other notion. As a single entity, the Marquis and Marchioness Northampton turned away, my civil courtesy unreturned.

Fanny gasped beside me.

The earl hesitated.

"Cornelius," his mother prompted, in tones so icy, it was if winter had swept in to suck the heat out of the overcrowded ballroom.

He turned away, presenting me his rigid back, and caught up to his parents in two long strides. Cut complete.

A buzz filled my ears; I was aware of a sudden flush climbing my cheeks. The room swirled around me, humming with the sensational scandal. Mad St. Croix's daughter had been cut, coldly and with surgical precision.

In front of all of London.

The ballroom turned upside down as my eyeballs throbbed. Humiliation clawed at me, and as I fought the pressure hammering at my ears, I turned and forced my way through the gathered crowd. Using elbows, shoulders, anything I could, I jimmied my way between faces I didn't recognize. I wasn't sure where I was going, whether I was half led by a sudden grip at my arm or if I dragged my escort beside me, but I couldn't stop. Wouldn't stop to face the eyes undoubtedly pinned on me.

I found the veranda doors, and a blast of cold air wafted over my face. I blinked hard, fighting back an angry strain of tears, to find Teddy hovering beside me, concern in his kind hazel eyes.

"Cherry? Cherry, buck up, there's a girl." He tapped my cheek as if I'd faint, and I realized he'd stripped off a glove; a terrible outrage in the ballroom.

A cold wind zipped over me, sharp as knives through the abysmal protection of my gown. My fists clenched so tightly, I heard each individual knuckle crack. "That horrible—" I began viciously, but got no farther as Fanny seized my shoulders and clutched me close.

"My poor child," she said softly.

But there was steel in her reassurance. A tone I had long since learned to recognize. Mrs. Fortescue was angry.

There simply wasn't anything to be done about it. I'd been cut.

I closed my eyes, allowing myself to sink upon the decorative iron bench beside me.

"What shall I do?" Teddy demanded. "Shall I fetch a glass of wine? Something to eat?" His fists clenched by his sides. "My pistols?"

I winced. "No." Fanny's stranglehold loosened, and I patted her arm as I disengaged myself. The cold beat against my skin, but my blood surged with anger and shame. Cut in front of *all* of London proper.

I wouldn't easily live this one down. My household would feel the sting.

"Something," Teddy insisted. "There must be—"

"Home." I smiled, but knew it was a weary thing as I reached out to take Teddy's bare hand in mine. I squeezed it affectionately. "Don't let your reputation be sliced to ribbons for me, Teddy. Go back in and find ladies to dance with. Pretend it meant nothing."

His lips thinned.

But he wouldn't argue. He knew the game as well as I. Better, for it was his world.

He squeezed my hand in turn, then bowed smartly. "Please take care of her, Fanny."

For once, she didn't scold him for his familiar endearment. She nodded, her expression incensed. "Come along, my dove."

I rose, locking my knees as they wobbled. "Will I see you on Wednesday next?" I held my breath.

He laid his hand over his heart. "Not for the world would I miss it," he vowed, and vanished once more into the ballroom.

That was my Teddy. With that single promise, something in my chest loosened. I could handle being cut from the Marchioness's social graces. I could take to the lack of invites, even the whispers when I moved in public now.

But if it had cost me Teddy's company, I would have gone in and challenged the woman myself. Not, of course, that ladies dueled.

But I would have tried.

"I'm tired," I said on a long exhale. Fanny laced my arm through hers, and I raised my chin, straightened my spine. I took a deep breath of the refreshing air, and added, "Shall we go home?"

"Can you face the crowd one last time?" Fanny asked kindly, and I hesitated. All those eyes. Judging, pitying.

Mocking, no doubt, as a cut from London's leading matriarch gave them permission to do just that.

And to think I thought the Earl of Compton handsome when he danced with me. How he must have laughed to know he charmed me before delivering the knife.

"Of course," I said coolly, and stepped once more into the crush to retrieve my things.

I'd be damned if I let the bloody-faced cow beat me now.

Chapter Four

The Midnight Menagerie kept extremely late hours. Fortunately, it was just before midnight when I returned home to change, and not too long later when I arrived below. As I crossed through the open gate, I searched the spot where I'd left Cummings tied and saw no trace of either his or my passing.

Someone had found him, and the odds were good that it was one of the Menagerie's people.

I huddled into my overcoat and breathed out a fog that contrasted with the haze around me. It was cold below the drift, lacking entirely the clarity that made stepping out worth the chill in London proper.

Fanny thought I was asleep in bed, nursing my hurt and temper. I'd told her I was worn, and retired promptly upon arriving home. Betsy had gone home to her husband, so there was no one to know when I changed into my collector's uniform and slipped away.

This time, I included a coat. I didn't expect to collect anything tonight, and I wanted to be warm.

The air around the Menagerie was clearer, noticeably different as I stepped across the boundary from street to garden territory. I still wasn't sure how they managed it, but something kept the worst of the lung-catching fog from infecting the grounds.

I shoved my goggles up onto my head, eager to be rid of the pressure around my eyes, and surveyed the estate.

A great deal of money had been put into the pleasure gardens. One part circus, one part park, one bit fair ground and all elaborate, it could provide whatever pleasure a man or woman with coin felt inclined to pursue on any given evening.

Exotic animals and strange foreign creatures from around the world? They could be seen. Midnight sweets, ripe for the taking and skilled in the art of love-making? Available for a price. Masquerades, drinking wells, elaborate dance halls where the corners were dark and the inhibitions few, all of this and more fell under the domain of the Karakash Veil.

Delicate paths crossed through elaborate fountains and sheltered groves. In the near distance, a large tent played home to the Menagerie's circus. Lit, tonight, which meant I'd stay away from it.

As usual.

I wasn't comfortable in circus tents. Even looking at it summoned to mind the din of chattering crowds, the cacophony of the music as it played out for every performer; the sticky sweat of fear and the dizzying rush of motion, of tensile strength and supple flexibility.

I remembered the tricks that had kept me useful. And well away from the bidding rings. I used them still, but never for applause.

Laughter, screaming and shouts echoed across the

grounds, rising and falling so suddenly, I startled. My eyes focused again on the paper lanterns strung across the paths before me. Red and gold, blue and orange and white.

I knelt in the circle of light from a blue paper lantern, picking up a discarded leaflet in one gloved hand. I squinted in the pale light, studying the print. Tonight's feature included sideshow freaks from the most exotic locations, aerial ballerinas and—I raised an eyebrow at the dark print.

His Highness Ikenna Osoba, the bold ink declared. Lion prince and far removed from the savage wilds of Africa.

A lion tamer, then. Dangerous work, even for the extremely confident. I'd only ever seen one, and this outside Monsieur Marceaux's rings. For his part, my employer had forbidden the act. Too dangerous. Too much could go wrong.

Underneath the gaudy announcement, the usual fare of sideshow attractions: bearded ladies, acrobatic midgets, the tallest man in the world and his Thumbelina wife. A tragic love story, I was sure.

I crumpled the paper in one fist and dropped it. No amount of nostalgia would coax me to enter the circus. Besides the usual whisper of anxiety skimming across my already stretched nerves, I knew my quarry wouldn't be there at the moment.

The ringmaster's role ended when the headline act took the stage. Micajah Hawke would be there again eventually, but I didn't want to wait.

And if I knew Hawke, he'd gone somewhere quieter in the interim.

I aimed for the private gardens, where I didn't often

go. For good reason. Where the rest of the Menagerie could be attained for some coin and eager company, the gardens were reserved for the truly decadent. There wasn't even a *pretense* of propriety here, though there was plenty of privacy to be had. And, as I recalled, they were the favorite haunt for many of London's gentlemen from above the drift.

Certainly the feeding grounds for more than one mistress.

Later, I would think back on this moment and consider that I was riding the crest of my anger *too* well. That I was feeling incautious and daring. For the moment, I only knew that I was tired of waiting. That I wanted my bounty, I wanted to replenish my depleted store of opium, and that I really, truly wanted to expend some of this restless, gnawing energy.

I approached the gate. Two men waited on either side: Menagerie footmen. Thugs, of course, and well paid. I'd never had to tangle with them.

Now, they both stiffened as they saw me.

I frowned as they stepped directly in front of the gilded gate. "Sorry, miss," one said, his Bow Bell accent lacking the education that softened Betsy's. "Ye can't go in."

"The devil I can't," I replied flatly.

Both men, taller than me but not too broad, exchanged glances. "Orders," said the other one, as if this would explain it.

"From?"

"Hawke."

My eyes narrowed. If the Menagerie was London's Garden of Eden, then Micajah Hawke was its serpent. A wickedly dark man whose power lay in his persona.

Hawke was ringmaster and director; foreman and tempter. He answered only to the Veil, which gave him free reign in the Menagerie he directed.

The man was sensual as sin. And just as dangerous.

I set my jaw. "He gave the order, did he?"

One nodded, his workman's cap set low over his bee-tled brow. "Aye, miss."

I sighed. "Well." Bully that for a joke. "I suppose there's nothing for it."

I half turned. Both men relaxed as I did, and one turned to retake his position by the gate post.

I spun, all the way around, quick as a snake. Before either could do more than draw themselves up, I seized the capped one's arm, jammed the heel of my hand into his elbow and heard it pop.

He was suddenly little more than a puppet as he bent over to save his shoulder, which gave me the leverage I needed to slam my foot back into the first guard's chest and send him clattering into the gate. I twisted the arm in my grip high. Height didn't matter when one had a man's elbow bent awry.

The man fell to his knees, strangling on a scream of pain.

"Stand—" The first guard didn't wait for me to finish my warning. He pushed off the gate, teeth bared and scarred fists raised.

I wrenched the capped man's arm up higher between his shoulder blades. His fingers nearly touched the nape of his neck, and he screamed, rough and guttural, his other hand flailing wildly as he danced in place.

The approaching man hesitated.

I met his eyes over the man's bent back. "I will," I said calmly, only breathing a little hard, "break his arm." I didn't know if I could, but he didn't have to know that. "Go get Hawke."

The guard met my eyes. Our wills clashed, but I was riding the surge of energy and a powerful triumph. Bracing my other hand on my captive's shoulder, I flexed my elbow. The guard locked his teeth and growled, "Do it!"

No contest. The first guard stepped back through the gate, turned and vanished into the dark.

I kept ahold of my man's wrist, just in case his friend tried something stupid. Like bringing more guards. Which, I knew, would be the end of me, but the bastard behind that fence had my bounty. It was mine. I earned it.

I needed it.

In short order, footsteps crunched on the imported polished stones lining the walkway beyond the gate. The guard in my grip had gone white around the edges, but he said nothing, breathing shallowly and silently. As if I would forget I held his working limb in my hands.

The gate swung open, and I looked up to meet the strangest eyes I had ever known. In any life I remembered.

Micajah Hawke wore the fashion of the day as if it were designed exclusively for him. His broad shoulders and exquisitely tapered chest set off a black tailcoat to utter perfection, and the scandalously crimson waistcoat only drew my eyes to his narrow waist. His trousers were black and pressed, his shoes without so much as a scuff. He wore no hat, carried no cane and wore red gloves, not white, and a red formal tie.

But it wasn't his choice in color that set him apart from the men above the drift.

The man was a fallen angel in disguise. As he stepped into the light, my stomach clenched as it always did, and my throat dried. His skin was swarthy, not fair, as if he carried Gypsy blood in his veins, and his shoulder-length hair ate up the light in a straight black gleam. *Beautiful.* The word popped into my head, a mere breath before I remembered that he was as dangerous as he was mouthwateringly devastating.

That was his skill. His strength. A ringmaster controlled the crowd and the performers, all with inhuman ease. All of my senses had to be on guard when he was near.

I raised my chin as his unusual dark brown eyes raked over the scene. The blue streak running through the center of his left eye gleamed almost as if the heart of a flame had burned a swath through it, and his full mouth pressed tightly together in annoyance.

"Let him go, Miss Black."

The man whose arm I held grunted as I released him. He scrambled out of my reach, rubbing his elbow with retribution in his scowl, but my gaze leveled on Hawke.

That smoke-and-velvet voice of his wouldn't lull *me* into any sense of complacency. Even if he was the only one to call me that. For my hair, I think, though he'd never said. "They wouldn't let me in," I told him.

"Under my orders." He towered above me, bracing one hand on his hip, the very picture of barely tamed nobility.

The knot in my stomach warmed. "Why?"

He raised one imperious black eyebrow. "Must you cause a scene wherever you go?" he asked, his tone just a shade away from reproach. As if I were an unruly child in need of discipline.

It took effort to keep my jaw from falling open.
What did *that* mean? Had the gossip already spread—I
caught myself as I watched the glint in his mismatched
eyes. Hawke was toying with me. As he always did.

There was no way he could know about the marchioness's ball, and certainly no way that he knew my identity above the drift. To him, I was simply Miss Black.
Just a collector.

I thrust out my jaw. "You owe me."

"I beg your pardon?"

A joke, that was. I couldn't imagine Hawke begging
for anything. And he knew it. "Cummings," I elabo-
rated. "You owe me his bounty."

The other eyebrow joined the first. "There was no delivery made," he replied, equally as even. "Therefore,
there is nothing owed. Now, if you'll excuse me—"

"Hang on a minute!" I took a step toward him as he
made to turn away, which proved to be my mistake as
Hawke stopped precisely where he was. I was suddenly
much closer to him than I meant to be, my head tipped
up to glare into his eyes, my balance shaky.

I sucked in a breath as one large hand curved over my
shoulder. Steadying me.

I smelled something musky. Foreign and spicy.

My stomach pitched again, and I felt warmer than
I should have in the dark and cold. My heartbeat
throbbed almost painfully loud in my chest.

His lips curved faintly. "Yes, Miss Black? Do you
have a problem with the terms of the contract? I thought
it rather standard. You deliver the man, and we pay you
for his delivery."

"I'm well aware of the terms," I snapped waspishly,
seizing for some semblance of internal equilibrium.

His hand fell away. "Then I fail to see—"

"Did he escape?" His eyes narrowed. "I left him tied to your front gate," I pressed on, flinging a hand back the way I came. "With my handkerchief in his pocket. You couldn't have missed it."

Hawke stared at me for a long moment. A breeze wafted across the grounds, bringing relief to my too-warm cheeks and stirring the tails of his coat. His hair was pushed back from his forehead tonight, held in place by a gleaming pomade. Under the lantern flame, his square jaw and high, noble cheekbones threw shadows that painted him in demonic light.

I swallowed as the silence stretched between us, thick with something I didn't recognize.

Finally, he stirred. "There was no man at the gate," he said with barely civil finality, "and no handkerchief."

He turned, and I stared at his back as he walked away. In front of me, one of the men sniggered.

I bared my teeth at him. His grin faded.

The shadows swallowed Hawke with ease, and I was left staring at both guards, each rubbing whatever part of their anatomy I had assaulted.

I didn't care. I rubbed my arms as I recalled the heavy weight of Hawke's gaze on mine. What had he been thinking as he stared at me?

What game was Micajah Hawke playing? Had Cummings gotten away? Had some helpful soul freed him?

Impossible. There were times when it seemed Hawke knew *everything* that happened on the grounds. There was no way he could have lost Cummings this morning. The man was lying to me.

The footmen watched me warily.

Flipping them a tight little smile, I turned and walked away.

I wasn't going to wander through the gate. Those men weren't entirely stupid. They'd dispatch a message to Hawke quick as a lick, and I'd find myself on the defensive instead. As soon as I could, I slipped off the path and into the shadows beyond the lanterns.

I knew of a half a dozen ways to get into the Menagerie, but I usually used the gates to maintain a certain element of propriety. The same could be said of the private gardens. The hedge walls were usually deterrent for average customers, but I was neither average nor a customer.

My feet rasped on the cobbles that comprised much of the Menagerie's walking ground. Although the area was less foggy than it should be, it was difficult to get plants to grow where the sunlight only weakly reached. That the Menagerie retained an entire army of groundskeepers was something, like the fogless air, I'd never managed to explain.

The place was a carefully guarded mystery, top to bottom.

I held my breath as I crouched by the bristled hedge wall. This was typical London fare, sturdy greenery that didn't require much more sunlight than what generally made it through the English winters, anyway. Most of London below didn't get foliage of any kind.

Shrugging out of my coat, I folded it neatly and shoved it out of sight beneath the hedgerow. The twigs poked into my back as I leaned into it, carefully counting footsteps as they passed just beyond hearing.

I counted silently again, and when no other footsteps reached my straining ears, I eased into the foliage.

This was one of many reasons I knotted my hair so firmly in place. I could only imagine what would have happened to my ballroom finery had I attempted this earlier.

The prickly hedge branches poked and prodded, and I had no choice but to move as slowly as possible. There was absolutely no way to do this silently. I was lucky that I could work my way through the foliage at all; a small bonus to being at least somewhat diminutive in stature.

As soon as my hand speared through the other side, I waited. A twig jabbed into my cheek, and I knew I'd have sap clinging to my hands, but it was a small price to pay. Catching Hawke off guard would be worth every moment.

Disentangling myself from the hedge took effort, as it attempted to cling to every hair, every fold of my shirt, even my trousers. I made more noise than I would have liked, even snapping a few determined branches, but there was no hue and cry around me.

I doubt, honestly, that anyone thought anything of it. The private gardens had heard much stranger noises than rustling.

The internal garden was a large courtyard, too big to see with a single lamp. Much like the greater Menagerie grounds, it was carefully maintained, and the hedges here were deliberately set in ways that provided the maximum amount of privacy with an occasional chance of discovery. Whispers and laughter drifted over the dark, cut by the murmuring trill of water fountains. Fires flickered here and there, carefully tended grates with the occasional silhouette beside them.

Or several silhouettes, I noticed through a sudden wash of embarrassment. The laughter I heard had a dulcet edge, husky and teasing, and I knew what was happening in the darkness around me.

Decadence. Debauchery.

A hauntingly sweet violin reached my ears as I hastened along the path, silvery and beckoning. Masterful hands stroked those strings, as sure as a lover.

The thought slipped into my head and I stumbled, caught myself hurriedly and swallowed down the awareness rising like a physical warmth in my chest.

The bloody gardens made me nervous. In wholly different ways than the circus tent, to be sure.

I resolved not to care. But my fists were clenched as I hurried through the vast courtyard. A helpful, wide-eyed young man in dockworker's garb directed me to the far buildings while a woman grinned indulgently on his arm—mostly clothed, thank God. But not for long, given the way her fingers laced possessively around his arm. And his purse, likely.

As I rushed through, I searched the boundary for more footmen. There was nothing. Hawke was all too easily lulled, I thought, and found myself vaguely disappointed by this fact.

Floating on wild energy and high fury, I pushed open the door.

And found myself in China.

It was as if someone had bottled up the mystical Orient and painted the interior with it. The walls were dark wood, adorned by silk screens and exotic weaponry. To my right, a fountain bubbled from mysterious sources. The water trickled happily among the unusually lush lilies floating serenely on the surface.

How did they get any plants to survive? These were indoors. What was the secret? A fertilizer, maybe. Something scientific in nature; I resolved to experiment when I could.

Across the room, a fire crackled in the polished hearth, which was made from wood as red as a cherry and engraved with an array of eye-boggling designs. Mirrors glittered back the flame in burnished gold, making the room seem larger and brighter than it was. There were no trinkets in the room at all.

A high, wide chair faced the hearth, its back to me, made of the same red wood as the mantel and draped with brilliant gold silk banners. Silhouetted in the transparent fabric, a tall figure remained still and unbothered by my abrupt entry.

To its right, however, was another chair of the same style, and Micajah Hawke rose from its depths with murder in his eye.

I meant to say something. I had the words, the clever accusations all ready.

But the sheer animal grace with which he stood took out every viable thought in my head and replaced it with blank terror. As the firelight painted one half of his lithe body in gilded shadow, my overactive mind painted him as a black hunting cat, wild and sleek and hungry as the panthers I'd read of in India.

He stalked toward me, disarmingly dapper; unmistakably dangerous. The muscles in his thighs flexed with every step, a ripple of black, his jaw was a rigid line of temper.

I jerked as his hand wrapped around my upper arm, tight enough that I knew it'd bruise come morning, and my teeth clicked together as he propelled me backward toward the door. "You are worse than a child," he said between gritted teeth, so low I struggled to hear him. "I thought I'd made it clear—"

I found my voice. "Get your hands off me," I hissed. My boots skidded on the lush carpet.

His greater strength was undeniable. Willing or not, I was bodily dragged toward the door, all with a single hand at my arm.

"Tíngzhĭ."

He froze. Not in the way a man pauses at a familiar voice and turns to look at the speaker, but as if he were suddenly a statue. Because I had no choice, I froze with him, and watched as a muscle ticked in his jaw. He stared at the door, features taut with . . . anger? Exasperation?

I couldn't tell.

I glanced at the chair, but the silhouette hadn't moved. Long, thin ornamentation wrapped around the figure's shoulders, making the shadow seem distorted. A spate of foreign-sounding gibberish filled the tense silence, speckled with the silvery whisper of delicate bells. The voice sounded higher than my English ears were accustomed to, but I recognized the language as some form of Chinese.

I made a mental note to learn the bloody language as Hawke's fingers tightened on my arm. I winced. Easily, he spun around to face the chair and crackling fire, hauling me with him. My teeth snapped together with the speed of it.

When he answered the silhouette in the same language, he didn't pitch his voice higher as they all seemed to do. Each foreign syllable rolled off his tongue in his husky, deeply rich voice. Short. Cut to the quick.

The voice responded; I supposed equally as short, because that muscle leapt in his jaw again. I watched the tanned column of his throat work as he struggled to swallow whatever it was that burned so intensely behind his rigid mask.

Without a word, he turned, shot me a quelling glare edged with dangerous warning and dragged me out. It was all I could do to maintain my own footing.

The door shut behind us. Just as fast, he let me go, shaking his gloved hand as if I'd burned him through the red fabric. I staggered. He didn't help. "You are a failure at comprehension," he said, his voice flat.

Finding my balance, I squared up as pugilists do, shoulders back, chin high as I met his glittering stare and stabbed a finger into his chest. "I know a lie when I hear it," I returned readily.

There. That tick again as his gaze dropped to my finger.

This time, my stomach yawned unsteadily as he slowly reached up and encircled my hand with his. His gloved fingers were warm. His touch exceedingly gentle as he pushed my hand away.

I snatched it back before he could feel it shake in his palm.

When I met his eyes again, they were weary. "Leave it, Miss Black."

I raised my eyebrows. I'd never mastered the art of lifting only one. "You expect me to just do so? That's my bounty!"

"I expect you to use your head," he said evenly. "I've told you there was no bounty delivered. Have I ever lied to you?"

I narrowed my eyes. "How would I know?"

His mouth tightened. "Wherever it is you call home, Miss Black, I strongly encourage you to go there."

And for the second time that night, giving me nothing but the iron obstacle of his will, Micajah Hawke turned his back on me.

I watched him reenter the door he'd hauled me so unceremoniously out of, kept my silence, and hoped no one but me noticed how badly my legs were shaking.

Leave it, he'd said first.

Like hell I would.

Chapter Five

I left the Menagerie after retrieving my coat, my mind circling around and around. Why had Hawke lied about my bounty? Had he, in fact? Was it even possible that he was telling the truth?

Of course it was. As much as Hawke made me nervous, and as much as I didn't *like* being made nervous, I had to admit that I was fixated on something that might well be nothing. I'd have to find Cummings, if I could. That was the only way to get the truth.

And underneath all of these thoughts yawned the void of the night's earlier events. What would happen now that the marchioness's family had made clear their feelings? Would my staff suffer? Would I?

I would have been happy to stay for the rest of my twentieth year in exile, inherit my father's estate and set off on a tour of the world.

But what would happen to Betsy? To Booth, crippled as he was?

Without me, Mr. Ashmore had no reason to keep the staff. As much as I loved them, they were his more than they'd ever be mine. I had no doubts as to the loyalty Booth felt for his employer. He doted on me, I knew. But it wasn't the same.

I trudged quietly, my breath fogging in the cold, my throat itching despite my respirator. As I passed under the struggling light of guttering lamps, I huddled into my coat and tried to make sense of my predicaments.

I'd made a muck of all of it, and I didn't even know how.

My feet took me through Limehouse, across the immigrant border and into Blackwall. I jammed my hands into my overcoat pockets for warmth, and peered through the goggles set firmly over my eyes. Even as I watched the road before me, I kept a wary sliver of attention on the shadows around me.

It never paid to be caught unaware. Even a single streetwalker could prove to be the bait for a footpad searching for a juicy pocket.

It wasn't until I found myself at the front stoop of a faceless door that I realized where my feet had taken me. With unerring precision, no less.

I looked at the worn druggist shop window and remembered the pound notes I'd put in my pocket before I left.

It was the last of my dearly hoarded allowance.

I rocked back on my heels, hesitated for the fraction of a moment it took to recall the emptied vial tucked under my mattress, and seized the latch.

I wanted to sleep dreamlessly tonight. And I wanted to do so without Betsy's worried stare.

The interior of this particular druggist shop was not as familiar to me as others, but it smelled exactly like its kind. Musty, fraught with the aroma of powdered herbs and thicker substances, dust and the underlying stench of coal smoke. The light was dim, the cobwebs thick in the corners.

I stripped off my goggles and mask, inhaling greedily as I paused in the entry. The door eased shut behind me. A bell's tinkling warning faded into the hushed silence of an academic's study.

The druggist—a short, rotund man with red caterpillars for eyebrows and tiny spectacles perched precariously on his nose—looked up at me over a collection of books and assorted tools of the trade.

Those eyebrows pulled together. "This here's a business establishment," he warned, and I held up a hand to halt him as I crossed the small, cluttered floor.

"And I am here for business," I replied, "with coin to purchase with." Albeit the last of such for the next fortnight.

It was as if I'd spoken the magical words. His expression cleared, and he beckoned me closer with ink- and herb-stained hands. "What may I do you for?"

"Tincture of opium, if you'd be so kind."

His eyes gleamed over half-moon lenses. "Opium eater, eh?"

The question wasn't entirely unsympathetic, but my back straightened. "Do I look like a Turk to you?" I snapped. "It's for sleeping." But I tasted the lie even as I claimed it with such authority.

It was never *just* for sleeping, was it?

Still, he hastened to smooth the offense. "No, no," he reassured me. "Apologies, miss."

I swallowed down my irritation with effort. Everyone knew only Turks ate the stuff whole, anyway. Civilized people distilled it. "I'd like to see your store," I told him. And smell it. I knew the flavors by rote, and some that came out of China were worse than others.

The druggist didn't argue with me, though he leaned ponderously back in his chair and folded his arms across his barrel chest. The buttons on his coat strained. "I'd be pleased," he replied, with a surprising grace of manners. "But I'm afraid that my store's run out."

"What?"

"Just yesterday. I only just replenished my stock when these two blokes be wandering in, looking to see my stores."

I grimaced. "And they bought it all?"

"Every last grain," the druggist said, raising his eyebrows meaningfully. That was a lot of money to be throwing about below the drift. A lord's servants, maybe? Merchants with an itch?

"Did you gain a name, by any chance?"

"Nothing," the man replied, shrugging. "But they seemed a scholarly sort. One old bloke, graying, patches at the elbows, you know the type."

"And the other?"

The man rubbed the side of his jaw with the backs of his stained fingers. I watched him shiver. "Can't say I much cared for the gent. Tall, thin sort. Couldn't see much past the hat and collar, though. Soft-spoken bloke. Called the other 'Professor.'"

"Professor?" I leaned back on my heels. "Professor of what? Perhaps with the university?" The man only shrugged again, and I sighed. "Well, thank you for your time."

"Come back in a few days," he added to my retreating back. "I'll have it in again. I sent out a man special."

A few days. The very thought fisted hard in my chest, but I only nodded as I saw myself out.

What in God's name would a professor be doing with that much opium?

I replaced my goggles, but left my respirator in the pouch. I was close enough to the docks, anyway, that I'd have no need for it. I gritted my teeth as I stalked into the street. I could have just as easily walked to the next shop, I knew of another not far, but I was exhausted. I'd worn myself into circles. Between the marchioness and Hawke, I was tired of dancing around the questions and lies.

I just wanted to sleep.

London had a feel, a thread of familiarity that persevered from the darkest underground tunnels to the heights above. So wound up in my own predicaments, it took me longer than it should to recognize the subtle shift in resonance. I wasn't alone.

I looked up just as a shadow detached itself from the coal-ridden fog in the alley beside me.

"What—Oof!" Long arms thrust from the swirling silhouette of a flowing coat, caught me square in the chest. I staggered over the pitted cobblestone, slammed against the corner edge of the brownstone shop and flailed for my goggles as they slid off my nose.

They slipped through my grasping fingers, clattered loudly to the ground, as loud as a pistol shot in the sudden darkness fogging my vision. Effectively blinded, I rolled off the building's wall and farther into the alley, praying neither my assailant nor I would step on the discarded goggles.

Fog swirled in front of my face, etched in darker whorls of dirty yellow and black. My eyes wide, I strained to see through the burning miasma.

The damp stone beneath my feet gleamed in flashes of light trapped in gray; the rubbish of forgotten passersby rustled as I stepped over it, and the sound was a scream in my too-sensitive hearing.

And in his.

He came at me from the swirling striations of mist. I received an impression of height, motion and the faintest reflection of light in eyes all but concealed by the wide brim of a bowler hat. A man, I thought as I danced back out of reach.

And a knife.

The long, thin stiletto slid from the folds of the coat like a silver whisper of death, and my heart exploded into my throat.

This was real. No foggy nightmare concocted in opium remnants. Not that I'd ever been prone to such things.

I sank down into a half crouch, my fingers tight at the base of my spine. The hilt of my own flat blade fit into my hand, but I hesitated before drawing it.

I shouldn't have.

He came at me wordlessly, his features obscured by his high coat collar and the low hat. Another collector?

A ruffian after the contents of my pockets?

I ducked low under his grasp, circled around him in fluid motion. I felt as much as heard the whisper of steel by my ear, and my blood surged. Playing for keeps, then. I snapped my fingers around his wrist, felt warm skin between the edge of his glove and cuff of his sleeve, and jerked hard with all my might.

At the same time, I rotated on the ball of my foot, jammed my shoulder under his armpit and hauled like the bellboys of Westminster. *"Allez, hop!"* I huffed.

The man didn't soar so much as tumble over my

smaller height, but he made no sound as he collided with the broken stone wall on the other side. With an agile twist, a flutter of limbs, the coat swirled and he landed not gracelessly, as I'd hoped, but on his feet, knees bent and one hand braced on the ground in front of him. Spiderlike and all too fast.

The head turned—I saw the silhouette of the rounded hat tip, a flash of paler skin between the collar and brim—and then he launched himself upward and past me, barreling his shoulder into mine.

I fumbled for my knife and my balance, but the road was too uneven, too eager to make my acquaintance. I sprawled on my backside, one knee pointed up, the other foot caught in rotted wooden crates, my braced hand sinking to the wrist in cold mud. I swore the foulest dockside oaths I knew as the fog closed behind the ragged slap of retreating feet.

I inhaled a shaking breath, wiping at my burning eyes with the back of my sleeved arm. My heart pounded loudly, so thick in my ears that it was all I could do to force myself to concentrate on the direction of my assailant's escape.

Who was he? What was he after?

And what the devil had I done to make an enemy from a stranger?

I returned home with my mind racing. And extremely angry.

The fall from my head had cracked the right lens of my goggles, splitting the glass into four distinct segments barely held within the frame. Although the yellow lens was unscathed, I'd have to fix the right before I wore it again.

I needed to scrounge some leather, and quickly.

I was too shaken to sleep without aid, but I tried, anyway. The laudanum sat too low in the decanter to risk Betsy's interest. For what seemed like hours, I tossed and turned. I'm not sure at what point my waking energy transferred to sleep, but I soon found myself in a feverish dreamscape.

Demonic light and a thousand mysterious colors haunted me as I slept. Ink-black strands of spun webbing, voices from beyond my memory or knowing. Fire sprang to life in a wild cacophony of orange light and furious sound, crackling, feasting, devouring all it touched. Footsteps rang out, voices shouted, glass and silver and damp stone reflected a voracious flame.

"Not the laboratory!" cried a desperate voice, hoarse with fear. "Please, not my girl!"

I thrashed inside this painted prison, watched it swirl into the aether as if pulled through a watery drain, and suddenly I stared into jade green eyes. I called for help—didn't I? Didn't I fling my hands for succor? *Please, my lord, help me.*

But the earl only turned away, cold and unyielding as marble. From the rigid line of his shoulders, feathers sprouted. Rending, tearing, they spilled from his back like a froth of lace and violent water, until angel's wings hung heavy to the floor behind him.

I awoke gasping, my breath heaving inside my chest. I clung to the crooked coverlet. My legs hung bare from my nightdress, tangled around my hips. I tugged at it, only half awake, trying to untwist the material from my sweat-damp skin.

My heart pounded. Blinking hard, I threw off what bedclothes I hadn't already kicked off and swung my feet over the edge of my soft bed. Daylight trickled through the closed drapes, and I rubbed my face. Every inch of my skin prickled, as it always did after a bout with nightmares. I felt drawn, horrid.

What in God's name would compel me to dream of the earl as some kind of avenging angel? He certainly wasn't anything of the sort. The earlier bits of my dreams were as familiar to me as my own name. My nightmares always held fire. Fire and a man's voice pleading for mercy.

My body ached, remnants of the scraps I'd gotten into below. I threw my arms over my head in a stretch that unkinked the tension from my body.

Energy flooded through me, as if by doing so I'd uncapped a dam from somewhere inside. "Aah!" I sighed, arching my back. Nightmares or no, today was a new day. There were mysteries to solve. I only had to await the night to once more travel below and locate my vanished quarry.

I could stop by another druggist when I was done. I'd be damned if I went through another night without aid.

And with that solid thought, the vague memories of my dreams faded away, replaced by that which I knew was real. I knew nothing of fiery laboratories or angels, after all.

The door swung open. "Cherry, wake up!"

Betsy all but sprinted inside, drawn up short as she saw me sitting up, the covers askew and my bare legs hanging over the edge of the bed. Puzzlement shaped her brow for half a breath before she flung out a hand. "Hurry!" she entreated. "We've got to get you ready."

"What is so," I began, only to yelp as she grabbed my arm and half dragged me away from the bed. "Betsy!"

"The earl," she hissed. "He's sent a card 'round, he has."

I blinked dumbly. "The earl?"

"*The* earl," she repeated earnestly, whipping my nightdress off without so much as a by-your-leave. I stood gaping as she added pointedly, "The Earl Compton. The marchioness's son!"

Ah. Then it all made sense. I stepped back out of reach as my maid tried to seat me at the vanity. Nude, I braced my hands on my hips and said flatly, "I'm not going down."

Her brown eyes narrowed. "Oh, yes, you are."

"No, I'm—"

"Fanny told me to tell you that if you so much as narrow your pretty eyes at him," Betsy continued over my stubborn refusal, "then not only will she take away your books, she'll donate them to the richest abbey in all of England."

My jaw dropped. "She wouldn't."

All Betsy had to do was cock her head, hands on her aproned hips, and I wilted. "There's a girl," she encouraged, but I ignored her.

Damn that Fanny Fortescue.

Not only would she remove my books, but she'd have them placed in a library so large that they'd never get read again, just to watch me bat my lashes at an earl.

An earl who had already snubbed me in front of all of London.

Bah. He wasn't even really an earl. His father was; but as the eldest son, he only gained the title as a courtesy. The land and holdings wouldn't be his until his father's death, when he'd inherit "marquess" and "earl" both.

It could be years.

Unlike me, who was only months away from independence.

"Is he handsome?" Betsy was saying as she hurriedly styled my hair.

My back teeth clenched. "No." Lie. Just the mere thought of him was enough to remember his lovely eyes meeting mine as he danced me across the floor.

I shifted as my stomach flipped.

"That's not what Fanny says," Betsy countered gaily. She jerked hard on my hair, forcing me to look straight ahead as I tried to glare at her. "She says he's quite possibly the most handsomest gentleman in all of London."

My jaw shifted. "Not likely," I muttered. Especially with Micajah Hawke about. But that was hardly fair. They were as day and night; fair and dark. Angel of the night and angel of . . . *Oh, for God's sake.*

Neither man was suitable for me, anyway. Not that either man was asking.

What the blazes was wrong with my head today?

"Quickly, hang onto the bedpost."

I obeyed Betsy quietly, breathing out as she placed a knee at my back and pulled my corset laces tight enough that for a moment, I saw stars. "Betsy!" I gasped.

"Your waist is not your strength," she told me firmly. "One more."

"Good Lord." I winced as she yanked with all of her strength. "This is hardly going to be a social—"

"It's never too late," Betsy interrupted me, and flung yards of dusky rose fabric over my head. The day dress all but floated to the ground at my feet. Trimmed with a rich wine and touched with creamy lace at my elbows, décolletage and hem, it was one of my favorites. And one of my most flattering. It contrasted beautifully with my hair.

"There," she said as she finished the last hook and eye closure. "You're pretty as a painting."

We'd see about that. Everything in place, Betsy thrust me out the door and downstairs, where Fanny waited as if afraid I'd bolt if left alone too long.

She surveyed me critically. "You'll do," was her momentous praise. I barely resisted sticking my tongue out at her as she took my arm and led me into the parlor. "Booth will be bringing tea immediately. Don't you dare ruin this, Cherry St. Croix."

"Me?" I glowered at her as I sank to the gold brocade settee, automatically arranging the folds of my gown. "I'm hardly the one that cut *him*, you know." Although maybe I should have. The beautiful, sonorous melody of chimes soared through the house as the door mechanism was engaged.

One of my favorite sounds, that doorbell. So much more pleasing to the ear than a simple ringing gong or bell.

I heard the uneven step of my butler approach, and my back straightened. Fanny sat on a far chair, knitting in hand, and glowered at me. "Not," she warned on a hiss, "a word. Not even a hint of your temper, miss, or so help me—"

Booth cleared his throat. "Miss St. Croix, my lord Compton, Earl Compton, is arrived."

It was as if someone had thrown some diabolical switch. Fanny's expression eased from severe to gracious in the space of a breath. She rose, shooting me a pointed look that I couldn't possibly fail to understand.

As tempted as I was to remain seated, my own brand

of snubbing, I knew Fanny would more than make good on her threat if I acted up.

I rose as well. We eased into a curtsy as Earl Compton strode into the room. Hatless as a courtesy and divested of his outer clothing, he cut a fine figure in my small parlor.

Too fine. Although the striped brocade chairs and heavy curtains were of excellent quality, and the dark wood furniture kept to a gleaming polish, it seemed to me as if it paled next to the earl's own refinement.

His bow was stiff, but precise. "I thank you for your hospitality," he said by way of greeting, and a shiver slipped between my shoulders.

I remembered that polished voice in my ear. And I did not like it. "We could hardly turn you away," I said sweetly. "Imagine the talk." Fanny's eyes narrowed a fraction.

His met mine directly.

I lifted my chin. "Please, my lord, sit. Tea shall be arriving." The sooner, the better. Booth had gone to acquire the service, and once a single cup was done, I'd have the pompous earl tossed out on his ear.

Or at least, I amended as we all sat, escorted out politely. I wasn't a fool, after all.

"Are you well, Miss St. Croix?"

I almost laughed at the polite query. "Yes, thank you," I replied, even as I locked down the surge of incredulity bubbling in my throat. He hadn't risked scandal just to ask after my well-being.

"Excellent." He hesitated. "I apologize for my early visit, but as I was passing through on an errand, I thought . . . that is, you must be wondering—"

The earl's words ended abruptly as Booth rolled the tea service in. I watched his eyes trail over Booth's missing limb, taking in the ornate prosthetic. Not a flicker crossed his expression. Not a pained wince or quiet judgment.

To my dismay, my estimation of the man rose. Just a notch. "Tea?" I asked, retaining the saccharine tone I knew Fanny would task me for later. I stripped off my gloves, tucking them into my lap.

"Most kind." Compton sat rigidly, as if every muscle were in a constant state of focus. His frock coat was a rich, deep blue, his waistcoat polished gray and his trousers to match. His tie was blue, as well, and the color did remarkable things for his brilliant eyes.

They remained fixed on me. If he was aware of Fanny's silent speculation above the gentle click of her knitting needles, he didn't show it.

I was all too aware of every nuance in the room, and I could add that to my silent litany of things I didn't like.

I poured tea—fortunately with more practiced grace than I expected of myself—and refrained from throwing it at him. I wanted to scream at him. I wanted to demand satisfaction for his behavior. I wanted to march into Mr. Ashmore's study and tear the matched set of pistols from the wall, just so I could throw one to him and watch his shocked expression.

I did none of these things.

Instead, I passed the delicate china politely into his keeping.

His gloveless hand cradled mine for the heartbeat it took to transfer the saucer. As if he'd laid an electrical charge against my flesh, I felt the brush of his skin clear to my bones. The china clinked as my hand shook, tea sloshing over the lip and onto my fingers. Hot enough that I jerked in surprise. "Oh!"

"Forgive me," Compton said at the same time, capturing my hand in his. "That was terribly clumsy of me." Without awaiting my permission, or even any response at all, he plucked a neatly folded handkerchief from his pocket and blotted at the liquid sliding over two fingers.

Fanny said nothing.

Some chaperone she turned out to be.

I watched him as he tended to my bare skin. His eyes were on his task, his posture still unbending for all his fingers curved into my palm. Gentle, but strong. Sure. Warm.

He glanced up to find me staring. Was it my imagination, or did I detect a trace of heat in those eyes? A whisper, something. Something focused and intense.

Whatever it was, it slipped over my skin and curled into a warmth low in my belly.

I snatched my hand back. "My Lord Compton," I said flatly, "with all due respect, why are you here?"

"Cherry!"

Fanny's gasp of outrage drew only a flick of eyes from my guest. The corner of his mouth quirked. A hint of a smile. "They say you are a woman to speak your mind."

I poured my own tea, ignoring the vaguely damp remnants of the same liquid between my fingers, and dropped two sugars into the steaming cup. "They also say that I am a madman's daughter," I replied evenly. "Beyond hope and help, with ambitions far above my place." I watched the almost-smile fade from his mouth and steeled myself not to care. The words were his mother's.

"They say you are a keen mind," he countered stiffly.

"I have my father's mind for science," I replied, "and my mother's love of the written word. Or so they say." I raised my eyebrows. "They say an awful lot. This does not answer my question."

He inclined his head. "So it does not. Miss St. Croix, I've come to apologize."

The word didn't stick in his craw like I imagined it would. He said it easily, graciously. He did not choke on the syllables, as I'd half hoped.

I blinked at him. "I beg your pardon?"

"As a point of fact," the earl continued, placing his untouched saucer on the service beside us, "it is I who should be begging yours."

I could only stare.

He rose, and with instinctual courtesy, I rose as well, but I neglected to put my tea saucer down to do it. My skirts rustled; I resisted the urge to smooth them. They didn't require smoothing.

I did. My hackles were up like some ruffled cat's, I knew that, but so was my awareness. Of him—his presence, his costly fragrance, the fit of his waistcoat. Awareness of my own pulse, loud in my ears.

He did not take my hand, as I suddenly was terrified he'd try. I kept all ten of my fingers curled around my saucer rim, white with strain.

Compton placed one hand to his heart and bowed deeply. "I indulged Mother's request without knowing who you were or why she would request such a thing," he explained, but rigidly. Uncomfortably, I hoped. "I was foolish, and humbly beg your pardon."

I stared at the sandy gold cap of his lowered head. "I—what?"

Hardly my most gracious moment.

But as he straightened again, taller than I and now closer for standing, he looked down into my face with such earnest appeal that my throat went dry. "You must allow me to somehow mend the rift, Miss St. Croix. It was undeserved scandal, that much I am sure of."

"You have no conception of who I am," I pointed out. Across the room, I could see Fanny gesturing frantically. *Stop talking! Forgive and forget.*

I wasn't ready to.

No matter how sweet the apology.

"I would rectify that, as well," Compton replied simply.

I pushed on. "You are aware that even now, you are scandalizing your poor mother, yes?"

Again, that corner of his lips twitched. His eyes remained on mine; we were close, but not touching. Squared off, but not for a fight. The tension seeping between us was all me, I was sure.

I should have just forgiven the man and removed him from my house.

But that near-smile. His eyes. His earnestness and utter control and propriety . . .

"As one good turn deserves another," he replied, "so can it be said of an incivility. Such feuds can last life-times." I was so surprised when he actually reached for my hand that I let him have it, his long fingers enclosing mine. He bowed over it, apparently heedless of the incongruity of my standing there with a teacup and saucer balanced awkwardly in the other hand.

"It is my hope, Miss St. Croix, that there will be no cut in my future."

Chapter Six

I retired to my room the instant the earl took his leave. Fanny thought me too overwhelmed to handle myself, that I needed a rest.

I let her think so. In truth, I was too vexed, too befuddled, too utterly bemused, and too eager to unloose this pent-up energy roiling inside my skin to bother with these new complications the earl posed.

I could have taken the laudanum I had left. There was nothing better to cure anxieties, but I didn't dare.

Locating Hawke's missing quarry could release this anxiety as well as acquire me a new batch of laudanum for future use. All I had to do was mend my goggles enough that the glass would remain intact inside the frame and I'd be off.

It was the work of an hour. I sacrificed a pair of corset ties, but the wrapping would hold until I found thinner leather.

It would be harder still to replace the glass. I silently added it to my mental list of tasks.

I didn't often go below by day, but there were times

when the risk seemed lessened by need. Whether this was true or not, I felt the risk justifiable today.

It was this, I thought, or I'd go snooping in Mr. Ashmore's study for books I hadn't yet found to devour, likely end up not reading them for all this restlessness, and leave them lying about as I often did. And as I was not allowed in such sanctified men's territory, I opted for the plan that seemed like much more trouble.

If only my guardian knew what it was I got up to when propriety banned me from the lesser evil.

Far below the drift, buried in the deepest center of the East End, there is a fog-ridden building. Once upon a time, it had posed as a rail station, but the rail had been moved farther south and the station long since abandoned.

Now, it hung empty and dark, its floors coated in the fog seeping in through the cracks. My strides displaced the heavy smoke, kicking up droplets of yellow-green mist with every step. This, unofficially, was where the collectors came to claim work.

I wasn't sure how it started, or who held the lease. I didn't know whether word of mouth created this epicenter of the trade or if it were some secretive business in the dark. All I knew was that we collectors came here when we wanted work. Miraculously, there was usually work to be had.

The crumbling station was empty this time of day. Sometimes, I came across other collectors surveying the walls for postings. We were a wary lot, mistrustful by nature, but also a cautiously supportive community. As long as a bounty didn't weigh in the balance, you could rely on a certain amount of secrecy and support from your fellow collectors.

Otherwise, we'd throw one another under a train for a purse.

I grinned as I approached the far wall, dingy with years of smoke and dirt. Papers were pinned in place, some torn as if from a scrap of a greater work, and others fairly neat at the edges. Some were clean scripts, in words educated and polished. Others were barely legible, with terrible phrasing and a complete lack of grammatical understanding.

But each offered coin for a delivery, a death, a retrieval.

I pulled my overcoat closer about my ears, made sure the brim of my street boy's cap shadowed my features from any eyes lurking in the dark corners. My goggles allowed me to scan the fluttering parchments with ease, though the yellow lens was fogging in the damp.

There were some calls for beatings. Men who owed money and needed a reminder of the fact. Some requests for lost items, general sleuthing. A handful came from the Menagerie, others from shop owners in need of aid. Some were from secretive patrons of the business, especially the killings.

There were gaps on the wall where bounties had been pulled; that was the unspoken way of the collectors. It was a competitive vocation, a difficult one already without adding other collectors to the mix. To ensure we didn't race each other to the pot, a collector would accept a job by taking the posted bounty.

It had taken me a few stolen quarries to learn this when I'd first learned about collectors' business. I'd been bored out of my skull at a ball, and wandered away before the master of the house foisted another boring dance on me. I found myself outside on the veranda, just over a knot of young men. One was a Society collector who'd regaled the young bucks with tales of his exploits.

I'd overheard his directions to find the laughably termed "offices," and thus began my secretive career. Of course, it had taken quite a lot of nerve to do then what was only habit now.

"Hello," I said to the damp, still air. "You're out and about, are you?" I reached up and pinned the corner of a ragged edge to the wall with a finger. Someone had sliced through the bounty notice with a sharp edge, leaving two halves hanging open. By placing them together, I could see that the bounty was a killing, a call for assassination. There were no reasons given, only a figure that made my fortnights' worth of allowance look like a pittance.

Claimed, then.

I didn't know who the bloke was, but his mark showed up like this now and again. The last time I'd seen it, it was for another assassination. Nothing nearly so heavy a purse as this, but the same tear through it.

A few days later, the posting was gone. Fulfilled, perhaps. I never knew for sure. But something told me that the collector did this on purpose. He wanted us to know what he was after.

As if daring us to race him for it.

"No, thank you," I murmured, letting the two edges part once more. I didn't take eliminations as a rule. And I had no intentions of fighting another collector for a murder.

No, what I wanted was to see if another posting had been made for Mr. Bartholomew Cummings. Surely, if the Menagerie were so keen on getting their owed money, they'd post another.

But there was none.

There was nothing for it. I left the collectors' offices and made my way through the idly busy streets. By day, there were more of the working and lower classes to be had. Women soliciting whatever coin they could; servants traveling to their homes below. Dock men looking for work or a drink, wagons creaking across the uneven cobbles, market stalls placed unevenly along the streets. Although the fog was deucedly thick, enough light filtered through to turn it all to a vapid gray.

Bright enough to see and be seen. Thick enough to choke on.

I preferred the streets at night—fewer people to see me, even with my disguise—but some things couldn't wait. And I knew where to look to find Cummings.

He was a barber by day; degenerate gambler by night. I would never trust a drunkard to hold a razor near my throat, but I hadn't heard any rumors of accidental throat slitting, so I supposed he got on all right.

It took me less than an hour to make my way to his small, but oddly clean, shop. I pushed inside, not bothering to remove my mask or goggles. There was no one inside save Mr. Cummings, wrapped in a stained white apron and focused on affixing a pinch of wax to his rather excellent mustache as he leaned close to a shining mirror.

As the tiny bell over the door jingled merrily, he straightened and turned, smiling.

It faded as he saw me. "Now wait just a moment," he said quickly, throwing up a chapped hand. "This here's a place for gentlemen."

I ignored that, stopping just inside, hands on my hips.

"Have you paid your debts to the Menagerie?" My voice, typically so feminine, came out raspy through the respirator vents.

His eyes narrowed. Then widened again, and he stepped backward so fast that he nearly tripped over his own barber chair. "Now, now, I paid my due last morning! You tell them—"

I didn't come any farther into the room, but something in my stillness must have made him think again about his belligerent order.

His tone softened. Pleadingly. "I got hauled in by some heathen foreign bloke and we made a deal."

"We?" I queried, but the angry buzz flowing through my veins already told me what he was going to say.

"My lord Hawke and I," he said, puffing up his chest as if designating that rooster a lord lent himself some credence. "We're square. Or," he added, very quickly, "will be soon. Honest."

I narrowed my eyes at him. "Your bounty?"

"He swore it'd be pulled!" he said, almost a squeak.

That lying, thieving bastard. I turned on my heel and stalked from the door, listening to its jovial jingle fade.

So much for fair dealings.

I pounded my fist into my other hand as I turned for the West India docks. Fine. I'd show him. So he thought he'd cheat me, did he?

I couldn't let it stand. If I did, word could get out that I was an easy mark. Gullible enough to take the work and never bat an eyelash if I didn't get paid.

That wouldn't do.

I withdrew my pocket watch, frowning at the delicate hands. I didn't have time to corner Hawke now, and even if I did, I didn't have a plan. I'd need one. For whatever reason, he'd decided to cut me out of the accustomed deal.

I'd need to think on it. In the meantime, my "rest" couldn't last too much longer, or Betsy would run out of excuses. I turned toward the docks, determined to come up with a foolproof method to shake my money out of the recalcitrant Hawke.

I spent half of a precious hour at the ferries, talking with the dockworkers who were inclined to spill a word or two for the right incentive. I didn't learn anything of too much worth—most of London society already knew about a certain lord's unfortunate interest in the gaming hells, and there were no rumors of anyone more suspicious than usual taking the ferries.

Still, it's good time well-spent when I can levy a certain amount of familiarity with the dock rats. They may be more inclined to talk again when real news comes calling.

Betsy was on the lookout as I arrived home, and the stark relief on her face was as obvious as if she'd shouted it to the district. She hurried me through the window.

"What on—" I started to say irritably, but she waved her hands wildly and wrestled with my coat.

"Hurry!" she hissed. "M'lord Helmsley is below."

"Why is—" I caught myself, slapping both hands over my dirty face. Buggery and blast! I'd forgotten Teddy utterly in my insistence to snoop and God only knew what he'd think if he found me dressed like a man—collecting corset aside.

Not that I expected him to bully his way upstairs and into my boudoir, that wasn't his style. As easily as he discarded the more onerous expectations of propriety, he wasn't a belligerent man.

Still, I'd promised him my company, as I did every Wednesday regularly, and I knew he'd be smarting over the invite that led to my social destruction. He'd be eager to see me.

While I'd all but forgotten. "Right," I said grimly. "Quickly, then."

Betsy worked hastily, disappearing while I bathed off the lampblack in my hair and scrubbed my face. She returned, helped me dry and coiled my still-wet hair up on my head. She pinned it viciously as I winced. "I told Mrs. Booth you'd been sleeping," she said.

I smiled gratefully. "You're a queen, Betsy."

"I'm a liar," she sniffed, but her grin flickered. "They thought you were still reeling from the earl's visit, anyway."

And wasn't I? But not in the way the rest of my household thought. My smile turned grim as I studied myself in the mirror. Since it was after tea, she'd chosen a new gown suitable for a cozy dinner at home. Teddy was a frequent guest, after all, and I had no desire to stuff myself into full dress for him.

Or, really, ever.

Fanny allowed me to get away with a somewhat less elaborate gown only with Teddy, and so I wore a simple dinner jacket in bronze poplin and a skirt to match. I clipped the pocket watch to my jacket, tucked the faded disc into the tiny pocket at the side, and nodded. "How do I look?"

"Why?" Betsy asked baldly. "Trying to charm the viscount's son?"

I snorted. "Teddy's easily charmed, and easily distracted, by much prettier women than me." And, I suspected, more readily available by the pound.

"Pish-tosh," Betsy scoffed, throwing out Mrs. Booth's favorite dismissal. "Off you go."

I grinned, adjusted the jaunty little hat I'd insisted she pin to my mass of still-wet hair, and swept out to meet my guest.

He rose as I entered the parlor, eyes narrowed. "Where the devil have you been?" he demanded.

"Sleeping," I replied easily, lying without a thought. "I had a rather long night, you know."

Any suspicion etched in his sharp eyes vanished, replaced by raw apology, and he threw himself back onto the settee with typical foppish flourish. "Damn that Compton," he swore vehemently. "Everyone was saying that he'd danced with you before the cut."

I sank into a chair, and though I'd intended to brush it off, my mouth twisted. "So he did."

"Didn't you know who he was?"

"How, exactly?" I asked. "Should I have asked him, 'Excuse me, sir, but are you in fact the Earl Compton and do you intend to cut me after this dance?' " I waved the very idea away as Teddy snorted. "Her Ladyship's been after me since the beginning."

"Maybe she saw you dancing with her precious son." He sneered the words, even as his long legs kicked out to cross at the ankle in easy familiarity. "Saw a spark? A bit of something?"

"Don't be daft," I said sharply.

But the memory of the earl's hands on my waist wasn't fading as quickly as it should have. I wanted to know why.

Even as I really didn't.

"Truth be told," I went on, treating the matter as if it were only a puzzle. A case to be studied, solved, and then discarded. "You know as well as I that any such invite must have been given with her blessing. She went out of her way to set me up in as public a crush as possible,"

"That much must be true," Teddy allowed. "The fine ladies of L.A.M.B leave a certain something to be desired in terms of kindness."

"She's hated me for years," I said, suddenly sullen. "She and her little salon think I'm the devil."

"Oh, come now."

"As good as," I replied, wrinkling my nose.

He raised a dark eyebrow, his grin edging in. Quick, far from innocent, and impish as he could be. "Maybe your raw beauty scared the woman senseless." I snorted, a most unladylike sound. "She happened to see her precious son dancing with the prettiest lady in the room and saw a future trapped in a dowager house, far from London. Exiled to the country."

Color swept into my cheeks, and I flung a dismissive hand at him. "Oh, be serious. You know I've no intent to marry."

His expression sobered. "I know. Why should you? Your estate is yours in a year's time." Then a kick of something at his mouth; a glint in his eyes as he lowered his head and studied me through lashes I'd always envied. "Don't think I haven't considered asking, you know."

"What?" I straightened. "For me? Why ever for?"

"We're friends, aren't we?" He shrugged fluidly, thin shoulders moving. Typical *laissez-faire* ease. "We'd be a good match. We get on famously enough, and you know I'd never touch your fortune."

He was serious. I looked at the honesty written clear

as day on his hawkish features and something softened inside me, soothing away the tension of lies, fatigue and worry. Heedless of propriety, I rose, crossed the parlor and settled to the cushion beside him. "Of course we're friends," I assured him, taking his gloved hand in mine. "And a kinder, sweeter, more courageous friend I couldn't ask for."

He squeezed my hand, and I saw the same softening reflected in his expression. Even if that lazy half smile lingered at his mouth.

"Which is why," I continued in the same tones, "I will do you the enormous favor of saving you from myself."

His half smile twitched. Widened. "You're sure?"

"Well." I paused, as if deep in thought. "How do you like the taste of arsenic?"

Teddy's laugh cracked like a gunshot. He threw his head back with it, letting it free with the forthcoming familiarity that I loved so much, and he squeezed my hand between his. "Your point is well made," he said when he could again, chuckling still. "What a bloody idiot, that Compton."

I blinked. "What?"

A finger tucked a stray tendril from my cheek, but there was nothing in Teddy's expression but lingering humor, that defensiveness he always displayed on my behalf, and a touch of devilish mischief. "He could have found in you an excellent companion," he told me. "Even if you do like to stick your face in the fireplace."

My hand flew to my cheek, even as my stomach turned over.

"Only a smudge," he told me. "I've gotten it. See? I'm a real gentleman, I am."

"So you are." But my chuckle wasn't entirely easy. Had I missed a spot of lampblack? Was it in my hair still?

"A fine catch," he added, but with a wicked, teasing grin.

I rolled my eyes. "I am going to send for Booth," I said evenly, without heat. "And he's going to bring this week's periodicals. Let us just focus on Mr. Horatio's theory of aether-to-oxygen ratio, shall we?"

"If you insist." Teddy laced his fingers behind his head. "You go first."

I smiled, innocent as an angel. "I think it's bollocks."

Another crack of laughter escaped from his lips, and everything was once more as it should be. "Which bit?" he asked, grinning.

"The one where he insists that aether can be lit in an enclosed tank," I said. "Enlightened men have proven time and again that if you enclose something without air, it will fail to burn."

"But aether itself is a compound that we know nothing about." This was the Teddy I know. Quick minded, sharp and opinionated. I flicked my fingers at him as I pulled the bell to summon my staff.

"Not true," I corrected swiftly. "We know what it can be used for, and what it is similar to, which gives us insight into its makeup."

We could go 'round like this for hours, and as Booth brought in the stack of periodicals painstakingly delivered from around the globe, we launched into a debate that could rattle the ears off a saint. Mid-debate, I snatched the fireplace poker from its resting place and brandished it like a sword at him, as if I'd pierce my point to his heart. "If *anything* contains aether," I said, "then it means we do, too. Is aether just *life* simmered down to a single compound?"

"Impossible," Teddy replied, watching me swing the poker warily. "Air holds aether, and air isn't alive. Aether is just *a* compound, one of many required to *make* life." He reached up, having long since stripped his gloves for tea, and I yanked the poker away from his grasp.

"Aether is not, in fact, life. Then we're agreed," I said triumphantly, and tossed the poker to him. "*Allez, hop!*"

Teddy snatched the heavy iron out of the air, his eyes narrowing on me.

I grinned, wiping my now sooty hand on my skirt heedlessly. "What?"

He turned the poker in hand lazily as he sat back into his chair. We were terribly opposite in that regard; I was always pacing, while he expended as little energy as possible. "What of alchemy?" he asked thoughtfully.

I screwed my face into an incredulous grimace. "Don't even start," I said, flinging a hand out at him as if to ward away the thought. "There's no such thing."

"No such thing as magic, no such thing as alchemy." He pointed the poker end at me. "For a scientist's daughter, Miss St. Croix, you are awfully closed minded."

I rolled my eyes. "Alchemy is what a bunch of old men called magic, just so we wouldn't think them crackers when they went looking for things like everlasting life and gold from metal," I scoffed. "Let's stick to true science, shall we?"

"Like aether?"

"Exactly."

He grinned, the way he did when he felt he'd scored

a point. "Aether," he repeated, "which until fairly recently was thought to be nothing more than magic?"

I narrowed my eyes at him, dropping into the chair across from his so smug scrutiny. "But it's *not*," I countered. "Ergo, it's science."

"And alchemy isn't?"

"It's not real," I said evenly. "Therefore, no, it's not science. It's a bedtime tale."

Even when he got a bee in his bonnet about such things, our debates were an excellent way to spend the time, and it focused me for the hours I had to let pass before my mission later that night. When Teddy finally made his good-byes, I was all but crawling out of my skin with anticipation.

I still had to sit through dinner. Every minute was an excruciating wait. Fanny seemed in decent spirits, however, and I blamed the earl's visit for that.

Finally, I could claim a headache and retire. I returned upstairs and found my collector's uniform. Only this time, I wore my corset on the inside, hidden under a man's shirt and working coat. It would be a bit of a struggle to get to my weapons in time, in the off chance I'd need them, but as I drew a cap low over my ears and covered my blackened hair, I told myself I wouldn't need them.

I left Betsy muttering darkly behind me, appalled at my appearance, and hurried below.

Chapter Seven

I had never traveled as much as I did today. I was always careful, mindful of followers or interested eyes. I had to be even more careful now; the more I took the ferries in a day, the likelier the talk.

I was several days out of a bounty, though, and at the end of my patience.

I made my way to the Menagerie. As it always was, the grounds were lit just well enough to see where one trod, and the fog remained at bay. Amid the colorful lanterns, a few patrons—mostly men—strode from one point to the next. I didn't bother wondering from whence to where, as the Menagerie could quite literally cater to nearly all tastes and pleasures.

And I knew more than most how well a façade could hide those deeply rooted desires.

Pulling my coat more firmly around me, I hurried along the well-tended paths, each Chinese lantern lighting my way in a multitude of hues. I bypassed the private gardens, and this time, I decided to make at least an attempt for courtesy.

A pair of women halted for me, but all beginnings of flirtation ceased when I lifted my hat in wordless introduction. Talitha and Jane, midnight sweets promenading arm in arm in gowns fit for a moonlit ball, were this shift's lure, then.

Pretty enough girls. Each golden-haired and fair-skinned, near enough alike that in the theatrical gloom, they could easily be sisters. Lures would stroll the grounds in apparent idleness, engage those in between pleasures, or those patrons who hadn't yet decided where to go.

Many is a man, gentleman or otherwise, who has been trapped behind the gates until dawn, lured back each time by the pretty temptations of the Midnight Menagerie.

I knew them both, albeit in passing. Asking for the whereabouts of their employer raised Jane's eyebrows, and her painted lips curved in a smile I was sure she practiced in her boudoir. Wicked, it was, and knowing. "He's out at the amphitheater, love," she told me, lacing her fingers over Talitha's arm. " 'Tis a feature tonight. You want to see this yourself."

"Isn't he—"

But Jane patted Talitha's arm, tipping her bright head toward the girl. "Let the collector do her business, then," she said cheerfully. "Come by and see us soon, won't you?"

There were evenings when I came by not for business, but to visit with the women I knew and pass an idle hour between collections. I had not, to my recollection, spent much time with Jane.

Still, my reputation here tended to invite speculation. A woman collector, and one the ringmaster tolerated.

"Of course," I said, and doffed my cap—as gentlemen do. Talitha's cheeks turned pink.

I took my leave, but did not have to change course too much. The amphitheater had been situated well away from the din of the main structures and circus tent. As I followed the lantern-lit path, I went over my questions in my head. Over and over, they flitted in and out, haunting my every step.

I passed others on the paths. Some working, some patrons. It wasn't until I passed a group of boisterous young men clad in Greek togas that the first inklings of trouble crept upon me.

Like much of the Menagerie's façade, the theater looked simple and elegant from the outside. The gilded edges were appropriately burnished, decoration stylish without edging into an eyesore, highly reminiscent of Vauxhall's now faded glory.

I pushed through the doors, murmured, "Collector business," to the men who guarded them, and was directed toward the interior.

At least Hawke hadn't ordered me kept out this time.

I didn't go through the front entryway, knowing it would lead me into the very front of the amphitheater. That was one of the many hidden tricks of the Menagerie. You were often placed in the eyes of those you mingled with. Though discretion came at a price, subtlety was not for sale.

So forearmed, I stepped into the servant halls, followed the faceless walls until I came to another door, and carefully cracked it open.

The strains of a violin slid through the gap, low and sultry. I saw a sliver of light, a brush of mysteriously healthy plants, and an alcove just beyond.

I would wait there, then, and gain Hawke's attention as I could. Quickly, crouching low, I pushed open the door just enough to let me through, and gently closed it behind me. As the unnatural warmth of the theater seeped into my clothing, I hurried into the shrouded alcove.

It wasn't until I'd situated myself just beside the lush foliage of a hanging plant did the scene shimmer into complete focus.

I stopped. I stared.

The theater had been transformed into a decadent bathhouse, with verdant plants hanging all about and steam vented through mysterious contraptions in the walls. Water sloshed from long, shallow bathing pools, and laughter mingled with the occasional husky cry of something less than innocent taking place beneath the water's surface.

My face flushed as I saw naked limbs and bared bosoms. Men and women entwined together; some lazily, as if luxuriating in the total absence of demand, and others tightly, impatiently. Skin gleamed. For the first time in my handful of years frequenting the Menagerie for business, I had an unfettered view of more flesh than I ever thought to see in one immoral tableau.

Men's flesh.

Women's flesh.

I gripped the pillar beside me, my fingers digging into the cool grooves. Unbidden by me, my eyes slid over the lengthy flank of a man's exposed buttock. The muscle flexed as he rose over a woman who rolled under his grasp in the water, laughing and splashing.

My mouth opened. It closed again.

I saw the rosy tip of a woman's nipple painted with

wine before it vanished into another woman's mouth. I recognized some; sweets, of course, earning their keep.

And how.

My throat went dry. My heart, once in my chest, now pounded somewhere lower than my stomach.

What the devil had I wandered into?

Sucking in a deep breath, I forced my attention away from the bathing pool and toward the dais raised in the center. Wry amusement slipped in beneath sudden, horrific embarrassment as I recognized Micajah Hawke upon the throne.

Like some reincarnation of the hedonistic god of wine, the wicked man sprawled lazily on a throne entwined with grape vines. A woman sprawled at his left, another at his feet like some nymphlike supplicant. The latter was draped in a sheer bit of nothing, lavender and damp with sweat, and the press of her breasts were obvious through the thin fabric.

The other, beautiful at his arm, was naked. Milk-white skin, flushed pink with the steam and heat, golden hair, luscious mouth. She was perfect.

I found myself envious.

Unlike his guests, he wore formal dress again. His trousers were black and molded to the powerful line of his thigh, draped carelessly over the vacant arm of the throne. His boots were perfectly shined. This time, it was a violet waistcoat, but as my eyes trailed up the perfectly accentuated line of his chest, I realized that his shirt was open to the waist, revealing the heavily muscled edge of his chest and one flat nipple.

I'd never seen Hawke in anything like this.

My legs squeezed together. The sensation this unconscious act provoked sent sparklers into my mind, and I clenched my teeth. This was the Menagerie, I reminded myself. This is what they did.

It was no different from the bidding rings of Monsieur Marceaux's circus. Much more expensive, to be sure, but the end result was the same. Flesh peddled; flesh owned.

I wasn't so stupid as to consider the sweets' role here as ornamental, right? Then certainly, the same could be said of the ringmaster.

My grip tightened on the pillar. Another low moan reached my ears, masculine and throaty, and I don't know why the sound curled into my skin and caught fire.

I leaned my feverish temple against the pillar, relieved as the cool stone soothed that bit of skin.

Then stiffened again as one of Hawke's gloved hands skimmed over the thigh of the woman beside him. She stretched languorously, the soft skin of her belly tightening, and his fingers danced across it lightly.

Someone called something to him, and he answered in his husky voice. Teasing, tempting. Doing what he did best; inciting and inferring. I don't know what. I couldn't make heads or tails of the tableau in front of me, inside me.

All I knew was that his hand slid over the woman's breast, over her throat, and his laughter rose rich and throaty.

I'd never seen him laugh before.

It changed him, softened the planes of his face without losing the edge that made him so mysterious and terrifying and beautiful all at once. It filled his eyes and spilled from his mouth and entered my skin as if it were his hands on *me*; his fingers in *my* hair.

I gasped.

And although I would swear the sound wasn't nearly enough to be heard across the vast, crowded theater, his head rose. His dark eyes pinned on my dark alcove; it had to be the opium that caused me to fancy that I could see the burning streak of blue from this distance.

His eyes narrowed.

I forgot how to breathe. Sweat gathered along my spine. The room was hot, too bloody hot, and if I let go of this pillar, I'd fall to a useless tangle of melted limbs.

And still I watched him as his smile started slowly. Stretched like a wolf's, all teeth and sensual, seductive leisure. He reached out an imperious hand, still gloved, his other still settled possessively at the sweet's narrow, naked waist. That hand beckoned me.

Come to me.

A demand. A dare.

Every nerve ending in my body shuddered. I met that gaze from across the amphitheater, no longer sure that he couldn't see me. That he couldn't see my pink cheeks, smell the salt and sweat of my body.

See my fear.

I withdrew. Forcing every limb into action, I peeled myself from that pillar, stumbled through the shadows of the alcove and fell back to the relative safety of the servants' halls.

I was used to tracking prey through all manner of conditions and environs. I had been in the ruins of Vauxhall at the stroke of midnight, stalked a ruffian through the Underground tracks and even caught a man just on the edge of my own district above the drift.

But I knew this wasn't the same.

Here, I was the prey, and I didn't like it one bit.

Or . . .

Did I?

As soon as my wobbling knees could support my weight, I fled the amphitheater entirely.

I didn't make it out of the Menagerie before I was caught.

I was halfway across the grounds, talking myself into coming down again another day to face—I mean, *confront* Hawke, when I heard a familiar voice. "*Cherie!*"

Turning, I scanned the dark stalls and cleverly arranged walls. On a market night, the stalls would have been brimming with wares, from the sublime to the sensual. Human or otherwise. Right now, everything was dark, and I had to strain to see the shadow flitting between the slats.

As it passed under the lamps, I relaxed. "Zylphia, what are you—?" Then I saw my friend's face, and I hurried to meet her. I wanted to reach for her shoulders, to grab her, make sure that she was as hale as she appeared, but Zylphia didn't like to be touched.

She got enough of that every night. Whenever I kept her company, I made it a point, a courtesy, to respect her wishes. So instead, I tucked my hands at my hips and demanded, "What happened? Whose fingers shall I break?"

Zylphia was a prostitute, a Midnight sweet. Retained exclusively by the Menagerie, she was one of many beautiful women to choose from, and I knew that they lived a much better life than many of the fallen women who worked below.

She was truthfully the most lovely woman I'd ever seen. An exotic mulatto, with skin the same color as my favorite black tea lightened with a dollop of cream.

Her eyes were shockingly blue, legacy of her unknown white father, and her hair a full mass of wavy black, with enough unusual kink to point to her Negro slave mother. It hung rich and heavy to her hips, thicker even than mine.

Tonight, it was twisted into exotic braids and peppered with speckled feathers. Much of her skin was bare to the cold, clad in some fur-trimmed frippery, but it wasn't a sight that shocked me anymore. I was used to Zylphia's unusual dress, for she often wore costumes designed to tempt the palate of whatever men—or women, she'd once told me—bid to buy her company.

The Menagerie maintained order on its own ground, and the women were not cruelly treated; but one look at Zylphia's grim expression, and my annoyance flipped to worry.

"I'm glad I found you," she said, bending to catch her breath. "Need . . . to talk."

I let her catch her breath, which allowed me to grab ahold of my own mind and focus it firmly on my friend. Of all the sweets at the Menagerie, Zylphia had somehow become a confidant of sorts. A friend where I hadn't expected to find many. While I'd never given her a name to call me, she liked to call me the French *cherie*.

It was close enough to *Cherry* that I had to keep from snickering every time I heard it.

She'd been here when I delivered my first Menagerie bounty, and I suspected she would stay long after I departed.

She straightened, her flushed cheeks fading as she took a deep breath. "I heard you'd come by the other night," she said, "but I didn't see you."

I winced. "I left rather quickly."

She nodded, braids sliding over her shoulders, and I waited. My friend was working up to something. As I took in the chill, I watched her hands work through the plaits. Then, looking once over her shoulder, she blurted, "There's been a murder."

It's impossible not to blanch at a statement like that. "What?"

"It's Annie."

I drew a mental blank. "Annie?"

Her long-fingered fists clenched in front of her. "Someone killed our Annie. That bastard killed her, he did, and I'm going to make him pay."

The only other murder I'd heard about was the prostitute in the East End. I frowned. "Do you know who Leather Apron is?"

Zylphia shook her head so hard, her braids fell over her shoulders like oiled snakes. "No, but he's like as not what killed Annie," she said, and I covered my face as my confusion only grew. "Bad enough the first was."

"Stop," I said through my fingers. "Wait. Let's go over this again, Zylla. There's been a murder, entirely different from the one in the papers?"

"Yes."

A cold wind swirled around us, and I shivered, suddenly all too aware of the dark pressing down from all sides. The lit path was only a few steps away, but I didn't walk toward it.

"You remember Annie?" Zylphia pressed. "Red-haired bit of a thing, had the youthful look about her. The men what like the innocent faces liked that one."

And suddenly, I remembered. Shorter even than me, with freckled skin and a laugh reminiscent of a child's.

I dropped my hands. "No," I breathed. She'd been sweeter than treacle and bawdy enough to keep me in stitches of laughter the few times I'd talked with her. "Zylla, I'm so sorry."

Zylphia nodded, once. "We aren't to talk about it."

"Why?"

She shrugged, her bare shoulders graceful and smooth. "But that bastard what killed her, he took her apart like she was a doll. We was wondering . . ." She trailed off.

"Wondering?"

She tucked her fingers under her chin, frowning down at me. "You're a collector. Did you hear of a price on Annie?"

I thought back to the wall of bounties; parchments and scrawling littering the surface. I made it a point to read as many as I could. I needed to be paid, after all, and some were easier to earn the coin than others. "No," I said slowly. "I saw nothing of the sort. And you know it's a dead man walking what puts a price on Menagerie employees."

Zylphia's face crumpled.

It was more than I could stand. "How can I help?" I demanded.

She took in a shuddering breath. "Annie wasn't our first," she admitted, and my eyebrows climbed as I stared at her. She hurried to add, "There's been three other girls, all murdered by the same bastard what did Annie. Three sweets and one common dove. That one, her name was Mary."

"How do you know it was the same killer?"

Her mouth set. "He's a ripper, that one. He took bits."

"Bits?"

"Bits of them," she clarified. "Liver and such. You don't forget a mark like that." Her white teeth flashed, all the more startling a grimace for her tea-dark skin. "We wasn't to say anything at all."

"By whose order?" I demanded, only half listening now.

She didn't answer. She didn't have to. That rotten, serpent-tongued two-faced thief. Not only had Hawke stolen my bounty, he'd gone and kept *this* from me, too.

Her gaze searched my face earnestly. Very slowly, she caught my hands and tucked them together, palm to palm. So surprised was I that she'd touched me, I could only stare as she said softly, "He's killed enough of us. We're scared, and we want him brought to justice."

I blinked. "I don't suppose you mean a magistrate."

"*Our* justice," Zylphia explained grimly, but said nothing else. She didn't have to. I opted not to ask. There were some things I needed to do with as clean a conscience as I could.

"What do you need from me?" I asked, frowning. "What can I do?"

Zylphia squeezed my fingers, then let me go, once more stepping out of reach. "We—that is," she amended, "the girls and I, we want to hire you to collect the ripper."

My stomach flipped.

"We can offer coin, but not enough," she continued hastily. As if by giving me time to think, I'd say no. "So we've gathered what we could together, and we can make up the difference with a ball of opium Preshea was given from one of hers."

I want it. It was the only thought that filled my head as Zylphia's offer registered. "What size?" I asked.

She held up thumb and forefinger, creating a circle big enough that I'd be set for at least a season.

But even as my greedy body yearned for it, I knew it didn't matter. There was such hope in my friend's eyes. Such fear.

And I'd already decided, even before offer of payment.

I nodded. "You and your girls have yourselves a collector," I said, but it seemed too sparkling, too brisk to my own ears.

This wouldn't be easy.

But for Zylphia, for the girls she befriended, for the simple fact that I wanted to see Micajah Hawke's smug expression fade as I dropped the murdering bastard at his lying feet, I said yes.

Let that teach the man to keep secrets from me.

Zylphia had precious little information. The sweets had been lured or stolen from the Menagerie grounds and found elsewhere in Limehouse. The first victim, the doxy called Mary I'd read about in the paper a month ago, had been found near her own rented rooms in the East End. Four murders over the course of four weeks.

Five victims, actually, if I could count the latest in the paper. All brutal. All done by the same man? God, I hoped so . . . To think there might be two horrifically unhinged killers stalking London below gave me chills.

But I knew one thing: I wasn't looking for an immigrant, and possibly I could release any of the more prominent gangs from my scrutiny. Say what you will about the criminals and the Chinese, none of them were stupid. Laying a finger on a sweet was tantamount to signing over your life, and I didn't know of a single Chinese man or gang leader who'd give the Karakash Veil reason to come calling.

How in God's name had the other murders gone unreported? The same papers that wrote about Leather Apron's latest surely wouldn't have passed up the chance to print something about mangled Menagerie sweets.

Unless the Karakash Veil had quashed it so thoroughly that no one else knew. That might have explained Hawke's recalcitrance at my presence. I was an outsider, and not even a paying customer, at that.

That meant Zylla had taken a major risk in hiring me. I'd have to tread carefully, lest I get my friend in trouble with an employer not especially well known for mercy.

The first thing I needed to do was get a lead. The problem was, I had nothing to go on.

Of course, I rarely had more to go on than a name and a motive. Sleuthing, I'd long since learned, came in different forms. The first was careful, cautious study. Evidence. Trailing folk and putting the clues together.

It didn't often come to fruition, and sadly, clues could so easily be manufactured. I should know, I'd done it enough times myself in the course of my youthful mischief.

The other, much more common method, was pure dumb luck.

It wasn't the first time I'd had to go fishing for leads. I knew just where to do it; there were all manner of establishments where tongues wagged and gossip flowed as easily as drink, opium, or both.

I took a direct route, one that led me through populated streets. Some were more active than others, even at night. As I walked, I scanned the faces of prostitutes and street rats alike. Many were filthy beyond repair. Some deformed. My eyes skated away from a young girl as she passed, head down and feet trudging through the muck.

The raw, open lesion eating at half her face stayed with me. They called it phossy jaw, a common ailment that plagued the girls what worked in the match factories. That girl could expect either surgical removal of her jaw, or death.

It was a hard life, anyway. Being poor only made it worse.

I rubbed the back of my neck as I walked, unhappily aware that my respirator and goggles were drawing more attention than I necessarily wanted. I braced myself for confrontation, but none came. Odds are, I was an uncertain mystery in the lamplight. Diminutive, sure, but there was an adage about small folk on the streets. More often than not, they fought the hardest. Would shiv you as soon as fight fair.

I wouldn't do either. But no one needed to know that. Still, the back of my neck prickled uncomfortably as I walked.

Finding no one I thought would be useful, I sidestepped into an alley I knew as one of the many paths that led to the Brick Street Bakery—an alliterative name for one of the many territories claimed by a gang by the same name—and surprised a boy preparing to urinate on a wall.

"Bugger!" he squeaked as I clapped a hand into his collar. Fierce brown eyes lifted to stare at my goggles and mask, fighter's eyes, for all he was certainly younger than Levi. He thrashed in my grip, hands and feet hammering. "Lemme go!"

I shook him hard enough to rattle his teeth. "Be still, you little rat."

"I'll take yer eyes out!"

"Do," I shot back, warding away his blows simply by holding him at arm's length. "I'll laugh to hear your pleading when Ishmael Communion comes a-calling."

He froze. All at once, the fight drained from his eyes, his body, and he hung limp as a starved puppy in my grasp. "You know Communion?"

"We're friends, he and I." I narrowed my eyes at him, for all he couldn't see them through the lenses. "If I set you on your feet, you won't run?"

I watched the notion sneak into his face, easily read despite the entire city's worth of dirt covering it. "Won't," he lied.

Poor blighter. I knew his language, and I used it now. "There's a shilling in it if you don't," I said, and watched his eyes widen. "And another if you deliver a message for me."

"Wot, really?"

"Really." I set him down, let him go and stepped back.

His little body tensed, taut as a bowstring as his instinct fought with greed. All but vibrating in place, he flipped me a look under stringy, unkempt hair and held out a dirty palm.

I delved into my pocket and produced a grimy shilling. I'd long since learned to dirty up my coin when I spent it below the drift. I held it between two fingers, where he could see it. "Good lad," I said, and tucked another beside it. "Where is Communion?"

"Somewhere," the lad chirped. "Can't tell." He tapped his nose. "Bakers only."

He didn't mean the sort who made bread. I frowned at him. "You're a Brick Street Baker?"

"Uh-uh," he replied. "Not yet. But I'll be soon."

So young, too. I refrained from the lecture welling behind my teeth—in the background of my thoughts, Fanny's voice was filling my head—and focused on the matter at hand. "Tell Communion to meet me at the corner of Emmett and Park. In one hour."

He watched the shillings as I held them just over his head. "Aye!"

"What is the message?" I knew this lesson well, too.

"Meetcha at th' corner of Park 'n' Emmett. One hour," he repeated dutifully.

"Good lad." I flipped him both coins with a flick of my fingers. He caught them deftly, one in each quick hand, turned and fled down the alley. I watched him almost vanish into the dark, pause, turn and look at me.

"Hey," he called. "Woss yer name?"

I smiled. "Tell him that it's collector business," I replied. "He'll know."

He stared at me for a moment. Finally, just loud enough that the alley fed the sound to me, he sneered. "Nutter."

Then he ran.

My smile widened as I left the alley. This time, I bypassed the busy street entirely. I took my time, knowing it'd take the rat at least half as long to locate Communion, and threaded my way through side alleys and inner lanes.

This time, I didn't feel quite so scrutinized. Was I overworried? I thought so. I'd never agreed to collect a murderer before, even alive. And it's not as if it were an official bounty posted, so there was no reason for me to worry about other collectors jumping on my back in the dark.

Of course, anyone else looking for a collector might luck out on my trail, but certainly no one would be dumb enough to try.

Unless it were the mysterious assailant outside the druggist's shop.

As the thought occurred to me, I damned my stupidity to perdition and melded back into the shadows. Of course, the chances of being located twice by the same man were slim at best, especially if he were just a footpad looking for coin, but I didn't need to risk it. I still felt overly anxious.

I hurried to my chosen destination and remained as hidden as I could.

I waited at the corner of Emmett and Park for over an hour before I gave up. Ishmael either hadn't gotten my message—I made a mental note to hunt down the little sewer rat—or he'd other business to attend to.

That made this evening's plans that much more dangerous.

Not that it'd stop me, of course. I'd go in alone.

I chose the poorer opium dens in Limehouse for my evening's snooping. Not only were they likely connected to the Karakash Veil's far-reaching influence, but they often catered to the lower classes more than the upper.

I didn't need to know what the gossip was above the drift. I was well aware, thank you.

Although it pained me to do it, I put away my fog-prevention goggles and respirator. They were remarkable things, and easily recognizable. Any working rat, as I was passing myself off to be, would have no such thing.

My eyes stinging and my nose filled with acrid smoke and fog, I hurried across the district and to a den I knew still plied its foreign trade. I'd spend the last of my money here, sadly, but all in pursuit of a greater bounty.

The distinctive smell assaulted me as I stepped inside its plain doors. One part spicy, mostly medicinal in flavor as it hit the back of the tongue. Blinking quickly, half blinded by the dimmed lamps, I looked around the entry hall of an unassuming brownstone.

There was nobody there. The furniture was shabby, the paper peeling from the walls. Beneath my feet, the carpet was worn thin, showing patches of grimy, scuffed wood beneath.

Same as it ever had been.

As if by some unseen signal, a small Chinese woman stepped out from behind a door. She was dressed in an unusual amalgam of Eastern and English attire, with a small bustle offset by the strange, wide sash her kind wore as belts or corsets. I wasn't sure. Her hair was a graying knot at the base of her neck, her rouge too thick, and her features wizened.

She said nothing, only gave me a quick once-over with beady black-eyed greed. I knew the steps of this dance, although I kept myself from knowing why. I recognize now what I hadn't yet admitted to then, and my familiarity with the subject has only grown threefold in the interim.

Producing a small purse, I tossed it to her as I'd seen so many other men do.

She caught it, lightning quick.

Not as aged as she'd like me to believe, then.

With brief gestures, she escorted me to another door,

opened it with the creak and groan of damp-rotted wood, and pointed me inside.

The patrons of an opium den are not usually the raucous sort. Conversation flows when a man or woman is just settling in, and as the opium is heating in the long, slender pipes. Then, as the resulting smoke is inhaled and begins to creep warmly, deliciously, to the mind, conversation ebbs. The better to follow the spidery trails of liquid gold; the warmth of it as it fills every nerve and sensation and paints the mind in shades of glorious awareness.

Once fully absorbed, conversation may start again, but it's not the rough, unrefined sound it was. It becomes something melodic and fascinating, and many things are said if only just to hear the sound of it.

Small lamps glittered in the hazy air, the devices by which the opium pipes could be heated. I inhaled deeply, holding the smoky remnants of used opium in my lungs for a moment.

I knew this smell.

Strolling in as if I belonged, I kept my stride easy but not polished. Like a man, or at least more like the boy I resembled. Men and women alike sprawled around the cramped room. Some on the floor in indolent repose, others in chairs or laid back in chaise lounges. Some slept, rocked into a gentle rest by the opium's lullaby.

All were poor. All worn and bedraggled and so at ease, it was as if the hard day didn't matter anymore.

And it didn't. That was opium's blessing.

The light glinted off of the pipes clutched in hands, passed from person to person, and I took one as it was offered to me in passing.

I didn't say thank you, though it sprang to my lips.

This wasn't the place for such niceties. Instead, clasping the pipe to my side, I found a bit of unclaimed territory against a wall where I could watch all the goings-on.

The murmurs around me continued unabated as I sank to the dirty floor. I tried to listen, but I found my hands running over the pipe instead. I had to light the opium and take some, of course. In a gathering like this, anyone who didn't partake would be seen as an interloper, or worse, a spy. Maybe a policeman in disguise.

It was as good an excuse as any.

I inspected the pipe swiftly. It was a lengthy bit of metal, copper but for the grime from so many fingers, and inlaid with jade too mottled to be the high-quality stones they likely reserved for finer dens. Everything touched by the Karakash Veil sported something of jade. A bit of an in-joke, maybe, or a calling card.

A bulbous sphere at one end was divided by a small basket, into which the brown glob of opium remained trapped.

I sank back into the woven mat beneath me, leaned fully against the wall, and supported the long pipe in both hands. The lamp beside me flickered as I held the sphere over the small chimney built over the lamp flame.

The end shook. Just enough that I set my jaw, firmed my grip. It wouldn't take long.

The chimney funneled the heat to the sphere at the end of the pipe. Inside, the pea-size pill of opium grew warm, then hot, barely retaining its shape as it turned to a vapor that could be drawn in through the pipe stem.

Around me, voices half whispered. Laughter crept in, but I watched the chimney. Watched the vapors trickle from the tiny seam.

When I had waited long enough, I fit my mouth around the hollow tube and inhaled deeply.

The vapors slipped into my mouth, my throat, my lungs and I could have danced for joy. Instead, my muscles relaxed, as if I'd been holding on to some unknown tension for too long. I closed my eyes, inhaling again before the vapors built too much.

My skin prickled. Ordinarily, this would cause me to look about, searching for the eyes that watched me, but I didn't bother. This was different. This was warmth and magic and energy all rolled into a small copper tube. This was raw aether, if aether could be taken into the lungs.

This was the means by which I'd track down my killer.

My killer?

I frowned, opening my eyes. Of course I meant my bounty.

I blinked.

Though I had no recollection of it, my arms had settled, the pipe drifting to my lap, and the flame in the lamp beside me had burned low. I sat up, languid with the lazy heat swirling under my skin, and it was as if every detail etched itself indelibly into my mind.

I saw the small knots of people around me. Twos, threes, even four and more. They leaned against one another, laughing, some even dozing. I saw missing teeth and pock-scarred skin; glittering eyes feverishly bright in the golden light.

And the rumors. Oh, the words that slipped through my ears to dance a heavenly waltz in gutter-worn shoes through my awareness. They sang choruses about the goings-on below. The adulterers and the thieves. The cracking cases, robberies and pox-less doxies. Sky ships seen hovering too close to the drift and the steamboats gliding through black water beyond the river banks.

And the Menagerie, I realized, as an aimless thread floated to my ears. These poor people, they didn't attend every night like many of the more well-to-do could afford. But when they did—a flush scorched a fiery path all the way to my ears as details of debauchery colored the tale.

I almost curled into the corner and caught myself, instead adopting one of Teddy's more leisurely poses—as a man would, I thought, and smothered a giggle.

Behind me, two men spoke of the growing tensions at the docks, both above and below the drift. "Me cousin," said one, "'e works th' above docks, but 'e sez ain't no better there 'n down 'ere."

"What, an' 'im makin' more?" demanded a woman.

"Threepence more, an' starvin' already, too," the man added.

I thought about this for a long time, drifting away on a scarlet wave of imagery and speculation. If the dockers were starving above and below the drift, why not pay them enough to feed them well? After all, they worked hard unloading the goods brought into port. And the airships that came in would be stocked with such lovely goods as silks and fine linens and crystal things from faraway kingdoms.

My fluid thoughts slid to the Menagerie once more, and Hawke rose in my idle thoughts like a specter, a haunting ghost without sound or form. His eyes, that damned blue streak aflame, laughed at me, even as his mouth curved up into a sensual line. Beckoning. Tempting me to step into the humid air of the ampitheater—

"I didn't 'spect this place to have any o' this," said a gruff, masculine voice in the lazy crowd. "Went lookin' for a few grains and most ev'ry shop's done out."

I blinked hard, straightening. Shaking my head, I looked down to find someone had taken the pipe from my hand, but restocked the flame in the lamp.

A fresh opium pipe, this one unmarred by the grasp of dirty hands, lay beside it.

My fingers itched.

"Me, too!"

"All over Blackwall," chimed a woman whose voice grated like shattered glass. In it, I heard the tinkle of a thousand shards, each like diamonds as they scattered across the filthy floor.

I felt as if I could take a deep breath and taste the world.

"All over th' East End," corrected another man, sounding not so much put out as mildly accepting of the fact. Opium made getting angry difficult, at best, and not worth the effort at any rate.

I smiled, reaching for the pipe.

"Think these foreign Chinese—"

"Shhh," hissed a younger female voice. "Rude."

The man snorted. "Jes' askin'. They make their own, right?"

The first voice rumbled through them all, not loud. Just noticeable. Raspy enough to make me think he'd inhaled more than his fair share over the years, for his tone now put me in mind of the smoke that hung low around us all. "Heard it was a professor."

"What, *the* professor?"

"That's th' one," murmured another. "But th' bugger's good and crazy, innit?"

A moment of speculative thought followed this, and my smile faded. So a professor *had* been involved. It figured. God only knew what a man of science would be doing with that much opium.

Deucedly interesting things, I was sure.

I pitched my voice low and asked, "What professor?"

Laughter met my inquiry. "Boy don't know," one woman said, giggling. I studied the room, searching for the woman and found her sprawled half up against a settee, her calves and worn stockings bared to the lazy eyes who admired them.

Beside her, a man in patched, fraying fustion took the pipe from her slack fingers and held it over the lamp. "Nobody knows," he explained, but with the inherently theatrical implications such a phrase always demanded. His bushy gray chops were wild as he bent to inhale the fumes.

"'e's a ghost," said another woman, but frightfully. She drew her knees up, hiding behind her skirts and displaying her knickers by doing so.

I blinked again. Yet couldn't find it in myself to say anything. She'd figure it out, I was sure. "A ghost," I repeated doubtfully.

"Bollocks," said the first gruff voice. Yet I couldn't make him out, shrouded in smoke and set apart from the others. "'e's no ghost. Woolsey's 'is name. They say 'e collects bodies."

"Bodies!" squealed the fearful girl.

I rolled my eyes. "A caretaker?"

"Worse," said the voice, and it lowered. The man's shoulders rounded in his overcoat. "A scientist."

Oh, *bollocks*. Unlike the faceless man, I didn't say it aloud, but I turned back and picked up the pipe I'd forgotten about. Holding it over the flame, I let them bandy the rumors about more, and held on to the thread binding them all: there *was* a professor. It was a small community, the academia of London. It was something, anyway.

"They say any man—"

"Or woman!" piped up another, much more distinguished, voice, loudly.

"Anyone," the man amended, "bold or brave enough t' go wand'rin' about at night is ripe for pickin'. Whole bodies." He paused. "In bits."

The crowd gasped, almost as one, and I smothered a smile. Whoever the man was, he had a decent sense of performance and timing. All but eating out of his hand, this lot.

I rose from my mat, taking a last breath from the pipe as I did. I held the smoke inside my chest and closed my eyes. A shoulder brushed mine, and I exhaled hard, coughing in surprise. The gruff-voiced man paused just by the door, one gloved hand on the latch, and didn't turn as he warned, "Careful, you lot. You stick to th' lights a'fore you fin' yerself missin' those same bits." His head tilted, and I saw a shadow of an ear beneath a low seaman's hat. "Bodies," he repeated with chilling inflection.

He slid out the door while I stared at him, and for a long moment, there was no sound in the den.

Then it erupted into a frenetic whisper.

Part of me wanted to applaud. Instead, I dropped my pipe into the lap of a decently dressed man with neatly barbered blond chops and half ran out the door.

He'd known something. At the very least, he'd known this Woolsey bloke. I could sense it, as if a shimmering thread connected me to his mind. He'd known some-thing, or I'd eat my hat.

The hall was empty as I pushed into it; not even the Chinese hostess in attendance. I sprinted through the entryway, pushed out into the damp fog, and spun in a hard, tight circle.

The details of the night screamed at me, but long practice allowed me to filter it into recognizable par-cels. The fog reeked of rotting river water tonight, sewage and rubbish conspiring to undercut the rough, gritty flavor of coal smoke.

The iron-worked gas lamps tried their best to shed light on my quarry's trail, but the fog roiled in a miasma as thick and reflective as mirrored glass, and I saw no trace of his silhouette in the dark.

The slick cobbles beneath my feet easily swallowed any trail, and as I spun in helpless frustration, I kicked at them.

A clatter echoed from behind me, and I turned to scrutinize the shadowed edge of the slick, faceless building. Gritting my teeth, I sprinted toward the noise, my fingers already slipping into the top of my shirt.

A form loomed out from the dark, and before I could find traction on the wet stone under my feet, I collided with a chest that didn't stagger half as much I did.

A midnight blue overcoat looked almost black in the lamplight, settling over decently wide shoulders. As I found my balance against the brownstone brick, I looked up into the rigid face of Lord Cornelius Ker-rigan Compton and felt my jaw drop.

He hesitated, the hand holding the fashionable walk-ing stick deftly brushing at his shoulder as if he could wipe away any stain I may have left, but he did incline his head sharply. "Your pardon," he said evenly.

The tone suggested bone-deep propriety was all that forced the courtesy. His gaze raked over me briefly, but didn't linger for longer than it took the words to leave his lips. He was clearly focused on whatever task brought him below the drift.

"Er," I managed, but he was already moving on, long before I had time to make sense of shock screaming through me.

I watched him enter the opium den I'd only just vacated and forgot how to breathe.

Could it be?

Did my Lord Compton's secrets go as far as mine?

It took me a long moment, but eventually, I remembered how to close my mouth.

It was as if I'd taken a draught of liquid sunshine. Running into Lord Compton, quite literally, had jostled my anger at losing the mysterious rumormonger into something frenetic and bright—glittering and full of vigor.

I shed my street clothing as I traveled across Limehouse, leaving my collector's garb open for all to see. I dug out my mask and goggles, needing them for the task I levied upon myself next.

At the same alley I'd found the would-be Baker boy, I paused in the dark and adjusted my various accoutrements. My tool belt was solidly locked in place, strapped down and unlikely to flap open. My fog-prevention lenses were secure, my gloves exchanged for ones with a particular molded substance on the fingers and palms.

Assured I was as ready as I could ever be, I spread

my arms, touched both ends of the alley easily, and kicked my feet up on either wall.

No matter what training I had as a youth, there are certain things the human muscles just aren't willing to do. Straddling an alleyway to climb to the roof is one. With my legs split wide open, I held myself straight, splayed my arms for balance and slowly inched my way up. My legs and hips burned by the time my head cleared the roof, and I hooked my fingers into the edge with a sigh of relief.

It would hold. I locked my grip, leveraged my weight over to one side and hung for a moment. Arms shaking ever so slightly, I bent at the waist, pulled my straightened legs up, up, up until my toes were pointed to the sky.

"Allez, hop!" I muttered, and bent backward almost double until my feet touched the rooftop. Completing the walkover was the easy bit, and soon I was on my feet and upright again.

My back complained. Just enough.

I was, after all, getting a sight too old for such antics. There was a reason most circus performers were children.

I studied the vista laid out before me, arranging the yellow lens over one eye until it sat more comfortably against my socket. The fog drifted like a living thing, pouring over the roof edge as if it could climb to the very pinnacle. The smell was somehow not as intense up on first tier of rooftops, and visibility seemed much clearer.

Around me, as far as the fog would let me see, iron structures climbed up and up and up. They were the feet of London above, brilliant architectural foundations that supported elements deemed too valuable or necessary to leave below.

I had heard the palace had been raised *en masse*, leaving only the crypts behind. I'd never looked.

There was something about tombs, even royal ones, that I found frightfully sinister.

I headed for Baker territory, but cautiously. They called the rooftops Cat's Crossing. The theory being that only the city's rampant strays were foolish, and dexterous, enough to attempt to travel by rooftop.

Cats, I supposed, and those of us with good reason to risk it.

I wasn't the only enterprising sort to use the rooftops as a safer means of anything—not that the slick roofs and steep peaks could be called safe by anyone but the terminally insane—and I knew for a fact that the Bakers posted men above.

Well, children, really. They were smaller, lighter and much more agile, as I'd mentioned. And lacked an appropriate fear of death from tall heights.

I moved swiftly, my feet sure, sometimes scaling the pointed apexes of the buildings I used like a path, sometimes leaping between them.

I saw the sentries before they saw me. It was one of many benefits of these goggles of mine. Dodging them proved to be as simple as waiting for them to move on, or moving around them on silent feet.

Once in the heart of Baker territory—you knew it because of the terrible smell of rotting fish, twice as thick here than anywhere in the East End—I paused.

Now the slower game.

I crept to the edge of the roof I hugged, foot by booted foot, inch by inch, hand over gloved hand. I waited for what seemed like hours—I would guess only about thirty minutes. I let my mind wander.

I lay on the edge of a yawning crevasse, and in my mind, I balanced a series of spinning plates. Light glimmered off of each one, and each bore a color. Blue for Compton, and his strange interest. Wicked serpent green for Micajah Hawke and his relentless lies.

Zylphia was a whisper in my ear, and a disk of bloody red spun just over my head. I didn't know what that was, but it tasted of murder and rage and I dwelled for some time on the matter as I waited.

A mind saturated in opium works twice as fast, and yet three times as slow. Caught on the edge of a thousand thoughts, I startled when I heard the cursing pitch of a masculine voice.

My grin was fierce. I was lucky. I could recognize Ishmael's dark baritone from blocks away.

I peered over the edge and saw a group of men, many in shabby dockhand clothes, a few in whatever it was they could scrape together. Some carried hafts of broken wood, others weapons I couldn't see well in the dark.

They were a short distance away, walking together, complaining, I think. Had I any skill in it, I could have summoned enough saliva to spit at Ishmael and likely tagged him from here.

Fortunately for us both, I was not a good spitter.

I eased the upper portion of my dark-clad body over the rooftop, hooked my feet against the ledge, and felt in my pockets for something to throw.

I found a single pence.

Eh, it was as good as anything else.

Taking careful aim, I threw the coin at Ishmael's feet. It landed with a soft *whup*, all but lost under the staccato argument taking place between three members of the group.

Frowning, I watched as they walked over it. Blast, I'd have to get down to street level to—

A large form detached itself from the group.

Victory! I resisted the urge to punch the air with my fist, tamping down the surge of elation I felt as Ishmael Communion stepped into clearer focus.

He was a very big, very broad man of color. His wide, flat features and pugnacious nose had always marked him as a bruiser, and if there were any doubt, his scarred knuckles would finish the tale.

He was an ox of a man, with a head he kept free of hair or hats. He wore a kerchief around his neck, overalls like I'd seen Americans wear in some of the more mocking caricatures, and a particularly large overcoat in patched fustion.

He stepped into my alley, not once looking up, and I heard clothing rustle.

I narrowed my eyes, soundless and unseen just over his head. If I wanted to, I could poke the very top of his skull before he let fly the stream of urine.

I reached out an arm to do just that, then froze as he rumbled, deep as a train car in the vast Underground, "What in God's own are you doing, girl?"

So he *had* seen me. I slowly withdrew my arm, my feet straining to hold me. "Where were you?" I hissed.

The voices continued to rattle back and forth, insults and demands, and he glanced over his shoulder. This time, when he glanced up, I caught a glimpse of dark, dark eyes. The whites were yellowed, as if tinged permanently by the pea soup that surrounded us. "You came," he whispered harshly, "to ask that?"

Ishmael had an unbelievable grasp of the King's English. I'd always wanted to ask why and how, but had never summoned the nerve.

Instead, I frowned. "Why are you angry?"

"If you are found—" He didn't need to finish it. If I was caught in Baker territory, I'd be killed. If they found me to be a woman, there'd be worse.

The Brick Street Bakery was a sweet-enough name, but there was nothing sweet about the men in it.

"That's why I sent a boy," I told him, conversationally reasonable, for all I was hanging ten feet above the ground by the flexed arches of my feet.

I didn't have to see well to note the grimace that split his thick, fleshy lips. "Girl, that boy got strung up in his own gibbets."

The blood, already pushed to my head because of my angle, suddenly pounded in my skull. "What?" I gasped.

Too loud. The voices stopped. Then, "Communion!"

"Lay off," my friend barked. "I'm taking a whittle."

I didn't giggle. I wanted to, the part of my brain still steeped in the calming cushion of opium thought his word comical, but the rest of me was still reeling. That boy? Dead?

"How?" I whispered.

"You had best be scarce for a while," Ishmael warned. "That boy—his name was Rufus. You were seen with him by several of the abram men." In the silence that followed, I heard a stream of liquid splat against the wall.

I grimaced as the odor reached me.

Abram men, I knew, were thieves and beggars pretending to be so mad that they could scarcely afford to dress themselves. They begged for coin amid *faux* fits.

They were also some of the keenest eyes and ears in London below.

"I swear to you," I said tightly, earnestly. "Ishmael, I swear on my mother's grave, I didn't kill your boy. Why would I? I don't take those contracts, you know that."

"I know that," Ishmael rumbled. The stream of relief continued unabated, thick and loud as it splattered. "And you know that. They don't know that."

I braced my hands on the wall, swallowing hard to get the knot of pressure and anger and guilt out of my throat. "When was he found?"

"Not long ago. Them?" He nodded vaguely toward the alley mouth. "They found him."

Damn it. How soon after I'd given him my coin had he been killed? And why? "I'll get out, then," I managed. "Just one thing."

"Communion!" roared a man from beyond the alley.

"Quickly," my friend rumbled, his gaze on the wall.

"Do you know anything about a Professor Woolsey?"

He thought it over as the stream of urine finally died. I thanked God I couldn't see that well in the dark. Ishmael's privacy was something I had no intention of ever breaching. The smell was bad enough.

"No," he finally said. "Try the Menagerie? Your sweets might have heard."

"They aren't *my* sweets," I shot back. I stiffened my body, caught one edge of the roof with the very tips of my fingers, and hesitated long enough to add, "But I'll send your love to Zylphia."

Ishmael's growl followed me over the roof. "Coming!" he intoned, impatient. "Can't a bloke relieve himself in peace?"

I scooted up on the roof as far as I dared, then counted slowly. I didn't move, holding my position far longer than strictly necessary. I didn't want to risk it, not until I was positive the men below had moved on.

The boy could have been killed by a rival gang. There were many below the drift, each fighting for territory or wealth or recruits.

But I remembered his fighter's eyes, earnest and crafty. That boy had been younger than Levi, I was sure of it. Clever and cocksure, but still just flesh.

I rubbed at my face, taking the time to let my limbs rest.

I'd learned two things tonight. One, not a soul knew about the death of the sweets, or else that would have been all the den would have talked about. Nothing got the blood surging like murder.

Two, the name of the professor who inconvenienced me was Woolsey.

But I could deduce a third: according to the rumors, that professor dealt in body parts, and Zylphia said those sweets had been missing organs.

There was nothing for it. I'd have to head home for the night and begin my investigations fresh. Without my original bounty. Without opium to sleep by.

My mood, bolstered as it had been, plummeted.

Chapter Eight

I returned home, my thoughts swirling around and around. How would I locate this Woolsey? What clues did I have to go on?

Well, nothing, of course. Just missing organs and a professor that could be committing the crime.

How would I catch him?

I could pose as a prostitute, I supposed, but the odds of meeting the right man at the right time were slim enough. Besides, he seemed to be targeting sweets now.

Why?

Perhaps Hawke or the Karakash Veil had made an enemy of him? Perhaps one of the sweets had turned him down?

No. That seemed too simple for the brutality of the crimes. And it didn't account for the two common doxies.

I got ready for bed on my own, washed the lampblack from my hair and studied the cards left for me on the nightstand. I didn't usually receive any; such markers of social interest weren't typically tossed my way but for a specific purpose.

There were two now.

I recognized my Lord Compton's seal, and I picked it up as I slid into the bed. The card rasped against my sensitive fingertips, textured as good silk was textured. The sheets were cool to the touch; I blamed that when I shivered.

He'd left a note on the back, in simple, elegant writing.

I humbly beg your company on this matter.

I wondered if he'd left me the cards on his way below.

As the lantern flickered beside me, I reached over and found the second card—an invite, I realized as the bold script danced beneath the flame's illumination.

A ball. *Another* ball. Lady Rutledge, I read as I skimmed the information. My eyebrows raised.

Lady Euphemia Rutledge was renowned for her library, and often entertained foreign dignitaries from various countries. She was a brilliant woman, and I had read many of her theories as reprinted in the periodicals that didn't shy from a woman whose mind lent more to science than fashion or other delicacies.

I had always longed to meet her, but her society circles were so far adrift from mine.

I *had* heard, however, that the marchioness had no love for the lady. But that for some unknown reason, the widow was safely out of Marchioness Northampton's vicious reach.

For that alone, I might consider going.

I tapped the card against my lips as I sank back into the softness of my pillows. If Betsy were here, she'd tell me that I was being foolish. Of course I'd have to go.

One didn't spurn an invite from an earl.

"Unless," I told the card in my hand, "such an invite is only designed to leave me once more cut at my lord's whim."

The thought stitched an icy knot in my stomach.

Then again . . .

A new thought unfurled. A mischievous thought, one trimmed in sudden sweetness of revenge. A picture of the earl rose in my mind, swathed in yellow fog and apologizing brusquely for a transgression not his. Ever so proper, my Lord Compton.

Even stepping into an opium den below the drift.

What would his lady mother say, I wondered?

But as I threw the card to the table, dimmed the lantern until the wick guttered out, I knew I'd never betray that secret. Not without some foolproof method to ensure my name was never dragged in alongside his.

A gentlemen could be excused his idiosyncrasies.

A lady would be packed off to an asylum or cast out below the drift.

Besides. We all had our secrets, didn't we?

Some were simply more involved than others. Much, *much* more involved.

Slam!

I was jarred awake from my nightmares, reaching for a weapon I didn't have and ready to fight the ruffian that didn't exist. Sweat clung to my skin, plastered my nightdress to my legs and breasts.

Booted feet echoed from somewhere in the house. Too rhythmic to be Booth's. A guest?

An intruder?

I began to throw off the covers, intent on confronting the foolish criminal myself if need be, when the raucous cacophony of barking dogs halted me as surely as if I'd been bathed in ice. The noise echoed, as feral as if the animals making such a racket had risen from hell itself.

I sucked in a breath. A masculine voice slid through the floorboards, too muted to hear more than the deep rumble, and the noises stopped.

All at once, the energy of a sudden waking flipped to an icy sliver of fear winding down my back. Instinctively and without reason, I threw the covers over my head, huddling beneath them as I'd used to when I was a child.

Step-thunk. The uneven rhythm of Booth's footsteps preceded the other's up the stairs, solid and defining. Booth murmured something. It was answered by the voice of a man I'd never grown to like.

Or to face.

For all my swagger, I'd once been much more of a terror in this house. At my worst, I'd left Fanny in tears and Mrs. Booth at her wits' end. Yet it was Ashmore who frightened me into submission.

He was, in my memory, a large man, giant in stature, with features carved out of stone and hellfire in his eyes. Which were, of course, gleaming red.

My memory of years gone by has never been what it should be. Flights of fancy often intertwined with fact, but in Mr. Ashmore's case, I was sure it was only a small stretch. I remember our initial meeting vaguely, and I am aware that it was not under the most cordial of circumstances. It had been a long night, and I was screaming at the top of my voice.

Wracked with illness, with pains through my body

and head, I couldn't sleep without nightmares and the fevers kept me restless and angry. I was frightened, above all. I wanted the opium that I'd been given all my young life, and couldn't understand why my new keepers would not allow me the salve.

I did not know Mr. Ashmore was home, and when he burst into the room my governess locked me into, I had no time to realize anything but that there was a demon presence over my bed and a hard hand at my mouth. He bent over me, growled something low and demanding.

Likely, that I would be silent.

There must have been more. I would never simply acquiesce to such brutality, but I no longer recall. There was only an empty void behind that memory. A suggestion of fear, of something terrible. Some certain knowledge of evil, I was sure, but I had no real recollection. I awoke the next morning, snug in my bed and certain that I'd escaped the gates of hell itself.

When he was home, I hid. Unreasonable as my fear seemed by day, it persevered.

Now, as I lay staring into the darkness beneath my bedclothes, that same weight of presence hovered just outside my door. A curious snuffling echoed too loudly in my ears; I stuffed the edge of my coverlet into my mouth before I made a noise. My heart pounded as the door thudded softly, as if something tested its solid weight.

Had I locked it?

I couldn't recall, and as my mind painted a picture of a large, perhaps clawed hand reaching for the latch, I balled my fists up into the blanket and pulled it tighter around my shaking body. Icy sweat drenched me.

I was a ward of the devil. I was sure of it.

Suddenly, that low voice murmured a sharp command. The door creaked, the snuffling stopped, becoming instead padded thumps that faded away down the hall.

Slowly, quietly, that presence eased away.

The dark closed in again, silent and thick. Now and again, I heard a muffled whisper from the small room Mr. Ashmore claimed as his own when he visited. Booth's polished murmur rose and fell in small bursts, and I suspected that as much as I loved the butler, he was informing my demonic guardian everything he knew I'd been up to in his absence.

I wasn't so foolish as to assume there were no spies in my house. Someone had to keep Mr. Ashmore informed, and the Booths had made no secret of their loyalty.

I eased from beneath the cover, poking my head out. I half expected it to be bitten off by some hovering creature in the dark. A thing with horns and leathery wings.

When only the usual patterns of my bedroom greeted me, I let out a silent sigh of relief.

If Mr. Ashmore stayed true to form, he would sleep nearly through the day to make up for his late arrival, and I'd be gone when he rose to leave again. In his wake, there'd be a new trinket or bit of foreign décor from across the world.

But my hand shook as I reached for the decanter upon my nightstand. As slowly as I could, desperate to keep the crystal stopper from clinking, I plucked the cap loose and held it clenched in one fist. I dared not set it down. It might make noise.

Alert the dogs, if not their master.

To . . . what? I silently scoffed. Would he tear down my door? Slither inside and ravish me in my sleep?

Bollocks. He'd left me well enough alone since the one and only time he'd ever set foot in my presence.

But even as I thought it, I tilted the decanter to my lips and drank the rest of the ruby liquid inside. Let Betsy click her tongue and report its vanishing to Fanny, this was life or death.

The laudanum ran a long, warm line along my throat, into my stomach. The burn was welcome. It signified sleep. Blessed, peaceful sleep.

And yet, even with the laudanum, it seemed a long time in coming.

Chapter Nine

I awoke with the awareness of pain dancing around inside my head. My mouth was dry, my body aching as I untangled it from the twisted snarl it had gotten itself into while I'd slept.

I reached over and pulled the rope to summon Betsy.

She arrived as I stretched, uncharacteristically quiet. Without fuss, I was bathed and dressed, my hair gathered into two separate braids and then pinned high atop my head in artful twists. The dress she'd chosen was striped poplin, peacock blue and white, with a typical froth of lace at the short, tight sleeves and trimmed all over with the same blue.

It was cheerful, crisp and light.

As she affixed a small bit of cerulean netting to my hair, allowing it to poof upwards in a fashionable net flower, I caught her hand. "Are you all right?"

"Just fine," she said, and flashed me a smile. "Tired, miss."

Guilt swamped me. Had I been working my friend too hard?

"Off you go, then," she added, and I had no chance to answer before she bustled me out the door.

Arriving at the breakfast table, I saw Fanny as usual, but no sign of my mysterious guardian. Mrs. Booth hummed gaily as she carried in the tray. "Good morning, miss."

I knew what made her so happy. She adored her employer, for reasons I couldn't fathom. I grimaced. "Is that what this is?"

Fanny looked up from her tea. "Cherry," she warned in dangerously dulcet tones.

Booth entered behind me, the paper tucked under his arm.

I slid into my customary seat. "Will we be foregoing the pleasure of my guardian's company, then?" I asked, obediently injecting my voice with bright cheer.

"Sir had a rather long trip and a terribly late night," Booth informed me. He set the paper down beside my plate, and I smiled up at him. "I imagine he'll be abed for most of the day."

"Lazy," I observed, smothering my mischief against the rim of my teacup. The brew was strong, just as I liked it, and lacking in all but two lumps of sugar.

"Cherry." Fanny sighed again.

"Well, we shan't be waiting on his presence," I said briskly as I reached for my toast. "I'm eager to go out today."

"Oh?" Fanny ate with delicacy. It gave her much more time to talk.

I needed my energy. Most of the time, she filled the silence as I filled my mouth and scanned the papers. I reached for the *London Times*, briefly meeting my chaperone's gaze over the crisp paper. "What?" I asked.

She studied me thoughtfully, her ice blue eyes measuring. "Have you an agenda in mind, or are you simply eager to be out?"

"Nothing in mind," I hedged, returning my attention to the articles. I skimmed through most quickly; reading had never been a difficult chore for me. "They say the *Ophelia* is skyworthy, now. Do you suppose we'll go to the christening?"

"I don't see why not," Fanny answered, but she wasn't so easily distracted. "You have no desire to greet Mr. Ashmore?"

I frowned. Of the many responses I could have said, I chose the lie with ease. "Booth said he's exhausted. Why, would you awaken him to dance attendance on us?" I didn't like to say his name, if I could help it. It might have been akin to summoning the devil.

I could just imagine the name sliding from my lips, a sinister green mist. It would sprout wings like something alive, flit upward, defying every attempt to catch it. Leading me on a haphazard chase around the house until it slid like poison into that dark hall. Beneath his dark door.

Into his dark, slumbering thoughts.

By the revealing light of day, my fear of the man seemed both ludicrous and something worthy of shame. In my logical assessment of my reaction to him, I believed that it was the man's own fault. What *natural* man would ignore his ward so thoroughly, remain gone from his own home for so long and go years without so much as a by-your-leave?

I'd had nothing but time to make up all sorts of fancies as to his whereabouts and habits, and it was no fault of mine that they strayed toward the grim and dark.

I repressed a shudder, snapping the paper briskly. "I'd rather he rested. I'll see him when he's awake."

Although I hoped not.

"Indeed," Fanny said, but dubiously. "Well, there's certainly the theater. I understand that Fidelia Larken is engaged for a fortnight."

I enjoyed the theater. Or at least, I enjoyed the lighter events at the theater. I'd tried to stay awake during some of the more ponderous operas and generally succeeded only in learning how to doze sitting up.

"Perhaps we can go," I suggested, finishing the article quickly. The Queen's new flagship wouldn't rest in the shipyard for long. If they remained true to form, she'd want the sky ship at the forefront of her navy right away. Rumor suggested she was quite the intimidating beast.

The *Ophelia*, of course. Not the Queen.

"The markets in Chelsea will be closing for the season soon," Fanny continued thoughtfully. "You'll want to visit once more, won't you?"

"Mm." My eye caught on an article. An advertisement, more like.

I could almost feel the ideas in my laudanum-soaked brain click into place. They fired up, one by one, like the pinging retort of an aether engine. "Here," I said abruptly. "I want to go here."

Fanny frowned. "What are you looking at?"

"Professor Elijah Woolsey is holding an exhibit at the Philosopher's Square." It was all I could do to keep the triumph from my voice. I lowered the paper, summoning my best, most innocuous smile, and added, "Can we go, Fanny? Please?"

She was nobody's fool, my Fanny.

"And what is he presenting?" she asked shrewdly.

Mrs. Booth raised her eyebrows at me as she refilled Fanny's teacup. I'd find no help there. She and her husband had read the paper long before I rose for the day.

Drat. "It's a scientific exhibit," I explained. I set the paper down, careful to make sure the article in question remained out of sight. "It involves electricity."

"And?" she probed, her gaze firmly on mine.

I shifted in my chair. "It's a study on the conductivity of dead tissue."

It was as if I'd thrown a rotten rat at her feet. She and Mrs. Booth both grimaced, but it was Fanny who set her foot down. "Absolutely not. That is no fit place for a young lady."

"It's only the Square," I replied, brow furrowing.

"It's not the Square," she returned, "although heaven knows that is bad enough. Any so-called exhibit involving dead anything is simply a circus act in thinly veiled disguise. No, Cherry. I will not allow it."

I threw my unfinished toast back to my plate, my temper spiking. "It's not as if I don't know what a circus act is," I snapped.

She winced. "And well I know it," she replied sharply. "That is, to this day, one of my great burdens. However, that doesn't mean you can continue to gallivant about as if you still"—her lip curled, aquiline nostrils flaring as if the very word singed her tongue—"*worked* for that scoundrel."

Although Society didn't know about my time between the Glasgow orphanage and London, my staff did. It was not gossip they relished getting out, and I wasn't anybody's fool. No good would come of anyone else knowing.

I sighed. "It's not a circus," I said, attempting for logic. "It's a scientific hypothesis."

"The answer is no, Cherry."

"What is so damaging about science?"

"Aside from the proven fact that it engenders in the female mind acute hysteria," Fanny said evenly, setting her own toast down with extreme precision, "you are talking about an exhibit of dead flesh."

My eyes narrowed. "Science does *not* engender hysteria."

"Your very behavior assures me—"

My palms flattened on the table, causing the china to rattle as I pushed up from my chair. It groaned as it slid across the wood floor, and Mrs. Booth winced.

I didn't care.

"Science," I said, very coolly, "is what will save this society from its own humors. Neither faith nor fantasy, it takes the very elements of this world and outlines them in ways that allow us to develop better tools with which to survive. This is, madam, an age of reason, you know."

Fanny rose as well, her lips thinned. "You have no pressing need to survive. You are an unmarried lady, and your only need is to settle upon a suitable husband. *That*," she said over my sharp intake of breath, "will guarantee your survival more than any tool or whim of electrical whatnot."

I strode from the table. "Fine," I bit off over my shoulder. My skirts rustled loudly as I seized them in both hands and darted into the hallway. "Then I'll ask my guardian!"

"Miss, please," Booth began, likely to entreat that I leave his sleeping employer alone. I darted past him, feeling a twinge of guilt as I knew he couldn't hope to catch me on his bad leg.

"Cherry St. Croix!"

I glanced behind me as I took the stairs, saw Fanny bearing down on me as Booth attempted to redirect his near-hysterical wife. Fingers pointed at me; I didn't care.

I was in high bloody spirits.

I usually was, after a day at the opium dens.

I strode down the hall, stopped just in front of the closed silent door of my guardian. I raised my hand as if to knock, held it theatrically as I glared at Fanny down the hall.

"Shall I?" I demanded, but even I lowered my voice to a near hiss lest I waken the demon in his bed.

Fanny splayed a long-fingered hand across her bosom, her features pale. "All right," she gave in, so much quicker than I expected. "We shall go, just be silent, you wretched girl."

I drew back my arm, as if ready to knock, and grinned fiercely at Fanny's gasp. Then I lowered it, demurely gathered my skirts once more, and sauntered away from the door. "I'll be ready to go immediately," I said primly.

"You'll finish your breakfast first," my chaperone warned, and preceded me down the stairs.

As I stepped out of the hall, a low, threatening growl rippled from the closed door behind me.

Something wild and primeval scored nails of fear across my soul. Every fine hair on my nape rose, and though Fanny reached the stairs before me, I very nearly beat her to the ground floor.

My heart slammed. How close I'd dared to get to the demon.

With the safety of a whole floor between us, I allowed myself a smile.

My whim wasn't entirely without reason, after all. Professor Elijah Woolsey was, obviously, the professor of rumor. He dealt in dead flesh. He needed samples.

The slain prostitutes had been found with missing organs.

And what better way to experiment on dead tissue than to get it from them that wouldn't miss the loss?

The Philosopher's Square was something of uncertain territory. Most of the peerage chose to ignore its presence, leaving it to the care of the academics and philosophers that filled its corners.

For a few years after the Great Exhibition, the Square had been popular enough with Society. For days on end, a curious mind could have found aether contraptions on every corner; a brilliant mind behind every door. Many was the scientist, thinker, educator and likely mad genius who bemoaned the trampling of academia by the delicately shod feet of popularity.

Like most fashionable impulses, the furor died and everyone else forgot the origin of such wonderful inventions as aether engines, hypotheses such as the long-distance transmissions of energy or the application of sound within the tiny structures of matter.

And, rather important, Professor Elijah's current work, which could revolutionize modern medicine. Assuming, of course, that the man survived Menagerie justice long enough to complete it.

Even suspecting his role as I did, I could appreciate the relevance and magnitude of the exhibition's experiments.

The Philosopher's Square was less a square than a collection of squat warehouses on the wrong side of Society's acceptance. Much of the city's brilliant minds came here, to study or lecture or, rumor had it, steal the ideas and inventions from one another.

Somewhat soothing to Fanny's sensibilities—and much to my relief—the Square was located in London's West End, although still below the drift. Once upon a time, it had been the home to one of London's great universities.

A fire had destroyed it, and the municipal decay of the lower city ensured the dean looked up to the heights for new ground. I'm told my father once held offices here. How ironic that he'd survived one fire to perish in another.

On days when they cared to make a go of it, there could be whole parties of education-minded ladies and gentlemen from above and below. Intermingling, to a certain extent, but only for as long as a tour ticket allowed.

Hardly, Fanny had said, a fitting place for a young lady. But fascinating nevertheless.

Fortunately, we could take the St. Croix gondola to the West End docks, and from there navigate ourselves below. As Booth rapped sharply on the box top, I reached across the small space and drew the shades specially designed to keep the worst of the fog from creeping inside.

It also kept any sharp-eyed ferrymen from peering inside.

Fanny hooked her parasol on one arm, wrestled the large lever by her side to the on position, and sighed when the clean air machine rumbled to life beneath our seats. A subtle draft crept through the box.

Silence continued to reign. Fanny because she hadn't yet forgiven my outburst, and I because I hadn't yet forgiven her venomous put-down of my academic interests.

Booth and Levi sat above, each armed to the bloody teeth. I wasn't positive that my houseboy knew which end of the small derringer to point at ruffians and which end to pull, but it was the only weapon small enough for his hands.

Not that I expected trouble. Not by day.

Eventually, with the quiet broken only by the laborious rhythm of the air machine, the gondola eased to a gentle stop.

I sprang out of the box without waiting for Booth's hand, shaking out my skirts and waving a gloved hand in front of my nose as the fog hit me square on. I was more used to it than Fanny, but I had forgotten how badly the damp clung through layers of skirts. "We're here!" I exclaimed cheerfully.

"And so is your escort."

I whirled at Fanny's smug pronouncement, covering my nose and mouth with one hand as I spied a large, sleek gondola with bronze plating and a dual set of double-finned tail pipes. The Northampton crest emblazoned on the side gave me pause, but not as much as the broad-shouldered man now striding our way.

"Good morning," he called, only somewhat muffled through the cloth set over his mouth. He pulled it down, as if politeness dictated it. "I came as soon as I received your summons."

"My summons." Although I did not phrase it as a question, my eyes flew to Fanny, who opened her parasol and looked back at me with steady, innocent regard. She blinked rapidly, almost ruining the effect.

"I understand you're in need of an escort," Lord Compton replied, and doffed his hat. "I am only one man, and not given to meanderings of the scientific mind, but perhaps I may serve for this outing?"

"My lord, we are ever so grateful for your company," Fanny interjected, eyes sparkling at the man. "Why, Cherry was so thrilled when we saw the advert for the exhibit. I would have been dreadfully saddened to deny her for lack of a proper escort."

"The honor is mine, madam," he replied.

My jaw shifted. So this was Fanny's answer to my outburst. The cunning woman. I accepted Compton's arm, tucking my hand gently in the crook of his elbow and sweeping my skirts out of the way with the other. "Grateful," I repeated, shooting my chaperone a narrow-eyed look behind his back. "You know how Society does talk."

Fanny coughed, but I was sure it was as much reproach as caused by the air.

He looked down at me, his mouth pulled down into a small frown. "Unfortunately so." His eyes were shrouded behind a pair of protective spectacles in the thick fog, but I remembered them all too easily. Green shot with gray. Sharp, but kind. Speculative.

Now staring at me. I resisted the urge to pat at my bosom like an overanxious miss. "Shall we, then?" I asked, false cheer.

"Certainly." He replaced his hat, tugging the brim over his swept-back hair. "Miss St. Croix, forgive me, but have you no fog protectives?"

It was on the tip of my tongue to assure him that I

possessed the finest in all of London, but hesitated. Of course I couldn't tell him about my goggles, and to be honest, it's not as if I stepped into the fog as a St. Croix very much. It hadn't occurred to me to acquire a pair of protective lenses for myself.

Well, for myself as *me*.

He must have read something in my pause, for his expression settled into something I couldn't help but read as determination. "Never you mind," he said before I could answer. "Let us proceed."

He guided me across the cobbled lane. "Have you come to the Square often, my lord?"

"Not at all since I was a boy." He matched his longer stride to mine, hampered by my skirts as I was. "Once I'd come to see a display of engines for the gondolas. They were early models. The first, I think."

"What, really?" I blinked at him, as much to clear my tearing gaze as telegraph my disbelief. "I thought you said you weren't given to science."

Behind the glass spectacles, his eyes crinkled, golden mustache twitching as he looked down at me. "You doubt my interest, Miss St. Croix? Or my attendance?"

"Your attendance," I responded, unable to help my grin. "Although I can easily imagine you as a boy admiring tiny engines on paper kites."

His eyebrows raised. "Certainly you were only an infant if you attended."

"It's true. I only read about it from the periodicals," I confessed, dropping my eyes to study the way my white glove rested ever so neatly against his dark sleeve. Shockingly contrasted. "There were articles of the prototype engines, and a drawing of Dr. Finch's first self-propelling aether tubing. Do you remember it?"

His chuckle startled me, rich and deep from his chest as it came. This was a side of Cornelius Kerrigan Compton I hadn't yet seen; something not completely relaxed, but at least somewhat more at ease. Something human.

He dipped his head closer to mine, and a whisper of surprise mingled with the feather-light shiver at my nape as he said lightly, "Remember it? I was there, after all. I watched as he lifted the yellow kite into the air. It shot out a blue stream, long as a snake's tail, and promptly set the paper wings aflame."

I laughed, then, because I knew it was true. Dr. Finch's first prototype wasn't a success in that it worked without a hitch. It was a success in that it worked at all.

"Oh, how I would have loved to see it," I sighed.

Our footsteps didn't echo in the Square. The fog acted like thick cloth, dampening every sound we made. Here and there, other figures passed around us. We exchanged only the barest civil pleasantries in passing, but Lord Compton kept one hand firmly over mine at his elbow. As if unwilling to release me to leave his side.

Or perhaps protecting me from the vagaries of the district?

Surprise forced me to tilt my head, studying him sideways from beneath my lashes. I knew, after all, that my lord came below the drift for the dens. Did he, too, develop a sense in the fog?

He looked up at the paint peeling from the surface of the warehouse we approached, studying the banner hung across the beams. "Professor Elijah Woolsey's Electrical Anatomy," he read. "What on earth is this about, Miss St. Croix?"

"Dead flesh," I responded promptly, and hurried to add as he blanched, "and the reactions of same when touched with electrical current. Do you know, my lord, that we are conductive to electricity?"

"Of course." His brow furrowed, handsome features torn between disgust and the propriety of good manners. I was losing him.

"In the periodicals," I continued quickly, "there are accounts of hearts beating when a low current of electricity is channeled through them. Beating, my lord! Without a body to support it. Does it mean we are creatures of electricity, too?"

"It is a . . . difficult theory," he said slowly.

I spun, letting go of his arm to raise my arms over my head. As if I would embrace the banner hanging above me. "Just think what we could do if we understood the body more. The medical advances we could make. Things to salve the wounded soldier on the field, a process by which the birth of a child could be made easier."

Compton's features tightened. Disapproval. "Certainly this is no fit topic for a lady?"

I resisted the urge to kick him. Barely. Lowering my hands, I said with some asperity, "And what would you have me consider, my lord? The state of flowers at the height of autumn? Perhaps the nature of my wardrobe when fashions come so quickly and fade as easily?"

I watched him look up at the banner again, then at Fanny. She trailed more than a few steps behind us, though it was only the illusion of privacy. She would hear every word, and was in fact watching me now with a warning in the set line of her mouth.

I put my hands on my corseted hips and asked baldly,

"Would you prefer me deaf and dumb, my lord? Or perhaps stupid and meek?"

He looked at me, then, meeting my eyes. His own were wary. But his mouth quirked at one corner.

The same as it had during our scandalous dance.

"Never stupid," he avowed. "Although perhaps Mrs. Fortescue would prefer meek on occasion?"

My smile was slow, but I felt it curve at my mouth. Reach my eyes, fill me with a quiet, insidious warmth. "On many occasions," I admitted. "My lord, despite all appearances, I am my father's daughter. It is not magic or willful ignorance that will assure our place in this world, but science. And science is not always . . ." I trailed off, searching for the right word.

"Proper?" he supplied, with more understanding than I ever expected from the eldest son of the marchioness.

"Or expected," I offered.

"Much like you, Miss St. Croix."

My heart skipped a beat. "Me?"

Compton offered his arm once more, and scarcely sure what to make of the events, I took it. "Neither exactly proper," he said conversationally as he led me inside, "nor at all expected. Perhaps unfashionable, but hardly without merit."

I stared up at him, at the clean edge of his jaw and the golden sideburns he kept so meticulously maintained. "I did warn you that I might be uninteresting," I said, appalled at how breathless I suddenly sounded to my own ears.

He smiled, but he didn't look down at me. "I never listen to ladies in the ballroom," he said simply. "I find them all too eager to impress. Ah! And here we are."

The many doors built into the façade were all closed,

marked simply by a plaque declaring the beyond to be for official guests and authorized attendants alone. Compton, ever the gentleman, bowed shortly as he swept a door open for Fanny and I.

I walked in first, unable to make sense of this new earl below the drift. What was he thinking?

And why did he agree so readily to come below with me?

Fanny gasped behind me.

Truth be told, even I was forced to stare.

The interior was large, much bigger than it seemed from outside. The ceiling soared high above, girded by solid wooden rafters even I could tell were layered in dust and cobwebs. The lighting was decidedly stark, and more old-fashioned than I expected given the Square's scientific background. Large twisted-iron lanterns hung from the beams on thick chains, each capped by an inverted dome of hammered metal. It focused the light like a bobby's lantern, forcing it downward to highlight rows upon rows of metal and glass containers.

Although I had known what to expect, my mind was not allowing me to think too hard on what floated in those tanks.

And how many there were.

Compton caught Fanny's arm as she swayed, but his eyes raked the warehouse interior with a sharpness, a readiness, I hadn't expected. "This is an exhibit?"

"It appears so," I replied slowly. I squinted, shading my eyes from a light centered directly above us. "It appears to fill most of the space." That was . . . well, quite a bit of dead flesh, anyway.

I looked up, impatiently brushing away the jewel-bright fringe of my hair from my eyes. A railing passed along each wall, designating some kind of walkway from the main thoroughfare. I spotted ladders here and there, metal rungs inset individually into the walls before it faded into darkness. "Hello?" I called.

A shadow detached from the musty edges of my vision. "You," whispered a ragged, frail voice. "Jo . . . Josephine?"

Fanny's gasp turned into a mild, breathy shriek. I spun, skirts rasping loudly as they swirled around my feet, and found myself face to face with a thin, stooped old man with a wild bush of gray hair like a thorny crown atop his head.

He caught my hand. His fingers dug into my gloved palm, too-long nails sharp and ragged. "By the Maker," he breathed.

"Now, see here," Compton snapped. "Unhand Miss St. Croix immediately."

The old man blinked wide, owlish eyes at me. Was he confused?

Obviously.

Pity stirred in me as I surveyed his white apron, stained with dirt and what looked to be old blood, and the rumpled fit of clothes at least a decade out of fashion and too large for his frail frame. Buried in the untamed jungle of his hair, a pair of thick goggles winked at me.

"Here," I said gently. "Let me . . ." Disentangling my hand, I delicately extricated the clear lenses from his scalp and set them carefully, cautiously, on his nose.

Suddenly, his eyes were four times the size, filling the brass frames and extraordinarily gray. They blinked at me, rapidly, and he patted the bridge of his nose with two fingers as if surprised to find himself there.

"No," he declared, with greater strength than his words earlier. "No, silly me, of course not. Miss St. Croix, the younger of course. The daughter!" His laughter was akin more to the rasp of dried hay across a barnyard floor than obvious humor, but it didn't keep him from once more seizing my hand to pump with great enthusiasm.

Compton bristled as he stepped up beside me. "And you are?" he asked stiffly.

I had an inkling. Turning, I offered, "Professor Woolsey, I presume?"

"You remembered!" he beamed. "Why, now, my pulse is all aflutter."

Remembered? I met Compton's searching glance, shaking my head ever so slightly. "Professor, may I introduce—"

Ladies did no such thing. Compton cut in before I could finish. "Cornelius Kerrigan Compton, Professor. Earl Compton. At my side are Mrs. Fortescue and, as you apparently know, Miss St. Croix."

"Oh, gracious me." The professor blinked at Compton's stiff, precise bow, attempted to mirror it and succeeded only in causing his hair to whip back and forth. "Madam," he said to Fanny, who was looking at him as if he'd sprouted wings from his head. "Cherry—"

"Miss St. Croix," Compton corrected coolly, and again the man rubbed at his nose.

"Of course, of course, forgive me," he said quickly. His magnified eyes settled on me, brimming with affection I wasn't sure I'd done anything to earn.

I found my tongue at last. "You *are* Professor Woolsey?"

"I am!" He paused, hands worrying at his apron, now. Plucking, straightening. "You . . . don't you remember me?"

I hesitated. "I . . . no, I'm afraid I was rather young when my parents were alive," I said, keenly aware of Compton's steady scrutiny.

Woolsey's weathered features crumbled. "Of course. Of course, well, you were barely knee-high. Truth be told, I only recognize you because you look so much like her, you know."

My mother. I summoned a smile. "Yes. So I hear."

"Were you told to come here? I rather thought—well, now!" Following his patterns of speech was equivalent to meandering a narrow maze. "Have you come to view my humble exhibit?" His eyes widened even more, until I had to look away before they swallowed the goggles that already made them appear enormous. "I'm honored! Let me show you!"

"Excitable fellow," the earl murmured as the gangly professor turned and hurried back into the shrouded darkness from whence he came.

"And . . ." I hesitated. "Apparently someone who knew my parents."

"You don't remember him?"

I looked up at him. "I was young," I said sharply, and flounced away before he could answer.

"Wait, I didn't—"

Metal ground against metal. The warehouse hummed, and all at once, the dark was chased away as the lanterns brightened. The very air hummed, crackled with a surge of electricity so powerful that I felt the fine hairs on my head lift.

The maze of holding tanks and display cases was suddenly bright as day. Each tank flickered, and I realized they did so in tune with the hum surrounding us.

"They're all on the same current," I breathed, awed. How much electricity could be generated by this single exhibit?

"Come in, come in!" beckoned that voice, and I left Fanny and Compton to sort out propriety behind me.

To be truthful, the displays I passed were rather grisly in nature. Single limbs and independent digits floated in large glass urns filled with a greenish liquid. Flesh hung from the severed stumps like miniature flags, and even my stomach twisted as I recognized the tiny curled fingers of an infant.

Fanny moaned behind me. "Cherry, wait."

"Come on, then," I demanded, impatient now.

"What macabre artifice is this?" Compton's voice was low, but sounds carried in the warehouse, and I glanced over my shoulder to find him eyeing an urn with a floating dismembered knee joint hovering at eye level.

"Not artifice. Science," I corrected.

The professor rounded a nest of tubing and beamed at me, the very picture of a deranged bird. "It's ghoulish, I know," he admitted, "but oh, the mysteries we are uncovering!"

I raised my eyebrows. "We?"

He blinked again. "We. The people, the thinkers." He spread his hands to encompass all of us. "The scientists! Tell me, Miss St. Croix, what do you think?"

I thought that Professor Woolsey was maybe more than a little mad. But I also thought that most scientists were, and so I turned to survey the large square tank he gestured to.

It seemed inoffensive. A round glass window revealed a small organ inset in what looked like glass. Copper tubes had been thrust into the flesh, the ends speckled with dried fluids, and a series of electrical devices appeared to run out of the tank, along the floor and to a switch in the wall.

I frowned. "What is that?"

He smiled. "A heart, miss."

Fanny groaned.

Compton stepped up beside me, and although I wouldn't admit it, I was glad for the solid weight of his arm against mine. "An actual heart?" he demanded. He removed his spectacles, folding them neatly and sliding them into a pocket. "From where?"

I silently thanked him for asking. That made my work here so much easier.

The professor's smile faded, and he scratched behind one ear as he thought for a moment. "I can't recall," he finally admitted, sounding more perplexed than anything. "But if you'd like, I could locate the records. My organs come from legal hands," he added quickly. "All done proper, I swear it."

"I'd be interested in seeing them," I said, studiously avoiding both Fanny and Compton's raised eyebrows.

The professor's smile once more split the dingy gray stubble at his cheeks. "I went to university with your father, you know," he declared, as if I hadn't just said anything at all. "That's how we know each other."

I stared at him. "You what?"

"Your father," he repeated, slower now as if I were dim. Or slow. "Abraham St. Croix. A fine man, your father." His eyes blinked again, hard and fast. "A fine doctor. A terrible shame about his laboratory. A terrible loss. Your mother was the best of us."

"She . . . was?"

"Of course," he said solemnly. "She was a brilliant mind, for all the university wouldn't allow a woman. That didn't stop her, you know. Truly the best of us . . ." With mounting horror, I realized tears glistened in his magnified eyes.

I hastened to reassure him with the only thing I knew. "She was much loved by Society," I said, perhaps a little lamely.

"Yes. Yes, she was. This is her idea, you know." The man waved at the tank, and I stared at it in surprise. "I mean, certainly the mechanics are mine, and the plans, but the theory was sound. It never would have come to pass were it not for her."

Compton lowered his head. "Is this man . . . all there?" he murmured in my ear.

"One never knows." I desperately wanted to ask more, but not in front of the earl. And certainly not until I could speak to the professor on my own, intellectual terms. Eager to distract him, I pointed at the tank. "Professor, what does this do?"

"Oh!" His expression cleared, even as he once more returned to wringing his apron between both hands. "A switch causes the electricity to enter the heart, and then it creates a loop by which the current liquefies—" He paused. "No, no, not liquefy, that's not correct, but the concept is sound. A better word is—" He stopped again. "Look, I can show you!"

But he didn't move, and I was left watching him as one would a dog that one wasn't quite sure was stable. Or toothless. "Professor Woolsey?"

"It's only. . . ." He shifted from foot to worn foot. "Are you . . . like him, Miss St. Croix?"

"Like who?"

"Your father."

I didn't know how to answer that.

"You look just like her," he said, seemingly unaware that he was repeating himself. "Just like her. It's just that one never can be too careful," he said over my sound of disbelief. "There's a great deal of rivalry in this world. Always has been, you know. Secrets, formulas." He cocked his head. "Why, I remember at university when I—" He stopped again, then darted to the switch. "Watch your eyes! Sometimes, the flesh catches fire. Just a spark or two, nothing to—"

"Oh." The sound didn't come from me.

Behind us, Fanny crumpled to the ground.

Chaos erupted.

Compton darted to catch my chaperone as the professor all but vibrated in place, the switch caught somewhere between on and off. The whole building shuddered; the tank pinged as if warming up. Somewhere in the depths of the warehouse power source, machinery groaned. I heard a terrible clicking noise, like an aether engine on the blink, and pink sparks flashed across the pockmarked organ.

Pink?

I clapped both hands to my face, torn between laughter at this terrible farce and a deep confusion.

A madman, certainly. But decidedly not a killer. I couldn't picture the birdlike Woolsey overcoming any healthy woman, even a doxy. It seemed this was another case of rumors warping fact. Someone else had to be killing the sweets.

Although, hadn't the druggist claimed *two* men? But here was only one. I needed to find out if the man worked alone.

"Air," I finally said, and turned on the professor. "Sir! My chaperone requires air, please."

"Oh, dear, oh, dear." Woolsey flung the switch fully to the off position and bustled to Fanny's side. She moaned weakly, pale and stricken as she sagged against Compton's side. "Please, madam, please, this way," Woolsey said, not unkindly.

He didn't walk so much as half scamper, as awkward as a crab with oddly spry legs. Compton followed, and though I made as if to hurry after them, I took a turn that pulled me wholly out of view.

So it wasn't exactly sporting. But I did come here to learn what I could, and though I doubted that the frail-appearing Elijah Woolsey could be responsible for overpowering healthy women, the man himself had engendered many more questions.

How well did he know my father? Where, in fact, did his organs legally come from? Did he work alone? Why did he say that my mother was the best of them?

With my head ringing with questions, I hastened along the aisles, searching for an office. A storage room. Something.

Unfortunately, I didn't count on Lord Compton's determination.

I made it across the warehouse, several empty shelves deep when a shadow fell over my shoulder. "Mrs. Fortescue is in safe hands." There was censure there. Mild, but apparent.

Caught, I stared into a tank labeled with LIVER, DISEASED. The tank, like all of them piled in this corner, was empty. "She only needed a breath," I said quietly.

"One might consider that she needs the safety of her charge as well."

His footsteps clicked against the floor, and I turned to frown into his eyes. "You must think me a lost soul."

"Lost?" He seemed to take this into consideration, easing beside me as I made my way down the aisle. I couldn't look for anything while he shadowed me, so instead I only meandered. Hoping something would stand out amid the ghoulish bodies dismembered all around me.

There was a statement on my life if ever there was one.

"Not lost," he finally said. "Perhaps just a little off course."

I chuckled. "Because I enjoy science and thought?"

"Because when reminded of your parents, your face betrays your emotions."

I stopped. Slowly, I turned to look up at Compton, bewildered and oddly elated to find him already facing me. My eyes narrowed. "Should I not?"

"Feel?" He tipped his head. "Or reveal that you do?"

"Do I reveal so much?"

"Not to all."

"Just to you?" I queried, trying and failing to inject levity into a conversation I had never expected. Not from the so proper Earl Compton.

"Perhaps not on purpose," he allowed quietly. "There is no shame in not remembering them, you know. By all accounts, you were quite young during the . . . incident."

The words bit deeper than they should have. I must

have winced, because he moved forward, taking a single step that closed much of the distance between us.

His eyes sought mine. Held them, as if he'd closed a shimmering cage around my attention.

A steel green net. Surprisingly understanding, and searching. Hesitant.

I swallowed, though my mouth had gone dry. "I . . ." What could I say? That I held no memories of my own parents? That much was obvious. That I had no guilt or shame or sorrow for the deaths of people I didn't know?

That seemed . . . too honest.

"All of London knows the tale," he said gently. "The papers carried the details, and of course much of the peerage hold estates in Scotland. There's no shame in any of it. Not for you."

"The tale," I repeated bitterly. "You mean that bedtime story they share when the children are feeling uppity and the dark is closing in. 'Behave, or Mad St. Croix will come to collect your bones,'" I mimicked nasally.

He caught my hand in his, pressing my gloved fingers between his palms. "You mustn't take it so personally," he said seriously. "The story is not a common one. People are drawn to the fantastical nature of it."

"It's not fantasy," I said impatiently, pulling my hand away. "It's science. His laboratory in Scotland caught fire, that's all. It was . . . it was a trick of luck that trapped them inside. It's happened to others."

"It has," Compton said soothingly. "Although perhaps to no others quite as engaging as you, Miss St. Croix."

I opened my mouth. Found no words.

He took my hand once more. "I must confess," he

said, and his voice slipped around me in this small pocket of light and electrical noise. I drew it to me, wrapped myself in it the way I imagined I would wrap myself in his coat should he offer.

In his hands, should he draw me closer.

I shook my head hard. "My Lord Compton," I began, only to gasp as the tip of one gloved finger settled across my lips.

It was warm. *He* was warm, his heat reaching out to mine through the constraints of his coat. I sucked in a breath, my eyes flying to his once more. They seemed so close. His hair settled over his forehead in a sandy curl and I found myself struggling not to brush it away.

"I must acknowledge how much admiration I hold for you, Miss St. Croix."

"Admiration?" I repeated the word dumbly.

His lips curved beneath his trimmed mustache. His handsome face seemed at ease, even shadowed as it was by the unusual light. "There are few ladies who could bear the burden of this society as gracefully as you. To have suffered and lost so much in the death of your parents, to have persevered with only a small staff to assist you."

"They . . . do well by me," I managed. When I inhaled, his cologne pierced my thinking mind. I smelled man and sweetening water; the affluence of his grooming and something warmer.

Long gloved fingers touched my cheek, soft as a feather. Unsure as a breeze. I swayed, drunk on the moment. The uncertainty. "You are a marvel," he murmured.

I hadn't realized how close he was. How warm his breath as it whispered across my lips. "M-my lord—"

"Forgive me," he breathed, and touched his mouth to mine.

The exhibit around us had been put together for one reason: to study the effects of electricity on dead tissue. But had the odd professor asked me, I could have written a proposal on the effects of electricity through live flesh on the spot.

The instant Lord Compton's mouth joined with mine, a current arced through my lips, down into my chest to set my heart pounding. It sizzled into my stomach, pooled lower into that soft, dark, wet place that had been so affected by my accidental view of the Menagerie just the night before.

My eyes drifted shut.

I think I made a sound; I must have leaned closer because Compton's breath caught on a low note—surprise, maybe—and those fingers curved behind my head. I felt my hairpins as they dug into my scalp; they didn't matter. All I knew was that his lips pressed firmly into mine. His chest was suddenly warm and solid against my own, and I curled one hand into the front of his coat.

His mouth was sweet, clean and warm and his lips tasted faintly of the tea he must have had before arriving. Softer than I expected. His lips clung to mine as they moved in a wordless inquiry, his mustache tickling.

"There you are!"

We leapt apart as if a spring had uncoiled, separating ourselves with as much grace and speed as we could muster. My fingers flew to my lips, tingling and too warm, while Compton cleared his throat and said perhaps too loudly, "Professor, how is Mrs. Fortescue?"

All I could do was stare in soundless disbelief.

"Good, good," the professor said, his eyes fixed on the ceiling far above. "Out with your footman, Miss St. Croix. Er, my lord."

"Right," I managed. Then again, stronger, "Right. Thank you, Professor Woolsey. Truly, I find your work fascinating. But I feel my chaperone should be taken home."

"Ladies," Woolsey replied knowingly. His fingers plucked at his rumpled apron as Compton offered a short bow, then extended his arm to allow me to precede him.

As I passed, the professor caught my hand, his fingers once more pressing into my hand. "Delighted to see you, Miss St. Croix."

A hard edge curved into my palm.

I smiled at him, though my ears burned as I curtsied quickly and hurried for the entrance doors. I was keenly aware of the professor's owlish stare in my back as I left, and Compton's warm, solid presence at my side.

As the earl escorted me to the gondolas, I clenched my fist around the small object the professor had pressed into my hand.

Curious, indeed.

The instant I was safely ensconced in the gondola, I lowered my hand to my side and, using my skirts as a shield from Fanny's smug, not unwell regard, unfolded the scrap of parchment.

10 o'clock.

I read the cramped, slanted handwriting, frowning.

Was I to meet the professor at ten that night? Surely, or else why risk being caught passing notes to me?

"Tonight's ball," Fanny said, breaking the charged silence, "will be the end of your isolation, my dove."

I bit my lip before I said something to ruin what tenuous truce my chaperone and I had achieved. The bloody ball. It seemed as if the skeins of my memory had become as ephemeral as a breeze; I was forgetting more than I remembered.

Ten o'clock. And here I was committed. Lady bloody Rutledge.

Damn and blast.

Chapter Ten

I spent the rest of the day arguing with Fanny and Betsy both. I drew the line at more flowers in my hair, compromising instead with a handful of soft gilt-touched feathers, and I wasn't inclined to listen to either woman's sly inferences about Lord Compton's intentions.

Marriage was not, would never be, and has never been foremost in my mind. At least, inasmuch as I resolved to spend my life a free woman. That both maid and chaperone seemed convinced it was only a matter of time before I found myself *settled* by the earl galled me.

Nevertheless, I was once more dressed and perfumed and bedecked in all manner of feathers and trim. This time, the gown was a daring chocolate hue, flattering my hair and turning my skin to milk. It was darker than strictly suggested, but the fabric shone with every step I took. As if I'd been sculpted in bronze.

It was also daringly low at the décolletage. I eyed Betsy as she affixed the pale ivory feathers into my hair. Each bob and sway of the delicate tines caught the light in glints of gold, gilded just for that effect. "Are you attempting to force me to snag a husband in here?" I asked baldly.

She burst out laughing. "I would pay good coin to see it."

"As would I. To someone else, please."

"Oh, nonsense. You look beautiful."

I rolled my eyes, but refrained from tugging at the bodice. To be truthful, I did look . . . well, rather eye-catching. My waist had been drawn to a narrow span, emphasizing the unfortunately broader curve of both hip and bosom. The shimmering fabric hugged my body as if the gods themselves had come down to paint me in their gold-flecked favor, and my hair gleamed with the fire of the darkest rubies from the far-flung Orient.

I took as deep a breath as my corset would allow, smoothed my hands over the bustle to ensure it remained flouncy. "I believe I am as ready as I can ever be," I announced.

Betsy wrapped her arms around me from behind, surprising me. "You look beautiful. Whatever happens, miss, you'll outpace them all."

I returned her embrace, but my look was suspicious in the mirror. "What's happening, Betsy? You're acting very strange."

She sniffed a little, but shook her head. "I'm just pleased to see you looking so grown-up," she confessed, fanning her reddening cheeks. "Truly. Your mum, she'd be happy."

"Hmph." Less than gracious, I knew, but as she draped my cloak about my shoulders, I kissed her forehead. "Good night, sweeting. Go home to your patient Mr. Phillips."

"When I've cleaned up," she assured me, and hastened me out the door.

Compton arrived precisely at nine. The very picture of cordiality, there was nothing in his carriage or word that even hinted at the impropriety of this morning's clandestine kiss, and I mimicked his care as I sank into a formal curtsy.

"I shall be the talk of the city," he declared simply, replacing his formal top hat upon his head. "With such beauties at my side."

Fanny couldn't hide her smile, or keep a little extra sway from her step as she followed us to the gondola. She wore a beautiful shade of violet, not so dark as to bring gloom to the event but not inappropriate for a widow, either.

My Lord Compton sat across from me in his spacious gondola, and Fanny beside.

All throughout the ride, I was torn between the knowledge that I had kissed the marchioness's son, the awareness of his eyes on me, and the realization that the haphazard professor would be awaiting my presence at his odd warehouse.

I would go back to the exhibit first thing tomorrow, I decided. Make my apologies.

Chatter was polite and appropriately light. Although it was comprised of absolutely nothing of consequence, I found myself enthralled with his voice—mild but not meek. Sure and polished and—was it my imagination? Did it warm when his eyes met mine?

How strange a man he was, I thought, who could seem so proper and kind, and yet whose footsteps led him—like me—to opium dens in the dark and smoke.

I resolved to find out why. I'd be lying if I didn't confess to a small hope that his desires might, even a little, echo mine. And when I idly pondered this, I caught myself frowning.

Why did I bother with this charade? What could the earl possibly give me, aside from an endless eternity of balls and soirees, that I would find interesting?

The gondola stopped, and he helped us alight with firm, sure hands.

Butterflies danced in my stomach. The instant my foot touched Lady Rutledge's spacious docking berth, they moved into my throat. My eyes narrowed as tiny spots began to dance in the corners of my vision.

I would have given good coin for even a tiny grain of opium.

As though he could read my apprehension, Lord Compton lowered his head to murmur, "I have never seen a more lovely lady. You shall be the talk of the ballroom."

"Of course I shall be," I replied smartly. "The madman's daughter has an earl on her arm."

His smile danced in his eyes. "The madman's daughter has every right."

It was as if he'd swept my feet from beneath me. Staring, I had no choice but to hasten my steps, follow his lead until I was divested of my cloak and blinking in the light of a thousand glittering shards.

The ballroom was already full, lit by two enormous chandeliers dripping with crystals. Color swirled around me, and I was only dimly aware of my name being announced to the throng.

That it came on the very heels of Earl Compton's was enough to set the room on its collective ear.

A murmur set up. My cheeks burned. I must have stumbled, or perhaps I simply failed to remember to walk as appropriate, because my toes were suddenly ensnared in the hem of my gown and I entertained a vivid picture of myself pitching face-first into shame.

A warm hand slipped into mine, raising it in formal display. Steadying me. I looked over the bent curve of our joined hands to find Compton's eyes on mine. Twinkling.

He was supporting me.

The thought came like a whisper, a dream. He knew I was uneasy, could sense the gossip starting around us, and here he was, showing what he thought of it. More, he was sending a very clear message to the gathered throng.

Whatever cut delivered only days ago, it was undone.

The butterflies in my stomach whispered to something much more insidious; terribly reminiscent of the warmth a draught of laudanum engendered from lips to belly. I stared at him as if he were a different man, and for the first time, I wondered if I'd done the man a terrible disservice.

In the corner of my eye, I saw a flutter of matronly fans, and I turned my head just enough to see the Marchioness Northampton furiously waving her fan at her reddening face.

"Oh, dear," I breathed.

"Your dance card," Compton said, ignoring the frenetic motions behind him. The music soared, quickly drowning the furious mutterings.

I blinked at the long, beribboned card thrust into my

hands. "There must be some mistake," I gasped. "My lord, this card is nearly full."

"No mistake." He let go of my hand, nodding behind me.

I turned, smiled ear to ear as I saw Teddy winding through the gaily dressed throng toward me.

"Save a dance for me." Compton's breath warmed my ear, and I clutched my card to my bosom as he added softly, "Perhaps I shall be so bold as to take two."

And then Teddy was bowing, handsome as a blade in his formal black tailcoat, and I was curtsying. He took my hand, his expression pensive, and led me to the floor. Within moments, he'd found the pace, and we whirled into the dance with aplomb.

My friend glowered at me. "Why are you here with *him*?"

"What?" I tipped my head back, smiling. "You sound like a child, Teddy. What's the matter?"

"Compton." His eyes tracked something over my head, and I glanced around to find the earl bending his ear toward his mother. She was gesturing sharply, but his expression remained inscrutable. "I thought we'd be clear of the rotter," Teddy added grimly. "Are you asking for more trouble?"

I shook my head. "He's my escort tonight. His invite, even."

His eyes narrowed. "Why?"

To be fair, I'd thought the same. "He's apologizing." I stepped lightly, broke hands with Teddy to turn with a young miss in lovely pale blue, then returned to Teddy's grasp as the dance dictated. "He's disagreeing with his mother even now," I added. "She doesn't look happy, does she?"

"Harpy," was all my friend had to say on the matter. We broke again, turned in separate circles with nearby dancers, and came together once more. "I don't trust him."

"Nor I," I admitted, and realized that it was true. Any man who frequented an opium den was suspect. Any woman, for that matter. I, of all people, knew this to be true.

Yet, was it this very knowledge that made him seem more . . . tenable?

Impossible. "But," I continued, smiling into Teddy's eyes, "he came to my home and apologized in person. To show he means it, he invited me here. My Lord Compton's grace has been enough to put me within reach of Lady Rutledge, Teddy. Perhaps if I impress her, I won't need him anymore."

Was it true? Even I didn't know.

Teddy's frown only deepened. "Will you still need me?"

I almost laughed. But somewhere, I think I realized how worried my dear friend really was. "Of course," I said solemnly. "I will always need you."

Finally, a smile shaped his mouth, and his demeanor seemed to ease. "Married or no," he told me as the music ended and the dancers thanked each other graciously, "I lay claim to our Wednesday debates."

"Always," I promised. "And I have no intentions of marrying. Why must I keep reminding everyone of this?"

He only levied an inscrutably indifferent look at me from beneath heavy-lidded lashes as he escorted me into Fanny's care.

I danced, it seemed, for most of the night. Gentleman after gentleman appeared before me, their names on my card. Old and young, finely dressed to a man, my night became a sea of faces and names and meaningless conversation. I remember laughing as one man, a tall gentleman with sandy blond chops barbered at his jaw, tipped his head to mine and complimented me most artfully on my stature.

"I am short, sir," I replied with matter-of-fact asperity. "It's not a difficult word."

"Too succinct for you," he told me, but his lips quirked in a manner I found most familiar. His dress was certainly fine and fashionable, every detail tended to with absolute precision.

His hair was darker blond than Lord Compton's, but there was something to the jaw maybe that caused me to frown at him. "Would you consider me rude if I confess to not hearing your name?"

"Terribly," he assured me as he led me into a sedate turn. His feet stepped among my many skirts with ease, but his muddy-brown-and-green eyes twinkled. "I think I shall leave you guessing."

He did, but I was certain I'd met him before. Somewhere. Perhaps on another ballroom floor, another night past? I couldn't possibly keep track of them all. A quick scan of my dance card told me I'd long since lost track of who I'd danced with.

But whatever his name, or his intent, my mysterious yet familiar partner left me with a moment's peace. I found a wall and braced my shoulder against it as if it, and not I, was the one needing support. Once more, I frowned at my dance card. The Honorable Fairbanks Fitzgibbons? No, I had an impression of a dark-haired man with an enormously bulbous nose.

I remember feeling his name a most unfortunate jest.

Teddy's name was clear, as was Lord Compton's. A bevy of gentlemen whose names I only vaguely recognized.

And then my eye hitched on one in particular. I stared.

"Was that young Lord Piers?"

I bit back a startled sound as Fanny's voice drifted over my shoulder. My fingers clenched over the card, guilty gaze rising to meet my chaperone's cheerful smile. "Er," I managed. "I believe it was." Lord Piers Everard Compton, the Earl's youngest brother.

No wonder he'd seemed so familiar.

What *was* it with the Compton men and their deuced love of anonymity?

"Dancing with both Compton gentlemen, are you?" She slanted me a raised eyebrow. "Daring the marchioness doesn't seem quite the thing, my dove."

Except I was positive I'd seen those elegantly barbered chops before. I sighed. "I'm not daring anyone," I told her.

Her mouth pursed. And then, as if flicking away the conversation, she said brightly, "Never you mind." She curled gloved fingers around my arm. "Come along."

"Fanny, where—"

"Smile, my dove." She pulled me into a group of other matrons. Her face was all but alight with excitement. Without so much as a by-your-leave, I was bustled off, introduced to Lady Rutledge—a massive woman with an impressive bosom and hair too dark to be naturally free of gray. Her gown was stunning silver, accented with a large cameo depicting three Greek maidens at play.

The lady inspected me through a single gold-rimmed monocle, raised her eyebrow and said baldly, "So you're the madman's daughter."

"I'm *a* madman's daughter," I replied immediately and without thought, "but if I'm the only one in existence, I shall requisition a banner to proclaim my exceptionality. Perhaps I shall drape it across Westminster Abbey?"

Gasps resounded around me.

Lady Rutledge's mouth pursed. "Your mother was a friend of mine."

"My mother was the toast of the ball, I gather."

"That she was, much to the dismay of *some*."

I tilted my head. "Who?" The words were exchanged too quickly for me to leash my tongue.

She squinted at me through the monocle. And then she smiled, but only enough that her eyes narrowed with it. Her fleshy cheeks raised up. "A certain marchioness, for one," she told me. "Don't tilt your head like that, you look like a rotund bird."

I resisted both the urge to compare her gray gown to the hide of a pachyderm and the sudden desire to look around me, scanning the crowd for icy green eyes and a pointed stare. The marchioness had disliked my mother? That certainly explained much of her disdain toward me.

Well, that and her son's determination to play the gentleman probably made her want to spit brass tacks.

I straightened my posture. "My apologies."

Lady Rutledge nodded, as if pleased. "Are you a reader, girl?"

I tucked my hands behind my back. "I am."

She sniffed. "Fashion and gossip, no doubt."

"I detest fashion," I returned, "although I'm quite taken with the concept of tea gowns." Her eyes narrowed. "Unfortunately," I continued gamely, "my chaperone refuses me to have any."

"Hmph. Gossip, then?"

"I hate, loathe and abominate gossip," I replied, but my civil tongue had developed an edge.

My throat dried as she stared at me.

"What say you about the current hypothesis of aether-to-oxygen?"

"Cherry," murmured Fanny beside me, her expression worried, but she subsided as Lady Rutledge raised a silencing hand.

"Well?" she barked. "Have you anything?"

With my knees shaking, and my stomach flipping over in the strict confines of my corset, I seized on the only thing I could. "I think it's bollocks."

Gasps became an outraged din. One or two ladies swayed, but Lady Rutledge's oddly pink mouth twitched beneath a beauty mark I wasn't sure was real. "Go on."

I sucked in a steadying breath, aware of Fanny's fingers tight around my upper arm. "As discussed with"—I mentally slapped a hand over my own mouth before I cast Teddy's reputation to the gossips—"acquaintances Wednesday last, I believe that it is impossible to ignite raw aether without any presence of oxygen. It's been thoroughly argued to death in the interim. Until I see evidence to the contrary, I'm of a mind that we should not attribute to aether any properties that we wouldn't ordinarily attribute to any other compound." I paused, then added, "My lady."

Oddly shaded eyes narrowed at me. Were they violet?

No, perhaps blue. I couldn't tell. "Interesting," she said. "Why must you see it yourself?"

"Why must I take the word of men who too often cannot be bothered to speak to a woman as if she has a mind of her own?"

Someone tittered.

Lady Rutledge leaned in, studying my every nuance through that single spectacle lens. "Do you hold with the hypothesis that aether is magic?"

"I don't believe in magic," I replied evenly. "Magic is simply what we mortals call a thing that science has not yet unraveled."

"And what of alchemy?" the lady asked baldly, and I blinked at her.

"I—what?"

"Alchemy, girl! Where do you hold?"

Dangerous ground. I didn't frown, though I had to force myself not to. "Alchemy is a hairsbreadth from magic, in my view. Useless theories dreamt by stuffy old men seeking answers at the looming end of possibly wasted lives. One never knows, really. Intelligent minds are better suited to science."

Her eyes crinkled. "You're not as gracious as your mother, I'm afraid, but you clearly have Mad St. Croix's gift of speculation."

"Science," I corrected, and then bit my tongue as someone inhaled sharply in the crowd.

"And his miserable grasp of manners," she added. She waved at something behind me. "Off with you, then."

I hesitated. "My lady?"

"Go on," she barked, raising the gold monocle to her eye once more. "I've already handed you an invite, must you demand special direction to enjoy my hospitality?"

"No, my lady," I whispered, and fled before I said something else I'd live to regret.

Had I *really* claimed bollocks to Lady Euphemia Rutledge?

The earl found me near the windows, sucking in the cool air as it drifted across the stately veranda. My legs had stopped shaking, but I was too hot. Too crushed and off balance.

He didn't seem to notice, offering his hand. "Miss St. Croix, would you do me the great honor of a dance?"

I wanted to say no. I wanted to invite him instead to the veranda, where we could enjoy the cool air and the privacy afforded by the cover of night. And, most important, where I could *not dance*.

Instead, as his eyes held mine in simple patience, I slipped my fingers into his.

For the second time that day, I felt the earl's body heat against mine. His gloved hands against my skin. In front of all, we danced a waltz; and though it lacked the secret thrill of a kiss amidst empty display tanks, I couldn't help but be exceedingly aware of every movement of his body against mine.

This was a man who wouldn't allow me to make a misstep. Whose guiding hand could steer me through the shark-infested waters of the society in which I lived. Here was temperance and stability all in one go.

Until now, I had never thought that such things could be so attractive.

But was it worth it?

I felt as if the world had been dropped out from under me. My stomach flipped around and around.

"Are you enjoying yourself?" he asked me.

"I am," I lied. I think I smiled. I must have, because his eyes softened as he gazed down upon me. "I met your brother, my lord."

That softness . . . changed, somehow. His shoulders stiffened, his grip tightened at my waist. "Did you? And did Piers behave himself, then?"

"What do you mean?"

"I mean, did he keep a civil tongue in his head?" he clarified, looking quite pained.

I wondered what on earth could be so bad that he'd worry about *my* sensibilities. "He was more than polite," I assured the earl. "Truly, he was quite kind."

He looked over my head, as if searching the crowd, and I was left with the distinct impression that the brothers weren't nearly as close as brothers should be.

"Are you all right, my lord?" I asked cautiously.

"Quite." And then, as if aware he hadn't even convinced himself, much less me, he looked back at me and allowed a small smile to curve his lips. Those lips that had touched mine. "Quite," he repeated, more warmly.

I didn't broach the subject of his brother again, but the conversation left me certain that the man held more secrets than even Society suspected.

It was one more thing that we had in common, the earl and I.

Chapter Eleven

here was no newspaper in the morning.

I sat down, feeling oddly thick. As if I hadn't slept at all. As if I'd woken with my bedclothes stuffed into my skull. I'd done neither, although the state of my nightmares was increasing. I had slept, but fitfully, and with visions of fires and body parts raining down around me.

I'd imagined the earl as a white-winged angel again, and this time, it was his judgment I'd been forced to endure.

In short, it had been a long, bloody night.

Bleary, I clutched my teacup at the table and ignored Fanny's overwhelming delight as she recounted the evening for Mrs. Booth.

In the cold light of day, I wasn't ready to examine anything but my paper.

"Where is the *London Times*?"

Fanny leveled a look at me that suggested this wasn't the appropriate response to her trilling excitement. "How on earth can you be so cool about this?" she demanded.

"About what?" I braced my elbows on the table. Lasted all of a breath before the weight of combined disapproval from both matrons coaxed me into removing them. "It was just one ball. And a disastrous one, at that."

The door swung open, foreshadowing Booth's uneven cadence as he carried in the breakfast tray. The housekeeper threw up her hands. "Just a ball," she repeated. "Just a ball!"

"Cherry," Fanny said, too calmly for it to be anything more than carefully maintained control in the face of my obstinacy. "You were escorted to one of Lady Rutledge's soirees by none other than the Earl Compton. That is *more* than just a ball."

"Is it?" All right, so it was. Maybe. But I was feeling spiky, and so I set my teacup down. "I flustered him, you know."

"Cherry!"

I shrugged. "Apparently, the earl doesn't much care for his younger brother."

She waved that away. "He's a younger son, and hardly worthy of attention," she sniffed. "I gather he prefers to remain nothing more than a wastrel. He's lost quite a bit at the gaming table, they say."

They. It always came down to *they*, didn't it?

"So Lord Piers is an inveterate gambler," I mused.

"That is not our business, Cherry."

I wondered if I could garner any more information from below. Surely, a young lord caught in the net of the gaming hells would leave a trail.

Wait, what was I thinking? Wander on down to become good friends with the earl's gambling brother? I must have been out of my head. I caught myself before

Fanny's infectious excitement fanned any more of these useless thoughts. It didn't matter. We'd see what would happen when and if the earl came by again. Brushing the entire conversation aside with a flick of my hand, I repeated, "Where *is* my paper?"

"It didn't arrive," Fanny said quickly.

Too quickly.

I narrowed my eyes at her. "It never fails—"

"Your pardon, miss, but your periodical was only just delivered," Booth interrupted smoothly. Features impassive—ignoring both my chaperone and his disapproving wife with equal aplomb—he laid the folded paper down beside my tray.

Fanny's mouth sealed, and she busied herself with arranging the toast and eggs laid out on her plate.

"Thank you," I told him. With short, sharp gestures, I unfolded the paper, making certain it crackled and rustled as much as humanly possible.

What the devil was my problem that morning?

Speaking of devils. I glanced at the table, and the empty chair at the head of it. "I gather my guardian will not be gracing us with his presence again?"

"I am sure he sends his regrets, miss," Booth said quietly. "He is not quite recovered."

I blinked. "Is he ill?"

"Cherry," Fanny said with a sigh. "Mr. Ashmore travels much too long and keeps unfortunate hours doing it. Allow him the courtesy of recovering in his own home in peace."

My back teeth ground together. It was *my* home he recovered in. I said nothing, shaking the paper to align the fold, and removed my attention from the table pointedly.

I only had to scan the headlines this time to learn exactly what was so important that Fanny didn't want me to see it.

The tableware rattled as I slammed the *Times* to the surface. "What is the meaning of this?"

"Cherry St. Croix, ladies do not—"

I cut her off, pointing to the bold print. " 'Professor Murdered,' " I read. Each syllable bitten off as if made of poison and swallowed bitterly. " 'Philosopher's Square now the site of an ongoing investigation. Has Leather Apron moved to more academic pursuits?' " I looked up. "Fanny, did you know?"

She avoided my eyes, concentrating on smearing her egg just so with the small tines of her fork. "I may have caught sight of the article," she allowed. "But I—"

I made a rude sound, once more rustling the paper loudly. Ignoring whatever explanations my chaperone, well-intentioned or otherwise, meant to frame for me, I read the article top to bottom.

Professor Elijah Woolsey had been found dead in the early hours of the evening. Just after eleven o'clock.

One hour after I was supposed to meet him.

Guilt slipped into my heart like a knife. If I had been there, would he still have died?

What if I could have seen that something was wrong? Warned him?

Saved him?

In a bitter twist of irony, half of the man's stomach had been carved free of his body. But unlike the others found in such brutal circumstances, it wasn't missing. Nor was it on display in one of his many tanks.

They found it strung across the floor. Sliced to ribbons.

None of the other organs had been touched. Just the professor's own. His face had been sliced to ribbons, unrecognizable beneath the damage. They were calling it a crime of extreme hatred.

I didn't touch my plate again. "Professor Woolsey," I murmured.

Fanny sighed softly. "I'm sorry, my dove." I looked up, met her eyes and the very real regret there. "I'd hoped to save you the sorrow."

The paper slipped to the floor as I rose. "E-excuse me," I murmured. "I don't feel well. I think I'll retire for a while."

"Do you need—"

"No," I hastened to say before any suggestions could be made. Booth's fingers caught my arm, a brief squeeze as I passed.

"Poor poppet," Mrs. Booth said behind me.

I hurried up to my room, gathering my skirts high to take the stairs two at a time. Woolsey was dead, murdered on the very night I was to meet him.

Like the boy I'd sent to deliver a message, hung with his own innards.

As I shut the door behind me, Betsy looked up. Something on my face must have translated my anger, because she straightened from the corners she was tucking at my bed and reached for me. "What is it, miss?"

I shook my head. "Lampblack," I said hoarsely. "Quickly. I'm going below."

"So soon?"

I caught her hand when she would have gripped my shoulder, shaking my head over and over. "Professor Woolsey is dead, Betsy. For me. He was killed over me."

Her eyebrows furrowed, her hand still in mine. Cautiously, she guided me to the vanity chair and I sat, my legs no longer willing to support me as the guilt rose like a bitter tide in my chest. "Certainly not because of you," she said, frowning. "The Square is not the most safe—"

"No," I whispered. "I know it. I'm to blame. I should have been there when he asked. He knew my mother and father, Betsy. He could have told me—" I met my own green eyes in the mirror, my gaze stricken. My mouth set into a thin, white line. With an angry sound, I tore the pins from my hair. "Lampblack, Betsy. Now."

By the day's half-light below the drift, the Menagerie became something much less exotic. Simple grounds, with simple workers. There was no violin this time, no laughter or cheers. Empty tents, abandoned stalls, and a ringmaster who became a foreman.

Micajah Hawke was no stranger to difficult labor.

"Put your backs into it," he ordered. From the full lawn away, I could hear the ringing authority in his trained voice.

In the company of three other men, he stood out even without the mystique of the nighttime masquerade. All clad in shirtsleeves and working trousers, it was Hawke that my eyes pinned on. His broad shoulders, the edged muscle of his arms as he hauled back on a rope affixed to something high atop the largest circus tent.

The queued tail of his dark hair, scraped back from his square features.

"And," rang out Hawke's calm order, "heave!" All four men pulled back on the rope as I approached. High above, barely visible, a pulley snapped taut. The whole side of the crimson canvas tent rippled.

Two of the men were white, notable for the lacquered circus spikes one had made of his hair and the unusual thinness of the other. The last was a dark-skinned man, as tall as Ishmael but only a fraction as wide. He was whipcord lean, shirtless even in the cold, and his rangy muscles gleamed with the sweat of his exertions.

"And, heave!"

I drew to a stop, glaring at Hawke. I waited for him to notice me, to say or do anything to acknowledge my all-but-vibrating presence.

He didn't. "And, heave!"

The men hauled back, muscles popping. The canvas tightened.

I opened my mouth, but then studied the tense rope worked between four sets of hands and shut my mouth. I didn't want to be responsible if anything broke loose.

I'd seen circus tents fall. Too many pounds of thick canvas could kill a man easily.

Stewing in my own anger, I waited. But I did not do so graciously, pacing as frenetically as a caged tiger.

Finally, the rope went slack, dropping to the ground. Hawke's gaze remained up, head tipped back even as the other three men sucked in air.

And watched me.

Hawke frowned. "Kelly?"

"All set!" came a high voice from far above.

My gaze flew up to the circus top. Was there a woman above? A child?

And why not? Monsieur Marceaux had proven time and again that women could do what men could on the rope. In the hoops, high above on silk scarves.

Although they fetched better on the auction table.

I saw no sign of the owner of that voice. But when

I dropped my gaze to the men, I found Hawke finally watching me. Silently. Weighing.

One of the men, the tall bloke with his lacquered sideshow spikes, adjusted the flat, worn goggles over his face. The lenses were tinted dark by a thin coat of something I'd never seen before, shrouding his eyes.

The pale, thin man cleared his throat awkwardly.

Hawke only held my gaze, and I knew that all of them were waiting to take their cues from him.

Bugger that for a lark.

"Why didn't you tell me about the murdered sweets?" I asked flatly.

Hawke's ungloved hands settled on his waist. "You have your tasks," he said quietly. The two white men suddenly scattered, as if they couldn't wait to be as far away from me as possible.

The third, the Negro I didn't recognize, studied me for a moment with tawny eyes nearly gold. His hair was long enough to reach the middle of his back, braided in a multitude of very tiny plaits and held back with a leather thong.

I glared back at him, raising my chin at the unspoken challenge in his expression.

Micajah said something in a language I'd never heard before, sounding not so much like words as a series of syllables and clicks. The man glanced at him.

His grin revealed even white teeth, startling against his dark skin. Nodding to me, he sauntered away, fishing the tail end of his shirt from its loop at the back of his trousers.

My eyes flicked to Hawke. He didn't move. He didn't address me, either, but that muscle in his jaw was pulsing as if he ground his teeth. His eyes pinned mine, razor sharp. I didn't know what kind of game he was playing, but I was sick of it.

Ignoring the now departed men, I closed the distance between us, raising a finger to shove against Hawke's solid chest.

"You lied about Cummings, too," I seethed at him, picking up the trail of thought where I'd left it.

He looked down at me, his eyes as inscrutable as ever. Save for the streak; that devil blue swath of flame. I'd swear it glinted. "Are you here on business, Miss Black?"

I lifted my chin. "Yes."

"Whose?"

I opened my mouth to say Zylphia's name, then caught myself before I could. Had she told him anything?

I doubted it. And I wouldn't be the one to get my friend in trouble. I didn't even know if the sweets were allowed to purchase or hire anything on their own.

It occurred to me that I didn't know a lot about Zylla's life.

I flicked my fingers at him, dismissing the question as unimportant. "That's twice you've tried to manipulate me," I said, flattening my voice to icy calm. I jabbed my finger into his chest again. "And twice you've gotten in my way."

"Is it?"

"At least."

"So you claim."

I snarled. "Do I need to go speak to the Karakash Veil, Mr. Hawke? Is that how you want me to open this discourse?"

By the gray light of day, I'd thought Micajah Hawke

would be bereft of the midnight mystery he wrapped himself in. I'd thought him just a man, any man. Flesh and blood.

I hadn't expected flesh and blood to be so real.

Or to get so close.

He moved into my space, a single step from long, powerful legs, closing even the whisper of distance between us with fluid ease. Before I could leap back, he'd snapped out a hand, caught the wrist of the offending finger I kept poking into his chest, and yanked me forward.

If I thought him close then, it was nothing to the sudden lack of oxygen I suffered as he cupped the long fingers of his other hand around my jaw and tipped my face up, up, up until my world was comprised of brown and blue.

Golden skin, black, black hair. Azure flame.

His white teeth bared. "Do you think this a game, Miss Black?" The very gentleness of his tone belied the aggression of his hold; his fingers were warm and faintly damp with sweat at my cheeks. Roughened, I realized with surprise. Working man's hands.

His body towered over mine, his breath warm against my lips, and I gasped. Seizing the front of his shirt in my free hand only gave me the barest impression of balance. Of control.

His fingers tensed at my jaw.

Fear and raw awareness flipped to anger. And the even sharper knowledge that his chest was solid with hard muscle. That the bare skin of his arms gleamed faintly with his exertions, and his breathing wasn't labored at all.

I swallowed the hard knot of anxiety balled in my throat and hissed, "Let me go."

A flex of one arm, and my face wrenched higher beneath the pressure he applied. Closer to his. I was drowning in the angry glitter of his eyes, vibrating along the awkward curve of my back as I fought to maintain my balance on my toes.

"You are worse than any child," he said, and I remembered the scathing words he'd thrown at me when I burst in on him before. "Is there nothing you won't meddle in?"

"I am *not* a child."

"Then stop acting like one," he growled, mere inches from my face.

I sucked in a shuddering breath. Smelled warm male, honest sweat and something raw. Something all him. Edged, angry.

I let go of his shirt to grasp at his wrist. Tendons moved beneath my grip. Muscle and sinew. "Let me go," I demanded again, but it wasn't more than a whisper.

"Will you behave?"

I opened my mouth to retort, but my voice lodged in my throat as his furious gaze dropped from my eyes to my lips. Traced them. As if it were his fingers sliding along my damp lower lip.

As real as any caress.

I gasped.

His eyes narrowed.

"My gardens are open to all manner of creatures," he finally said. I stiffened, but he bent his wrist, forcing my head to the side. I saw only the bare skin of his shoulder in my straining vision as he lowered his mouth to my ear to murmur, "All manner of monsters, Miss Black. You are not the most dangerous pet in my Menagerie."

His breath ghosted against my sensitive skin. Goose-flesh rippled over every inch of my body and I shuddered. "I am not your pet," I said between clenched teeth. "And I don't belong to the Menagerie."

"Not yet." And suddenly, he let me go. Left me standing alone, so fast that I stumbled. When I regained my balance, he had already put distance between us, half turned away. "And for that reason, Miss Black, you'll turn around and return to wherever it is you come from. I'll give you the promised payment for Cummings, but leave the murderer to better men. This is not your problem."

Better men? Red colored my vision. I *was* "better men." *I'd* accepted the bounty. *I'd* made the deal.

I'd found the evidence leading to Woolsey, who had died because of my interest. I was sure of it.

I glowered at him, rubbing at my cheek. At my still-tingling skin. "People are dying, Mr. Hawke."

His shoulders moved, a powerful roll of indifference. "People have that tendency."

"They're dying because of me!" I realized only once the fog sucked it from my lips that I had shouted it, but as I took a step—perhaps to grab his arm, perhaps to gesticulate expansively, even I didn't know—his head came around. As sleek as a predator. Aggressive and intent.

His eyes glittered again, telegraphing something I wasn't capable of translating.

Menace, I thought. Or warning.

"Don't," he said quietly, "flatter yourself. Go home."

"I cannot," I told him. Threats hadn't worked. Perhaps honesty would. "I need to find this killer."

"You won't find him here."

"How do you know?"

His jaw ticked. Once. "This is not a charity. You'll get nothing for nothing, Miss Black." He looked away. "Go *home*. You cannot pay this fee."

I frowned. "What fee?"

His lips curled. Mockery. A sneer. "Exactly my point." As was his wont, he turned his back on me, dismissing me so thoroughly that I could only stare. The nerve.

The sheer bloody-mindedness!

"Very well," I said, drawing myself up. Lifting my chin, which even still ached from his grasp. "If you won't help me, Mr. Hawke, I'll find somebody who will."

He turned, then, a graceful spin of powerful, lethally sinuous grace, and I was reminded once more of the fallen angel he truly was. The bow he sketched me was contemptuous at best. "You will not find someone to help you here, Miss Black. Good day."

I stared at him, fuming silently as he strode away.

And wishing desperately that I wasn't imagining the bare expanse of that muscled chest, slick with humidity and rippling with muscle as he tipped his dark head back and laughed beside a nude woman.

"Satan, indeed," I muttered.

I'd show him. I'd solve this bloody riddle, and show him once and for all.

With or without his help.

But perhaps with someone else's.

Chapter Twelve

The last child to run a message for me into the Brick Street Bakery had been murdered. I could have gone in myself, but Ishmael had been clear in his warning.

There was no jury of my peers to convict me here. Or to exonerate me. If his lads found me on their beat, I'd be as good as dead. Even I couldn't take on the Bakers and hope to survive.

With misgivings, I found another child to run courier for me. I paid him handsomely to ensure he was careful, bid him to run swiftly and trust no one.

I was on tenterhooks the whole of my wait. I didn't dare pace, but every fiber of my being strained to do something. Anything. I was antsy. Nervous.

And I was wholly out of opium.

Finally, my patience—or at least my stubborn hope—was rewarded. I heard Ishmael Communion's distinctively heavy tread long before he loomed from the dark.

I stepped out of my vantage point. "Ishmael."

"There you are, girl." Like everyone else, he had no name to call me by, but it didn't bother him. He'd always called me *girl*. One day, I assumed I would have to give him some kind of *nomme de plume,* but I hadn't found a good reason.

I answered to *girl* easily.

"Thank God," I sighed. "The kinchin cove found you." That was Ishmael-speak for, I had always assumed, *grubby yet useful young criminal.* I'd picked up some of his vulgar street language along the way.

His broad, flat face split into a smile. "Easy." It faded quickly. "You've never called by day."

"I know it." Quickly, I outlined the circumstances. His features registered no recognition as I said Woolsey's name, nor any flicker of familiarity when I described the exhibit warehouse.

But they darkened as I got to the bit about my plan. "You want us to crack a case in that Square?" he asked, frowning. "By day?"

"It's not as if you haven't worked by day before," I pointed out, dry as a desert in summer. I waved my hand in the gray air. "Day's not exactly bright below the drift, right?"

He grunted. After a moment's silence, I realized Ishmael was studying me oddly, and I barely kept from wincing. It was statements like that, which sounded as if I had the knowledge to contrast this world with the one above. Ishmael may have been part of a brutal gang, blessed with a face only a kind soul could love, but he wasn't stupid.

I hastened to add, "I'll pay you for it."

He still looked unconvinced. "I'd have to get my cracking tools," he rumbled. "Bess and glim, just in case."

I looked up into his dark face, made all the more so by the soot that invariably clung to everything. I widened my eyes, as innocuous as I could manage behind my goggles. "Zylphia hired me to take in this murderer. And I think he's the same what murdered Rufus and Woolsey. This rotter's killing sweets, Ish. I want to pin him."

If possible, his expression of unease knitted even tighter. "That's something else, girl." His huge hands, larger than the whole of my face, fisted against each other. "This hang-in-chains, he's long past the point of any old miller. There's no call to be messing in his way."

I blinked. "Er . . ." Hang-in-chains. I got that one. After a murderer was hung from the gallows, he'd be hung on display from chains for a while. Gruesome business, but *hang-in-chains* was vulgar dialect for "murderer." Miller? I wasn't sure. I frowned. "Wait, so you knew about the dying sweets?"

He nodded once. "One of mine, he found the first dove. Zylphia, she told me the rest."

And yet I was kept in the dark? I didn't like that thought. But I'd have to address it with Zylla later. "And he's not known to yours?"

"Bakers?" His teeth bared, but it wasn't a smile. Not even close. "Bad as we are, girl, this cove's worse. That's a whole other monster, much bigger than us."

Monster. Ishmael was the second man to use that word to me today. I didn't like the frisson of apprehension it caused.

If this murderer could keep the Bakers in line, he'd have to be a frightening monster, indeed. I rubbed at my cheeks beneath the line of my goggles, hoping it would

suffice to ease the brewing headache from behind my
eyes. "Zylphia and her girls, they're scared, Ish. I need
your help. *They* need your help."

"Everyone needs help," he rumbled. But then he
sighed like a gust of wind. A heavy hand came down
on my shoulder. "I'll get my tools."

"Thank y—"

His thick fingers tightened. "Just stay the bleeding
hell away from the ripper by yourself, are you hearing
me?"

I didn't need reminding. "Oh, yes." I blew out a hard
breath. "I hear you."

The immediate difficulty presented itself upon arriving
at the Square.

"What the hell is this," Ishmael muttered, not a
question. We were wedged between two of the warehouses, half-hidden behind a pile of discarded crates
and up to our ankles in alley muck. Ishmael towered
over me, which meant he could see much more than
I could.

I frowned at fragments of rotting wood, and the blurry
patches of fog-smeared Square beyond. "What?" I demanded. "What do you see?"

"Traps."

"Traps?"

He didn't look down at me, but he didn't have to. I
could sense his patient effort from where I knelt. "A
constable," he clarified. "And bobbies."

I wanted to smack my forehead in frustration. I didn't.
I was acutely aware of the lampblack I was determined
not to smear today. "Of course," I sighed. "And why
not? It's a crime scene, isn't it?"

Ishmael wasn't the type of man to speculate. "We'll have to go in a back way."

"Is there a back way?"

He grinned down at me, but said nothing. Wordlessly, he inched his barrel-chested frame back along the alley we'd come, completely unbothered by the green and black splotches of grime rubbing off against his overalls.

Grimacing, I followed, though I checked over my shoulder often.

Only the faint murmur of masculine voices ghosted through the fog behind us, but it was enough. I didn't know what they were saying—what sort of clues would they find, I wondered?—but I worried an officer would walk by and spy us creeping along like common criminals.

Which, really, we were.

For all his size, Ishmael moved like a bloody ghost. I almost lost him twice as he bent low and darted from shadow to shadow. Much to my relief, we made it to the back end of the exhibit warehouse without any hue or cry, and Ishmael squatted by the scarred door inset a meter up from the muddy cobbles.

I let him do his magic. Ishmael was one of the best crackers I'd ever known, which largely explained the foundation of our relationship.

Within moments, he'd selected a small pry bar from a worn leather satchel he wore over his shoulder and fit it into the seam between door and stained wall. With his other hand, he wadded a thick cloth against the joint.

A sharp tug, a careful twist and the lock split.

The cloth muffled the worst of the sound and the door swung open.

I leapt lightly to the stoop and patted Ishmael on his bare head. "Brilliance."

Again, he grinned, though he was quick to carefully replace his tools. He was, after all, a craftsman. Of sorts.

The door led directly into the warehouse proper. I recognized the mazelike array of shelves, though it was terribly surreal without the electrical hum I remembered. The lanterns were dark, suggesting the power Professor Woolsey had been using had been turned off. Perhaps by the bobbies?

Ishmael tugged the door closed, cutting out what hazy light filtered through. "Where?"

"What, rather," I replied, my voice a low whisper. "I'd like to find a study, or some sort of storage provision where he'd keep all records."

"Split?"

"Up ahead," I agreed, and led the way in.

Ishmael eyed the tanks as we passed by them, but the interiors were dark. If he picked out any details, he made no noise to tell me, and we didn't have the time to speculate on the matter. I wiggled my fingers at him as we approached a crossroads.

The very place where an earl had kissed me.

Clearing my throat, I tipped my mouth to his ear as Ishmael lowered his head to hear me. "I'll take the left wall. Have you a timepiece?"

The look he gave me suggested I was daft to ask.

Of course he did. His mother had been the slave of a watchmaker. I'd forgotten.

"Ten minutes, here," I said quickly, wincing at my lapse. My mind was worthless of late.

"Be careful, girl."

"You, too. Mind the bobbies, they'll be in and out if they're still investigating."

"I know what bobbies do, girl."

I grinned. He probably did, better than most.

We split without another word, and Ishmael became nothing more than a soundless shadow in the dark. It amazed me that someone so large, so vital, could vanish so easily.

He could take care of himself.

I had to do the same. I traversed the dim interior as swiftly as I dared, passing row after row, tank after tank. I paused by one, cupping my gloved hand against the glass and straining to see through it. I saw no hint of its contents, and a quick scrutiny revealed no sign or label.

Had the police taken it all?

The warehouse was large, and even small sounds could echo with disturbing ease. I caught myself straining to hear every tiny sound. I felt isolated. Alone. Perhaps I was just remembering how full it had sounded with the electricity running through it.

Perhaps I was just recalling the professor's earnest eyes, owlishly large behind his spectacles.

Ten o'clock. And I'd failed him.

Somehow, I'd come to think of the man as a victim, not a suspect. But it was hard to consider a corpse anything else. I set my jaw, hurrying across the floor. The air was cool inside. Darker than I liked for easy vision, but just dark enough—I hoped, anyway—that I had a measure of freedom from prying eyes. If the police came through, I'd hear them long before they saw me.

Sooner than I expected, I came upon one wall, its bare woodgrain dingy from lack of regular cleaning.

Silhouetted crates provided a haphazard obstacle to the right, so I turned left.

Pipes thrust from the wall at various increments, some attached to flexible tubes and others left raw and unfinished. None were warm to my touch; whatever they were used for, it hadn't been recent. Eager to find my hoped-for records, I stepped over a twisted nest of tubes.

I didn't see the step inset just behind it. My mind expected to find floor, but my foot encountered thin air and I staggered. The pipes groaned as I caught one in each hand, swinging my body in a graceless tangle of flailing limbs. "Oof!"

My backside hit the step. Pain slammed through my tailbone, zipped up my spine and I saw stars as I stared at the ceiling, my feet splayed out in front of me.

Utterly inelegant.

For a long moment, I didn't move. I barely even dared to breathe.

The air pulsed with anticipation. I held my breath, but there was no sound of alarm in the distance. No sign that my clumsy misstep had alerted anything but my own exasperation. Carefully, my teeth gritted and every nerve jangling in alarm, I eased up from the nest of tubes. They creaked and rustled.

Who the devil would leave something so unsafe as a *stair* behind a bundle of tubes?

Well, that was easy enough an answer: a preoccupied professor, clearly.

I stepped away from the clutter, dusting myself off with as much dignity as I could muster. Not that there was anyone to see me.

As if in answer, I heard a clang behind me. I froze,

searching the shadows. For a long moment, even my breath stilled as I imagined all manner of things in the darkness beyond the shelves: men with weapons, monsters with fangs, even the bobbies carrying their truncheons.

I turned slowly, eyes wide behind my goggle lenses as I strained to see.

It came again, somewhere out of reach. Almost out of hearing.

"Ish?" I hissed. And immediately felt foolish. It probably *was* Ishmael, all the way on the other side of the warehouse. He'd likely put his cracking tools to work again.

Regardless, the sound didn't come again. Rubbing my aching backside, I very cautiously tested the floor ahead of me with a foot. No gaps met my searching toes. No more ledges.

Grumbling under my breath, I reached for the wall and froze.

My hand passed through open air.

I'd found another room.

And I should have brought a lantern.

The room was darker than the warehouse proper, and I got a sense that it was nowhere near as large. My footsteps didn't echo, and even the very air felt more contained.

My goggles were useless in this darkness. I set them carefully atop my head, blinking rapidly in the gloom.

Nothing moved; or at least, I didn't hear anything. I waited for my eyes to adjust, all too mindful of the treacherous ground I'd already found by accident. Without knowing what waited for me, I didn't dare risk falling into a hole. Or over metal piping. Or into a strange but incongruously placed collection of chimes.

One never knew, with scientists.

Over time, my eyesight began to adjust, clearing enough detail that I could walk forward in relative confidence. My initial assumptions proved to be correct; the room wasn't terribly large, lacking entirely in windows or—near as I could tell without traversing every centimeter—other doors.

Strange shapes loomed from the murky interior as I stepped deeper in. I recognized the bulky, rectangular shape of a gurney as I came closer to it. There were no sheets atop it, no sign it had ever been used. The bare metal facing had been stripped of anything that would tell me what the professor had ever used it for.

I crouched, running my fingers along each leg. I found the wheels locked in place.

Curious, indeed. Perhaps a repurposed work table of some kind? Or a method by which his crated organs and limbs had been transferred. The tanks looked heavy. Surely Woolsey would have needed help. Barring an extra pair of hands, a gurney with wheels would do.

I was back to my theory of a second person. Perhaps, then, Woolsey wasn't the killer at all but a victim in more ways than the obvious? Did the second person, if there was such a thing, collect the organs and pass them to the unsuspecting scientist?

I rose again, my clothing rustling faintly—the only noise daring to break the weighty silence. To my left, a wide table seemed home to a carefully cultivated morass of . . . rubbish, I thought. A tangle of twisted wires and sharpened cutters sat beside a pair of metal goblets smelted together.

I could see no viable purpose for fused goblets.

Dirty cloths and stained rags were piled on the floor beside the table, and I kicked them aside curiously. There was nothing hidden beneath. Copper coils had been left scattered across the table's surface, some bent and others joined together by brass fittings.

It was as if the professor had only absently worked on this or that, picking it up and leaving it as the mood struck. No organization. No purpose.

A tinkerer?

The worst kind. I saw nothing of value amid the debris, nothing useful or even particularly clever. It was as if the truly useful items had been . . .

I covered my eyes with one hand. Of course! Whomever had killed Woolsey *must* have taken anything of value. Granted, most items a tinkerer made probably wouldn't look like much—I still remember my first few attempts at fog protectives.

Maybe it meant, I thought slowly, that the person who'd killed Woolsey was also a tinkerer? Or familiar enough with such things to know what was useful and what wasn't?

Or had Woolsey's mysterious partner killed him?

It was a thought, anyway. I left the table, passing the gurney once more. As I did, a faint glint caught my eye.

I paused. Had I imagined it?

No. Something had winked, I was sure of it. A tiny, glittering gem? A sheen of paint? I crouched, surveying the gurney surface with a critical eye.

There. Again. I bent until my cheek was almost flush to the surface, my eye aligned just so. As I blinked, the light flared off tiny, almost invisible motes of . . .

Dust? Pink dust?

I touched the spot with the tip of my gloved finger. The gurney shifted, just a twitch. At the same time, I heard something that put me in mind of a footstep crunching on fine grit. I jerked upright, whirling to stare at the empty room.

Had the constable come in? Found me?

Certainly not, I thought almost immediately. I'd be arrested on the spot.

Nothing moved behind me. Or at all. I heard no other voices. I was alone. Still, my skin was prickling most uncomfortably, and time had to be ticking closer to the designated minute of reunion.

I left the gurney again, approaching a wide shape arrayed along the far end of the room. It turned out to be a large and rather awkwardly designed switchboard. Nothing quite so ominous as it seemed in the shadows. The whole was made of metal and entirely without labels of any kind. I scrutinized the array of switches, levers and pulleys with some wariness.

If I had learned nothing else from my forays into scientific theory, I knew this: never assume a scientist's gadgets were harmless. Many was the article about laboratory accidents, explosions or injuries caused by the unwary fumbling of the ignorant bystander.

I walked the length of the switchboard, found the pipes and tubes crawling out of either side, and thought it looked awfully similar to the smaller tank Woolsey had attempted to show me before.

But this was so much larger than the individual switch he'd pulled. What was so complex that it required this much . . .

I hesitated to use the word *finesse*, but the concept remained sound. This had been designed to levy as much control as possible over the electricity I was sure had been funneled through the whole structure.

As I studied the silent and still dials, my gaze fell on a small oblong shape tucked amid a series of five levers. It was crooked. Not as uniformly set as the gauges just above it.

Not a dial at all, I realized as I plucked it from its unusual nest. A brooch of some sort. I couldn't make out any details in the gloom, but my fingers found raised edges and a beveled surface.

Squinting, I backed up toward the door, seeking even a shade more light to see by. The piece seemed . . . familiar? No, not as such. It put me in mind of something my memory was struggling to grasp; I could sense the idea just beyond reach.

As I passed the gurney, squinting at the object, the ambient light brightened just enough that I realized what I held.

Quickly, I stripped my gloves off, tossing them to the gurney to better explore the palm-sized cameo. I was wrong; there was no pin at the back of the odd piece of jewelry. It wouldn't fasten to any bodice or ribbon. There were no hooks by which to string a chain. It was too large for a necklace, anyhow, and there were strange raised marks along the edge. Hinges? Or knobs.

Who would make a useless piece of jewelry?

Although whomever had, he had certainly been a craftsman. The make was exceptional. Delicate gold filigree framed a burnt umber oval, striking in both design and color. Polished to a beautiful sheen, it set off the black silhouette raised in the center.

The tips of my fingers skimmed over the features of a lady I couldn't see. I could feel the cut of her cheek, the graceful sweep of her neck and her shoulder. I traced what seemed to be a wealth of hair, or perhaps the folds of a gown.

It felt expensive. And thicker than a bit of jewelry should.

And warm.

A clue?

Most assuredly so. I caught myself as I started to grin. Surely someone would remember making it, seeing it. Even hearing about it.

I had to go find Ish. I turned.

"No!" The rasping, oddly muffled voice sliced through the dark. "*Give it back!*"

I whirled. And then the world turned white.

Chapter Thirteen

Stars ricocheted across my sight. I found myself careening into the gurney, grunting with the impact as the metal edges dug into my stomach. Pain licked along my skull with sudden, shattering force.

The cameo spun from my hand as I clutched at the surface.

Energy flooded through me. Fear and raw survival combined inside my roiling veins to send an urgent message to my limbs. I let go of the supporting edge, dropping my weight solidly to the floor just as the gurney shuddered beneath an impact that rang through the small room like a tinny gong.

I rolled, gasping for breath.

My skull echoed with pain and the ongoing rapport of metal on metal. Whatever had been used to strike me, I could already tell that the result would hurt horrifically. Just as soon as I stopped trying to survive long enough to pay attention to it.

Metal clanged once more, and I caught a glint of

copper tubing as it dropped to the floor. It rolled list-lessly away. A black shape flitted between the gurney legs, scrambling to collect the cameo I'd dropped. Much too quick for my pain-blasted eyes to see more than a vague impression of a dark coat. A bowler hat pulled low on his head.

"Stop," I gasped, and launched myself to my feet. I wasted no time in attempting to dart around the gurney. I vaulted over it, one hand braced on the surface, legs kicked out.

My aim was good. My fury did the rest.

With my feet lodged squarely in his back, my assail-ant collapsed under my weight. The cameo sailed from his grip. I teetered as I caught my balance, the cameo spinning wildly in front of me, but the man wrenched himself back with superhuman effort.

The top of his head smacked into my chin, dislodg-ing his bowler hat. My head snapped back even as my fingers closed on the thick oval.

Sprawling on my backside on the cold floor, I tried to roll away, but he was quick. And much more determined than I expected. No wilting flower, he leapt on me, and I realized that this wasn't the same opponent who had cornered me outside the druggist's shop. This man was bent, reedier beneath his bulky coat and wearing some-thing that covered his mouth and nose. His hair was an iron gray corona around his head, his eyebrows bushy over fierce eyes I couldn't see the color of.

We rolled gracelessly, each struggling to maintain a grip on the cameo. I didn't know why it was so impor-tant to *him*, but for me, it was a clue. A link.

And more important, I didn't want the bloody bas-tard who'd coshed me to have it.

I grunted as his knee found my ribs. He didn't seem to notice the fist I drove into his covered cheek, but my knuckles caught on the sharp brass rods built into what I realized was a respirator. Pain sliced through my hand, jarring a muffled sound of surprise and anger from my lips as he latched onto my other arm.

My head cracked against the floor as his elbow planted itself into my cheek. For the third time in only a handful of minutes, sparks once more shot across my vision. Like a writhing, many-jointed spider, my assailant twisted and kicked and drove everything he had at me.

The cameo skittered across the floor, glittering.

He rolled off of me, but I caught the back of his coat in my grasping fingers, hauling back with everything I had. I heard a masculine voice growling something, wheezing through the mask and utterly indistinct. "No, you don't," I shot back.

His boot caught me square in the stomach. I let go, gritting my teeth, and scrabbled after him. Digging the toes of my boots in to the floor, I launched myself across his back. A rush of exultation lanced through me as his chest hit the ground, legs akimbo.

We reached for the cameo at the same time. My fingers closed over it first, his locked tightly around my wrist. He wrenched me to the side. My legs hit the side of the work table. Metal rained from the surface, pinging and clanging loudly. Something hard rebounded from my knee, sending aching shockwaves all the way to my spine, and clattered loudly amid our struggles.

At the same time, the man slammed my fingers against the floor. I locked my jaw. Tightened my grasp, my other fist flailing for the man's head.

He slammed my hand again. The cameo dug into my palm.

And again. My fingers went numb.

A tiny, almost imperceptible *click* undercut our desperate panting as we struggled for the damned thing.

The man went still, his fingers tight around my wrist.

Perhaps something about the way he froze translated across the tenuous, violent contact between us; I went still as well, my face level with a tiny gold dial turning cog by cog in the cameo's edge.

His fingers spasmed around my wrist. "No!"

It was the only word I actually understood since the fight began, hoarse and muffled behind the copper- and brass-fitted respirator.

This was my only opportunity. I bucked hard, managed somehow to splay my free hand over the man's face. His respirator caught on my fingertips, cracked even as a thin seam split along the cameo edge.

The man groaned. To my surprise, he let me go so suddenly that I found myself flailing against nothing at all. A foot planted firmly on my back, driving my face down against the cold ground once more.

In the suddenly too-acute focus of my right eye, the seam at the cameo's gold edge widened. There was another click, a *puff!* as if something had blown through a narrow channel, and a wisp of pink and gold wafted into the air.

Into my face.

I sucked in a breath. Too late. It slid into my nose, and it was as if I'd inhaled a head full of raw brandy. It slipped into my mouth, my throat. My lungs. I knew this feeling.

It was as if I'd inhaled raw opium. Only not just opium. It tasted . . . different.

"I'm so sorry," the man said over me; pleading, I thought. Raging? "I'm so sorry, forgive me, forgive me . . ." And then I saw his feet beside me. I struggled to get to my feet, made it only as far as my knees before the cameo dropped from suddenly nerveless fingers.

I blinked. Sparklers filled the corner of my vision. I took another deep breath. Once more, it tasted of . . . of something thick and faintly bitter. Like medicine. Like smoke.

The cameo vanished into gloved hands. I reached for the man, but his back was to me. He was fleeing. His footsteps echoed all around me, crashed like a wave long after his body no longer moved in my sight.

What sight I had.

Pink glittered across it. Pink and gold, like the warmest summer sunrise.

I shook my head hard. Saliva pooled in my mouth. I could hear my heartbeat, feel it throbbing inside my chest. I reached for the edge of the worktable, found it and held on as the air turned to spun sugar around me.

I croaked out a sound. Maybe I only thought about it.

I'd been drugged. I had enough presence of mind to realize that much, and I could taste the opium within it. Opium, I could handle.

But this was different.

"Girl?"

The deepest night would never be so rich as the sound of Ishmael's voice.

I shuddered as it rolled over me, an ocean of resonance and opulence. My blood exploded inside my veins, suddenly warm. Too warm. I pulled at the high collar of my corset. "C-cameo," I managed.

"Girl, where are you hurt?" Large, callused hands pulled at my arms, wrenching me upright.

I gasped. "Cameo! Where—" Even speaking sent vibrations along my throat, my lips and tongue; it was as if I were suddenly *alive*. More alive than any human body could stand. I shuddered. "A m-man! I saw him, g-gray hair . . ."

His full lips turned down as he studied me. "Cameo? What man?"

"Drugged," I managed. My cheeks felt flushed. My breathing came in shallow gasps.

My blood surged. I felt full. Too full, as if the drug pushed against my skin from the outside. Threatened to split it. To rip me open. The first spasm hit me low in the stomach. I bent over as the world went crinkled around the edges. Waves of pain radiated from somewhere inside my belly. My lungs. "Oh, God," I managed. "It hurts!"

He grabbed my wrists. "I got you," he rumbled, suddenly all too grim. "But damnation, girl, you hold on."

I gritted my teeth, biting back another moan of pain. Around my gasps, the muffled voices of men echoed from the warehouse beyond.

"Damn it to bloody blue," he growled. "Sorry 'bout this, but we're running now." He caught one hand at the back of my neck, swept the other arm under my knees and hauled me over his shoulder like a sack. It sent the room into a slow, pink swirl.

Every motion squeezed me from the inside. Nothing like the sweet, clenching feeling I'd experienced in the Menagerie amphitheater, this was vicious and raw. This was being fed, toes first, through a washer-woman's wringer.

I had no chance to struggle, to argue or think before the spasms started again. Filling me. Stretching me. Tearing at my insides.

I screamed as Ishmael sprinted between shelves. He barreled through the door, out into the Square, and didn't stop for anything. I retained only the vaguest impression of startled men, of shouts and commands behind me, before the tide of pain overwhelmed me and I stopped caring about anything but the pressure locked beneath my skin.

I tossed and turned on the bed. My body was on fire. It raged inside me, worse than any fever I'd ever had. I turned over, tangled in the blankets someone had tried to cover me with.

I turned back again, limbs moving. I was moaning. It hurt. I was filling up with pink and gold; I was dying inside. It had begun in my stomach, in my veins, in my chest. Now even my fingertips hurt, pulsing as if there was too much pressure trapped inside my flesh.

I had to let it out.

I had to let it go.

I clawed at myself, desperate to release the golden light from the trappings of my body. Flesh tore, blood gleamed slick and eerily crimson against my skin. It glowed.

I glowed, as if lit from inside by a soft light. I cast my own shadow, turning the light inside the bedroom to something eerily alive.

A Chinese man stood over me. I didn't know him. I didn't care if I did. He was short and frail-looking, with long black hair pulled into a knot at the very top of his head and a full mustache growing straight downward on either side of his moving mouth.

"You must be still," he was saying. I didn't care. I arched, sweat gathering across my shoulder blades. My clothes were gone. It wasn't enough. I was burning up.

The man flung a handful of verdant dust into the air. It glittered, sparked like emeralds, and settled over me like a cloud.

It sizzled, but not against my skin. It didn't even *reach* my skin. I gritted my teeth as I struggled to make sense of what was happening to me.

I couldn't. This was like no drug I'd ever seen. None I'd even heard of.

"What caused this?"

Another voice. This one slid over me like the rough velvet of a great cat's tongue. It soothed the pain. It nursed the ache. I gasped for breath, my heart pounding so hard and fast inside my breast that I felt it would explode out of me.

"*Móshù.*"

"What?" I gasped, struggling to raise my head.

"The devil it is!" Warm, callused hands gripped my upper arms. I found myself wrenched up, staring into eyes that burned. A river of blue flame cut through one. Cut through me; scored a path from my sight to my core and twisted. "Miss Black, can you hear me?"

I clenched my teeth. "C-can't hold . . . been drugged."

He looked over my head. "What kind of magic?" he demanded.

I managed a sneer. It bit off on a hard, painful sound as I jerked at Hawke's hands. "No such—" I couldn't finish. The man threw another handful of dust into

the air. This popped and sizzled over my head like the
green dust had, but only portions of it settled to my
skin, to Hawke's skin, like a fine layer of gold.

The rest flickered, scorched the air for a single
second. Flashed wildly. And in the sparkling reaction,
I saw the shape of a woman.

She stretched her arms to me.

As if in answer, my heart slammed wildly. Something twisted hard inside of me, kicked outward as
if it would tear free of my body and surge into those
ghostly arms. I writhed in Hawke's grip, half screaming and half sobbing. My nails found my chest, dug so
deeply I felt the fibers of my own flesh give way.

"Jesus Christ!" He caught my hands, wrestled me
back and slammed them to the mattress beside me. He
glared not at me, but at the man with the dust.

"Watch," the Chinese man told him.

Hawke dropped his eyes to mine. To my breasts, full
and bared under his scrutiny.

His eyes widened. "It's healing?" Narrowed just as
fast. "What kind of sorcery is this?"

The Chinese man shook his head, releasing a string
of syllables that grated across my skin. I sucked in a
long breath, howling, twisting against the shackle of
Hawke's implacable grip.

"Get it out," I sobbed. "I can't—I can't take it, get it
out of me!"

Hawke stared at the Chinese man.

And then Ishmael's voice, resonant like the deepest
bell at Westminster Abbey. "She said something about
a cameo. And a man."

"Where?" he demanded.

"The Philosopher's Square."

Hawke's eyes shifted to me, angry and tight. His sculpted mouth compressed. "Too many spirits?" he asked, but he wasn't asking me. I thrashed against him, kicking the blankets free, wresting every inch of control I could.

The Chinese man put away his dust. "Only room for one," he said in English so heavily accented that it was almost its own language. "Another one want in. She waits there." He pointed to the ceiling above me, but I saw nothing. Felt nothing but fear and anger and pain.

And pressure.

Hawke's lip curled. "Get out."

The man stiffened. "*Wǒ xiǎng*—"

Hawke let me go. I arched into the bed, naked and uncaring, grabbing at the pillows around me. Searching, struggling to find something, anything that could soothe my feverish brow. That could protect me.

Footsteps clattered. Voices rose. The Chinese man hurled invectives as the commotion passed me, and all I knew was that they were leaving. The pain slammed home, stole my breath; I could only gasp as it welled inside me. A deep, viscous fluid, a rising sense of . . . of *other*. Of *not me*.

"Don't let anyone in," Hawke ordered.

"As you wish." Ishmael hesitated. "Cage, will she . . . ?"

"She's ignorant and a fool," Hawke said flatly. "But I won't let her go."

"The Karakash Veil—"

"You let me handle the Veil," Hawke said.

Ishmael sighed deeply, and I felt it drag against me. Inside me. "I had nowhere else to take her."

Hawke swore. Then, curtly, he said, "You saved her life." The door shut.

The bowstring of my body snapped. Throwing my head back, I screamed, dragging my nails along my body in a desperate bid for release. It hammered inside me; filled me, overflowed from my body and my mouth and my thoughts until I was nothing but pink and gold and bloody red and *not me*.

Hawke's hands closed around my wrists again. Pinned them to the bed above my head. Hawke's eyes glittered down into mine. "I told you," he seethed, his voice strapped taut. "I told you to leave it alone."

I wrenched against his grip, but could only gasp as every nerve under the seal of his flesh around mine compressed to wild points of heightened awareness. No words made it through the wild cacophony of my thoughts and feelings.

"Miss Black." He shook me. My gaze snapped back into focus, but it was hard. So hard. "Do you recognize me? Do you know where you are?"

"Menagerie," I managed around a tongue thick and dry as cotton. I swallowed with effort, and my eyes once more darted around the room. "What . . . what's wrong with me?"

Hawke hesitated.

I clenched my teeth as another vicious cramp swept through me, toes to forehead. "I feel . . . I feel like I'm going to tear apart. I feel like I'm going to . . . to burn away."

"Too many spirits," he said grimly. "You wouldn't believe me if I told you."

I laughed. It sobbed on a wild note of amusement. "T-try me," I gasped.

He held me as I wrenched beneath him, his grip implacable. His eyes glittering dangerously while he waited me out. I sank back into the bed, sucking in air. "You're being haunted," he finally said, as flatly as if he spoke of collector's business. "A ghost of a woman." His eyes narrowed. "Have you been mucking about with the dead, Miss Black?"

This time, my laugh bordered on hysteria. "People . . . dropping dead."

The thick sweep of his lashes was like a fan, I realized. Lacy and black as the hair sliding over his shoulders like a velvet curtain. I could see each individual hair. Some were traced with gold. Lingering gold dust.

What was it?

And was it the opium within the drug that caused my senses to react this way? It had to be. I could *almost* think through it. Almost.

I wasn't so far gone that I'd swallow the tale of a ghost so easily.

My stomach twisted. My eyes widened. I yanked against his hold as the first spasm crept over me. "N-no," I whispered. "Hurts. Help, p-please—Augh!" I clenched my teeth as it rolled through me. A fist made with shattered glass and hot knives.

He flinched, but he didn't let me go. He transferred both of my wrists to one large hand, easily shackling me in place, and dragged his thumb by my nose. As caresses went, it wasn't kind.

He raised his finger to my eyes. It shone, vaguely pink. Vaguely gold. "What is this?" he demanded.

I squeezed my eyes shut. "Hurts," I begged.

"Miss Black, where did it come from?"

He was relentless. As my pain climbed to excruciating heights, I managed, "It's . . . the drug. Came from the cameo."

Rough fingers slid behind my head. Cradled it. "God give me strength," he muttered.

"What?" I gasped. "Please, Hawke, what?"

He shook his head, his gaze tipping up to the ceiling. His eyes narrowed once more, that fine line I'd seen at his most resolute. Usually, it was directed at me. Now, he aimed it above my head. "You won't find purchase here," he told . . . nothing.

There was nothing there.

Even my hallucination in gold dust had gone.

"Hawke," I gritted out between clenched teeth.

"I will not let you fade so easily," he told me, almost conversationally were it not for the implacability of each word. And then he let loose a stream of Chinese that felt thicker than anything I'd ever heard; pulsed as if it lit the air. It didn't, of course it didn't, but every hair on my body rose as if with static discharge.

In answer, the pain slammed through me. I opened my mouth to scream.

To my undying surprise, he covered it with his own.

And it was if he'd found a switch; as if he'd flipped it with a casual flick. Electricity sparked somewhere deep inside me. A shower of blue and yellow sparks collided somewhere in my mind and there was only Micajah Hawke. His mouth, warm and demanding and coaxing against mine. His body heat, so close but still too far. The pressure of his fingers locked around my wrists.

The smell of him, spicy and hot and masculine.

The pressure eased. A fraction. Distracted. I gasped and his tongue slid between my lips, rough and wet. It touched mine, rasped against it, coaxing. Daring.

Beckoning.

As dangerous as a hand lifted in a humid bathhouse.

I craved. Moaning, I opened my mouth to his kiss, to his demand. My back arched; his fingers tightened around the back of my head, tangled so deeply in my loosened hair that I couldn't get away even if I wanted to. The overly sensitive tips of my breasts brushed his clothed chest and I heard him gasp in turn.

He drew back, panting. Color darkened the taut skin over his cheekbones. He studied me. His mouth glistened, damp from mine.

Did mine look like that?

He cleared his throat. "Are you with me, Miss Black?"

I shuddered. "More," I breathed.

A muscle leapt in his jaw. "Are you *with me*, Miss Black?"

The *other,* the only name by which I could call the heavy sensation struggling inside my skin, roiled. *Not me.* I felt it as if it were its own voice. Its own mind.

This was the worst opium flavor I had ever in my life encountered. Cut with . . . a hallucinogen of some sort? I bit my lip, hard enough to draw blood. Hard enough that his arm flexed, pulled me up on my knees. I sank against him, my hands now locked behind my back.

My nipples brushed his still-clothed chest. It rocked me to my core, flooded my body with liquid heat.

I sucked in a breath. "I'm here," I said. Was that my voice? Was that me, sultry and breathy and pleading?

Or was it the thing that filled me?

He grabbed my jaw between thumb and fingers, tilting my face up to his. His gaze searched mine. "This isn't you," he said tightly. "You wouldn't be here if it weren't for this magic." I opened my mouth; he didn't let me say anything. His voice rough, he shook his head and said angrily, "Whatever you got into, it's not *you* begging for it. Don't think I don't know."

I laughed. It hurt, even as it uncoiled inside me like a lush, fragrant flower. "I can't fight it alone," I whispered. "There isn't . . . there's too much. There's too much inside me. This drug . . . opium and something. Pink." Tears gathered in my eyes as pain slid burning tendrils up my spine. My fingers flexed, nails digging in. "Help me."

Hawke gasped, teeth baring. His nostrils flared, a hound scenting a bitch in heat, and I watched stark arousal fill his features. Watched it and didn't understand.

But it was his wrist my nails had found.

His blood now trickling down the curve of my hip.

"Save me," I pleaded.

He laid me back, grabbed my hands as I struggled to dig them into the center of my chest. To peel away the flesh and bone trapping my stampeding heart and let it go. "Stay with me," he ordered. He leaned over me, once more holding my hands down beneath his.

His lips were a breath from mine. "You hear me, Miss Black? Focus on me. If it hurts, fight back. Force her out."

Her?

I clenched my eyes shut. "What will you—"

"Patience be damned," he cut in savagely. "I'll do whatever I must." And then his tongue slid along the corner of my lips. It was a faint trigger at first. The slightest pressure. It did nothing to combat the furious battle raging inside my skin. His lips traced the curve of my jaw. I tilted my head back, inhaling deeply as I struggled to find a path through the pink-and-gold violence of my mind.

His tongue trailed a warm, wet line down the column of my throat. A different sort of pressure gathered low in my belly. A different kind of burn.

I gasped as his whiskered jaw rasped against the sensitive flesh of my breast. He tongued the pale upper slope, and my eyes flew open. The world shimmered in vibrant color. Diamond white, shimmering gold. Black onyx, sapphire blue, bloody, vibrant crimson.

My stomach quivered, and I looked down to see Hawke's dark head against the pale skin of my breast.

His mouth closed over one nipple and the *other* inside me struggled to surface. Arrowed in with such focus that I moaned.

It was distracted? God Almighty, *I* was distracted.

Sensations shot from breast to groin, flooding us—me . . . *us* with pleasure. With warmth. Raw satisfaction. I arched into his mouth, surged out of my skin as his teeth closed gently around the hardened point.

He gave the other breast the same attention, and I barely remembered how to breathe. He slid down my body, and I thought somewhere that I should have protested. That I should have argued, fought him, protected—

What?

He was muttering something against my flesh. Each word skimmed across my too-sensitive nerves, scored as if branded there. Across my ribs, my belly. My hips lifted as he tongued the hollow beneath my left hip and I jerked against his steely grip.

He didn't let me go.

He raised his head, looking at me from along the length of my own body. My eyes widened.

The man was beautiful. I'd always thought so, but here with the world lit by fire and God's own colors, I knew him as the dark angel he was. His hair was loose around his face, strands of black pulsating with an eerie lack of light. His skin was burnished gold, lit as if the sun itself burned within him. Control shaped every nuance of his strong jaw and set mouth. Of his eyes, hooded and so guarded, but glittering with such intensity that it took my breath away.

And as if that was the opening it needed, the *other* erupted into life.

I had no chance to take a breath. No real chance to scream; it strangled in my chest half formed as pain ripped through my body. I felt it; I lived it, I struggled against it as the pressure built and built. As it thrashed against the boundary of *me*. As it fought for purchase.

It was trying to overtake me. It was trying to *devour* me!

And even as I fought it off within the hallucinating cages of my own mind, the ringmaster of the Midnight Menagerie firmed his grip on my wrists, lowered his head, and covered my most secret and sensitive flesh with his mouth.

My back bowed. The cords in my neck stood to abrupt attention as I threw my head back, screaming in mingled pain and pleasure. In forbidden delight and raw terror.

His tongue dragged across my wet flesh, and without my control or command, my knees lifted. My legs fell open. The pressure slammed into place somewhere I'd never known it, coiling higher and tighter and hotter as his lips closed over a tiny nub of flesh and nerves.

My hips lifted almost off the bed, so hard and sudden that Hawke was forced to let me go. My hands moved of their own accord, fingers spearing into the luxurious silk of his hair. I held his head as he licked at me, pulled him closer as he tasted me where no other man had ever tasted me. Where I'd never imagined any would dare try.

Where I'd never even considered letting any man near.

High, keening pants filled the room and I realized somewhere that it was me. That I struggled to breathe and had no ability to censor myself. That I was shamelessly encouraging him with every dip of his tongue, every rasp of his lips and soul-shocking skim of his teeth.

When the dam burst inside me, I screamed with release. The pressure flowed from me, burst from me like a spring released from extraordinary tension. Every muscle in my body snapped at once; every color in the world conjoined into one glorious vision. Wave after wave of pleasure crashed into me, a cooling spray against my fevered skin, a tidal wave of sensation.

Somewhere beyond the drug-addled confines of my own mind, I heard a woman scream in fury.

Strong, muscled arms came around me, steady and gleaming faintly with sweat. I was shifted, repositioned so that I was cradled against his chest. Held in case I slid bonelessly into unconsciousness? I didn't know.

I took a slow, deep breath. Smelled spice and musk and something indefinable.

I swallowed hard, my cheek pillowed against Hawke's

chest. The even rhythm of his heart steadied mine, and I set my palm over the taut muscle by my ear.

He stiffened.

Somehow, I found words. "It's . . . better," I whispered. "You still glow."

The statement should have been incongruous. People didn't glow. Humans didn't light up rooms, save in the metaphorical sense.

There was no such thing as magic.

But I looked down at my fingers, shaking and still covered in blood against his shirt, and saw that he was right. A faint, shimmering light pulsed from my skin, turning my flesh into something whiter than milk. Brighter than moonlight.

What could I say? Nothing. For a long, silent moment, I only allowed myself to breathe. I could actually breathe.

I was *me*.

Oh, God, I was *mortified*.

Despite all the conflict I'd ever had with the man, despite the flutter he caused in my stomach, I'd never dared to even *imagine* what a night in his arms would be like. I had no basis upon which to compare. He'd never even *kissed* me, not like Compton had, but I had nowhere to hide now. Nowhere to look but at myself. My own mind.

My own demons, strengthened by an unknown drug as they were.

They taunted me. I had no choice but to admit then that a dark part of me was always tempted, but I'd never even considered the reality.

There would never have been a reality, I was sure of it. I was just *Miss Black*. A collector. And he was the serpent of an earthly Garden of Eden. He tempted everyone. That was his job.

And I'd gone and . . . he'd . . .

Would the bed open up and swallow me whole? I prayed so. Even as I thought it, my chest twisted. My stomach spasmed, fainter, but there.

I shuddered. "It's n-not over."

Hawke slid his fingers into the tangled, half-tumbled knot of my hair, cradling the back of my head in his broad, callused palm. He pressed his mouth to my temple. "It won't be. The drug must run its course. Until it does, the magic will find a way in."

"God help me."

His chuckle, strained as it was, vibrated against my ear. "No need. I'll stay with you."

I wasn't sure that would be any better. I clenched my teeth, but the pain didn't begin right away. Into his chest, desperate to hide my burning face from Hawke's too-acute scrutiny, I mumbled, "How long?"

He didn't answer for a moment. And then, as his fingers pushed through my blackened hair, he asked, "How long have you taken opium?"

I jerked, but his hand flattened against the back of my head, keeping my body pressed to his. My face against his shoulder. I stiffened, to no avail. "I don't—"

"How long, Miss Black?" There was steel in the question now.

My fingers clenched into his shirtfront as my skin tingled. Prickled as if it would find seams and peel itself open. "All my life," I whispered.

He stilled. And then, all at once, he let out a long, wordless breath. It stirred my hair, cooled my still-feverish skin as his arm tightened around my back.

"Then take heart," he said against my temple. "Those who eat it for many years must eat more to find the same peace of mind. Your body will run through it quicker than if you had never."

"Thank God," I gasped.

"If you must." But I wasn't listening. My fingers were already searching for the hem of his working shirt. Tunneling under to find the hot, smooth flesh I knew waited for us . . . *me*.

Me. Not me. I was losing myself.

His stomach clenched under my seeking touch.

"It's starting again, isn't it?" he asked roughly. He didn't need to wait for an answer. Despite my own mortification, it was as if my addled mind had joined the rising pain and Hawke's touch, as if it knew how to save itself. "I'll keep you grounded," he said again.

I didn't know what Hawke was talking about. I desperately wanted to ask. But my fingers slid over his belly without my command and I gasped. Swearing, he caught my hands, forcing them out from under his shirt, and laid me once more on the bed. This time on my stomach. As my body started to writhe, involuntarily twisting against the growing strain of whatever it was struggling to claim me, his lips came down on the nape of my neck.

His teeth caught the flesh there. Bit down hard enough to draw an aching gasp from my lips.

"It will end," he whispered against the pulsing spot.

I grabbed fistfuls of the bedclothes beneath me. His tongue dipped into the small hollows along my spine, but it wasn't enough.

The force, the weight, slammed into me. Again and again. Inside me. Twisting, clawing. Filling me until the room glowed once more and light spilled from my eyes in shimmering green.

My own hair slid over my shoulder, muted by the lampblack I'd coated across it, but the occasional glimmer of ruby and flame flickered as I twisted and turned.

Hawke remained by my bedside. In my bed. For what seemed an eternity, he battled my demons from the outside as I screamed and fought them from within.

I don't know when I fell. Something in me gave up.

Oblivion replaced pain, and that was the last I knew.

Chapter Fourteen

Although a lady could maintain a certain elegance of appearance while in public, I'd always felt that among the many hazards of marriage, that time between finding sleep and waking up is the most dangerous for appearances.

Case in point, I woke up with my cheek pillowed into damp bedclothes. I'd been drooling.

My eyelashes scraped against the cushion beneath my head. I blinked slowly, aware that among all of my usual waking complaints, aches and pain always seemed to be at the top of the list.

This time was no different.

My head throbbed. My mouth was dry, my tongue felt like it was swaddled in cotton. My body ached from forehead to heels. It was as if I'd been clubbed and beaten and stomped on by angry men wearing wooden shoes. Nausea clamored in my belly, which felt unsettled and wrung out as if I'd spent the night losing the contents of my stomach.

I didn't recall that.

I struggled to raise myself to my elbows. Slowly, the details of my surroundings swam into focus. White cotton. Black silk. Smudged black stains, as if someone had taken charcoal and ground it into the pristine sheets. A faint glimmer of gold.

Browned stains. Disappearing into the bedclothes beneath me.

"God in heaven!" I scrambled away from the streaks of dried blood, then flailed for the sliding bedclothes as I realized I was nude beneath the sheets. I grabbed at the trailing material, gathering it to myself in whatever shred of modesty I could possibly have left, and glanced quickly at my surroundings.

A large room. Much larger than my own above the drift, and displaying a decidedly masculine flair. The furniture was sparse but elegant, reflecting elements of Oriental design merged with English sensibilities.

The bed I knelt in was large, much too large for a single body, and the black silk coverlet was patterned with uniquely Chinese embroidery in shades of red, green and gold.

The sheets beneath were white. White as snow, save for the lampblack rubbed from my hair. And the brown stains of dried blood.

My dried blood.

I backed off the edge of the mattress, my knees suddenly weak. That was *my* blood. Mortification warred with anger. Tears pulsed behind my eyes, ached in my jaw, but I gritted my teeth and tried desperately not to think about the dull pain centered low in my body.

What had I done?

I staggered as my feet found floor. My toes sank into

the brilliant Oriental carpet, but it wasn't the master-fully woven pattern I saw as I stared at it.

A vision of Micajah Hawke, his bare chest rising above me, his eyes focused and brilliant in his taut features, was suddenly all I could see.

All I could remember.

Had I—I'd *begged him*, hadn't I?

"Oh, God." My cheeks caught fire as I buried my face into the trailing ends of the bedclothes. I was ruined. I was more than just a girl astray; I was *impure*. Never fit for marriage, now. Who would want me?

I wasn't fit for anything but the streets below the drift.

My knees buckled. The nausea roiled, yawned wildly in my stomach and I swayed. I was going to be sick again.

A light knock slid through my muddled, chaotic thoughts, and I jerked my head up as the door swung open. "Wait, I'm not—"

It wasn't Hawke. Even as I realized it, as Zylphia stepped inside, my legs gave out. I sank to the floor in a tangle of silk and fine cotton, my eyes squeezing shut.

She hurried to me. "What's wrong?" Small, cool hands cradled my face.

I clenched my teeth as tears welled up in my throat. Behind my eyes. "Where," I rasped. "Where am I?"

"The Menagerie." Her voice was low and soft. Pity-ing, I thought. Knowing. She knew. She *knew* what I'd done with that . . . that *man* and she—"How are you feeling?" she asked gently. "You gave us all a terrible scare."

My eyes snapped open, and though hot words of abuse and recrimination sprang to my lips, I found her studying me with such worry in her blue eyes, such heart-wrenching concern, that I couldn't let them fly.

I sagged. Her arms came around me as I wilted. She pulled me close as the first spasms wracked my body, splayed a hand at my cheek and set my head against her shoulder.

I didn't fight it. I cried. I let the tears loose and she held me, whispering nonsensical things that soothed and did not judge. She let me sob, great wracking heaves of muddled air and tears, until I was reduced to nothing but blotched skin and the occasional, wringing hiccup.

I was spent. Exhausted and feeling ill and so very alone.

And angry.

That I'd lost my virginity to Micajah Hawke wasn't truthfully the root of my upset. Truly, I'd never considered it one way or the other. The Church of England would have an impure woman cast aside, fallen and beyond redemption. Society would be the first to send me to the streets for my sin, but I was neither overly dependent on the clergy's favor nor particularly interested in the peerage that would see me cast aside one way or another.

The men who'd propositioned me in the past had never succeeded simply because I'd spent too long among the doves who peddled themselves. I knew what came of such things. To my way of thinking, there was always a price for that sort of behavior, and I was in no hurry to pay it.

Somewhere along the way, my virginity had simply become a part of who I was. And now it was gone. I couldn't even remember the event.

One more thing to lay at the feet of my drug-addled memory.

Zylphia smoothed a hand along my loose hair, her other supporting the bedclothes she held to my naked back. "There," she soothed. "A good cry does wonders. You're well again, that's all we can ask right now."

I sucked in a shuddering breath.

And raised my head. Her gaze was steady, not a shred of recrimination in them as she took the edge of the sheet and wiped at my cheeks. It came away smudged with gray.

Her lashes flickered.

"Where is—" *Hawke.* "—everyone?" I somehow managed calm. Wrung dry, but calm.

"Working," Zylphia told me. "It's nearly midnight, and there's a show to put on." For the first time, I realized that she wore a draping confection that was *almost* sheer. Just opaque enough to keep a man guessing. It gathered at her shoulders, hugging her lush body, made of a pale blue gauze that made her skin look rich and inviting.

And the cut of its draped collar revealed the outermost edges of raw, scabbed lines at her back.

My gaze narrowed. "Zylla—"

She rose to her feet, suddenly overly brisk as she fixed the collar to cover the dark lines. "You're a mess. Your wounds are gone, but you're still smeared with the aftermath." The word made me flinch. "We've got to get you cleaned up. My employers want to see you."

"Wait, they what?" My voice rose two octaves in the space of a breath.

Zylphia picked up a handful of leather and linen from

the edge of the bed, and as I watched her, trying to get a better glimpse of what I feared were whipping marks, she bustled to a small basin and collected dampened cloths.

Slowly, feeling even sicker than I already had, I shut my mouth.

She'd seen my hair; her palm was black with it. She'd noticed the stains I'd left on the pillow, and she'd let me cry. She didn't ask. And she quite obviously didn't want to talk about the wounds on her back.

I looked down at my unmarred, bare flesh beneath the blanket and repressed another shudder.

I could respect her privacy. I would have to. At least I wouldn't have to meet the Karakash Veil nude. Would I be whipped, as well? Like some slave?

Like Zylphia?

I got to my feet, swallowing back a knot of raw anger. "The Karakash Veil wants to see me, then."

The look Zylphia shot me as she helped me dress was filled to the brim with worry. And dark warning. "Mind yourself," she said quietly. "This isn't a lark about. Whatever happened before, it's gotten the Veil's attention, it has."

"Whatever happened before," I replied, straightening my work shirt while Zylphia sponged off my face, "it got *my* attention."

"Is it related?"

"To what?" Then I met her direct gaze and remembered. "It might be," I replied, taking a deep, steadying breath. I shrugged into my corset, waving away her hands as Zylphia tried to help. I'd designed it to be a one-woman affair, easily pulled tight by my own efforts. The plating slid into place.

"The professor I thought might be the murderer . . ." I hesitated. "Well, *wasn't*. In fact, he was murdered in a spectacularly brutal fashion." I fastened the corset's high collar around my neck, quickly running my hands down the leather facing tailored to protect me from chin to waist.

"You think the sweet tooth did it?"

I blinked at her. "The . . . sweet tooth?"

Zylphia shrugged, but sheepishly. "We needed a name. We couldn't just call him *him* all the time. There's a lot of *hims* in the gardens."

The sweet tooth. It was too macabre to be funny. "I think it's possible," I finally replied, "but not proven. I was hoping to find something at the Square."

Zylphia's lush mouth compressed. "So you did."

And how. "A man drugged me, and that's telling enough. I was getting close to something." I took a deep, steadying breath. Then another. "But all I've got is a hangover and—" *Patchy memories.* I flinched, rubbing my face. "Nothing I can use." I checked my hands.

"It's gone," she assured me. Speculation lingered in her features, but she very deliberately collected the blackened cloths and said nothing else. As I watched, pulling on my boots, she stripped the bedclothes with brisk efficiency and balled it all together.

I bit my lip. "Zylla, I—"

"Some of the girls have said that Micajah Hawke is a fierce thing between the sheets," she said offhandedly.

I froze. My cheeks warmed.

"But you wouldn't know, would you?"

"What?" I croaked.

"You," she said as she bundled the bedclothes under her arm. "And him. Rather, the lack of a you and him. They say all he did was keep you from giving in."

Giving in? I stared at her as if she'd lost her mind. Of course, I felt more like I'd lost mine. "I don't follow," I said carefully.

She flicked me a glance. "Really? You think—Oh," she finished on a knowing sound. "You think he lay with you." She shook her head. "*Cherie*, I've seen that man after a night of lovemaking."

I bit my lip before I asked if she'd been the one in his bed that night. Or any night. Then caught myself imagining Hawke in the very bed I stood beside and looked away.

"Trust me," she said, "he didn't ravish you in your haze."

"He didn't?" I was beginning to sound stupid, even to my own ears. I cleared my throat quickly. "Of course he didn't, he only—" But I couldn't finish the sentence. I had very distinct images rattling about in my mind, and I wasn't sure I could steady myself long enough to explain them.

Not to her satisfaction, and certainly not to my own. It was a relief to know that Micajah Hawke might not have actually ruined me, but he'd come close enough that I wasn't sure where the line was. He'd seen me nude. He'd put his hands on me. His *mouth* on me.

Where had he stopped? Did it matter?

I just wasn't sure.

"He'd be in a finer mood if he had," she added tartly. "They call him Cage, by the by."

I blinked my friend back into focus. "What? Why?"

"I suspect it has to do with the fact that it's a natural

shortening of Micajah, isn't it?" But a corner of her mouth slid upward as she gestured me to the door. "Or it may be a so-subtle reminder of his circumstance. A tiger, that one is. Caged but not tamed, trapped between iron bars."

I swallowed hard, rubbing my suddenly chilled arms. Gooseflesh peppered my skin.

"But then," my friend continued, oh so nonchalantly, "aren't we all?"

I did not look back as we left the room.

Zylphia held on to the bundle of soot-stained cotton as she escorted me through a vast, elaborately decorated hall. Here and there, Chinese men and women bent to servile tasks—cleaning, sweeping, polishing, carrying—and the occasional white or mixed face worked among them. Servants, indentured or slaves.

Slavery wasn't exactly the thing these days. Not officially. The Queen had abolished the ownership of slaves and the Anti-Slavery Society had long since lobbied Her Majesty to outlaw slavers as pirates.

But signing a writ didn't make it so. And the Veil had a long reach.

Zylphia paid them no mind, hastening me past several other rooms and doors. I caught glimpses of rich furnishings and affluent décor, all flavored heavily by the Orient.

Finally, she stopped outside a set of polished wood double doors. The carvings on each were exquisite. Dragons and tigers and ornate birds tangled together in a frenzied dance. A war? A struggle?

"I'll be here when you come out." She knocked smartly.

The door swung open, without any hands that I saw. A faint mist of perfumed smoke rolled out to greet me.

I blinked.

"Best never to keep the Veil waiting," Zylphia whispered.

With my heart in my throat, and my stomach roiling uncomfortably, I took a deep breath and stepped inside.

The floor was utterly bare.

The walls were not.

I had never seen such ornate paper as that which covered the walls of the Karakash Veil's chambers. It gleamed like silk embroidery, reflected back the firelight in a thousand shades of crimson and gold. It was as if I'd stepped into the heart of a furnace, only it was dragons and tigers that reared at me, not flame.

In front of me, two stocky men in red trousers and odd, undecorated tunics bowed to me, their hands in their wide bell-like sleeves. Each sported a black topknot of hair.

They didn't look alike. One had a long, hooklike nose while the other had lips so wide his mouth was almost fishlike. But they moved alike, each in step as they gestured an arm to the interior—the opposite arm, so that I stepped through them like two halves of a gate.

The room had been divided by silk screens on polished wooden frames. The fire crackled merrily behind one, and almost immediately, I found myself sweating. A soft haze clung to the air, oddly sweet but with none of the properties I'd come to associate with Chinese opium. Incense, I think, but spicier than I'd ever seen them use during Mass.

It was vaguely reminiscent of Cage.

Hawke. Of course I meant Hawke. We weren't so intimate—*friends*, I hastily corrected myself and gave it up, shaking my head. I didn't know what to think. Not about that, not about this room.

Another set of dividers had been placed halfway across it. More of that opulent crimson silk, with ornate gold scrollwork embroidered along its length. It comprised three panels, much like the other screens I picked out.

I saw no one else. I frowned. "Hello?" I called. "Is there anyone here?"

There was no answer but the pop and sizzle of wood sap.

My frown edged deeper. I didn't have time for this.

I turned, took one step when a whisper of sound behind me caused me to pause. I glanced over my shoulder. Though nothing had moved, I was almost certain that I wasn't alone.

I looked at the Chinese men, who looked upon me with blank eyes. Then again at the screened room.

I cast my cards to the wind.

"I've no time for games," I told the men, moving toward the door.

They didn't move, but they didn't have to. I caught the subtle tension in both as they grounded their weight. A simple shift to the balls of their feet.

A fight? I could fight.

Although if they fought at all like the storied Chinese warriors I'd heard about, I was in trouble.

"Take no more steps, Miss Black."

That wasn't Hawke's voice. It wasn't any voice I recognized, either, and it had come from behind me. Or, I realized as I spun, behind the crimson screen.

There was no silhouette. Only a disembodied voice. Male? Female? It was impossible to tell.

"Who are you?" I demanded. "Come out where I can see you."

"That will not be possible," said the calm voice. Not a trace of an accent graced the English words, although the inflection was . . . off. Too careful, almost too precise. As if the speaker had practiced until every last trace of dialect was erased.

I narrowed my eyes. "Are you the Karakash Veil?"

Something drifted from behind the screen. A muffled laugh? A sigh? "So eager, are you? So impatient. Where are your manners, Miss Black?"

"I have no face to which I must be polite." And no way of ascertaining to whom I was speaking, for that matter. Maybe I *should* have been more cautious.

But I was exhausted, and ill.

"Ah." The tone remained all too calm. "A very English point of view. We shall, as they say, get to the point. We understand your life was saved by members of this Menagerie."

Saved? I said nothing, my hands settling to my corseted waist.

"A great deal of magic—"

I snorted. I didn't mean to, but it escaped before I could muffle it, loud and most unladylike. The voice paused.

Was it amusement I heard as it asked, "You do not believe in magic, Miss Black?" Was it curiosity? Or was it something less forgiving?

I cleared my throat and said curtly, "Magic is simply the word people use to describe something they have no explanation for." I was beginning to feel foolish, standing in the middle of a bare floor and addressing a silk screen. But I wasn't so impolitic as to use the terms *unenlightened* or *ignorant*.

My host was not so kind.

"Ah. Regrettably, this very unenlightened belief does not erase the fact that you brought *móshù* into the Menagerie."

The word slid across the faded remains of my memory like a sharp blade. I flinched. "Mo-shoe," I repeated. It didn't sound at all the way the disembodied voice said it.

"The word, broken to its basest point, means 'magic.' More precisely, it is someone *else's* magic brought into our home. Dangerous, Miss Black. Dangerous to all parties involved."

I narrowed my eyes, but I didn't have to look to know that the men behind me hadn't once shifted position. They were waiting. For an order to take me down? A command to kill me?

I squared my shoulders. "I didn't see any of this mo-shoe," I said flatly.

The voice sighed. "Please, Miss Black, show the language mercy. You may use your native tongue. We shall endeavor to keep up."

My stomach pitched suddenly, and I was spared the effort of responding to the thinly veiled insult by the necessity to keep from throwing up the bile rising in my throat. I swallowed hard, teeth clenched, shutting my eyes as if blocking out all the red and gold could salve my insides.

It didn't work.

"Are you feeling unwell?" asked the voice, not wholly unkindly. Decidedly, I thought, clinically. As if I were a specimen in a glass cage. "That's to be expected. You were barely saved from a most unfortunate end."

That was too melodramatic, even for my taste. "What do you want?" I demanded tightly.

"As was mentioned, you brought outside magic into the Menagerie. As well, one of our *wūshī* was forced to expend a great deal of energy to ascertain the nature of your . . . dilemma."

Dilemma. A delicate word to describe the hell I'd gone through. I inhaled as silently as I could, trying to force down a rising tide of nausea.

Then I blinked. "One of your what?"

"Such magic is not easily obtained, Miss Black," the voice continued, unruffled by my sharp question. "In other words, you owe us."

My fists clenched against my waist. "Like hell I—"

"Need we discuss what *might* have happened had Mr. Communion not taken you here?" There was nothing delicate about the steely edge in the faceless voice now. I glared at the screen as it continued. "Let us be clear: you would not have survived. Oh, your body would be ambulatory, as it is now, but your mind would no longer be within it. Your very soul ripped asunder by the creature that assaulted it."

I had no words. None. Was this person as barking mad as I was beginning to suspect?

"Shall I translate into words your *scientist's mind*"— the voice sneered the words—"can understand? Pay attention, Miss Black, we are not accustomed to explaining ourselves."

Bully for the Karakash Veil. "I'm listening," I said evenly.

"The . . . drug, as you so called it, weakened the bond

between your body and your soul." The voice behind the screen said this in easy conversational tones, as if every word didn't sound like something out of a penny dreadful found in a gutter. "While so weakened, your body was as undefended as an empty castle, do you understand? And like a castle, it was under assault."

Impossible.

"While we're sure that the ma—the drug acted as the catalyst, Miss Black, we lack proper understanding of how. Rest assured, however, that if left to your own devices, you would now be something not dead and not alive. A revenant, enslaved."

"Fine," I bit out. "You kept me safe while I was out of my skull, thank you *ever* so much." He—she?—was talking debt. I couldn't help my sarcasm. "So I owe you. I'm a collector, I can easily repay."

"Easily?" The word stretched out, a thoughtful sound. "Perhaps."

"I won't perform," I told the screen. "If you've any thought of dressing me up in pretty paint, you may as well strip the payment from my hide now."

I'd swear the room dipped in temperature suddenly. There was no sound, but gooseflesh tore over my arms, rippled down my spine.

For a long, aching moment, silence reigned.

Then a breath. "Do not ever," the voice said, so softly, so icily that I repressed a shiver, "presume to tell us our business, Miss Black. You are our employee. You will do as we command. Should we choose to, as you so quaintly suggest, strip the payment from your hide, that is exactly what we shall do, and we shall do it on our terms."

My weight shifted, and I heard the rustle of movement behind me. My shoulders went rigid as I pictured the Chinese guards reaching for me. Ready to obey any directive.

I set my jaw, but before I could force any graciousness from my tight throat, the voice continued in the same cool tones. "Despite your apparent desire to be so used, you are not fetching enough to garner the same price as even the plainest of our sweets. It would take you far, *far* too long to redress your debt in that manner."

My head reeled. Saved and insulted all in one breath? I bit my lip.

"Therefore," the voice continued crisply, "we agree to those terms. In exchange for saving you from the rings—"

"But you just said I wouldn't fetch a price," I cut in quickly.

"We said you would not fetch as *swift* a price."

This was rapidly spiraling out of control. *Nothing for nothing*, Hawke had said. My own need to assure I'd be left out of the ring was dropping me farther into debt.

I gritted my teeth, one hand splaying across my stomach. "Is that what you told Zylphia?" I demanded. "Pay with her body or pay with her hide?"

The voice was silent a moment. When it spoke, I was given the undeniable sense that my host was answering me only because he or she—bugger it, *he* would do— wished. "Zylphia already fulfills the role of garden flesh. Punishment must take another form."

So she had been whipped. "Why? What had she done?"

"There are no secrets from us, Miss Black. We do, however, expect a certain amount of decorum from our employees, which now includes you." The voice steeled. "Do not attempt to hide anything from us, and you will not feel our bite."

My eyes narrowed. So they'd found out Zylphia had hired me.

"Fine," I said evenly. "I won't—" I caught myself.

I'd already said the word *perform* once. The Karakash Veil, if that was who my host was, had taken it to mean I chose not to sell my thinly retained virtue.

I bit down on my tongue, hard enough to hurt. I didn't market my unique skills. I never have. But if I bartered for immunity from the circus as a whole, I could lose even more. I'd have to step carefully. Cautiously, I amended my statement. "So, I won't become a sweet. What is the price of that reprieve?"

"In exchange, you will take Zylphia."

"Take her? Take her where?"

"Clearly, you are meddling in affairs of magic and lacking entirely the ability to understand it." I locked my lips closed before I argued further with the Karakash Veil's outmoded sense of thinking. "Therefore, in order to fulfill your duties to us, you require someone who can. Zylphia's bloodline will ensure she is useful."

Her bloodline? I frowned. "What bloodline?"

"A *useful* one, Miss Black."

Unlike my mysterious host. Except I couldn't take Zylphia anywhere. I needed to get home, and I needed to do so without spilling my secrets any more than I already had. I shook my head. "Zylphia is a sweet, not—"

"If you do not take and keep her with you, we shall sell her."

Ice pitted in my stomach, and suddenly, I was too angry to be ill. "You wouldn't dare," I said, taking two steps toward the screen.

Hands grabbed at me, much faster than I ever expected possible. I didn't sense even a whisper of motion behind me. Although I was allowed to keep my own balance, the implacable grip at my upper arms told me *that* was only a matter of courtesy.

I glared at the screen, for the moment ignoring both men at either side of me.

"She is ours to do with as we please," the voice said, as if I hadn't just caused any sort of interruption. "We will sell her, Miss Black, and we will ensure that it is to the lowest possible creature. Are we clear?"

I almost snarled. Fighting the urge with everything I had, I spat out, "Clear."

"Excellent. You may repay your greater debt by bringing us the *móshù.*"

"Bringing . . . what?"

"The magic, Miss Black," the Veil sighed, and I heard impatience in the breath. "The drug. We shall expect it directly. Good day." A string of Chinese syllables peppered the air, and I suddenly recognized the high, sharp tones of the voice I'd heard in the private gardens. The very voice Hawke had argued with.

I didn't get a chance to say anything else as those hands tightened, and I was literally dragged from the room. I fought their direction, wrenching at their combined grip, but it was as if I were nothing more than a child between them. The door swung open, and on some unspoken communication, they both pitched me out to the hall.

I stumbled, wrenched one foot and staggered to my knees.

"Good Lord!" Zylphia caught my shoulders. "Are you all right?"

It took me a moment to find words in the rage and helpless frustration filling my skull. I bit my tongue until the small pain sawed through my tunneled focus, and I realized I was staring at a small patch of floor between my splayed fingers.

I pushed up to my feet. My friend's hands fell away. "Collect your things," was all I trusted myself to say.

She was silent.

I turned, and noticed for the first time that she'd changed. Her jacket, although plain, was almost proper. It buttoned to her chin, hugged her generous curves to her waist—my trained eye picked out the unmistakable cinch of a corset—and narrowed to a *V* at her waist. She even wore a bustle beneath her matching skirt.

My mouth fell open.

Zylphia patted a hand along her dark, kinked hair, coiled up into an elegant chignon. "I received orders," she said. But her tone was self-conscious. Her eyes remained cast to the floor.

She was worried. Comprehension was slow to dawn, but when it came, I reached out and took her hands in mine. She winced. I held them tighter. "This isn't your fault," I told her. "So you're required to shadow me, that's all right." I summoned a smile, ducking my head to look into her clear blue eyes. "I could think of worse shadows for your Veil to slap on me."

Zylphia's too-generous mouth curved faintly. "You don't believe in magic." She knew me well enough.

Which might explain why she'd never told me of this so-called bloodline of hers. I wouldn't ask now, not in the Veil's own halls.

I shrugged loosely. "I don't believe in magic," I

agreed. And then I gave in. Just a titch. "But you do, it seems, and so does your Veil. And whatever the correct term is, *something* infected me. We shall find what."

With a sigh, Zylphia picked up her valise. "I don't like it."

"Nor I, but we're to make the best of it."

And in the interim, maybe I'd find a way to free Zylphia from the Karakash Veil's garden.

As we left the Menagerie, I saw no sign of Hawke. It was well past midnight and the pleasure gardens were well occupied. The circus tent glowed like a blood-red jewel, but Zylphia led me along the quieter paths, where the Menagerie staff often went unseen. I walked quickly, exhausted and spent.

I didn't dare take my time. Every step of the way, I felt the prickle of eyes upon my back.

Nothing for nothing, Hawke had said.

And didn't I understand now? My time was limited, and the metaphorical collar placed on me all too real for my likings. I needed to get out from under my debtor as soon as humanly possible.

I needed to find that bloody cameo.

Some of the ferrymen knew Zylphia. I shouldn't have been surprised. A great deal was going to change now that I had an unwitting partner in crime.

Fortunately, Captain Abercott was already too deep in his cups to bother with polite conversation. We sat in silence as he devoured the sweet with half-lidded eyes, and I hurried her off and away.

We were nearly to my home before she spoke, her voice hushed and very carefully restrained. "I never took you for gentry."

And there it was. The moment I'd been dreading.

My fingers flexed as I stopped. She stopped beside me. "I knew you colored your hair," she added after a moment.

"Listen to me very carefully," I told her, my voice tight and thin. I wasn't feeling any better. My head had exploded like an aether engine somewhere between the Menagerie and the ferry, and I still felt as if I wanted to climb inside the nearest basin and lose my insides.

She said nothing as I turned to face her.

But whatever she saw in my eyes forced her a step back, her own gaze widening.

"My name is Cherry St. Croix," I said. "I am *not* a member of the peerage, but I walk among them as a well-to-do miss of at least semi-decent reputation. I live in Chelsea, I have staff—of which you are now one, might I remind you—and if you so much as breathe a bloody *word* of this to anyone, I'll feed you to the sweet tooth myself."

It ended on a note so hard that she flinched. Her gaze banked, mouth tightening, but she nodded once. "I won't tell a soul."

"Promise it, Zylla." I didn't touch her, but every fiber of my being strained to grab her by the shoulders and shake. "Promise me, on pain of death, that you'll tell nobody."

Her shoulders squared beneath her plain brown jacket. "They told me I'm to tell them everything," she said evenly. "That I'm to share every detail of your life with them."

I would swear I saw red cracks forming in my sight.

But Zylphia surprised me. She reached out, touching my cheek with two fingers, her expression softening.

"You're my friend, *cherie*. Doesn't matter to me what side of the drift you're on. I'll only tell them the bits we agree on, right? Lies or no."

My mouth twisted. It was good enough. Given she'd only recently been whipped for keeping secrets, it was better than I could have hoped for. She'd soon learn how unforgiving London proper could be, even among the servants, and she was a fine-enough actress that she'd learn her way among them. I nodded once, fighting back tears of frustration and anxiety and exhaustion, and led the way home.

Every light in every window blazed.

I stepped through the back door, gestured Zylphia in behind me, and made it three steps across before the kitchen door swung wide. A woman screamed.

I clapped a hand over my ears and squeezed my eyes shut as my head threatened to shatter into a thousand bloody pieces of agony.

Mrs. Booth seized my shoulders. "Washington Barrett!" she shouted. I'd never heard her use her husband's name before, she'd always been the very model of propriety. She shook me, then pulled me to her bosom. "Oh, bless me, she's home safe!"

I found myself propelled into the dining room, protesting. Only to stop cold. I stared blankly at the array of weapons laid out on the dining table. Rifles, pistols, even two sets of matched fencing rapiers. Booth lowered the dual pistols he held aimed in each hand as soon as he recognized me in his wife's grip.

The stark, unmitigated relief on his old, weathered face filled me with shame.

"We have been very anxious, miss," he said, his baritone mildly reproachful.

"Cherry!"

I braced as Fanny's wail lanced through my ears.

"Betsy, she's home!" And then she shrieked, loud enough to wake the dead. "Trousers? Lord have mercy, your *hair*."

And suddenly I was surrounded by every member of my staff, and a hysterical Fanny. Betsy watched me from the side, her features tight and worried, while the others clamored around me. I was pulled this way and that; questions peppered at me from all directions.

"Stop, stop!" I begged, disentangling myself with effort. "Please, I'm so sorry."

"Miss, you look quite green," Mrs. Booth said worriedly. "You, girl—" She frowned at Zylphia. "Who are you?"

I forced down a roiling ball of queasiness to say, "Mrs. Booth, this is Zylphia. She's . . . a new member of my employ. Please set her up as . . . as . . ."

The blood left my face. My skin broke out in a clammy sweat and I swayed.

Betsy whistled sharply. "You, girl, get me a pot of fresh tea. The green bin. Mr. Booth, sir, can you carry her to her bed?"

I struggled against the hands grasping at my arms, my shoulders. All this noise, it would surely wake my demon guardian. "Ashmore," I muttered, only half aware I'd said anything at all.

"Gone, miss." Without warning, Booth bent and swept an arm behind my knees. I crumbled like a paper doll. With surprising strength, and shaky dexterity, my butler carried me awkwardly up the stairs. "He left early this evening."

Fanny fluttered behind us, and as I glimpsed her

shockingly pale face over Booth's shoulder, guilt sliced almost to my soul. I pressed my face against his chest and squeezed my eyes shut. "'m sorry," I whispered.

"Now, there's no need for that." Booth's deep voice floated over my head, gentle as a summer breeze. And just as sweet. To my horror, tears pricked behind my eyelids. "You gave us a fright, but we weren't all that ready to give up on you. Betsy?" he called back.

"Just behind you, Mr. Booth," I heard.

I sniffled. "Were you looking to outfit an army?" I asked, my smile tiny.

"Ah, just some souvenirs from the old infantry days," Booth said, a little more than sheepish as he set me down on my bed. "Rest up, now." He backed stiffly away. His gaze remained awkwardly on the ceiling, as if setting eyes on me in my own bed might somehow prove impolite.

I closed my eyes, heard Betsy shoo everyone out. Everyone but one. "She was sick all day," I heard Zylphia tell my maid. I curled into the bedclothes, hugging a pillow to my chest.

Betsy sighed. "It's something below, isn't it? You, all this? It's caught up to her."

"I wish I could say," Zylphia said softly.

"Don't. I don't care to know. Bring the tea. We've got to get her presentable, though Lord only knows why it matters now. They've seen the lampblack and trousers and—" My maid's voice broke. Firmed quickly. "The whole house is in disarray."

"Is that laudanum?"

Crystal clinked. Cold, edged facets pushed into my fingers, and eager for the oblivion of sleep, I drank the entirety of the draught Betsy poured for me.

"Mrs. Fortescue—that's her chaperone," Betsy explained. "She sent the houseboy out to purchase some. We thought the miss might need a bit of help when she returned."

I knew what Betsy didn't say. Laudanum was a powerful reprieve from pain; opium direct was better. Lacking in the ability to barter for opium above the drift, Betsy found the next best thing. Dear Fanny had loosened the purse strings to acquire it.

Just in case I came home near enough to dead to warrant it.

Betsy instructed Zylphia quietly, and I let them undress me without argument. The laudanum soothed my stomach in increments, wiping away all trace of illness and hunger and shame and fear until I drifted slowly off to sleep. The whispered voices of my two friends were my lullaby.

But sleep was not my savior.

I dreamed. Feverish, anxious dreams plagued with memories of black, black hair and golden skin. With fangs dripping crimson in the shadows. I heard Micajah Hawke screaming hoarsely in the dark; pleading, I thought, or threatening.

I dreamed of white angel wings and woke gasping, only to find Zylphia's arm cradled under my shoulders and a glass of laudanum at my lips. "Take it slow," she whispered. "It's not as strong as you like it."

How did she know? "Betsy," I croaked as soon as my mouth was clear.

"Gone home, love. Sleep. It'll do your body a world of good."

Her blue eyes were understanding.

Until they ran down her caramel cheeks like melted

wax and I was once more cast adrift in an unrelenting tide.

I gave up hope and all sense of self as I dreamed of everything and nothing at all. Clinging to what little flotsam of identity I had left, I slept.

And in my sleep, I relived it all.

Every. Screaming. Note.

Chapter Fifteen

I didn't wake slowly. It was more as if I crossed a threshold, stepped through some formless door and all at once, I was awake.

And I was filled with boundless energy.

I knew this feeling. I threw off my blankets, blinking in the daylight creeping through my drawn curtains. I patted my chest, my stomach, my cheeks, and found myself all there. I suffered no twinges of pain. No twitches of nausea.

Kicking my feet over the mattress edge, I took a deep breath and stretched. I often felt like this after a bout with opium. I attributed it to the laudanum I took at night, or to the rare occasions I was able to get to an opium den for business.

That only cemented it for me. The madman below the drift had used opium in his drug. I still refused to call it magic, no matter what a faceless voice behind a silk screen said.

It came in a dust, a powder, like any other chemical agent. Science would unravel it long before magic could ever be proven.

I stretched the kinks out from my spine. Truth be told, I was a little stiff. I hadn't slept easily, although only the vaguest shadows of my dreams remained.

Getting to my feet seemed easier than it should, and I spent some time stretching my leg muscles and hips, as well. The key to continued success below the drift would be in keeping limber.

I padded barefoot across my bedroom, foregoing my slippers, and sat on the vanity chair. "Bloody bells," I muttered. I looked frightful. No matter how much vigor flowed through my limbs, my reflection painted a wholly different picture.

Betsy had worked to get the lampblack from my hair, and had admirably succeeded on that front. My hair was braided tightly in a thick plait down my back, once more restored to its red, if somewhat dulled, hue. I flicked the end over my shoulder, leaning forward to study the shadows beneath my eyes.

Clearly, though I'd slept, I hadn't slept *well*.

My eyes looked somewhat glazed, as if covered over by a sheet of glass. My skin was slightly too sallow. I looked, in a word, exhausted.

But I felt wonderful.

I braced my hands against the vanity mirror and leaned in as close as I could, studying myself with fierce concentration. Tremors vibrated through the soles of my bare feet. Masculine voices slammed through the floorboards, and I straightened so fast that the mirror rocked dangerously.

"I'm terribly sorry, my lord, but Miss St. Croix is still unable to receive visitors." Booth's voice, impeccable as ever.

"Still ill, is she?"

The voice snapped hard around me, as brutal, as unforgiving, as any cage. I sucked in a breath.

"My sympathies to the house," Lord Cornelius Kerrigan Compton said, his rich, educated voice clear as day beneath me. I squeezed my eyes shut, but it wouldn't help to block out the raw apprehension in his so-polished voice. "Would it help to send my personal physician?"

"Thank you, my lord, you are kind to offer. However, Miss St. Croix's physician is of the highest caliber."

"Of course. I will not . . ." He hesitated. "I shall take my leave. Please give my regards to your lady." The footsteps faded once more as Lord Compton said his farewells.

My forehead hit the vanity with a dull *thunk* of bone on wood. The crystal vials of my various perfumes clinked and clattered. Anger bit deeper than any blade, any *mo-shoe* I could have dredged from the depth of hell itself. Anger, and guilt.

He had kissed me. He had professed to admire me, to tell me how much he enjoyed my company.

And I . . .

I what? What did I want? What could I expect from a member of the peerage, one so fine as the Earl Compton?

Nothing. Of course, nothing. No more or less than anything I expected from the rest of Society. I had already been cut once, though the harpy marchioness had found her machinations undone by her very own son.

If word of the night's events ever trickled out of the Menagerie?

Images of the night flashed through my mind, suddenly daylight bright and too vivid to be a dream.

Micajah's hands on my breasts. Callused fingertips plucking at the rose-tipped flesh of my nipples. My skin flamed. I squeezed my eyes shut even tighter, until pain pulsed through my eyelids, but he was still there.

Are you with me, Miss Black?

"Devil take it," I whispered. I was so confused. I stared at my hands and tried to concentrate on the facts. The facts of the situation. Hawke had . . . seen me in the flesh. He'd touched me, but I was . . . I'd needed his help. I'd practically begged him, hadn't I? This was forgivable.

The blood on the sheets after had been from my own wounds, I remembered making them. I remembered Hawke's surprise as they'd vanished. There was something truly mysterious about the drug the madman had given me.

Hawke had done what he'd needed to do. At least, that's what I told myself now.

But then I thought of Compton and it was as if I couldn't breathe. Why? Why did I let the earl capture my thoughts so thoroughly?

It shouldn't have mattered. I did not want to marry, and surely there was no call to assume Compton would *ever* ask for my hand. And even if he did, I'd long since resolved to deny every man who would try. I was assuming a great deal about Compton, and I had no reason to assume anything of the sort.

Why, then? Why did I feel as if I'd made a terrible mistake?

The door slid open on silent hinges.

Zylphia stepped inside, so tame in appearance I almost didn't recognize her. Her tea-stained skin was scrubbed clean of everything even resembling rouge, her eyes lacking in the dark kohl she'd worn so often below the drift. Her hair was tightly coiled once more, and her clothing identical to Betsy's in every regard. Her dark dress and white apron were clean, her shoes polished and the tea service in her hands remained steady.

But her eyes. They were so blue, startlingly colorful in her dark skin, and so full of sympathy that I was seized with a vicious urge to throw something at *her*.

How dare she approach me with so much knowledge in her face?

I dashed an arm across my eyes, though no tears had fallen, and turned resolutely away. "Just leave the tray," I ordered stiffly.

She complied, though she took a slow, deep breath. "It's difficult, isn't it?"

My back went rigid. I sneaked a glance through my lashes, saw her staring at the delicate teapot with such sadness on her face. I bit my lip.

"We all have secrets," she told me, but she didn't look at me. "Some of us, it's worse than others. Them that's without, they're always on the out and looking in. You think you'd be better sticking with them like you."

Them like me. Like Zylphia.

Like . . .

Hawke.

My fists clenched so tightly, pain speared through my palms. "At least my Lord Compton is concerned," I said flatly. "At least *he* cares enough to bloody well ask after me."

"Is that what you think?" She looked at me, then, her eyebrows furrowed. Her hands settled on her aproned hips. "You believe he simply left you? *Cherie*, Cage was—"

I couldn't stand to hear his name. Embarrassed, my pride damaged deeply, I shot to my feet, my nightgown swirling around my ankles, and flung a hand to the door. "Get out," I ordered, each word bitten to the quick.

The vanity chair tumbled backward as I strode across the room. Zylphia passed me, her lips tight with disapproval. With anger.

I didn't care.

The door shut behind me as I poured myself a cup of tea. She must have been listening for my stirring, for the brew steamed as it hit the china cup. Fresh from the kettle. And she'd left only sugar on the tray. No cream.

My hands shook as I brought the cup to my lips.

What kind of awful creature was I becoming?

The kind that could lie with ease. That could blame others for my own shortcomings.

"Damnation," I seethed, and scalded my tongue on the tea. It was a small pain.

It did nothing to overwhelm the hole in my chest.

I was angry. I was mortified by my own behavior and acutely aware of how petty I was acting. It only worsened my mood. I was frightened, I admit now what I couldn't then, feeling out of sorts from all of it. Compiled with the restless energy I always felt after a bout of strong opium, and I was beyond help.

The events with Hawke were only a portion of my frustration. The things he'd made me feel seemed somehow . . . unnatural. I was no closeted miss unaware of the ways of the world, but I was virginal in the strictest definition and entirely too embarrassed by the subject matter in regards to myself.

I'd never summoned the nerve to ask Zylphia about such things.

To feel the same whispered urges when I heard Compton's voice? This was deucedly unfair, and baffling beyond. Micajah Hawke sold his soul to charm the stars from the sky—and more than a few ladies from their stays, I was sure. That he could engender such feelings from a girl like myself was unsurprising.

The earl was no ringmaster. No wicked tempter in the dark. Why, then, did I think of him?

Bah, I was back to this again. I needed a distraction.

I spent as much time as I possibly could in the relative safety of my room. I paced, I curled up beneath the covers. I called for a bath, scrubbed myself until my skin turned pink, then soaked until the water turned cold and my fingertips wrinkled.

I dressed, decided against the pretty rose-colored day gown and found something instead in charcoal gray. Much more somber.

Much more to my mood.

I brushed out my own hair until it shone, dry and vibrantly lustrous. I began to weave it into a plethora of tiny plaits, like I'd seen on the dark-skinned man beneath the drift, then impatiently gave up and twined it all up into a simple coil.

When I couldn't stand my own company a moment longer, I seized my courage in both hands and left my bedchamber.

The house was quiet. Not empty; not even pared down. I waited at the top of the stair, gloved hand gripping the banister tightly, and strained to hear every sound trickling through the tomblike silence.

There was motion in the kitchen. Betsy and Zylphia, perhaps? Or simply Mrs. Booth with early preparations for the afternoon tea. I stared at the foyer beyond the stairs, willing myself to take the first step.

Just one, and my other foot could continue the motion. Step by step.

Guilt gripped at my throat.

I gritted my teeth, took a deep breath, and forced myself to move. Daintily. Skirts held just so. A proper lady.

What a liar.

I stumbled on the last step, caught myself with both hands around the lion's mane newel and shook my head hard. Enough of this. As far as anyone else knew, I was still just me. All right, so I'd tipped my hand to my staff, but they were my staff, weren't they?

Only Zylphia knew what had happened below.

But she'd never stand for a character witness. I had to be certain that my secrets stayed below. I spoke often of choosing to live as an exile, but if it ever came to that, I preferred it on my terms. If news of this—any of this—ever reached my guardian's ears before I came of age, I could lose everything.

I squeezed my eyes shut.

I could do this. I was Cherry bloody St. Croix. My father was a notorious madman. I'd been through worse, I was sure. A knife wound I'd sustained years ago surely outweighed embarrassment. A childhood spent in the circus rings certainly mattered more than a week's worth of inconveniences. In less than a year, I'd have everything I ever wanted.

I straightened, shook out my skirts, and strode into the parlor.

Fanny started, her knitting needles clacking together in surprise. "Cherry!"

I waved a dismissive hand at her as I crossed to my favorite settee. "Don't get up," I said quickly. "I feel fine. I was just ill."

Her eyebrows furrowed, thin lines of deep suspicion. "Ill, then?" Her lips pursed. "How ill?"

"Just ill," I said, carefully arranging my skirts so I didn't have to look up at my chaperone's all-too-sharp scrutiny. "I believe I ate something below that disagreed with my constitution."

It was as if I'd slapped her with the word *below*. Her indrawn breath hissed. "Yes," she said after a taut silence. "Below." She chewed on the word slowly. Cautiously. "Cherry, what on earth—"

I looked up, already shaking my head. "It's a long story, Fanny. I'm tired. Can't it wait?"

"You spent all day abed."

"I was—"

"Ill, yes," my chaperone finished for me, but her tone was dry. "So you said. My dove, do you have any idea how close your reputation is to lying in tatters?" Her needles clicked, once, twice, before she gave up and set them aside. Standing, Frances Fortescue began to do something I had never in my life seen her do.

She began to pace.

I blinked at her as the rustle of her heavy poplin skirts filled the silence.

"You vanished for an entire day and almost all of the night," Fanny pointed out, her gloved hands twined together. I bit my lip. "Betsy was beside herself; we practically had to force it out of her by a switch," she added grimly.

I stood so quickly, the blood left my head in a dizzying rush. "You didn't!"

"Sit down, Cherry," Fanny snapped. I sat, but only because it was that or fall. "Of course we didn't," she added irritably. "What do you think we are?" She pointed a gloved finger at me before I could answer, though I hadn't the faintest idea what to say. "We're your family, that's what! How dare you, Cherry St. Croix?"

I flinched.

It wasn't enough. My rail-thin chaperone was nobody's idea of a formidable foe, but as she stared me down across three feet of elegant parlor, every quivering inch clad in elegant navy blue poplin, I thought even a seasoned pugilist would quail.

"How *dare* you," she demanded again. "How dare you place Betsy into such an untenable position? How long has this been going on?"

I opened my mouth.

"Trousers, Cherry!"

I shut my mouth again.

Red-cheeked and all but vibrating in high dudgeon, Fanny spun and stalked to the mantel, her thin shoulders rigid. "And your corset! Good heavens, what on earth was it doing being seen by anyone who could look at you?"

"It's plated," I began, then threw my hands up in surrender when she spun, fury glinting in her pale blue eyes.

"You are a disgrace," she snapped. I winced. "A disgrace to your father and mother, God rest their dearly departed souls, and a disgrace to this very house!"

I shot to my feet, impatiently scraping away tendrils of my less-than-expertly pinned hair. "Now you see here," I began heatedly.

Fanny had no mind to see anything. She covered her eyes with one hand, groaning, "If this gets out, you're ruined. Don't you see that? All the hard work and effort we've put into you—"

I'd had enough. "*Madam* Fortescue," I said tightly, my voice pitched to a dangerous edge. "Will you shut your bleeding mouth!"

Fanny gasped, her cheeks draining of all blood. Her eyes widened, and I swear she swayed.

It was, I reflected later, likely the first time anyone had ever used such a word in her presence. And it coming from me, no less.

I forged ahead before she could collect herself. "My parents are dead, thank you very much. I can't possibly disappoint them as they're rather beyond caring." I strode to the window, but didn't reach for the drapes. I spun, my skirts frothing around my feet, and pointed at her. "They should have thought of what I'd become when they bloo—" No. I censored myself before the word escaped again. One such shock was enough for the old woman. "Before they died," I amended tightly. "You have *no conception* of the life I've led, the choices I've made."

"Of course we don't." But it didn't come angrily. Fanny sat back on the settee I'd abandoned, her tone—her very demeanor—weary.

I blinked at her, my anger suddenly trapped between walls of uncertainty.

I could handle yelling. Even the too-sharp barbs that were Fanny's way of keeping me in line.

I didn't know what to do with . . . this.

"How could we possibly know, Cherry?" She looked at me, and her eyes were so large in her thin features. Brimming with tears. "You've never told us."

My mouth closed once more. What could I say?
Nothing. She was right.

I tried anyway. "I've never told anyone. Betsy only found out that I'm a collector by accident, and I swore her to secrecy on—" I winced. "On pain of losing her post."

"Oh, I think that girl enjoyed the secret," Fanny said wryly, but it lacked every trace of humor. My chaperone rubbed at her cheeks, pale and so delicate, I was suddenly seized with the awareness of how old my chaperone suddenly appeared.

Were those wrinkles always there?

Were her veins always so dark in her translucent skin?

Something cracked in my chest, and I crossed the room, sank to the cushions beside her and took Fanny's fragile hands in mine. "I'm sorry," I said. I wanted to give her something, anything. So I began to speak. Quietly, calmly. As if I were only recounting the plot thread of a book, I spoke to her of Monsieur Marceaux's Traveling Circus. What little I could remember, I told her. Of the acts I participated in, the quota the vile ringmaster required of his acquired children. I mentioned the thievery, the threat of failure, but I left out a great deal more. Like the auction rings. The loss of limb or life when an act went terribly awry.

I avoided all those things I knew would bring pity to her eyes as she listened to me, her hands tight in mine. To her credit, my dear chaperone listened in silence, her gaze steady.

"Oh, my poor child. And now?" she asked when my voice fell to silence.

"Now, I collect," I admitted. "I have for nigh on five years, Fanny. I was afraid you'd force me to stop."

"Stop?" Her chuckle strained. "I don't even pretend to know what it is you do." She blew out a hard breath. "Nor," she added quickly as I opened my mouth, "do I wish to. Please, let this old woman live in as much ignorance as possible. I know what I *think* a collector is, I'd rather leave it at that."

That ache in my heart tightened, and I raised Fanny's hands to my cheeks. I loved her. She was as close to a mother as I'd ever had, and I knew that I'd betrayed her trust in me.

In so many more ways than she even suspected.

She turned her hands, cradling my cheeks in her gloved palms, and ducked her head to meet my eyes. Her regard was steady. Worried. "But you must be ever so careful now, my dove. Your reputation is only a whisper away from ostracizing you from everything you know."

"There is nothing to be ostracized from."

"You know better, Cherry."

I did, and I gave in. "No one here will breathe a word," I said firmly. My staff trusted me. So much more, I realized, than I had trusted them.

That would have to change.

"And besides, Fanny," I said lightly, patting her hands as I pulled away. "No one else even knows."

"Ahem." A masculine throat cleared itself of nothing at all, and both Fanny and I jumped.

Teddy hovered in the doorway, his hazel eyes sharp within a carefully tempered expression of indolent curiosity. "Knows what?" he asked.

Fanny's lips moved, but I was quicker than she. I had to be. That's what I did, after all. "Teddy!" I said brightly. Then, glancing sidelong at my recovering chaperone, I added, "That is, my Lord Helmsley."

"I prefer Teddy, thank you." His rejoinder was quick, but not entirely distracted.

Fanny harrumphed softly as she rose to her feet. "I shall see that tea is arranged," she announced. She sailed past us both with her nose firmly in the air; the very model of a proper Englishwoman.

Too proper, really. I'd have to work on her, I thought.

Teddy's hands clasped my shoulders, and I half turned in surprise, eyes wide. "Are you all right?" he demanded.

"Yes?" I looked down at myself, at my perfectly boring gray dress, and back up to meet his gaze. "Do I appear not to be?"

He let me go with a sigh, crossing the parlor in three long strides to throw himself into his favorite overlarge armchair. "They said you'd been ill," he half accused. "You still look worn. I was rather afraid that I'd arrive to find you'd passed of some mysterious plague."

This made me grin, morbid as it was. "You should only be so lucky." I once more found comfort on the settee, arranging my skirts neatly. "I'm well. I came down with some touch of the ague, but I'm quite recovered, as you see."

Lying came ever so easily. A pang of guilt clanged once more in my chest.

I ignored it.

I couldn't afford to give in now. There was a murderer to be caught, after all. And a cameo to locate. Above all, I was a collector. I'd given my word.

Fanny returned, her eyebrows arched high and a colorful bundle in her hands. I blinked. "Flowers?"

"Your pardon, my lord," Fanny said, ignoring me for the moment's courtesy.

Teddy rose to his feet. "Not at all, Fanny, there's no need to stand on courtesy with me."

"Charmer," I muttered, pitched so he could hear.

He flashed me a grin.

Fanny handed me the bouquet. "This was left at the stoop for you."

"Me?" My gaze flew to Teddy, who shrugged.

"I saw no such thing when I arrived," he replied. His eyebrows furrowed. "Red roses, eh? Perhaps it's from that ruddy earl."

Fanny had the grace to ignore this.

I did not. "He's not a ruddy anything," I replied in exasperation. "Teddy, really."

"Maybe it's a farewell gift."

This gave me pause. "Farewell?" I was acutely aware of Fanny's suddenly sharp stare. "What farewell?"

Teddy leaned back, ankles crossed fashionably. "He didn't inform you? He and his younger wastrel of a brother have left Town." His eyes glinted. "Rather suddenly. All the tongues are wagging, at least out of the marchioness's hearing."

Compton had left London without so much as a by-your-leave, then? I couldn't even begin to speculate on this. Such a leave-taking was bound to provoke gossip. And though a small, bruised part of my heart ached at the realization that I did not warrant a proper farewell, or even a polite explanation, I quashed my hurt with a careless gesture of the nosegay. "Regardless, why on earth would he send me roses?"

"You were quite the model of beauty at Lady Rutledge's ball, you know. Perhaps he's simply admitting his deep and abiding pas—"

I coughed.

Teddy snapped his mouth shut before he said something entirely too scandalous for Fanny's ears.

Fanny chuckled as she once more took her seat; a sound that eased some of the anxiety wrapped inside me. It wasn't as it once was, and I didn't know that our relationship ever could be, but it was a start. "Cherry hasn't received many flowers in her time," Fanny said lightly. "My lord, you may need to translate."

"Surely you've received many a nosegay, madam," he replied with a wicked grin. "Your translation skills may be equally as important."

"Not for many years, now." Fanny's knitting needles clicked quietly. "And as all things must, the terms have changed with time. Although red roses," she added with a pointed look at me, "still indicate a deep love, unless I am grossly misinformed. Are you sure it's not from your earl?"

I eyed the bundle. "It seems . . ." Not his style? I shook my head. "What are these white flowers?"

Fanny frowned. After a moment, she retrieved a pair of spectacles from a chain about her neck and placed them firmly on her nose. "Aside from the roses, it looks like . . ." Her eyebrows knitted. "Foxglove? And white verbena."

"The pink is sweetbriar," Teddy pointed out. "Ah, I do love a mystery."

"I didn't expect you to know flowers," I teased my friend.

He didn't look even a smidge repentant. "I shall teach you one day. There's much to be said with flowers."

"Of flowers," I corrected.

"No, dear," Fanny said, smiling. "*With*. In my time, foxglove meant the sender had ambitions only for the recipient. A declaration of intent, if you will."

Teddy craned his neck to study the bouquet. "Is there a card?"

I carefully separated the boldly crimson roses from the morass of smaller white and pink blooms. It was a lovely nosegay, admittedly.

And lush enough to mask a small, folded piece of card stock beneath the flower heads. I fished it out with only minimal loss of petals. "Found one," I crowed triumphantly.

"Ah! Of course. Sweetbriar is a flower of sympathy," Fanny said, then glanced at me over the top of her spectacles. "Why would someone declare love, ambition and sympathy all in one go?"

I opened the card, squinted at the slanted handwriting. The ink was tobacco brown, decently dark, but the lettering too cramped for easy deciphering.

"I'm afraid," Teddy said slowly, "that foxglove is an entirely different message from what you recall, madam."

"Oh?"

My dear, I read slowly. *Know that you are in my thoughts, and that we look forward to your prompt perception in this matter.*

A dull ache began to throb behind my forehead.

"It carries an accusation of insincerity," Teddy was saying. He leaned closer, peering at the bouquet I still held loosely in one hand. "But what are these?"

A knock resounded from the back of the house.

Fanny once more crossed the small parlor, her mouth pinched in deep thought. She bent to study the tiny white flowers Teddy captured between two fingers. The five-petaled blooms were mostly white, with a hint of darker pink at the center and dusting the stems. Three petals curved down, and two up.

This once, I read, my lips moving, *I shall skim the bounds of propriety and direct you to Whitechapel Station. Tick tock, Miss St. Croix.*

"Geraniums," Fanny said after a moment's thought. "Nutmeg geraniums, unless I miss my guess." She hesitated. "I don't recall this one."

The trains stop for no woman. Yours faithfully.

There was no name. My fingers tightened on the card, bending the edges.

"Cherry?"

I looked up.

"The geraniums," Teddy said, frowning. "They indicate an expectation of meeting. Have you made plans with some upstart?"

There didn't have to be a name. There was no one else it *could* be. The madman must have followed me to the Menagerie. Someone must have let slip about my hair, perhaps followed me and Zylphia home.

I didn't know how it got out, but it seemed my secrets were destined for revelation.

The bastard had all but demanded I accost him.

I rose. Teddy stood abruptly, alarm written clear as day over his sharp features. "What is it? What's wrong?"

"Cherry?" Fanny asked, her own voice reflecting the worry I couldn't do anything to salve.

Teddy caught my arm. "Cherry, what is going on? You've been acting awfully—"

Footsteps scurried down the hall. We all looked over as Zylphia caught herself on the door ledge, her cheeks flushed. She didn't bother with formality of any sort. "Come quick!" she demanded.

I picked up my skirts, card and flowers crushed to

the fabric, and pursued Zylphia to the kitchen. The man who waited there did so uncomfortably, his cap in his hands and his plain, undecorated coat still on. He was a tall man, given to breadth and uniquely suited to his employ as a blacksmith's journeyman. Soot stained his hands, had settled into his pores from a lifetime of work, but he loved his wife.

"John," I greeted, as worry clawed at me. "Is something the matter?"

He bowed awkwardly, that somewhat clumsy bob of one not quite sure of the correct mode to address a lady of any standing. I had met Betsy's husband only once, and I had no call to be calling him by his Christian name, but damn propriety.

"I'm sorry t'be botherin' ye fine folks," he stammered uneasily, his thick Scottish brogue strained.

I waved that away.

His eyes widened, and I realized I'd swiped a mass of flowers in his direction. I tossed them to the table. Petals scattered. "What's wrong, Mr. Phillips?" I pressed. "Is Betsy all right?"

And then I saw it. The flicker; a wince. "I was hopin' t'be askin' ye th' same, miss." John clutched his cap tighter, all but folded in his work-chapped hands. "She didna come home last night, like she does. I thought maybe ye'd kept her over . . ." His voice trailed away as his gaze flicked to three sets of suddenly worried faces.

Teddy looked confused.

"She's na here?" John asked.

A wealth of pain, of heart-stopping fear rested in that single question.

"She left for home last night," Zylphia said softly.

John's shoulders sagged. "God help me."

My hands shaking, I smoothed out the card. The brown ink blurred. *We look forward to your prompt perception . . .*

My gaze fell on the nosegay. The roses gleamed like blood against the white flowers. Sympathy. Blood on the snow. There was no snow in London, but there were places where the fog was so thick, it was akin to walking through a blizzard.

The trains stop for no woman.

Whitechapel lay in the very heart of such a place.

Dear God in heaven. "I have to go," I said suddenly.

"Wait just a bloody minute," Teddy said, but I shook off his hand and sprinted for the door.

"I'm sorry," I called over my shoulder. "But I must ask you to leave, Teddy. I shall explain everything later!" Lie, more like.

"Cherry, wait!"

I didn't. I didn't dare. I had no time to waste changing, none to waste explaining. The warning was clear. It wasn't sympathies for my debt to the Karakash Veil the rotting bastard was actually sending. It was sympathies for the death of my friend.

He had Betsy.

And it was her blood that I'd mistaken for tobacco ink.

Chapter Sixteen

Zylphia caught up with me halfway to the West India docks. She had enough presence of mind to bring a cloak, which she handed to me wordlessly. The hood draped over my hair, hid enough of my features that I could travel unmolested in London below.

"Go back," I told her, pulling the cloak closely around me. I didn't dare stop to converse.

"Not likely," she replied, and I realized she kept one hand curved around a long shaft hidden beneath her own cloak. "The gent left, and Betsy's man went home to wait for her, in case she returns." Her jaw set. "She won't, though, will she?"

"She bloody will," I said grimly. "Zylla, go home. This one's only after me."

"You don't even know who it is," my friend said as she easily matched her longer legs to my brisk pace. "I saw that note you left. He doesn't leave a name."

"It's that man who drugged me."

"Or it's the sweet tooth," she pointed out. "Or it's another bloke you've gone and collected in the past. Or it's a group of them, *cherie*. You want to go down there alone?"

"Yes!"

"Well, you can't." She turned slightly to show the satchel over her shoulder, the like of which Fanny would take to markets. "I brought you trousers to change into, and Mr. Booth sent me with a little something extra." She hefted the hidden shaft, distinctly rifle-shaped.

I shook my head. "No time to change."

"There will be time on the ferry," Zylpha said, her caramel features as intent as I imagined mine were.

My lips flattened, but I said nothing.

Although it would have been faster to take the most direct route and hire my own gondolier, I instead took the route through the West India docks. Captain Abercott was already accustomed to my comings and goings, and for the right incentive, he didn't bother with any schedule.

Once the ferry was moving, Zylphia pushed me into the captain's tiny hold. It smelled of old seawater and beer. I shed my voluminous skirts quickly, stepped into a pair of my own trousers and—God bless her— my collecting corset. My kid boots looked too fancy for the rest, but there was nothing to be done about it now. They'd be ruined in the damp below. I just didn't care.

I adjusted my hood and stepped out of the cramped little room.

"Better," Zylphia murmured as I sat beside her.

Abercott's slitted eyes glared daggers into my back. "What did you tell him?" I asked, frowning.

"He wanted twice the fee," Zylphia said, her gaze

steady over the railing as the fog slipped up to caress the deck. It was like sinking into a stew pot, but without the heat. Thick and viscous.

"And?"

"And I told him I'd curse his bollocks blue if he so much as thought of it."

I wanted to laugh, but there was something so serious, so steely, in the sweet's expression that I snapped my mouth closed around it.

She glanced at me. Then away.

That was the first time that something about Zylphia made me nervous.

The captain set us down. "Thank you," I told him.

"Hmph."

Once on the street beyond the dock, we worked quickly to secure one of the hackneys still in service below the drift. Though the ride was jarring, it was as fast as I could possibly like.

Every minute was like a knife inching closer to my throat.

My friend's throat.

I sprang out of the hackney the instant it slowed. Zylphia swore a vulgarity, but I couldn't dwell on it now. My mysterious opponent wanted a meeting, he'd get his meeting.

The hackney driver cursed behind me as I spooked his horse, but Zylphia had already paid him. My sanity—or lack thereof—was not his concern.

The cloak around my shoulders seemed to get heavier with every step I took, leaching the damp from the air. The lantern hanging from the retreating hackney quickly faded to nothing behind me, leaving me standing in a miasma nearly too thick to breathe, much less see through. I hadn't brought my fog-prevention goggles, and I cursed myself for my lack of foresight. Zylla didn't know where I kept them, or else I hadn't given her enough time to look.

No goggles, no respirator. I was as blind as a babe in the dark. What the devil had I intended?

"Where are we headed?" Zylphia asked behind me.

"This is a large rail yard," I mused, squinting through my tearing vision.

"Split, then?" she asked, already sounding as if she were prepared to argue.

I glanced at her. "Split," I agreed. "I've got my knives. Keep the rifle." The Springfield officer's rifle she carried glinted dully in the fading light as she raised it in acknowledgment.

"I'll take the right, then," Zylphia said, and her pale eyes narrowed as they flicked to the fog behind me. "Be careful, *cherie*. Whitechapel's already been host to a murderous sort."

Leather Apron. Maybe the same killer we were after. Maybe not. I nodded once, and set off into the fog, only now and again picking out details as the coal-laden stench roiled and shifted. Here the corner of a building. There a pocked and pitted sign proclaiming the site as Whitechapel Station.

My toes rammed into the raised metal bars of a railway, and I stumbled.

Whitechapel Station, although not one of my usual haunts, was not wholly unfamiliar to me. I'd been here before on occasion. Usually on the trail of a quarry. Once or twice via the railway lines.

Fortunately, the yard was quiet. I'd spent so much time in my rooms that dark had to be less than an hour away, which meant there was precious little light to spare already. I squinted against the fog, yellow black and shifting so quickly, it was like walking through a filthy blizzard.

The station took up a wide parcel of land, and nothing had been raised above it. It connected many rails to various posts throughout London below. Most of the passengers never set foot into the rail yard, and the trains didn't run as often by night. One or two per the hour.

Which meant, for all intents and purposes, I would be alone with my opponent.

I picked my way along the rails, pushing my hood off to better see around me. Everything hung still and heavy; there was no whisper of voices, no movement. Now and again, I stepped over a rail that vibrated subtly, as if a train moved over it somewhere down the line. The distant echo of a whistle came back to me, but nothing close enough to matter.

Somewhere else, near enough that I suspected it came from a mechanism for the rail yard, steam hissed. After it spat, I heard a dull clank of metal shifting.

It was all so surreal. A fog-shrouded dreamscape comprising acres of iron-strewn land, and I was alone inside it. Seeking, straining to hear, trapped.

Bugger that for a joke.

"Betsy!" I called. The fog sucked at my voice, all but ripping it from my lungs. "Betsy, where are you?"

A wall loomed suddenly out of the mist, and I reared back. My heel came down on broken rubble, loud as grating rock could be, and I swore under my breath. This was ridiculous.

"Betsy!" I shouted, striding past the building's

grimy façade. An alley mouth yawned open beside me, filled to the brim with the same black miasma. "Elizabeth?"

Nothing. Frowning, I turned away. What if she was unconscious? Dead, already?

No. I wouldn't let myself think it.

I pulled the cloak tighter around my shoulders and turned back to the open yard. Here and there, the shape of a silent steam engine thrust from the cloud. A smokestack, a still caboose.

It was as if I'd stepped into a train cemetery.

"Bet—"

Fabric bunched at my neck, and suddenly I was choking on my own voice as my cloak dug into my throat. Something pulled hard, yanked me back into that alley so fast that it was all I could do to lodge my fingers beneath the clasp to keep myself from strangling.

My back collided with the wall, sharp and damp, my head rebounded with enough force to make me cry out. Heart thumping, I struggled, only to grunt as rough hands seized my shoulders, my cloak, and spun me around.

This time, my chest slammed into unforgiving brick, my cheek grated against the pitted stone. A hand flattened against the back of my head, holding me still. Grinding my face against the surface.

The pain at my cheek was nothing to the sharp point digging into the small of my back.

I wasn't the only one with knives. Unlike me, however, my opponent had already drawn his.

"I'm delighted you came," came a low, soft-spoken voice. It was masculine, I could hear that much. Even pleasant, nonchalant, for all the knife at my back was neither. I didn't recognize it; to be fair, it was barely a murmur.

My hands tightened against the wall, but I didn't dare push away. I'd impale myself on the rotter's weapon if I didn't play the next few moments carefully. As I took a deep breath, I smelled damp grit and the choking stench of coal. No cologne or fragrance; or at least nothing strong enough over the rail-yard rot. Nothing helpful to identify my assailant.

"Good evening," I greeted, as drolly as I could manage with my face crushed against a wall.

"Why, Miss St. Croix." The knife shifted, and suddenly it was at my neck. The warmth of a man's body slid in behind my back as his breath tickled my ear. "So polite." He chuckled, and though I couldn't see his face, I didn't have to. Every fiber of my being hissed a wild, panicked warning.

I'd heard laughter. I was familiar with the sound. But I'd never heard anything like this.

Subtly unhinged. Mildly threatening.

Every breath of it so easy, so uncaring, as if the man uttering the sound was beyond any comprehension of human understanding.

The hair on the back of my neck prickled. "Why did you take my maid?"

For all he encroached on me, keeping me still against the alley wall, the man didn't press. He didn't take advantage of my position, though I knew he could. It was only the blade at my throat. The hand at the back of my head.

His words soft in my ear. "How else was I to gain your attention? Subtlety had failed spectacularly."

"What?"

"A mad one, that professor," the voice said gruffly, and I frowned. Why did that voice, those words seem so familiar? "They say 'e collects *bodies*."

A smoky room. A faceless rumormonger.

I gasped. "You were in that den!"

"As were you, naughty girl," he said, once more in his soft-spoken tone. My opponent was a chameleon, then.

"Why?" I demanded. "Who are you?"

"Which should I answer first?" The point of the knife lessened, just a touch. "I followed you to the den. You looked ridiculous, you know."

I gritted my teeth. "Charmed," I muttered. "If all you wanted was an introduction, you didn't have to take my maid. The flowers were a fine start."

"Flowers are trite and inconsequential. Hardly fitting for you."

I flinched. "You don't know me well enough t—"

The edge at my throat tightened, and I bit off my acidic admonishment. "More than you'd think," my assailant whispered. "Shhh." His breath ghosted warm and damp against my ear. It smelled faintly of tobacco.

I shuddered in revulsion. But because I couldn't help anyone with my throat slit, I fell silent.

When day turned to night in London below, even in areas where there was nothing but fog and sky above, the light faded suddenly. Rapidly. Even as I stared out at the murky fog, I recognized the subtle changes in the color of the gloom.

I was running out of time. Soon, it'd be full dark. I had to find Betsy first.

All I heard was the rapid beat of my own heart. The faint, almost obscured sound of wheels grating on rusted rails and the constant hiss and *whoosh* of steam traps venting to the open air.

I shifted my shoulders. "I don't hear—"

"Tsk."

The knife at my throat vanished, and with it, the man. I didn't push off the wall, I lurched hard to the side instead. Away from the alley, my stomach launching into my throat as I expected to feel several inches of razor-sharp steel sink into my back.

It didn't come.

At the alley mouth, I spun, fog swirling around my ankles. The damp clung to my hair, forcing it into a frizz. I wiped at my cheek with the back of my arm. "Where did you go?" I demanded.

The alley remained dark and still in front of me.

I swallowed hard. The man wanted me to follow. That much was clear. But I knew what waited for unarmed women in alleys such as this.

I looked around, forcing my brain to push through the fear, the frustration. The shiny edges where the events of the night past hadn't quite worn off.

There. A piece of piping tucked just inside the mouth, discarded and broken at one end. It was clumsy at best, but sharp. And it afforded me much greater reach than my knives. It would do.

Quickly, I loosened the clasp and let the cloak puddle to the ground. Shivering in the immediate damp, I knelt swiftly and picked up the pipe. "Come out and face me!"

My voice faded into nothing.

Summoning every ounce of courage I had, I strode into that shadowy alley.

My footsteps echoed as I followed the narrow lane.

I heard a faint *drip, drip, drip* of puddling water, and the scurrying whisper of things on tiny claws and feet. Steam whispered its release somewhere beyond the walls rising high on each side of me, nearly black with slime and coal-choked moss.

Gripping the pipe end in both hands, I eased along one side, mindful of my back.

He was tricky. That much was certain.

As I came to a corner, I paused. My palms were damp, and I reaffirmed my hold. My nerves all but climbed out of my skin, I was straining so hard to see, to hear. To be anything but simply defensive.

I didn't like what I couldn't see.

Holding my breath, I rounded the corner, pipe raised. There was no tall figure in black. Only a dank, narrow lane stretched out ahead of me. An iron gate closed the lane behind me, locked fast. I hadn't heard the sound of what was sure to be rusted hinges, so I turned again to the open path.

My footsteps slapped against the broken cobbles, echoed back to me in a thousand directions as I sprinted down the open lane. I burst out of the small alley route and found myself once more in the rail yard. Here and there, a small lantern guttered, allowing just enough light to see nothing but shadows and fog. Bloody bells.

"Betsy!" I called, knowing full well it'd mark exactly where I was.

But the faceless man didn't need my voice to find me.

I passed two trains, still and cold side by side, and froze as his chuckle echoed from between them. "Where, oh, where is the dear little maid?" he asked in a lilting tune. "Is she on a train? Perhaps she means to leave London forever."

I whirled, my pipe raised in both hands. I saw a glimmer of white, maybe a flash of teeth. A whisper of a handkerchief. It could have been anything. He leaned indolently against the engine, his hat still too low to see anything.

"Tell me where she is," I demanded, already losing patience.

"Perhaps she huddles on a church stair," he continued conversationally. "Cold and alone. Why, oh, why won't her lady find her?"

I laughed, though there was no humor in it. "I am no lady."

He straightened, and I backed up quickly, my sweaty palms already slipping on the pipe. "No?" And in that single syllable, something sick curled into his voice. Something sharp as a razor and hungry for it. "If you are no lady, Miss St. Croix, you must be something else entirely."

"You don't frighten me," I spat, shaking my head. Tendrils of my hair clung to my fog- and sweat-damp cheeks.

"Come now," he said dryly, and eased back along the train. He vanished into the dark, and I rounded the two engines carefully. "You aren't so foolish as that."

Now he was a disembodied voice, leading me from the dark.

My throat ached, but I swallowed down a knot of uncertainty as I cautiously made my way across the uneven ground. A glint of metal became another railway, this one set next to three more and all merged together.

We were nearing a switching station.

I steeled my voice. My nerves. "I'm not playing with you."

"Yes, you are." It came from everywhere. Nowhere. I spun, turned again as only shadows and fog swirled around me. "Tell me, Miss St. Croix, why would I lead you to dear Professor Woolsey?"

A shrill whistle split through my confusion. A train was coming in.

"Because you . . ." My voice faded to silence as my eyes darted from whirling patch of fog to shadowed pockets shrouded and revealed with each eddy. My forehead furrowed deeply. "Because you knew I would suspect him?"

That silken laughter slid out from the dark again. "And rightfully so, wouldn't you agree?"

I tilted my head, but didn't look directly, as something flickered at my peripheral. Instead, I half turned my body away. "Did he kill those women?" I demanded.

"No," the man said lazily. "I did."

There. Just behind me.

"But then, you knew poor, fragile Woolsey couldn't have overpowered strong doxies like pretty Annie, didn't you?"

I set my jaw. Even hearing him say Annie's name made my skin feel mired in grime; desperate for a bath. "What of Mary?"

Silence.

"And the dove just a few days past?" I pressed.

A sound of disgust trickled out from the dark. "Useless, and a complication."

That made no sense. "Did you kill them?"

"I have no need for the pocked doxies of the East End." He practically snarled the words. "I shall race you, my dear Miss St. Croix."

"Race me?"

That laugh again. "To that ripper of the East End," he singsonged. "Talentless lout, eager for attention. Desperate for glory. *My* glory." Barking mad, then.

This was leading me nowhere. "Who are you to Professor Woolsey?" I demanded, searching for the light of sane reason in the morass of confusion he spewed out from the shadows.

He made a small, mournful sound. "Partner. Friend. Murderer, of course. He is quite a brilliant man, you know. Truly on the verge of something marvelous. I'd always thought him talented."

"Talented," I repeated, my tone desert dry.

"A genius, almost." But there was a thin sound in those words, as if he smiled in razor-edged humor.

I backed up slowly, as if watching the shadows play in front of me. "Who are you?"

"A scientist of sorts," he tossed out. Too easily. Laughingly. "A connoisseur."

The whistle came again, shrill and brassy.

I sucked in a harsh breath. "Were you the second man seen with Woolsey?"

"Ah, the apothecaries," he breathed, and his voice circled around me, carried by the shifting banks of black and gray and yellow. I didn't need sound to pinpoint him. "It was only a matter of time before someone saw me. Do you know, Miss St. Croix, you threw me for *quite* a loop outside the Blackwall druggist. To think it was you with all that black hair."

The whistle shrieked once more, and in it I heard the murderer's mocking laughter. Laughing as he killed the sweets. As he butchered them like animals. All for an experiment that his friend, his partner, developed.

It all collided in my head in a whirlwind of sparks. "You're a monster," I whispered, the sound all but strangled as my chest wrenched painfully. Anger knifed through me, sharper than any blade. Suddenly I spun, leapt on the shadow and swung my pipe. The metal caught on something solid, fleshy. It jarred all the way to my elbow, and the man grunted.

Something glinted, something wicked sharp, and I spun. Though my shoes skidded on the gravel, I neatly avoided his thrust, caught his knife hand between my arm and side, and wrenched hard.

He staggered. I seized his collar, pushed with all my might and slammed into his chest as his back plowed into a discarded train car. His breath gusted over my face in a surprised sound.

I jammed the broken edge of the pipe under his chin. He stilled.

"Now," I said, panting breathlessly. "Why are you after me?" Everything else had become an afterthought in my head. All I saw was the shadow of his features, thin and barely more than a blur.

I had him now.

"Ah." The sound was a sigh. The dark thickened, almost absolute, and all I could see was the merest hint of light reflected in his eyes. Against my body, I could tell that he was thin beneath his swirling overcoat, but it wasn't enough.

I needed to know more.

"You are magnificent," he said, and I stared at him. That sounded like . . . pride? Was he *proud* of me? As if aware of my confusion, the man very slowly opened his hand. I heard the knife drop to the gravel.

"Why?" I demanded again. "Who are you?"

He wasn't at all intimidated. "Can you kill an un-armed man?"

I glared up into his face, wishing I could see more than the flash of his teeth as he smiled over my rusted weapon.

"Of course you can't," he continued. Aside from a faint tremor of strain as he labored to keep his chin steady, he seemed unconcerned. Truly, not even a whit frightened.

What kind of monster was he?

"You're Cherry St. Croix, you don't kill."

"You don't know me," I whispered, but every word he spoke slipped into my ears. Danced around in the fringes of my exhaustion.

"Oh, my dear." So bloody kind.

A whistle blasted, and I gritted my teeth. "Where," I demanded, slow and as sharp as the broken barbs at his throat, "is Betsy?"

Again, that flash of teeth. "The trains wait for no woman."

"I don't want a train, I want—"

"Cherry," came the masculine sigh. "Use that brain of yours." My arm stiffened, and his voice cut off on a sudden note of caution, his chin lifted higher as the pipe ground against it.

No matter my fury, my intent, my anger, I knew I couldn't do it. And so did he.

His chuckle grated. "Do you hear the train coming? It's me or your Betsy," he rasped. "There's only time for one. If you strike me, I will struggle. I will waste precious moments, and your Betsy will be nothing more than a bloody memory."

My grip at his collar loosened.

"But I promise you," he said, so softly I almost didn't hear it under the train's shrill warning. "If you save her, I shall wait in the Underground."

"You bastard," I breathed.

His head inclined, the merest fraction that my impromptu weapon allowed. "Like you," he allowed, "we all have a price. And a motive. What *is* mine?"

I didn't know. The man was mad as a hatter, clearly, but he'd taken my friend and left her out on a track, of that I was certain. The train whistled.

For God's sake, why?

I pushed away from him, sprinted past the silent engine and onto the track beside it. His laughter followed me, crept over my back in a prickle of unease. Sweat centered between my shoulder blades, much like I imagined his knife would.

It still didn't come.

He was toying with me.

The whistle shrieked, and I dropped the pipe as I ran along the uneven girders. "Betsy! Betsy, talk to me!"

And then I heard it. A low moan. Not a word, but a question nonetheless. Just ahead, nearly invisible, a lump of motionless gray huddled on the track.

Relief nearly overwhelmed me.

Only to send my heart plummeting once more as I heard the unmistakable crunch and screech of railway wheels. The train would wait for no woman.

"God help us," I whispered, and threw myself along that track. "Betsy!" The oncoming train's whistle blasted, so close I couldn't even hear myself scream her name.

I sank to my knees beside my maid, quickly taking in her sallow cheeks, her glazed eyes, her white lips.

The blood smeared across her forehead. "Betsy, sweeting."

Her lashes fluttered closed as she moaned. Opened again, as if forced.

"It's all right," I said, as reassuringly as I could while I tore at the rope pinning her hands to the rail slats. They refused to give. A knife, I needed a knife.

Betsy's eyes widened as the dull roar of oncoming wheels filtered through her uncertainty. "Train?" she breathed, and then twisted. "Oh, God, help me!"

The whistle shrieked. The wheels seemed louder, faster, and wrenched the knife from the front paneling of my collecting corset. The fibers gave under the sharp edge, and with my arms wrapped around Betsy, I wrenched us both off the track.

She was heavy in my arms, but alive. Sobbing, but dear heaven, she was breathing.

The train whistle blew, long and loud, ear-piercingly close.

And I stared down the empty track.

As I gasped for breath, clutching my friend to my chest, I listened to the rhythmic hiss of steam and the roar of the engine and saw nothing.

What devilry was this?

Only now, with my friend safe and my slamming heart slowly finding a quieter rhythm, did I realize that I'd felt no vibrations on the rails. I'd seen no lights.

As if on cue, the whistle cut off mid-shriek.

I'd been had.

I buried my face in Betsy's hair and took a deep, trembling breath. "You're all right," I said fiercely, rocking her as her arms tightened around my chest. She cried so desperately, I felt every tear as a burning ember in my heart. A twist of a guilt-ridden knife, sunk to the hilt in my breast.

"You're all right," I whispered again. It was all I could say.

And it wasn't true. For as long as that bastard lived, no one would be all right. Not my friends. My family.

Not me.

Gravel crunched behind me. I stiffened, my knees drawing up around Betsy's sprawled form as if it would help protect her.

Something large, funnel-shaped and brassy crashed to the ground beside me. I jumped, my arms tightening around Betsy.

Etched metal gleamed dully.

"I found this." Zylphia's voice brought tears to my gritty eyes. "It's the top of some machine what makes noise."

As her words sank into my shocked, exhausted mind, I recognized the metal tube. "A gramophone," I whispered. I laughed, but the sound seemed flat and tinny even to my own ears. "A recording."

"What?"

I couldn't stop laughing, even as I clutched Betsy to me. Even as another whistle blew shrilly, clear across the yard. "He recorded the sound of a train and played it," I explained between hysterical gasps. Bloody hell.

The gramophone certainly wasn't in wide distribution, I'd only seen it once or twice in London above. And that at the occasional salon. I never would have expected its use below.

My unnamed opponent had reach.

I turned my head as Zylphia sank to a crouch beside

me, reaching out a bare, dark-skinned hand toward Betsy.

Whatever she saw on my face, it forced her to pause mid-reach. "Let me see how she is," she said softly. "No need to get your back up for me. All right?"

Her voice seemed too out of place. The rocks cut into the backs of my legs, the fog seeped into every pore of my skin. Cold and dank and hopeless. We were surrounded by rusting metal and empty trains and God only knew what dangers beyond. In her other hand, the outline of the rifle gleamed wickedly against the ground.

I should have taken that and shot the bastard.

I swallowed, shaking, and nodded. Held on to Betsy as Zylphia smoothed her fingers over her face, into her hair.

My maid moaned.

"A head wound," Zylphia said, frowning as her pale eyes flicked again to me. "It's still bleeding. We need to get her home."

A head wound could be nothing. Or it could be fatal. If she slept now, if my maid rested to heal, she might never wake again.

Rage lit like a match inside my heart. "Can you take her up?" I demanded.

She nodded, her beautiful face calm. I could only imagine what demons twisted mine, but as I rose, allowing my maid to sink into the crook of Zylphia's arm, I didn't care. "I'm going after him."

"Are you sure?"

"He won't stop, Zylla."

Zylphia rose, her supple muscles supporting the lolling maid with more ease than I would have expected. She held out the rifle. "Take this. Can you shoot it?"

I didn't smile. My fingers closed over the stock, and though I wasn't as familiar with such things as I desperately wished, I knew how to fire one.

There are certain things required of any collector. A passing familiarity with whatever common weapons may be seized in moments of opportunity is one.

I ran my hands over it in the gloom. A breech-loader, then. I'd have one shot apiece. "Ammunition?"

She unhooked a small pouch from her waist, handed it to me. "Mr. Booth sent extra."

I found it remarkable that I'd never known of Booth's propensity for firearms. I'd ask him about it in the future.

Right now, I only wanted one thing. "It's the sweet tooth, all right," I said calmly, cracking open the trapdoor of the rifle and checking its load.

Zylphia said nothing.

"I've got him dead to rights. He worked with Woolsey," I continued, strapping the ammunition belt across my hips. "Until he killed the man."

Cradling my maid, Zylphia watched me prepare in the fog. "Do you know who he is?"

Betsy moaned.

My fingers clenched on the rifle's barrel. "I don't." The man clearly thought he knew *me*. I met her eyes, pale as stars. "I intend to find out."

They flickered. "Should I—"

"Take her home," I told her. "Get her above and make sure she's all right, Zylla. I'm going after him."

"Where?"

Of that, I wasn't certain. Rubbing my face with a dirty, coal-smudged hand, I braced the rifle under my arm and studied the track as it vanished into the foggy dark. "He chose this station for a reason," I finally said. Was that my voice? Tight and angry and so taut, it vibrated like a spring. "Heading into London proper might afford him a greater chance to hide, but the rotter doesn't want to hide. He's leading me somewhere, and he told me he'd be underground. Whitechapel Station only leads to one Underground route."

"Wapping isn't far." Zylphia followed my gaze, her eyes narrowed. "The Thames Tunnel?"

I nodded. "It's the only Underground entry for miles."

She didn't need my explanation. Anyone who made a living below knew the legends of the tunnel. Not only was it a rumored entry into the London Underground, most of it remained abandoned by all but the meanest rogues.

Her lips pressed together. She stooped to collect Betsy against her side once more, and threaded my maid's arm around her shoulders. "I'll be at the tunnel as soon as I can. Try not to engage him until I arrive, *cherie*."

I said nothing to that. There was nothing to say. By the time she made it back, I'd either have the bastard by the throat, or have died trying.

Trusting in Zylphia, placing my dearest friend into the hands of a Menagerie spy, should have been so much harder to do. But as I ran along the dark tracks—as I passed the broken remains of a device so extraordinary I'd allowed myself to be fooled by it—all I felt was anger.

Chapter Seventeen

Fortunately for my fraying patience, I made it to the Whitechapel platform just in time.

That is, just in time to slip into a freight car attached near the rear of the train as it slowly built steam. The whistle shrieked, and now that I was practically beneath it, I could hear the difference in pitch between the genuine thing and the copy.

Had I not been so wound up, maybe I would have heard the difference then, too. Knew the trick for what it was, made the better choice.

But wasn't Betsy the better choice, regardless?

I forced myself not to stew on the matter. Bring down the sweet tooth; that's all I had to bother myself with.

The train rumbled beneath me as I stared out at the passing fog. It whipped past at an alarming rate, raking through my hair and sending loosened hanks streaming in the wind. Even in the dark, it gleamed like blood on black glass.

The man knew who I was. How? How had he known me to be a St. Croix?

There were ways, I supposed. I stared out into the passing dark and ticked them off on mental fingers. The easiest was that he'd followed me to my home. It was possible I'd missed a tail in my hurry.

Perhaps it was time to acknowledge my arrogance in believing I was so . . . bloody *clever.*

Then, there was a chance of a Menagerie link. I imagine it wouldn't be so hard to picture me with different color hair, once word of my lampblack trick got out. But this meant someone would have had to share. Zylphia? Or Hawke.

But until recently, neither had known who I was. Hawke still didn't, as far as I knew.

I didn't like not knowing this for certain.

Or perhaps it was a man I'd met below, who had a keen eye for facial features? Few ever looked past the obvious black hair and goggles, but some could, I supposed.

All right, so I couldn't know how he'd learned of my identity yet, but maybe I could figure out why he'd targeted me. And he clearly had done just that, even so far as kidnapping my maid in order to secure my attendance to this debacle. Why?

I didn't know that, either.

I was coming at this all wrong, wasn't I?

The train shrieked, and I grabbed the wall behind my back for support as the cargo creaked and groaned around me. Frowning, I dug my feet hard against the boxcar floor and tried to think of it from a different angle.

What did I know?

All right, I knew that five women had been killed. Although the sweet tooth had only claimed the Menagerie women. He'd killed them and taken their organs, and then given them to Woolsey. *Partner*, he'd said. And friend.

Some friend. He'd killed the poor professor.

What is my motive?

Me, apparently. All this to get me down here. Damn, but I wish I knew for sure what the devil was going on.

The train screeched as it approached Wapping, brakes engaging. Sparks flew into the air, and I wrapped my hand tighter around the rifle as I gauged the moment.

I had to time this most carefully. Large warehouses planted side by side left little enough room for the tracks between them, and the station itself was no more than a cramped collection of minor lanes tucked between.

The ground rushed by me, slower now. Squinting, I barely made out the Wapping station sign as it whipped past on a fog-shrouded smear.

It was now, or I'd miss the landing.

"*Allez, hop!*" I whispered, and leapt out of the boxcar.

For a moment, a heartbeat, I flew.

In that eternal breath, it was as if I were once more safe in bed. Snuggling into my pillows, dreaming things so fantastic that even a child would be hard-pressed to believe.

And then my body remembered.

My legs loosened, my back twisted. Rotating in an easy spiral, I clutched the rifle to myself and kept my eyes on the ground. For all it felt like an eternity, the uneven cobbles approached all too swiftly for careless-ness.

As I hit the ground, I slid fluidly into a crouch, rifle across my thighs, and jammed one hand against the cobblestones for balance. I felt the shock all the way through my ankles, my knees and hips, but I'd made it.

Tomorrow, I'd take the time to hurt.

Like a cat, I launched immediately into motion. Wapping was desolate at best, a district whose only claim to civilization lay in the Thames docks surrounding it. The smell of the river oozed into everything, like something sour and spoiled. Once upon a time, Wapping been a veritable nest of sailors, boatbuilders, craftsmen and other such maritime folk.

Then the London docks were built, and all of Wapping was swept away to make room for the warehouses now looming around me. God only knew what they held. Goods, one could imagine. Items ferried along the Thames.

I darted between the warehouses, following the curve of the railway. It thrummed under my feet, echo of the train continuing through the tunnel. Now and then, a whistle shattered the silence. Sometimes another answered, from somewhere beyond.

The rest of Wapping slept, I was sure, somewhere beyond the fog obscuring my view. One of the greater differences between London above and below was the sense of time. At home, we'd only now be engaged for dinner, whereas the poor folk below would be well on past supper. They worked hard, much earlier than I ever did.

Well, much harder than Cherry St. Croix ever did.

Wapping's homes, arrayed along the Ratcliffe Highway beyond the railway, often remained oblivious to the events of the Underground, less than half a mile from their beds.

All these thoughts drifted through my mind as I approached the Thames River Tunnel.

It yawned like a great, gaping mouth, black as pitch

and spewing forth coal-black mist. The very air rattled as I approached it.

Sweat dampened my face, gathered under my arms. Nobody had ever said a collector's life was delicate. I took a moment to wipe my forehead with my sleeve as I studied the dual tunnel entry.

The Wapping train had just entered, well on its way to Rotherhithe. There wouldn't be another for some time. I'd be free to follow the tracks as long as I needed to, although I suspected—hoped, really—that the sweet tooth would find me before I had to step off the path.

I shivered, partly from cold but at least some from the knowledge that once I set foot inside that black cavern, I'd be well and truly alone.

But for a murderer. And whatever vermin, bipedal or otherwise, scurried around beneath untold tons of mucky river water.

I pulled the rifle stock against my shoulder, hand firm near the trigger, and clambered down the small decline. The darkness swallowed me without fuss.

It reeked. Coal mixed with the humid wash of steam, with the hair-curling stench of sewage. And something else. Something that smelled as if it had died ages ago and only now settled into putrefaction.

Unable to cover my nose, I firmed my grip on the rifle and forged through the miasma, guided only by the faintest trace of light from lanterns lit sporadically between girders.

It was as if I'd stepped into some terrible dungeon. Dank and all too humid. Within moments, my shirt stuck to my back. Sweat pooled across my upper lip, but I didn't dare wipe it away.

I walked slowly. Cautiously. Every footfall crunched on the gritty remains of fallen rock or broken cobbles. Before my time, the tunnel's use was relegated strictly to pedestrian passage. Curiosity brought droves of lookers and gawkers, but it didn't last. Inevitably, it became the haunt of prostitutes and tunnel thieves.

Remnants of this history lingered everywhere. Rubbish discarded along the track line, rotting cloth and worse. It had been cleared for the train more than twenty years ago, but that sort of business never stopped the really clever ones.

Rumors of entry into an Underground unrelated to trains persisted.

They were true.

My fingers slipped on the rifle. I took a moment, wiping my hands on my shirt, and blew out a hard breath. Where to start?

Well. There was the obvious tactic.

"Hello!" I shouted, and listened to my own voice taunt and jeer in the echoes that followed. "I'm here!"

I wouldn't be able to see a bloody thing.

As I passed one of the few lanterns, I paused, squinting in its weak light, and studied the chain fastening it in place. I don't know who kept them lit—it could have been Metropolitan District Railway authorities, or perhaps the shady coves who used the tunnel more frequently—but it was an opportunity for me.

Casting a hard look down both ends of the tunnel, I set the rifle down against the wall and reached for the lantern hook. Rust had soaked into it but good, eating away at the finish it must have once had. Wrestling it off the iron hook took some effort, and in the end, I was forced to seize the bottom in both hands, stick my arms straight up, balance on the very tips of my toes and manage an undignified wriggle and hop.

The weight of it pulled me lopsided.

The rifle clattered to the ground as I yanked the lantern back from a flame-killing tilt, and biting back a sharp incivility, I seized the crusted iron loop at the top.

The light flickered dangerously.

I held my breath, as if by doing so I could keep any drafts from blowing out the dancing flame. And expelled it on a sharp cry as arms slid around me from behind. Rough hands seized my wrists, yanked me backward.

I swung the lantern on instinct, but the gloved grip around my wrist was unshakable. The light guttered, dangerously low, and I found myself wrenched off my feet, maneuvered as easily as if I stood in a ballroom with a masterful dancer.

The air slammed from my chest as my assailant thrust me against the tunnel wall. Damp brick gouged into my cheek, dug sharply into my wrists and knees.

How did he manage to put me in this bloody position every time?

"You called, Miss St. Croix." Pinning the wrist with the lantern to the wall, the man curved his other hand around my throat. "Didn't your mother ever teach you not to taunt devils in the dark?"

"You're no devil," I spat.

He laughed. I struggled futilely against the weight of his back against my shoulders. Too heavy for me to hold at an angle, the lantern scraped across the brick as it fell from my fingers, and the sound echoed back at us like a primordial shriek.

I flinched. "Let me go."

"So you can attempt to *capture* me?" He chuckled, lightly. As if he didn't hold me like a butterfly to a laboratory board. "Why should I do such a thing?"

"You deserve it," I hissed. "Murderer."

"Ah." That sound, again it came like a sigh. His weight shifted against my back, and his fingers tightened around my neck. He pulled my head back, forced me to stare up at a ceiling mired in damp grime. His breath wafted hotly into my ear. "Why do you fight me, my dear? We are the same," he whispered. "You and I."

I bared my teeth, muscles straining as I attempted to push away from the wall. His hold. "Not hardly."

In my peripheral vision, I saw teeth flash. A smile? A grimace? It was impossible to tell. The lantern's dim light only painted more shadows over his face, shrouded by a high collar and low hat.

"We are both collectors, are we not?" His fingers clamped on my wrists as I struggled, our feet clattering against rock and rubble. He didn't seem perturbed at all by the noise. "All that differs," he explained softly, "is the size of the parcels we deliver."

"Prepos—"

He pushed me aside. The brick scraped my cheek, and I cried out, flailed as I tripped over a foot so cleverly placed between mine. I clung to the wall for balance, fingernails snapped to the quick, but when I turned, I was alone again.

Only the rapid echo of footsteps deeper in the tunnel assured me I hadn't dreamed his presence.

"Damn you," I swore, and jerked the rifle into my hands. Heedless of the illogical attempt, I cocked it and fired into the dark. The muzzle flared, the report echoed back like thunder, but I knew I'd missed.

I knew I'd *wanted* to miss. I didn't kill. I never have, anyway, and the thought—

No. I wouldn't have that bastard's blood on my conscience. I'd leave it to the Menagerie to do that much.

But to do even that, I'd have to capture him. Alive.

Seizing the lantern, I hurried down the tracks. Followed the sound of footsteps.

He taunted me. His laughter slipped out of the dark like a buzzing net, drawing me in. I knew it even as I followed the sound. In minutes, I was soaked to the skin with remnants of steam and the sweat of my own anger. And fear.

The tunnel was a straight burrow right under the river. Or at least, it was supposed to be. One or two bright souls had carved entries into the Underground along its path, though I'd never been in without a guide. I hoped now that he wasn't leading me that far below.

As I walked, quickly but just shy of a run, I reloaded the rifle. "Show yourself, then," I shouted into the dark.

My voice rebounded on me, undercut with his laughter.

"Why should I do that?"

I spun, long-gun aimed back the way I'd come, but there was nothing in my faint circle of light to shoot. And no real guarantee the tunnel wasn't distorting the direction of his voice.

I needed to draw him to me. "Because you and I have unfinished business," I said evenly.

"A bullet does not count for business," he responded, but fainter. More echoes traveled with it, garbling the syllables.

Fine. I'd try for tact. Setting my jaw, I strode forward. I tucked my rifle under my arm—easy to get to, but not primed for quick firing. "Because I've questions only you can answer," I yelled.

That laugh. That deucedly cold laugh.

Muttering silently, I stepped over the remains of what looked like an old bundle of discarded cloths and followed the path he laid before me. Because I was helpless not to.

Because I wanted those answers.

Too much, I think. I wasn't paying attention, lulled into the complacency of following his trail. By the time I realized the echoes had stopped, he was on me.

I *felt* him, sensed his presence as he slipped into place behind me, but I wasn't quick enough.

One hand curled around my ribs, half lifting me from the ground. I drove an elbow into his chest, a foot into whatever portion of his leg I could reach, but he didn't let go. I had always prided myself on being a decent scrapper when required, but this man was far and above anything I could manage.

"Have you considered my motive, Miss St. Croix?" he demanded at my ear.

I smelled it seconds before it covered my face; bitter as medicine, sharp as the most pungent swill.

I gasped, and the smell filled my nose, my mouth, my throat. Laudanum on cloth. A tactic I'd used myself, on occasion. To take the fight out of my quarry.

"I'm a collector, just like you," he said, his voice filling the tunnel. My head. "Remember?"

I held my breath, struggled wildly. The lantern clanged as it fell to the cobbles. Glass shattered. The lantern rolled, light flickering violently. It leapt to blue flame as the gas within caught fire.

The hand at my mouth tightened, smothered me.

Blocked my nose and mouth and I clawed at his gloved fingers. Warm, damp skin pressed to my temple as the sweet tooth murmured, "Delightful as you are, in the end you *are* just my bounty."

It was no use. My lashes fluttered shut. In the darkness behind my eyelids, ghosts danced in wicked blue.

At first, I thought the walls whispered to me.

"Just you wait, my girl," came a voice, dry as autumn leaves and thick as the gutters they crumbled in. "All will be well, all will be like it was . . . Won't that be lovely?"

Would it?

What was it like, when it was?

My thoughts came at me as if through honey, sticky sweet and wrapped in a layer of fine cotton. My lashes fluttered open.

Where was I?

You are just my bounty.

All remnants of lethargy vanished beneath a surge of adrenaline so swift, so sharp, that I went rigid. Flat metal bands dug into my shoulders as I tried to struggle upright. A heavy lock clanked loudly beside my hand, hinge protesting as I wrenched my upper body.

It was all I *could* move.

I looked down at my feet, saw the bands across my ankles. My knees. My waist and, finally, my ribs and shoulders. The brass gleamed dully in the lantern light, tinged with a patina of age and use. A rigid band around my forehead clattered faintly, and I felt something shift and drag with every motion. Cords? Weights of some kind?

The inexpertly pinned mass of my hair had fallen

loose, tangled by my shoulder in a pin-strewn nest, and it blocked most of my vision to my right.

My left arm throbbed steadily, mirrored counter to my heart, and I tilted my head as far to the side as I could. The last moments of my single-minded chase through the Thames Tunnel seemed like a dream. It was possible I'd wounded myself before—

"Dear God," I breathed.

There was a glass tube in the crook of my arm.

My mouth went dry with terror.

The liquid inside was murky, but colorless. It flowed through the glass, sucked in to the open wound carved into my arm, and I visually traced the flexible tubing attached to the other side as it coiled its way around a tall structure made of brass, copper and iron.

There was a *tube* buried into my *flesh*. And it was attached to something. Forcing something into me.

A drug? A poison?

I didn't feel any different.

My gaze traveled to the nest of cords protruding from the metal connector, sharpened on the table beside me. More tubes draped across the space toward it. The light flickered wildly as the lantern beside me popped and sizzled, preventing me from seeing anything beyond the shroud draped across the table. The tubes vanished into the dingy fabric.

I sucked in a breath, forcing myself to breathe. Calm. Coolly. I was awake, which meant whatever was happening to my arm wasn't enough to sap my consciousness. There was hope.

Where the bloody bells was I?

The open room had a hollow, impenetrable feel to it, as if it were a protected bunker or somewhere far out of reach of casual intrusion. Fixtures loomed out of the murky edges where the lanterns failed to illuminate, alien to me and brimming with handles, dials, levers, gauges. Even the table I was strapped against boasted a series of cords and tubes inset into the panel beneath me.

A laboratory. It had all the hallmarks of the small room I'd seen in Professor Woolsey's exhibit, and as I thought of it, I realized the arrayed tubes reminded me exactly of that.

Not the laboratory!

I flinched as echoes of something forgotten shuddered across my memory.

Every sound bounced from walls shrouded in darkness—whispers of motion and movement from somewhere in the dark, the tinny clanks of unknown metal bits, even the sputtering oil in the lamp.

And the muttering. Half under his breath and ever coming, the thin figure hunched over a worktable and continued speaking. To himself? To me? I didn't know. I caught glimpses of motion as his quick, dexterous fingers flashed and fluttered like a manic butterfly to the tools near him, seizing this or that and always, always muttering.

My heart thudded, painfully loud against my ribs as I jerked against at my restraints.

This time, the clanking alerted my captor.

He straightened, quick as a lizard sensing trouble. "So I see." he murmured. "You were right, she lives enough. All right, all right, penance due . . ." He trailed off, and as he half turned and frowned at the object cradled in his dirty hands, I glimpsed the outline of gray hair. Beetled eyebrows over wide, thick goggles.

My stomach twisted itself into an icy, forbidding knot. "Professor!" I gasped.

"Ah, you remember me." Although Professor Woolsey made no motion toward me, my heart tripled its dance, sending my blood surging out toward my limbs as if desperate to be used. To move.

What was going on here? "I thought you were dead," I told him, accusation shuddering in each word. I was beyond confused.

And just a little bit angry.

"Yes, well, yes." The meandering way the man spoke hadn't changed, and it dipped from quiet to clear to a murmur all in the same breath. "That was rather the intent. The powers of deduction evidenced by the police leave something to be desired, don't they? Ah, come on, then, get your money and be gone."

Money? I set my jaw, mercifully free of restraint, and wrenched my head around as far back as I could. The band around my forehead pinched painfully. I saw more flickering light, swallowed by the gloom above me. That shrouded figure, still and quiet on the table next to mine. And a flutter of movement.

A whisper of a footfall.

My entire body startled as a tall, greatcoat-wrapped figure detached itself from the shadows pooling behind my fettered prison. I blinked rapidly, unconsciously clenching my left hand as the tube shifted inside the hollow circle cut into my skin to accommodate it. It hurt.

I growled as the man I'd been hired to collect paused just out of my direct view. I could see his gloved hand rising. I could sense his eyes on me, still hidden beneath that bloody bowler, and I swear I *felt* his smile.

"As requested," he said, his oddly soft-spoken voice nevertheless creating a barrage of echoes in the darkness around us. "One Cherry St. Croix, whole and in her right mind." He paused, thoughtful. "Perhaps a few bruises," he allowed after a moment.

I twisted, wincing as my flesh ground against the metal bands in my fervor to look at him. As my arm throbbed angrily in protest.

I wanted to know his face, damn it. "Show your face to me!" I demanded.

The hat tilted; a nod, or a dip to hide a smile I couldn't see, anyway. "I will not."

"Coward," I spat.

"Now, now." He rebuked me as if I were a child. "Young ladies must behave for their fathers, musn't they?"

I jerked my gaze back to the old man. Then scowled. "Stop playing games," I snapped. "Professor Woolsey, release me this instant!"

The darkness ate my voice, swallowed it as neatly as if the sweet tooth had carved it from the air with his knife.

Or maybe the professor wasn't listening. Without so much as a hitch in his demeanor, he seized a billfold from the worktable beside him and threw it toward me.

No, toward the collector.

It arced through the air, flapping open over my head. I saw pound notes. A great many pound notes. My quarry picked it out of its trajectory as if delicately fishing for something beneath his contempt. His lips twisted, no longer even close to resembling a smile.

"Get out," the professor demanded, and for the first time, there was nothing distracted to it. He glared at the collector, something oval glinting in his hands as he raised it threateningly. "Out!" he ordered again. "Out! Out!"

The faceless collector shrugged, such an elegance of movement as he turned. Away from me, damn him. "Payment received," he said, and pocketed the billfold. "Contract fulfilled. Cheerio, Miss St. Croix."

"You . . ." Words failed me as bile rose like acid on the back of my throat. "You *toad*," I spat. "How dare you!"

"Cherry, really. Young ladies musn't behave in such ways."

This admonishment did *not* come from the collector, who silently faded into the shadows like the vile creature he was. He whistled a jovial little tune that died away even as I snapped my gaze back to the professor, my eyes wide, my mouth hanging open.

"Or must they?" He paused thoughtfully. "I must confess, I haven't the foggiest."

I stared at the man as if he'd grown two heads, and in my opinion, he may as well have. "Professor Woolsey?" I wanted it to come out sure and certain, but instead, my voice trembled.

"That man," the fragile-looking professor said with a flick of his fingers. He sat back on his stool, slicking his free hand over his wild hair. The large spectacles over his eyes glinted as he shook his head. "Woolsey was no better than a lab assistant, and a poor one at that," he scoffed. "The fourth time he singed my pots, I had him expelled."

I wriggled under the bars, but the lock securing the longest bar held the whole cage firmly in place. "Why am I here?" I demanded. "What do you want of me?"

And then, because I couldn't help myself, I blurted, "Did you really know my parents or was that a lie?"

"No lie," he said hastily. "Not really. I know your mother, ha ha, quite well—Yes, yes," he added, his tone testy. But his gaze was fixed on the table beside mine. The silhouette beneath the cloth remained still. I hadn't heard anything. "Now, then. Where was I?"

The world had gone mad while I slept. Or maybe I had. There was no other explanation. "Professor, perhaps you should release me," I said slowly, summoning my best, most winsome smile. "We can talk about—"

"Still confused, girl?" The professor propped his head upon his thin fist, his wired spectacles winking at me as he flipped a thick gold disc through his fingers. "Ah, yes, I suppose I musn't be too disappointed. You were only a tiny thing when last you saw me."

"Yes," I said, gritting my teeth as my patience wore thinner by each passing second. I wriggled my shoulders, my hips, to no avail. "We established that at the exhibit."

"Oh, for the—I'm not Woolsey, that fool," the professor snapped, sounding waspish and . . . familiar. Surreally so. I stared at him as he stood, adjusting the crinkled apron protecting his patched trousers and shirtsleeves. "Woolsey has been dead for years."

"Hours," I croaked.

"Years," the professor repeated. He pointed two fingers at me, the oval held squarely between them. My eyes widened as I recognized the clockwork cameo. "I am rapidly reassessing my level of disappointment, Cherry."

I jerked my head, flinching as the band pinched my temples. "Why am I here?" I demanded.

"A better question," he told me, his beetled eyebrows drawing together. He crossed the floor, the golden disc vanishing into one weathered palm. "You are here because you are your mother's daughter. With your help, all shall be as it was, isn't that lovely?" He beamed at me, smiling a toothy thing that looked permanently torn between sunny disposition and the grimace of the deeply unhinged.

"I don't understand!" I cried, wrenching at my bonds. They clanked, but failed to give.

As if I were merely a precocious child, his chuckle filled the air like a warm fire, cheerful. Deeply . . . disturbing. I'd *heard* that laugh before.

Hadn't I?

Where?

Every touch, every movement, sent twinges of pain through the wound sucking at that glass tube. I winced. I wasn't thinking. I needed to stop, I needed to push aside the foggy remnants of the laudanum and *think*.

The clues were here.

I stared at him—at the thin hands reaching out for the tubed connector between the tables, at the shape of his thin lips framed in a genteel gray mustache— every nerve, every memory, every fiber of my being screamed that I knew this man.

I wracked my mind. The opium den?

The Menagerie?

Something went *click*. I shook my head, the back of my skull grinding against the hard table, and then gasped as I realized he'd set the cameo into a copper-plated slot in the cabble-ridden fixture set between my table and the one beside me. "There," he said cheerfully. "Isn't she lovely?" There was another click as something fell into place, and a faint *hiss*. A pink puff wafted into the air.

My skin turned to ice. "What are you doing?" I demanded. My voice no longer obeyed me; high and shrill, terror thickened my tongue.

"Poor poppet." Wide gray eyes met mine as he bent over my prone form, and I couldn't summon the will to flinch as the professor touched my cheek with gentle, oily fingers. "You won't feel a thing." And then he frowned, brow furrowing. "That's your mother," he said, gesturing to the cameo. "Didn't you know? She's so beautiful, isn't she?"

"But I don't—" *Remember her.*

Only I did. I knew her face, the shape of her cheek. Her mouth. It was mine. Hadn't everyone said it? I looked just like her, and now I recognized the profile on the wide cameo. So like *me*. I narrowed my eyes at the madman, my fists clenched, glass tube pinching. "Who *are* you?"

He sighed. "Your father, Cherry. We are your parents."

I could only stare, my mouth falling open.

"And though we've been absent from your life for too long," he said, once more sliding into a frenetic kind of cheer and gesturing manically to the greater lab, "Providence has brought us together again! Never you fear. All shall . . ."

Be what it was.

But he didn't finish it, frowning as he stared down at my hand. No, the tube. I forced my chin down as far as it could go, peering at the inner bend of my elbow. A droplet floated serenely through the glass, a pink pearl bobbing lazily closer and closer to the raw red hole in my arm.

My teeth clicked together before the scream in my chest found escape through them. "What," I gritted out, "is this? What are you doing to me?"

His eyes remained on the tube. One hand flattened on my shoulder, pressing my left side to the metal table. All trace of good humor left his tone. "Preparing you, my dear. You are going to be your mother's salvation. Isn't that lovely?"

No. No, it was . . . it was madness!

I jerked, struggled to escape the immovable restraints, wrenched at my arm as if I could jostle the glass loose, but I only succeeded in sending waves of pain through my limb. I cried out, and the man who called himself my father took my hand firmly in his. "Shh," he soothed, as if I were that child he thought he knew once more. "There, there. There—" He stiffened, his fingers tightening around mine, and glared at the musty silhouette. "There's time," he snapped, eyebrows drawing together in a wiry gray line over his spectacles. "There's still—"

Again, he stopped talking, his eyes narrowing.

He let go of my hand. "Be good, poppet," he added absently. His voice was only half directed at me, I was sure. It was the same tone I often used when Fanny tried to speak to me while I read. Not wholly paying attention. Saying only what one thought was expected.

He left me staring at the innocuous pink droplet as it bobbed and swayed closer to my arm. My skin.

The hole inside it.

Please, I thought, feeling my eyes widen. Feeling them ache inside their sockets as if I could glare the droplet away. *Please, please, don't . . .*

It bounced lightly against the edges of the wound.

I couldn't feel it, but my mind didn't care about such technicalities. My entire body seized as it rebounded. Hovered for a breath, a wild heartbeat.

And vanished into the wound.

"No!" The word choked as the bend of my arm began to tingle. All at once, another glistening bead dripped from the end of the solid tubing. It danced along the same route, and led another behind it. And then another.

They slipped into my bloodstream one by one, ignoring my cries for help, my desperate pleading. The tingle became a burn, and then a slow, bleeding smolder as the droplets became a ribbon, and the ribbon became a pink stream.

Around me, lights brightened as the professor shuffled from one lantern to another and turned up the wicks. He didn't have to bother. Where the pink chemicals went, my skin began to glow.

I knew what would happen next. *The drug, as you so called it, weakened the bond between your body and your soul.*

The Karakash Veil had told me what the drug did. Told me, and I'd failed to believe.

Now, assaulted by the same pink substance—at the hands of a man claiming to be my own father, no less—and I didn't have the strength to argue the facts now.

I'd become an experiment in my own father's laboratory.

I threw back my head and clenched my teeth, waiting for the pain. But it didn't come. Not as quickly as the last.

"Rest easy, my girl." St. Croix's voice drifted across the room like an autumn wind. Too warm to be winter, filled with the promise of dying things. Of empty things. Of long nights by lonely fires.

Oh, God. It was starting.

My stomach clenched as the burn slid into it. Beyond it. And with it, that sense of *other*.

Remember.

I didn't dare. Along the pink and gold path laid out in my mind were memories I didn't dare unleash. Memories that beckoned from within the opium-clouded vaults of my own mind; images and sounds and words I'd kept locked away for so long.

Was I imagining them now?

Was the opium within the drug already affecting me?

The first twinge plucked at my stomach. Twisting slowly, like a coiling spring. Too far, and it'd snap. And oh, God, the pain that would accompany it.

"All will be as it was," the professor said happily as he raised the lantern over me. His eyes gleamed, wicked diamonds in my suddenly too-vibrant sight. His teeth flashed in a smile that sent shockwaves through my head.

My heart.

My girl.

Me? Was I his girl?

He ducked out of sight. I turned my head, feeling as if I had to force myself to do so. I was trapped in honey, thick and sluggish and so sweet it made my bones ache, and my eyes blurred as I stared at the veiled shadow arrayed beside me.

Something creaked from the shadows, something groaned and pinged. I heard it hum—*was that my blood?*—and snap and crackle—*was that my blood in my veins?*—and I heard it explode.

It wasn't me. Any of me.

You would now be something not dead and not alive. A revenant, enslaved.

A woman. I remembered . . . a woman.

Light erupted into long, blue streamers around me, crawled across the metal rafters I could now see clearly. Electricity snapped and sparked from metal rods soldered into the walls. Snaked across the tubes covering the floor.

My skin prickled, every hair on my body rising as the air crackled.

Rest easy, my girl.

I clenched my eyes shut. Not me. I'd never been his girl. I was loved, of course I was loved—what scientist's child couldn't be, when she had so much potential to offer to the St. Croix name?—but he'd called me . . .

He'd called me . . .

My eyes flared wide again.

Poppet.

The table shuddered. I swallowed a scream as pain flared inside my belly, my chest. It knocked. It prowled beneath my skin, *other* and *not other*.

Me and not me.

The room tilted. *I* tilted. The table shook and wobbled, inclined slowly.

My girl.

Me. Not me. The *other* slammed into my chest with so much force, I choked on my own breath. No, not on air, on something thicker. Cold as ice, formless as a fog.

A woman! I remembered her, now! She'd hovered above me in Hawke's bed.

The table stalled in its incline, its creaking echoes

swallowed by the ear-splitting cacophony of so much energy. I was left half upright, bound in a slant. My hair slid over my shoulder, every brush of the fine filaments torturously palpable. I sucked in a shaking breath, clenching my teeth in a world sheened by blue lightning and pink glitter, and looked on the face of Abraham St. Croix.

"I remember you," I managed between my teeth. "I remember your face, now."

His eyes were wild as he stared at me. "Do you remember your mother?" he demanded.

No. But I didn't need to. I knew her face. I bared my teeth. "What does this drug do?" I yelled over the noise. "*What did you do?*"

"I found it," he told me, but his eyes glittered madly behind his thick lenses. "I found the formula. It only took years, it only took the sacrifice of pretty, pretty women and their so-clean organs, but I did it. I used aether—"

I jerked. "Why?" I demanded.

He paused, and then stared at me like I'd lost my mind. Me, the mad one. Laughable, but I was too angry, too frightened, to laugh. "Only the prettiest for your mother, poppet. That pleasure garden, they keep the women healthy and pretty and safe."

What logic. What cold, alien logic. "All in the name of an experiment," I spat.

"No," he demurred. "Not at all. In the name of love!" He breathed the word. "I harvested the raw aether. Pulled it from the living and distilled it into something no man has ever discovered before . . . Cherry, I have done it. I have discovered the alchemical truth!"

The alchemical truth?

Alchemy. The man wasn't talking *magic*, the Karakash Veil was wrong! There wasn't any such thing as magic, I'd known that. But alchemy . . . Maybe some would call it magic. Rumor, dark rumor, whispered alchemy could do what science alone could not. Strain the borders of humanity itself. Lady Rutledge had asked me about my thoughts on the matter, hadn't she?

But I had never, *ever* in my life heard rumor that suggested Mad St. Croix dabbled in the dark field.

The light crackled, cast blue shadows over the laboratory and deep into my retinas. I lacked the protective lenses my mad father wore, and each flare of light drove knives into my head. "Papa, please!"

"Soon, Josephine," he breathed. But he wasn't looking at me.

Suddenly filled with dread, forcing myself to *think* through the pink ribbon filling my veins, I slowly turned my head. Stared at the figure draped in dingy gray beside me.

A skeleton flashed beneath an arc of virulent blue. Gristle clung to the bones in ghastly shadows of flesh that no longer remained. And I knew.

There *had* been a woman. A ghost. Hawke had said it himself. *Have you been mucking about with the dead?*

No. But I knew who had.

Mad St. Croix's wife rested on a slab beside me. My beautiful mother.

Or what was left of her.

Chapter Eighteen

Ripples of blue lightning crawled up metal rods. Sparks shattered across wires strung between carefully bolted knobs, popped and sizzled as electricity climbed across the metal rafters like a jagged tide.

The world swam in shades of blue fire, white heat, pink-and-gold *mo-shoe,* and I was helpless beneath it. The drug, sweeter than opium but so reminiscent of it that I swore I tasted it in the back of my throat, left me limp. Aching. Barely cognizant of myself in my own skin.

I bent my right arm, and even that much effort left me feeling as if I were floating in a warm river. Every flex of muscle, every twitch, every breath turned me into something fluid and warm.

Beyond warm.

I was hot. Feverish. The metal bands holding me in place fogged over with condensation, even despite the dry electricity crackling through the air.

I watched my father—watched the madman that I'd

once known as my father—as he pulled and shifted and replaced the tubes in the large metal conductor between the tables. Pale pink puffs of air wafted above the cameo as he jimmied and jostled elements into place. The light reflected from his goggles.

Why all the energy? I wasn't sure, but as my brain danced along the opium- and aether-ridden pathways trapped within my own pounding head, I couldn't help but draw the parallels. Woolsey's—that is, Abraham St. Croix's—exhibit had been about the effect of electricity on dead tissue.

My mother was certainly dead.

The cords and the drug, the alchemical compound, connected me to a corpse. It should have horrified me even worse than it did; I blame the cushioning glow of opium for my grim rationale. Was he attempting to infuse the corpse with electricity to mimic life?

Or to use the leashed power for something else?

My lashes lowered of their own accord. I took a deep breath, felt it shudder all the way to my stomach. I felt as if it were opening me up. Loosening those bonds of spirit and flesh; to think I'd laughed then. Mocked it.

Well, I was a believer now, wasn't I?

The alchemical concoction shrieked through my body, head to toe, cycling around and around as the equipment popped and sizzled around me. It would consume me. It would force me out; it would devour me.

I forced my eyes open.

Gasped as my gaze crashed into eyes so like mine that for a lurching, sickening second, I felt as if I'd pitched out of my own body. Was I staring at myself?

"Mother," I whispered. So beautiful. She hovered

inches above me, exactly the way I'd always pictured her. Serene and lovely and so much more graceful than I.

Her hair floated in blood red waves around her head. Her lips were curved in a sweet, maternal smile that turned my stomach even as it wrenched at my heart. I had no recollection of this woman, I swore I didn't, but everything in me yearned for that smile as I stared at her, *through* her.

She shimmered in place, her chest scattering like droplets in water as Abraham reached through her and touched my cheek. "So beautiful," he whispered.

My lips moved. I *felt* every stretch of my skin, every shudder as I whispered, "Why opium?"

Abraham's smile stretched like a jester's across his thin face. "That's a good girl," he crowed happily. "Yes, yes, opium. What better compound to act as a carrier? Always so smart, just like your mother. Your mother . . ." The light died from his eyes, faded like a guttered lamp as he groped at something at his waist. A tool belt? An apron pocket. I couldn't tell.

"Josephine," he muttered. "So beautiful. My girl."

Opium. No wonder. It teased me, it always teased me, so far out of reach even when it rested in my hands. I inhaled deeply, gasped as my chest expanded. Opened, flowered like a rose in bloom. Could he see inside it? Could he seize my heart—*not me*—and hold it in his hands?

My own father?

I cried out as my stomach twisted. "Why?" I demanded. My fingers clenched hard around the band over my shoulder. It dug into my palms, and I felt it.

Felt it more surely than I expected.

I gasped again, my eyes dropping to my own fingers.

They wavered, but I peeled them off the bar. One by one. Wiggled them. They were mine.

Why were they mine? *Not other,* I thought desperately. Me. Mine.

Why could I focus this time?

Those who eat it for many years must eat more . . . Hawke had told me. He'd warned me. I'd been given opium all my life; for only the second time in all my twenty years, I *wanted* to shake it off.

Metal clanked to the ground. It slammed through my head like a bell, silvery and sweet. I flinched. *Stay with me, Miss Black.*

I didn't need Micajah Hawke. I was me.

Not me.

I could think!

"Papa," I cried, hoping to stall him further. "Why are you doing this?"

Abraham's back straightened so quickly, it was as if I'd snapped a coiled spring with my call. He didn't look at me, his gaze fixed on the bank of levers in front of him.

Slowly, so slowly I felt I'd die of the pins and needles sweeping across my skin in the interim, I let go of the brass band clamping my shoulder. My fingertips sank into the fall of tangled hair. Groped blindly.

My mouth filled with saliva. My throat with velvet. My heart with pink diamonds.

Focus! I was so close.

"You were so young," my father said, his chin sinking to his chest. The electricity arcing across the ceiling glittered wildly in his goggles as he stared at his gloved, clenched fists. "So young. My darling girl."

I didn't have it in me to cry. The words slid into my heart, delivered by my father's unerring thoughtlessness, but he wasn't mourning me.

Had he ever? Even as a child, had I realized that all his love was for his wife?

I swallowed the thickness in my throat, inhaled sharply through my nose as I strained to reach a hairpin. I shook my head hard, flinching as the bands cut into my forehead. The crook of my arm.

He turned, and I froze, my fingers mere millimeters from the curved joint of the metal pin. I stared at him. Both of him.

All four of him.

No. I squeezed my eyes shut. There was only one madman.

"You were only five," he said, and the lost waver vanished from his voice. I opened my eyes to find him staring at me, and my heart surged into my throat. "Maybe six." He propped his hands on his hips, but he didn't seem to notice my desperate reach for the pin. So close. Closer still. Pain ratcheted down my arm.

Swallowed by a wash of heat. A fevered flush.

"She was sick, you know," he said, sudden and sharp. "So sick. No doctors could help her. I tried. I took her everywhere. I took you both to every doctor, and then I took it upon myself. I could mend her. I could," he repeated, this time with an upward arc of intensity that revealed so much more of that madness I'd been accused of inheriting.

I hadn't. Not like this. If I knew nothing else, I was not my father's daughter.

How could I be? My fingers closed on the pin and I wrenched my arm down. My hair, tangled in the haft, pulled tightly. Ripped as I let out an angry cry. I remembered. I did. "You . . . you used bodies!"

"Organs," he corrected, his gray mustache shifting up into a rueful half smile. "Organs, first. I wanted to cure her, so I tested on the organs I purchased." His smile faded to a tight scowl. "Of course I purchased them, first, but the supply is not infinite. And so many shriveled and died. Withered away, like she was. My Josephine, your darling mother, wasted away with every failed experiment."

"How did you learn of alchemy?" I demanded, pin held tightly between my trembling fingers. "It's a myth!"

He waved impatiently at me, and turned back to his bank of levers. "Myth, pah! There are men, poppet. Brilliant men. Alchemy is the key. It's the secret to life! Life and death. And after death . . ."

I gritted my teeth, fingers cramping as I inverted the hairpin in my palm. "There *is* no after death."

"There is!" And with that wild pronouncement, Abraham St. Croix yanked a lever down. Gears crunched. The whirr of machines high in the ceiling almost drowned out the crackle of electricity.

Slowly, my hair began to lift. My teeth ached, and it wasn't pleasant and pink anymore. I bit my tongue, focusing on that pain with everything I had. Desperate to fit the pin into the lock holding the bars in place.

My father's hair mimicked mine, a gray corona lifting wildly from the charge. He reached up and adjusted the clear goggles over his eyes. "They didn't like my methods," he said after a moment. "The Scots, brutal barbarians that they are, they didn't understand. Their loved ones were *dead!* What use were they rotting in the ground? I gave them *purpose.*"

He darted across the room, skipping over the nest of tubes and copper wires. I glimpsed a manic smile as he sprinted between the tables, reaching for the cameo.

Please, not the laboratory!

The pin slid into the lock. "They burned it down," I gasped.

Abraham's hand stilled over the golden disc. It shook. "Yes. They . . . they came with torches, carrying those . . . those implements they use for farming. *Farmers.* And they destroyed everything!"

I twisted the pin. Wiggled it, searching desperately for the tumblers. The air thickened. The flashes seared into my eyes, and I feared they'd sizzle right out of my skull.

"My girl." I watched as the old man I didn't recognize as anything more than a ghost reach out his other hand toward the shroud that covered my mother's skeletal remains. "It's time. It's almost time."

I set my jaw. I had to keep him talking. I had to . . . I had to concentrate. "Papa—"

"I had only just found it," he said, his trembling hand hovering over the shroud. "Only just found the key that would prolong your mother's life, at least that much more. That much longer." His teeth bared. "And then *they* came. Barbarians . . . I had no choice!"

"You left me." I hadn't meant to say it. It shouldn't have mattered. But the words wrenched out of my chest, and I watched his head tilt.

"They took you," he told me, without once looking at me. "They took you, and I let them. I had no choice. No choice but to take the serum, to assure my life continued so that I could save her . . ."

Always his girl.

Take the serum . . .

"You what?" I gasped.

"But they stole it all," he said over me, and suddenly, he whipped back to the cameo. His fingers danced over the gilded edge, twisting and pushing tiny knobs. "Stole her life from me!"

The tumblers clicked.

I held my breath.

"And because they destroyed my laboratory," my father seethed through his teeth, "my girl died. *Died*, frightened and frail. Too weak to eat! Too weak to move. Too weak. Flesh is weak. But you—"

He paused. I watched the planes of his face soften as he turned to me. His eyes were hidden beneath the goggles, but his mouth turned up. Ingratiatingly sweet. "Ah, poppet. You look just like her. But the black . . . the black hair. Clever, girl. I didn't know it was you until you inhaled the treatment."

My skin crawled. "What did that matter?"

He stiffened, straightening his shoulders and staring down his nose at me as if I were a student in some lecture hall. I stilled, forcing my hand to bend at a painfully awkward angle to hide the pin projecting from the lock. "Alchemical formulae are exact, Cherry. It should have only worked for Josephine. I had no idea it would work for her daughter, or else I'd have never let you leave that exhibit with that fine fellow. What was his name?" he asked, suddenly all too crafty with his wide, gleeful smile. "Terrible choice of beaus, poppet, you need a thinking man."

I pushed through the chaotic stream of his words to focus on the topic at hand. "You . . . You knew? You knew what it was doing to me, to your own daughter?" It ended on a high, trembling octave, but I couldn't believe it.

Or maybe, it was one more thing I had no choice to believe, given the circumstances. My father was truly mad.

"Once I saw the psychoactive compound take effect," he said happily, "I knew. I knew!"

My chest rose and fell much faster than I wanted, feeling as if it struggled to inhale enough. To breathe deeply enough, fast enough.

I forced myself to slow it down. "Let me go, Papa, and I'll help you bring her back."

The devil I would. Dead was dead. And the woman hovering just at the edge of my vision was a hallucination courtesy of opium and aether and God only knew what else.

Nothing could bring the dead back!

Not even the love of a man who worshipped her.

"I've already unlocked your . . ." He tapped the tube by my arm. I didn't feel it. Instead, I looked down. Cried out as I realized the tube was filled to the brim with pink liquid. Streaming, pulsing, sliding into me. "Well, let's just say, you're much closer to your mother than you ever hoped to be." I was no longer sure this was as impossible as I'd hoped. "Now lay back and be at ease, Cherry. Your mother wants inside."

Something cold filled my heart. My chest. Replaced the feverish weight with something so icily *real* that I knew it wasn't my own wild emotions carrying me away.

I jerked my gaze up. Locked on shimmering green eyes once more floating above me.

My mother's hand lodged in my chest, buried to the wrist. Like a . . . like . . .

I had *no* frame of reference for this.

The doctor walked away, clapping his hands together like a giddy schoolboy. "Soon, my girl, you'll be mine again!"

I wrenched at the lock with one hand, even as my lips went numb. As my nose began to lose sensation. As my fingers began to ache and throb with so much trapped beneath my skin. I was going to burst; I was going to split like an overripe tomato as the vision of my mother pushed her arm deeper into me. Up to her forearm. Her elbow.

Although she was silent, I have never to this day seen anything more disturbing.

I tried to scream, but my throat went numb under a surge of icy pressure. My chest bowed; slammed into the bar and felt no resistance. I was in me, I was not me.

I was floating over me.

The drug was pushing me out?

No, my mother was *pulling me* from my own skin! I gritted my teeth and fought her with everything I had. Just a few more moments, a few more precious seconds was all I needed as I fumbled with the pin.

Stay with me, I heard Micajah Hawke snarl in my head. A memory, only a memory, but it was enough.

I'd beaten this once. I'd beat it again.

The tumblers caught, then clicked apart completely.

As metal groaned, it seemed to me as if the whole laboratory shuddered. The first of the currents traveled through the table, into the brass bands, into the plate wrapped around my forehead.

Into me. My brain, my heart, my body.

I screamed, back bowing as I struggled to throw it all off.

The gesture forced the lock free. Slammed the bars upright. With every ounce of willpower I had—feeling as if my skin, my nails, my teeth and heart and lungs and *all of me* strained to tear itself loose—I wrenched myself to the edge of the table. The band around my head tightened painfully.

The icy grip in my chest . . . *moved*. The foggy image of Josephine slid over me, gesturing with smooth, languid strokes. As if she were trapped underwater, held by something I couldn't see. Her pretty mouth twisted, and I fought back tears of pain and anger and . . . Oh, there was too much all at once for me to handle.

I had to focus on getting away. Get away, I told myself, get away and I could figure out the rest after. When I could think. When I could step away from it all and study it objectively.

Just *get away*.

She flitted like some oversize bat; a creature of light and airy grace framed in glittering blue. The figure rose over me, angry, I think. Demanding.

Demanding what? That I obey?

My fingers pulsated like overstuffed sausages, filled to bursting, and I sobbed brokenly as I clawed at the wires, the tubes.

A glint of reflected blue turned to a shooting star in my swimming, drug-addled vision. It arced, only to wink out as my father stiffened. His mouth widened. Twisted.

Blood trickled from his lips as he swayed.

I gave up on the band, managed to get my aching fingers under the glass tube, and tore it from my arm. Pink fluid sprayed like a fountain, splattered over me, the table.

The blue-lit shroud.

Abraham St. Croix wilted, sinking to the floor with his bloody mouth agape. A scream split the air; it wasn't his. It wasn't mine. Josephine rose to the ceiling, hands outstretched, mouth wide and teeth bared, and I think the scream came from her. It sliced through the electric crackle, through the painful slam of my own heart in my ears, through space and time and all thought. A primordial thing; a shriek of fury so violent and inhuman, I wasn't certain that I didn't imagine it.

The table edge was too close. I slid off, my limbs unwilling to obey me any further. The ground rushed up to meet me as the scream echoed and re-echoed; a crescendo that shattered glass in its wake. Machines sparked and shuddered.

My temple slammed into the ground. My limbs twitched helplessly.

A shadow leaned over me. Raked cool, gloved hands over my head and pulled the metal strap from my brow. Convulsing violently, I retained only the impression of a dark overcoat. A thin, angular jaw.

The metallic, overly sweet scent of blood high and tight in my nostrils as I was gathered up like a child.

As the scream faded into an altogether different sound, something that crackled and smelled like oil and smoke, my vision stretched out in front of me. As if I waited at the end of a tunnel. As if I could only listen through thousands of tons of water. Murky, frozen—pressing, and sucking at me and . . . I jerked.

"Funny thing," said a low, toneless voice above my head, "I'd made it all the way out of the tunnel before I turned back." A hand smoothed back my hair. "I suppose you're not just a bounty, after all."

I opened my mouth to scream. The collector I thought had abandoned me to my fate reached down to cover it with a bitter cloth. In my opium-riddled sight, his smile grew teeth long as knives. His hand wrapped around my jaw, my head, slid into my throat to reach for my heart.

I didn't scream. I couldn't. Instead, I drowned. Smothered in pink-and-gold lunacy.

Chapter Nineteen

y cheek was damp.

I surfaced from sleep slowly, this time. As if emerging from a vat of molasses. I became aware of subtle details first, varying nuances that warned me I no longer played in dreams.

The smell, first. Something spicy, something musky.

The linen under my cheek, although moist—bloody bells, I'd been drooling again—was soft. Fine. My lashes scraped against the pillow as I opened bleary eyes.

White sheets.

Black silk bedspread.

Red-and-green embroidery.

I jerked up so quickly, the room spun wildly in protest. I felt the blood leave my head, drain into my twisted stomach as I clenched the sheets in both hands and stared wildly around the all-too-familiar confines of Micajah Hawke's sleeping quarters.

"Damn and blast!" I hissed, and jerked the sheets away from the mattress I knelt on.

There was no stain. No sign of blood, so I hadn't clawed myself again. No . . . other . . . what would I even *look* for?

It was only as I glared at the innocent sheets beneath me did I realize I was fully dressed.

Relief swamped me. I sagged, bracing my weight on my arms and letting my head hang for a long moment while I relearned how to calm my rapid heartbeat.

My head throbbed, filled with brain-addling fuzz and a viscous goo too thick to think through. I cradled my forehead in my palm as I slowly straightened again. The room was quiet, darkened by heavy drapes.

What had happened?

The last I recalled, I'd been kidnapped by the murderer I was supposed to collect, and bound to a table. I'd seen . . .

I'd seen . . .

My mother?

My father . . .

"Blast." I knuckled at my eyes as the images warped and danced through my mind. Everything seemed too shiny. Too bright, too bloody loud. Even my own thoughts.

Slowly, every joint creaking with the effort, I slid off the bed. My bare feet sank into the lush Oriental carpet and I took a deep breath, spreading my arms as my balance wavered.

I felt terrible.

I was sure I looked it.

Where was there a mirror? There had to be one somewhere. Micajah Hawke was too much a peacock to go without. I spun, forcing myself to squint through the miasma of pain pulsing through my abused head. I felt as if I'd imbibed an entire barrel of bourbon.

"There," I muttered, and winced. Even the sound of my own voice grated as I staggered toward the tall vanity mirror inset behind a discreet screen.

My reflection, I realized as I stepped into view, had seen some rough days.

But it wasn't obvious to anyone who didn't know me. There were no signs of wounds upon me. Not even a circle where that glass tube had been. I frowned at the neat braid my hair had been plaited into. I touched my clean cheek, studied my hands as if by searching hard enough, I'd find the grime I knew was supposed to be there. Even my clothes were clean.

Someone had dressed me while I slept.

Someone had *un*dressed me while I slept.

Flushing, I turned, strode back across the empty, silent room, and found my own kid boots by the door. I struggled into them, fumbling for the door latch at the same time, and threw open the door.

The hall was empty. Not even a servant present.

I knew the way out. I took it hurriedly, my head down and shame bundled tightly in with my hung-over confusion.

As I pushed into the muted, fog-free daylight of the Menagerie, I blinked hard, shading my eyes with an open hand. Now I saw where the servants had gone.

They bustled to and fro across the lawn, carrying baskets, loads of washing, props, racks of clothing, trays and more. A full dining arrangement had been set up, tables and chairs and cloths and empty platters all extremely reminiscent of the adventures Mr. Carroll had written in Wonderland. A theme, I realized. An event was preparing.

It was business as ever at the Midnight Menagerie, and I clung to the door frame for a long moment as I struggled to wrap my head around my own memory.

What had happened? How did I get here?

Once more in Hawke's bed, no less?

And what had I done there?

Dread curled into a sick knot in my chest. I disliked not remembering. More and more, I felt as if my mind was going on a walkabout without me. But the images that rose to the surface were too fantastical to be real. Somewhere in there, in the shouting and the ghostly reflections and uncertain memory of my father's face, I knew I'd find the truth.

Opium twisted everything.

And alchemy; God only knew what my father had done.

I swallowed hard, my tongue gummy and sour in my own mouth, and wiped my lips with the back of my hand.

"I said, *git off!*"

The sudden roar of it lanced through my inward focus, and I jerked as the angry masculine voice was swallowed by gasps and jeers. I grabbed the door frame, peering across the lawn toward the knot of men by the private garden entrance.

One man—a broad, squat, heavily muscled sailor, by the looks of his tattooed arms—had dropped his load of polished furniture. It lay scratched and forlorn as he leapt at a Menagerie footman, this one equally as muscled but taller and lacking entirely in hair.

The gleaming chair he'd been carrying went sailing into the private garden gate, splintering loudly. The men didn't care. As the other servants taunted and jeered and screamed around them, the two men hammered at each other, locking up until muscles bulged and threats became curses.

"That's enough!"

I caught my breath.

Micajah Hawke waded through the nest of cheering footmen without fear, his sculpted features tight with anger. With intensity. My fingers tightened on the wooden frame as I watched him seize one brawler by the nape of the neck, the other by his collar, and wrench them apart.

Bared in just his shirtsleeves, the muscles of his arms rippled and shone. Bronzed and perfect, as if he'd been sculpted by Lord Pennington's mother-in-law with distinct precision. The moss green fabric draped over his shoulder did nothing to ease the power he displayed as he shook each man violently. The men separated, not entirely of their own accord, and glared at each other as Hawke's too-quiet voice tore into each.

I didn't know what he said. Whatever it was, the men grimaced, and the crowd dispersed as quickly as it had knotted. I watched money exchange hands.

I watched Hawke fold his arms over his broad chest and stand like a conquering statue as the men set about collecting the broken chairs.

I swear I *felt* it when his gaze lifted to me. All at once, he strode toward me, and a river of blue flame slid to my belly. And lower.

I closed my eyes. Took a deep, steadying breath.

Fabric rustled. Something displaced the air over my head, snapped like a sheet in the wind, and my eyes flew open. Startled, I jumped as verdant folds settled around my shoulders. Draped to my feet, soft and warm.

I drowned in mismatched dark brown eyes, towering over mine.

Hawke pulled the cloak tight around my shoulders. His ungloved hands were warm beneath my chin, his gaze intent on mine as his fingers slid the clasp in place.

I wet my dry lips. "Mr. Hawke, I—"

A muscle leapt in his jaw. Deftly, he flipped the hood up to cover my hair. "We can't have all of London knowing what it is you do as a hobby, Miss—" He paused, and I reached up to ease the lined hood away from my eyes. Just in time to see his mouth quirk. "Miss Black," he finished, with a wealth of meaning I'd never forget.

Or be allowed to.

I wrapped the folds of the loaned cloak tighter about myself. "What happened?" I asked.

"Zylphia found you outside the Thames Tunnel," he told me, but it wasn't a pleasant revelation. Anger tightened his features. "Despite having searched the tunnel thoroughly prior."

I winced. "There was a . . ." My dry mouth failed me, and I was forced to wet my lips before I said uncertainly, "A laboratory, I think."

"Not in that tunnel."

"There has to be," I countered, my fingers curling into the fabric. "I didn't just disappear."

His jaw set. "You were smoldering, Miss Black. Like a fire log."

I looked away. How much voltage had that lab used? Woolsey—I caught myself, knowing it wasn't in time to keep the wince from twisting my features. Not Woolsey, was it? My father.

"That's right," I murmured.

"Miss Black?"

I glanced up at him, at the man who'd helped me overcome the very thing my father had created, and realized that I owed him more than just my gratitude.

Damnation. I did not *like* the feeling.

"Thank you," I said, even if it sounded much more stiff than maybe he'd like to hear.

His eyebrow arched. "No thanks are required. You failed in your collection."

I had, hadn't I? I looked away.

"Are you still intent on your fool hobby, then?"

"It's not a hobby," I said, and even to my own ears I sounded petulant.

His hands enclosed my shoulders.

So warm, even through the thick cloak. I knew they were callused. I knew he hid working hands beneath his gentleman's gloves.

I imagined I knew what they felt like on my skin, but as I stared up at him, as his fingers tightened and his eyes banked with something I didn't know how to read, I realized that I couldn't be sure.

Opium muddled it all, and I was quickly growing tired of the realization.

Hawke let me go, only to tuck a finger beneath my chin. He forced my head up, until I was nearly on my tiptoes and half-seized with the urge to bury my fingers in his thick black hair as it stirred in the mysteriously fragrant Menagerie breeze.

"I did warn you, didn't I?" he asked, but there was not so much a question as a growl of . . . of *possession* in the words. A thread of, what, smug pleasure? "Now, Miss Black, you *are* a pet in my menagerie."

I clenched my hands beneath the cloak. "Unhand me, Mr. Hawke."

He ignored the order. "This time," he said softly, his finger unyielding beneath my chin, "you *will* go home."

Anger gave me the surge of energy I needed to pull away from his finger. Allowed me to turn away from the heat of his body and the odd feeling the sight of his bare arms was having on my insides.

I was just feeling ill from the events of the night, that was all.

"Your point is well taken," I said coolly. "If you'll excuse me, I shall—"

A sharp crack cut me off as surely as if he'd snapped his fingers and frozen me in place. My heart pitched into my throat, my stomach flipped and for a moment, I swear I turned as green as the cloak shrouding me from view.

I turned, slowly. He *had* snapped his fingers.

And the lazy smile shaping his mouth told me he was equal parts amused and appeased that I'd stopped. Like a dog to heel. My eyes narrowed.

"Your debt is still outstanding. See that you make progress." His eyes glittered. "Before we're forced to place a bounty on you, of course."

I scowled. "I won't forget."

"See that you don't. Zylphia will escort you home." His gaze rose above my head.

I turned again, the cloak brushing across the ground, and found Zylphia waiting behind me. How? *How* did the members of this thrice-damned circus move like cats in the dark?

I glared at her.

Once more clad in a demure dress and clean white

apron, she avoided looking at either of us. "At your ready, miss," she said quietly.

I'd just bet.

I refused to look over my shoulder. Wrapping the cloak tightly around myself, I hiked the hem off the ground and tried not to feel like an awkward child wearing adult clothing. I *was* an adult. I didn't need Hawke's appreciation.

Or his permission.

I stepped off the stoop and strode toward the gate, Zylphia quickly beside me. I caught a glimpse of her pale-eyed study as she unlocked the pedestrian door within the wider gate. "Are you all right, *cherie*?"

I didn't dare stop. If I stopped, I had a very real feeling that I'd forget how to walk again. I wanted sleep. I wanted my own bed, I wanted to forget this had ever happened.

Instead, stumbling over the green hem, I asked, "You found me?"

"Don't you recall?"

I shook my head.

Zylphia was quiet. Then, as she guided me slowly through Limehouse, she said, "Betsy will be all right. Her head hurts and she's frightened, but she's more inclined to be angry right now."

Thank God.

"I found you outside the tunnel, feverish and out of your mind. I took you to Cage," she added. "You weren't wholly unconscious, but I think it wasn't as . . . difficult as your first bout with the magic."

This time, I did stop. I stared at her, my fingers aching with the strength of my hold on the velvet cloak. "It's not magic," I said flatly.

Her lovely blue eyes shifted. "I'm only—"

"It's not magic, Zylphia," I repeated, aware that I sounded like a stubborn child. But I couldn't call it magic. I couldn't. Science, chemicals, even *alchemy* was more tolerable than faith or magic or monsters.

Monsters were people. Not magicians.

"Fine," she said softly, but I knew that wouldn't be the end of it. She had a heritage, too, didn't she? The Veil had said so. "Whatever happened, you vanished in that tunnel. I don't know how you got out, either."

This, I could cope with. "When you found me," I said slowly, "was there . . . anyone about?"

She reached into her sleeve and withdrew a long, thin blade. Nearly a straight razor, but for the hilt. "This pinned your hair to the ground."

Reflexively, my hands went to my head.

Zylphia caught them, her eyes flashing a warning as she pressed the knife into my palm. "Don't go fussing in plain view. You lost some, but a little resourceful styling won't show it."

I looked down at the knife. Studied its keen edge and blood-flecked hilt. I traced it with my thumb, studied the dried flakes it left behind.

Not just a bounty, after all. My arms spasmed.

I remembered. The sweet tooth. He was a collector, like me.

But a killer, unlike me. It came back, thick as treacle. Slowly. Sticky and muddled, but I . . . I'd watched him . . .

"Cherry?"

"He killed him," I whispered.

Zylphia said nothing.

I looked up, met her forthright stare. To my shame,

eyes filled with tears. Exhausted, angry, helpless tears. I could feel my face reddening even as I fought back the inescapable urge to cry. "The professor is dead," I managed tightly. "Woolsey is dead for sure, now."

Woolsey, who was St. Croix in disguise. I couldn't say it. I couldn't even frame the words.

She flinched, and curled an arm around my shoulders. Gently, as cautiously as if I were a lost child, she guided me toward the West India docks. "There's other days to catch the sweet tooth, love. You'll get your revenge."

Would I? As I allowed my spying friend to make the sky ferry arrangements, as I sat quietly and watched the fog thin from the bow of the *Scarlet Philosopher*, I wondered if it were my vengeance I owed the collector.

Or my gratitude.

It took me three days to find my feet once more. I spent a majority of the time in my bed, mulling over the incident below the drift. Slowly, strained through the frenetic whisper of my own thoughts and the outrageous dreams that plagued me by night, I threaded some of my memories together.

But I wanted *answers*.

I knew that the compound given me had been opium and aether. But it was likely distilled with other things I wasn't sure of. If aether was found in all things, I reasoned, then perhaps it wasn't that far off to speculate that it was an *indicator* of life. Perhaps there was no aether in *dead* things.

But a rock was dead, wasn't it?

I ignored that for the time being. If aether, in fact, was

already in a living thing, and my father's—I couldn't bring myself to so coldly call him my father while speculating about his attempted murder of me, his only child. Right, then. If Abraham St. Croix's intent was to replace *me* with Josephine, but in my own body, then he'd need to force me out—how strange was it to talk of my own self like a box?—and ensure that the transfer didn't damage my body.

Thus, perhaps he utilized the opium to weaken my resolve, and aether to fill my anatomy so full with . . . well, with *life* that any damage sustained would be repaired by the . . . the what? The drug? The compound?

How would I even go about testing this theory?

And then I caught myself thinking of the words *test* and *experiment* and curled up in my bed with the pillows over my head until I remembered how to think like a human again.

I couldn't possibly test these theories. Not without severe loss of human life. And soul.

I was not my father's daughter. I simply wasn't.

Yet no matter how calmly, rationally, *logically* I could think during the day, every night plagued me with dreams. I'd never seen the like. Black- and white-winged angels fought for territory inside a dungeon jammed with blue lightning. I heard my father's laugh, and it changed as I chased it down eternal hallways covered from wall to ceiling with Oriental carpets and jade figurines.

I drank more laudanum those nights than I had the entirety of the past fortnight, and I told myself that it was only to help with the after-effects of the . . . *incident*.

I think even then, I knew it for the lie it was.

I'd given all of my staff a terrible scare. I recognized the scars my adventures left when my maid gave her notice. Through a film of tears, she curled and combed and pinned my hair and explained that she'd decided to resign from her post.

"I'm going home with John," she told me, her fingers trembling against my neck. Her eyes were filled with worry beneath a fading bruise across her brow. "To Scotland. His family has land there, and there's always work for a blacksmith and trained lady's maid."

I reached up and covered her hands with mine. "I understand," I whispered. My maid, my friend, had a life of her own to lead. I'd scared her, and badly. I couldn't drag her into any more danger. Not when she had her own family to worry for.

And as long as she lived out in the country, she'd be out of the mysterious collector's reach.

I made certain to speak with Mrs. Booth about generous severance pay.

When I surfaced at the breakfast table, nobody spoke of anything untoward. The newspaper waited by my tray and Booth's *step-thunk, step-thunk* once more punctuated Fanny's brisk recitation of the week's schedule. We'd missed the appointment at Madame Toulouse's.

Teddy had been by twice, apparently. I'd been asleep for both, but he'd left cards, each with a threat of hurt feelings and worry scrawled on the back. I'd have to reach out to him, soon.

I still wasn't sure what I was going to tell him.

There were no letters from Lord Compton. With the earl's abrupt absence, the invites to my door stopped abruptly. It worried Fanny, I could see that; she was disappointed, concerned for my well-being, and I think that she quite enjoyed her taste of what Society life could have been to her. Worse, with the halt of invites to my door came the ceasing of invites from the other Society chaperones and mothers.

She said nothing, of course, but I knew Fanny. Society could be hurtful. For all that it provided protection of a sort, a foundation of care, it could also be cruel and unkind. I understood that the marchioness hated me—or, more like, my dead mother *through* me—but it bothered me that it affected Fanny so. I didn't know how to help.

So we pretended that nothing at all was awry.

Amid the usual articles of interest in my morning reading, there were gossip columns that spoke of me in thinly disguised references that would fool no one. I began to read them, for all they caused my teeth to grind and head to ache. If there were any hints of my true behaviors, I would need to know. But as I scanned them, there was only rampant speculation that I'd lost favor with the earl entirely, and was considered, quite firmly, *no longer the thing.*

The marchioness and her L.A.M.B. society were certain to be dancing a jig over it.

I wondered where the earl had gone so suddenly. Why he'd left no word. Had I done something to offend? Did it matter?

No. Perhaps it was better that Lord Compton tend to his own affairs. Between whatever issues might linger with his brother, his potential problems with opium—as if I were one to judge—and the demands if his mother, I told myself it was best that he remain out of my rather complicated life. With his lessened attendance, it was as if my logical thoughts once more placed him squarely under a category of simple acquaintance.

If only I'd stop dreaming of him.

Oh, who was I fooling? If only I stopped dreaming *at all.*

I skimmed over the periodicals at the table, making all the appropriate sounds as I nibbled on toast and jam. Among the bold, black headlines, I found an article detailing the failed theft of the H.M.S. *Ophelia* from her own dock. It earned a passing chuckle, and a brief flurry of patriotic blarney from Booth. "Mark you," he rumbled as I tried to muffle my amusement against the rim of my teacup. "Any thieves get it in their heads to take what belongs to Her Majesty had best reconsider, hup!"

"I certainly couldn't agree more," I murmured, desperately avoiding meeting Fanny's narrow-eyed censure.

"Why, when I was in the service, not a pirate around would dare show so much as an eyebrow," he told me seriously. "Mind, we were armed to the teeth at all times. Different times, then."

"Of course," I murmured, forcing myself not to laugh as he took his genteel indignation back to the kitchens. Sometimes, I wondered at Booth's memory of his "infantry days."

"Pirates." Fanny sniffed. "Cherry, really."

"I still would like to attend the christening," I told her. "This article says it's in a month."

"Perhaps."

It was almost . . . *normal.*

Almost. I didn't explain what I'd learned in that laboratory below the river. How could I? What could possibly make less sense? My father had abandoned me to a life of petty crime and exploitation, taken on the identity of a man he'd once known, opened an exhibit to better fuel his experiments on my mother's corpse, murdered himself in the eyes of the public, and then tried to kill me, too.

Impossible. It was up to me to carry this burden alone.

Well, almost alone. In too few days, Betsy would be gone, but Zylphia was already taking her place. I saw little enough of her while Betsy taught her what duties she'd be expected to fulfill, but as dark once more fell over London and I prepared myself to go below, it was Zylphia that helped me with my hair.

Was it terribly sad that she was the closest thing I had to a confidant? I knew that she had to be reporting at least some of my movements to the Karakash Veil. I hadn't told her everything about the laboratory below for that very reason. I didn't trust her not to try to retrieve the cameo with its alchemical secret herself.

But I told her just enough to make me feel better, enough to work through some of the details I still found difficult to recall. Like the whereabouts of that damned laboratory.

Hawke had claimed there was no such thing in the tunnel. I hadn't quite found the courage to check myself.

I would have to. Soon.

"Are you sure you're ready for this?" she asked, meeting my eyes in the mirror.

I wasn't. But I'd rather shave my head bald than admit it. "It's just a collection," I reassured her, surprised by how easy the words came. "Regardless of circum-

stance, I failed. Until I locate the alchemical serum"—
which I swore upside and down I'd *never* let the Veil
claim—"or pay off my debt, I can't afford to stop now."

"I don't like it," she told me, tucking the end of my
braid up into a tight knot. This, I think, would hold
through anything.

But she didn't say anything else. She didn't have to.
As she tossed the ladder over the sill and threw her leg
over the edge, she shot me a look over her shoulder that
told me she was as aware of my position as she was of
her own. Both of us, indebted. Owned, really.

We shimmied down the ladder and moved quickly to
the docks. I let Zylphia finagle Captain Abercott; she
had a way with him that surpassed even his irritated
bluster.

I left her waiting at the usual corner where I would
meet Ishmael, unwilling to take a noncollector to the
offices. Part of me worried that she'd get it in her head
to try her hand at collecting.

The rest of me still didn't wholly trust her.

I moved as hastily as I could, keeping to the shadows
and the dark paths well away from any of the guttering gas lamps, but I admit that my hackles prickled the
whole time. I couldn't shake the feeling, the paranoia,
of being watched. Which was ridiculous. No longer
content to assume I was untouchable, I backtracked so
often, rounded back around on my own trail so convo-
lutedly that I was *sure* no one could follow.

But the events past had left me . . . jumpy.

No longer quite so arrogant.

Once at the empty collectors' station, I focused only
on those bounties put out by the Menagerie.

I had a sinking sensation that it would be weeks of

tightening my metaphorical belt. As long as I took only those bounties that would free me from debt, I wouldn't get paid. That meant I'd have to skimp on the laudanum that I'd once more turned to with a vengeance.

Zylla noticed, of course she noticed how quickly the ruby liquid was depleted. But she said nothing.

"Hello," I murmured, my voice sinking to rasping whispers in the fog-filled station. I reached up, very delicately, and pinned a fluttering note to the wall with two fingers. The bifurcated halves came together into a call for murder.

Despite myself, my mouth twisted up into a rueful smile. "Come and get me," I murmured. And as I did, something clicked into place inside my scattered thoughts.

Was it possible that the collector who left his mark so boldly on the wall was the very same who'd collected the sweets' organs? Murder, after all. And he was a flashy devil, wasn't he?

I jerked my hand away from the note so quickly, the paper tore loose. One half fluttered to the ground, buried in the shrouded fog. Suddenly all too aware of the darkened corners around me, I pocketed the three notes I'd pulled and hurried back to meet with Zylphia.

She eased out of the shadows as I arrived. "Did you find some?"

"Three," I told her, and showcased one between thumb and forefinger.

My heart kicked in my chest as I recognized the gesture. My own, yes, but exactly like that of my father's. Only he'd held a thick cameo, a carefully modified flask for his alchemical compound.

"Cherie?"

"I'm fine," I said hastily, staring off into the roiling devil fog through the uncracked lens of my goggles. "I'm all right. Let's go find this bloke, shall we?"

Fortunately, it wasn't hard. "I know that one," Zylphia said as I told her the name. "And I know exactly where he likes to go. Are you sure the Veil will accept bounties in lieu of the cameo you described?"

No. I wasn't sure at all. But devil take it, I had to try. "They'd best," I said grimly. "It won't be my fault if the stuff vanishes for good."

"They won't see it that way," she pointed out. Her eyes, covered behind a pair of plain goggles, were unreadable. "In fact, I bet they'd prefer to have their own pet collector."

"I'm not a pet," I snapped, and strode away.

I heard her sigh before she hurried to catch up.

We didn't talk again until we reached the vantage point where I intended to set a trap. After a brief exchange, I found myself locking my knees and peering between my splayed legs at the fog-ridden alley below. The bald head of my quarry was just easing by, and I weighed my options. It was a cold night; autumn closed in with a vengeance. It felt almost like snow in the air, curling vicious cold into my bones, but no matter how much I wanted a fire and warm tea, I didn't have the luxury of returning empty-handed.

It was my hope that when I delivered my quarry to the Menagerie, his payment would come out of my debt. The unfortunate consequence here was that I'd see nothing but empty hands and a wasted night for each bounty, but I'd rather chip off every bit of owed compensation as I could.

My knees flexed. The short, muscular man passed

beneath my wide, straining legs and I recognized him as the sailor caught fighting the day I woke from the laboratory fire. So he'd only gotten into deeper trouble, then.

Quickly, I loosened the cosh from its place at my belt, and skimmed the fog-ravaged depths of the alley laid out like a serpent beneath me. The one working lens of my goggles painted the cobbles lurid yellow, and I enjoyed my unfettered view while I could.

My neck prickled again. The fine hairs at my nape lifted, and it took all I had not to let my imagination run with me.

Perhaps I'd start taking opium for my nerves.

The sailor whistled jauntily. The tune's echoes slashed across my memory, and I stiffened. The sudden imprint of memory clashed with the cold and dark and damp, but it felt so real. As if I *must* have experienced it.

I'm sure I'd heard a whistle in the dark before, that it was nothing at all to worry about, but my heart was suddenly in my throat and I couldn't breathe. My foot slid, grinding against the pitted brick and sending fractured rock clattering to the alley.

The whistle died.

Bloody bells. I had no time for this. "*Allez, hop,*" I muttered under my breath, and dropped silently down into the fog.

I had work to do.

It was just nearing dawn when we crept back in through Lord Pennington's hedgerows. Zylphia's face was smudged with black, and for a moment, I was struck with a fit of the giggles. Normally, it was *my* face that looked as if I'd been rolling in the chimneys below. On her dark skin, it looked more as if she'd slept in tar. And she didn't even have the excuse of lampblack in her hair.

But she wasn't laughing with me.

Instead, as we hurried across my small yard, her blue eyes narrowed. "What is that?" she whispered.

Too tired after two successful bounties and one fruitless back-alley footrace with a third, it took me a moment to understand what she indicated. The sky was lightening in that strange way London above did beneath a blanket of morning clouds, and my mind was still too sluggish for my taste.

I kept thinking of ways, *reasons*, to find more opium. As if the thought were a magnet and my head were filled with iron.

But then I saw it. A dab of red beneath my window. My smile died. "The devil?"

"Cherry, wait—"

I ignored her, sprinting across my yard to seize the dangling rope ladder in both hands. Scaling it with much more ease than Zylphia had yet mastered, I reached the top before my friend managed to reach a third of the way above.

Tucked against the glass, bold as blood on the muted green window sill, a single red rose beckoned.

My stomach sank.

"What is it?"

I looked back over my shoulder, scrutinizing the hedges behind us. The shadows slowly lightened to shades of blue and violet and gray. Nothing moved. In the distance, I dimly heard the beginnings of life in a district that never truly found its bed.

I'd had a visitor, clearly. "A message," I said. "From a mysterious benefactor, it seems."

"Get inside, then," Zylphia said impatiently beneath me, and with the rose clutched in one gloved hand, I slid open the window and crawled inside. She was a breath behind me, voice kept to a serious whisper. "From your earl, you think?"

I tried to imagine Lord Compton running about at dawn, climbing ladders hanging out of young ladies' windows, and snorted loudly. "Not likely. He's not in Town, for that matter."

"Then who?"

I could only think of one. "Blood on the snow," I muttered. "That rotter."

"What?"

"Never mind," I said, and tossed the flower to the vanity surface. It plinked across my perfume bottles and stayed there, crimson against silvered glass.

Only one man had ever sent me red roses.

Zylphia stared at me. Then at the flower once more. "It's him, right? The sweet tooth. Him what's a collector."

"Possibly." Most assuredly. The man knew where I lived, I'd known that. But he also knew how I escaped from my home. Knew about the ladder, which window was mine.

Ice slid down my spine.

"Cherie?"

I set my jaw. "Summon a bath, Zylla," I said evenly.

"But—"

"Summon a bath," I repeated, and drew the curtains with a sharp tug. If he was out there now, watching and waiting, then I hope he enjoyed the view of damask rose fabric. "Whoever he is, I can't do a thing about it right at this moment."

But there was tomorrow. And the subsequent days and evenings after. The collector hadn't killed me yet; he'd certainly had plenty of opportunity. He could have just as simply let St. Croix end my life, but he hadn't. Heaven knew why.

He was waiting for something, maybe. Waiting for me to find him?

Not just a bounty, after all.

Fine. Challenge accepted. I would find him.

There was, after all, an outstanding bounty on the man.

Zylphia slipped out of the room to order my bath. As the door slid softly closed behind her, I picked up the bruised flower and strode to the window. I pushed aside the drapes, wrenched the window open, and flung the rose out into the cold. It tumbled to the ground below, a sad little blot of bloody red.

Clapping my hands together, I once more closed window and drapes and breathed out a shuddering sigh of anxiety. I suspected my message would not go unnoticed. But was I prepared for the consequences?

Grimly, I reached for the decanter by my bed. The remnants of ruby liquid glittered like fire beneath the crystal facets.

I would have to find this collector. Find him and deliver him to Zylphia and the girls. I would have to go below, to the Thames Tunnel once more, and search for this laboratory. The very thought made my stomach churn with fear.

Of course, I'd have to keep a close eye on Zylphia. Whatever her *useful* heritage really was, it hadn't come to my attention just yet. Given I was still struggling to come to terms with anything even remotely termed *alchemy*, I wasn't ready to give her any more benefit of the doubt than what I already had.

And somehow, I had to do this all without forcing my staff to worry.

One good night's sleep, I thought. Just give me a few dreamless hours, and I'd be ready for anything.

As the liquid slid down my throat, medicinal and sharp, I called myself a liar.

Acknowledgments

At the risk of overstating the obvious—which I am rather prone to doing, both on the page and off—I must mention that this is a work of fiction. Please, delicious readers, believe me when I say that most changes made to the placement, description, events and residents of London are done so deliberately and with an eye toward the simple fact that this is no longer the London once known. That said, I'm positive that with the inclusion of mad scientists, aether, *móshù* and more, we all know exactly on which side of the True Story line this book will fall.

I must take a moment and thank those who came before me: those adventurous, imaginative men and women who penned such brilliance to initial critical disdain. The authors of penny dreadfuls, of Victorian adventure tales, and those who continued to tell such stories over and over, each more fantastical than the last. From eras past to modern affairs, Gothic to Steampunk to classic to horror; thank you for paving the way for me.

Nae earns my undying gratitude for allowing me to drone on and on about the things I wanted to do, would like to do, didn't know how to do and had yet to figure out how else to do, and for her patience, she has earned a certain reward that will, in time, make itself clear. Kyle—and most notably, his Changeling players—earns a nod for the inspirational use of the term "Brick Street Bakers." Thomas de Quincey's honest, often dryly amused extract entitled *Confessions of an English Opium Eater* provided much of my source material for opium addiction, and what he failed to explain, Ali—a nurse who knew all too much about the gory medicinal details—filled in.

And lastly, because this book would be nothing without either, Laura and Esi each deserve the unending riches of the universe. For taking a chance on an unapologetic opium-eater, on a new genre, a strange concept and on an author who spends her time dressing in odd costumes for little reason.

Look for

𝕲𝖎𝖑𝖉𝖊𝖉,

the second book in
The St. Croix Chronicles,
in Winter 2013

Love Karina Cooper's
Dark Mission Series?
Be sure to check out

SACRIFICE THE WICKED

On sale October 2012
from Avon Books

Next month, don't miss these exciting new love stories only from Avon Books

Lessons from a Scandalous Bride by Sophie Jordan
Miss Cleopatra Hadley goes from poverty to plenty virtually overnight: her true father is willing to share his wealth *if* she marries into high society. Wary of marriage, Cleo avoids Lord Logan McKinney's advances until their attraction proves too powerful, and her worries dissolve with one passionate kiss . . .

Return of the Viscount by Gayle Callen
Desperation drove Cecilia Mallory to seek union with a stranger, one who would wed her sight unseen. Bracing herself for an older, undesirable husband, Cecilia is shocked to find her fiancé to be quite the opposite—Viscount Michael Blackthorne is young and devastatingly attractive. What could such a man *really* be after?

Night Forbidden by Joss Ware
Bruno emerges from hiding after the apocalypse to find the world run by the malevolent Strangers. Scouring the savaged landscape for answers, Bruno stumbles upon Ana, an Amazonian ocean-dweller. Ana and Bruno are tempted in ways they never knew possible . . . there's only one problem: Ana holds a secret that could mean Bruno's undoing.

The Warrior Laird by Margo Maguire
When Lady Maura Duncanson steals Dugan MacMillan's treasure map, he has no choice but to hold her hostage. After one look at the handsome laird, Lady Maura has no intention of returning to her dreadful fiancé, and Dugan finds that the more time they spend together, the less he is willing to surrender her to any man . . .